Stories I Like to Tell
– Book 8 –

80 Candles

Stories I Like to Tell
– Book 8 –

80 Candles

JERRY PETERSON

WINDSTAR PRESS

The Legal Stuff

This book is a work of fiction. Names, characters, places and incidents are the products of the author's imagination or are used fictitiously. All characters in this book have no existence outside the imagination of the author and have no relationship to anyone, living or dead, bearing the same name or names. All incidents are pure invention from the author's imagination. Any resemblance to actual events or locales or persons, living or dead, is entirely coincidental.

ISBN: 9781702555760

Cover Design c 100 Covers at
100covers.com

November 2021

Printed in the U.S.A.

DEDICATION

To Marge, my wife and first reader.

To the members of my writers groups, *Tuesdays with Story* and *Stateline Night Writers*, sharp-eyed readers and writers who demand the very best of me in my storytelling and craft of writing.

To a friend and one-time colleague who wishes to remain unnamed.

WHY THIS BOOK

Back in the spring of 2017, singer/songwriter Stephin Merritt issued an album for his 50th birthday, the album titled *50 Song Memoir*. For the album, he wrote 50 songs, one for each year of his life, each song somewhat autobiographical. His album triggered the idea for this book.

I'm a writer, so for my 80th birthday, here's my newest anthology, a collection of 80 stories, one for each year of my life starting with 1940, my birth year. I've anchored each story either to something that happened in my life that year or to some important event in that year.

Enjoy my gift to you.

Jerry

80 Candles

Note: I was born in 1940. Like most people, I have no memory of that. I suppose I could make up a story about being born, but how does one make that interesting? So for a story for my birth year, I looked elsewhere.

To China.

Japan invaded China in July of 1937. By 1940, the two sides had fought to a standstill. Now units of the Japanese army were probing, looking for weak points in the battle lines where they might break out and resume their offensive. The border between Zhejiang Province and Fujian Province in eastern China was one of those areas. The Japanese occupied Zhejiang Province and were looking to the south, to Yandang Mountain in Fujian. They wanted the mountain for a fire base.

There was a time in the 1970s and '80s when I was a newspaper reporter. That got me to thinking that wouldn't it have been something to have been a war correspondent back there in 1940?

Meet Clint Boone.

Escape to Wenzhou
– 1940 –

CLINT BOONE and Jiao-long, his interpreter, stopped both huffing for air.

Boone leaned hard on his bicycle's handlebars, his head down. "How much further, do you think?"

"To the orphanage? Maybe five kilometers . . . maybe."

Boone wheezed, his cheeks puffing out like a chipmunk's with each exhale. "I'm getting too old for this."

"How old are you, Mister Boone?"

"Fifty-two. Does anyone drive this rotten road?"

"Few."

"So we're not gonna get to thumb a ride."

Jiao peered at his employer, his head cocked to one side. "Thumb?"

"Hitchhike, boy." Boone raised his eyes. "Stop someone. Ask them for a lift."

"A lift?"

"A lift. A ride."

"Oh." Jiao kicked his sandal at a stone. "No."

"Well, let us then be like Sisyphus and push on, push these damn bicycles up the mountain." Boone stepped out. He plodded on, one hand on the seat, the other on the handlebars, a canteen swinging beneath his fingertips and a hard camera case and a bedroll hitched behind the seat.

Jiao, a kid of the streets in short pants and a sleeveless shirt, both in need of laundering, threw a leg over his bike and pedaled on, upward.

"Show-off," Boone muttered.

Ahead, the grade eased. The trail, hardly wide enough for three goats to walk abreast, bent to the right. It disappeared behind scrubby junipers, those more exposed to the winds looking like bonsai. Boone heard Jiao, already out of sight, call back to him.

"Yeah, kid, what?"

"Mister Boone, we're not alone."

"What'd you find, Billy Goat Gruff?"

"It's one of the Sisters and a truck."

Boone pushed around the bend. Ahead stood a high-wheeled truck of a vintage his father had driven back in the States a decade and a half ago, the truck snugged up by the mountain wall where the trail widened enough for two vehicles to pass. Was it a Kissel? A Studebaker? More likely a Chinese knock-off, Boone thought. It did have hard-rubber tires, he liked that. No chance of a blowout on roads like this.

Boone stared at the profile of a woman in black, the woman bent over, poking into the innards of the truck's motor. He sidled up beside Jiao already there and kicked down his bicycle's stand. Boone leaned his bike onto it. "Excuse me, Sister. You having troubles?"

She turned to him and Jiao, her face framed by a white winged cornette that looked like a bird in flight. "Most observant, aren't you."

"Good, you speak English."

"And Dutch. And French. German, too. And the local Chinese dialect. You?"

"Enough Chink to get an egg for breakfast." Boone rocked back on his heels. "Forgive me, are you with the orphanage?"

"What's left of it."

Boone extended his hand. "I'm a reporter with the INS—International News Service. Clinton Boone. I've been looking for you for the better part of a week."

She let him shake her hand, the shake tepid on her part.

He brought his hand back and glanced at it—grease stains. Boone grubbed out a handkerchief.

A pair of eyes peeked out from beneath a canvas tarp behind the cab. Boone took them in as he polished his hand clean. "Sister, do you have children back there, under the canvas?"

"Seventeen. The Japanese attacked the orphanage this morning, attacked us and the war wounded we look after."

"The Kuomintang?"

"Terrible. If I had time to cry, I would."

Boone took out a pocket-sized spiral notepad and a pencil, the pencil little more than a stub. "Why?"

"My sisters killed—absolutely senseless—and a house full of children, dead in a mortar burst."

He scribbled notes. "How did you get away?"

"Chan—our handyman—we were loading the truck, to get the children out. He was to drive them, but refused. Said I had to, that he and the wounded would hold the Japanese off. They had rifles."

"And did they, hold the Japs off?"

"Yes."

"Uh-huh."

"I took a back trail out. I heard shooting for three, maybe four minutes. Nothing since."

Boone wrote faster, his handwriting becoming a scrawl. "Sister, do you think the Japs are after you?"

"The Japanese," she said, the words spoken with the formality of a teacher, "most likely. And now Huizhong is dead."

"Huizhong?"

"Our truck. That's what the children call her. Huizhong—loyal, dependable."

"Of course." Boone peered over the nun's shoulder at the motor. He pocketed his notepad. "Huizhong, has the old girl got spark?"

"Crank her motor and she sputters."

"Gas?"

"Two tanks. Both nearly full."

"Any chance the gas could be bad? Maybe dirt or water in it?"

"I was just about to examine the carburetor."

"You know about this stuff, huh?"

"I grew up with three brothers, all mechanics."

Boone hiked a foot up on the bumper and rested his forearm on his knee. "You know, there may be something else we should check first. Any big rocks in the road above here?"

"Certainly."

"A wheel could kick one up, and, if it were to hit the gas line just right, it could crimp it." Boone stepped down. He elbowed in beside the motor and felt around the carburetor, feeling for the gas line, touched the block and yanked his hand back. He shook his fingers. "Damn, that motor's hot. Oh, well—"

Boone plunged back in. He found the gas line and traced it back and down to where it disappeared. Boone crawled under the truck, behind the front wheels. He found the line again and followed it back to where it turned up toward the gas tank. "Oh, yeah, here it is." He felt around a dent in the line. More than a dent, his fingers told him. A pinch. A crimp. "Sister, do you have a pliers?"

She swished to the cab and rummaged in the truck's toolbox. When she found a pliers, she knelt by Boone's legs and reached the pliers to him.

He situated the jaws on either side of the pinch. Boone squeezed. He felt around the pinch and squeezed some more. "Sister, if I squeeze this too much and break the line, we'll be in a helluva a lot more trouble than if I had left it alone, pardon my English."

"I'm sure our Lord will forgive you."

Boone glanced over his belly at the nun still on her

knees. "Have Jiao get up in the cab and pump on the gas pedal, would you? And you get by the carburetor, see if you can smell gas coming through."

The nun disappeared.

Boone heard some conversation with the boy, then came a pushing on the accelerator.

"We have gas, Mister Boone. I can smell it."

"Praise Jesus." Boone wriggled out from under the truck. He came up slapping dirt from the seat of his pants. "Jiao, throw our bikes on the back of the truck and get up there because we're going down the mountain with the Sister."

As Jiao jumped from the cab and scampered away, Boone passed the pliers to the nun and pointed her to the driver's side of the cab. He dropped the hood, secured the turnbuckles that held it closed, then went around front. There Boone bent down. He seated the crank sticking out from under the radiator onto the motor's crankshaft. "Switch on, Sister," he called.

She answered, and Boone yanked up on the crank. The engine belched. It kicked back, kicked the crank into a backwards spin out of Boone's hand. On the spin, the crank handle whacked Boone's knuckles.

The nun peered over the steering wheel. "Are you all right, Mister Boone?"

He massaged his hand. "I'll live. Let's try it again, shall we? The switch still on?"

"Yes."

Boone leaned down once more. He flexed his fingers before he reseated the crank. He yanked up. This time Boone carried the yank over the top and down the far side, spinning the crankshaft and the cylinders faster and faster with each turn.

The motor fired.

Boone pulled the crank out. He pulled it free of the

crankshaft, the motor sputtering and stuttering to the rhythm of the nun stamping on the gas pedal.

The motor, clattering on all four cylinders, rose up to a roar.

She let off on the gas, and the motor settled back, settled down into a high idle.

Boone swung up onto the passenger seat. "Sister, let's boogie."

She jammed the transmission into first gear and got the truck rolling. She steered it out onto the goat track.

Something pinged off a rock above the truck.

Boone twisted back. "Someone shooting at us?"

Another ping and a stone chip hit the hood.

The nun shifted the transmission up into second. "You have your answer."

She herded the big truck around a descending switchback and a second.

Boone glanced up at a cluster of rocks ahead. He touched her arm. "Sister, stop down there beyond that overhang. Now you wouldn't happen to have a spud bar, would you?"

"Spud bar?" The nun stepped down on the brake pedal, the brakes squalling as the truck rolled to a halt.

"Spud bar. That's what we call 'em in Kentucky. You might know it as a pry bar."

"In the back of the truck."

Boone climbed down. "Jiao."

The boy popped up over the stakeside.

"There's a pry bar back there, a big, long iron bar. Get it and join me for a climb."

Boone hurried away from the truck. He scrabbled up among the rocks, some the size of refrigerators. Boone hauled himself higher, the boy dogging after him, dragging a bar as long as he was tall. Boone took the bar from Jiao and rammed it behind a rock, basalt by the color and texture. He drew the bar back and rammed it in between the rock and the sheer-faced wall with even more force. "Ever see a rock slide?"

The boy shook his head.

Boone braced his foot against the wall and pulled on the end of the bar. The rock moved, less than half an inch, but it moved. He pulled again, straining, the dirt under the rock giving. Boone repositioned the bar. He made it a lever and pulled again, his face reddening with the effort. "Jiao."

"Yes, Mister—"

"You push. I'll pull."

The boy wedged himself between the wall and the bar.

"On three now. One . . . two . . . three."

The rock tipped, tipped downward. It let loose and rocketed down into the rocks below, dislodging a jumble of them, sending them sliding, tumbling, piling into a heap still further below, on the goat trail. Boone pitched the bar after them. "Some days things really do go your way, don't they? Let's get out of here."

"SO," BOONE SAID as the nun guided the truck around the last switchback and out onto a valley floor, the valley lush with silver grass shoulder high undulating in the breeze, "two years on the mountain. Why?" He again took out his notepad and pencil.

She glanced at him as she shifted up to second. "Is this for your story?"

"Yes."

"It was God's calling, to take care of the children. Do you remember Shanghai and Nanking?"

"Shanghai, yes. My wife and child were killed there."

"I'm sorry."

Boone went silent, the only sounds filling that silence the rumbling of the truck and the chattering of martins and laughing thrushes darting after insects scared up by the truck rolling by.

The nun focused ahead. "War, it is a terrible thing. In Shanghai, the Japanese killed tens of thousands of Chinese. More in Nanking. The children, those who survived, there was no one to look after them."

With the back of his hand, Boone wiped moisture from the corner of his eye. He cleared his throat. "So, I suppose you were in Holland at the time."

"Yes. We heard about it on the shortwave."

"Uh-huh."

"Reverend Mother decided we must do something, start an orphanage. So sent us—Sisters Ilse, Dunya, and me. We are the Daughters of Charity." She waved her hand at her headgear. "You probably gathered that from my cornette."

"It does give you away. In the time you've been here, how many children have you taken care of?"

The nun's eyebrows pinched together.

"Sister?"

"I don't really know."

"Why is that?"

"There have been so many that I ceased counting after the first six months. You see, we keep them only a week or two."

"So short a time?"

The nun steered the truck around a bend in the ocean of green and silver, the birds still winging and jinking along. "Mister Boone, it is like a river, all the children coming through, now mostly from Zhejiang Province to the north of us."

"So what do you do with them?"

"Work with the Kuomintang to move them further

9

inland, to other orphanages, to get the children as far away from the fighting as we can."

The road rose up out of the valley, the incline a hill. The motor lugged, and the nun shifted down a gear.

Boone waved his pencil stub at the near horizon, where the road met the sky. "Sister, stop at the top. From there, we'll be able to see Wenzhou and the ocean. It would be nice to know, don't you think, if the Japs sent out a greeting committee for us?"

The nun nodded. She guided the truck off the road, toward a grove of cinnamon trees, and eased the truck forward until Boone signaled for a stop.

He motioned at an intersection downslope, several hundred yards away, an intersection of the village road coming out toward the mountains with another road moving north and south. "You wouldn't happen to have some binoculars, would you?"

"Under the seat."

He reached under, wriggling his fingers from one side to the other until they touched a leather case. He brought it out and stared at the manufacturer's name stamped in the leather—Zeiss. "German, very good," he said.

"Better than good. The best. I brought them with me from Holland."

Boone took the glasses out. He pressed them to his eyes, humming 'La Marseillaise' to himself while he fiddled with the focus ring, bringing the intersection into a sharp relief. Satisfied with what he saw, Boone passed the glasses to the nun who peered through them at the intersection.

"Sister, that tank wasn't there this morning when Jiao and I came out. That's a Jap Ha-Go, a light tank they send out on scouting missions. Everyone I've been with calls the Ha-Go the Dragon. Three guns. Very dangerous close in."

The nun handed the glasses back. "We can't get to the port, then. Mister Boone, there is supposed to be a steamer there waiting for us, the Bagatao."

"Oh, so all this was planned."

"Yes, by the Reverend Mother. An evacuation."

Boone put the glasses to his eyes again. "The town looks deserted. I'm willing to bet my paycheck that everyone packed out when that tank showed up."

"Mister Boone, is there anything in the harbor?"

He raised the glasses a tad. "No. No fishing boats tied up at the wharf, but I do see a junk." He raised the glasses further. "Well, I spy."

"Do you see something?"

"Yes, I do."

"Well, what is it?"

"A steamer. It's out in the estuary. Sister, it appears to be at anchor. Maybe it's yours."

"But we can't get to it."

"Well, if we had a carbine—"

"We have one, back under the canvas. Chan insisted I take it."

Boone leaned away from the nun. He studied her, a grin poking up the corner of his mouth. "Well, Sister, you are something. Now you wouldn't happen to have a hand grenade, would you?"

She reached inside her habit and brought out a grenade.

Boone recognized it—a Japanese Type Ninety-seven, a pineapple. He took it and hopped it in his hand. "Sister, I do like traveling with you."

He slipped off the seat, calling out for Jiao.

The boy peered over the stakeside.

"Jiao, how would you like to go to work? Well, again."

"Doing what?"

"Somewhere under that canvas is a carbine and probably an ammunition pouch. Find them for me."

Jiao disappeared under the tarp. When he surfaced, he held up a rifle and handed it over the stakeside to Boone.

"Isn't this a beauty," he said as he took it. Boone placed the stock against his shoulder and peered through the eye piece. "A sniper rifle. The Japs do know how to make a good one."

"You're going to shoot something?"

"I'm going to try. Get your bike down and come with me." Boone strolled forward, the rifle in one hand, the ammunition pouch in the other. When he passed the front of the truck, the nun called him back.

"Mister Boone, what are you going to do?"

"Sister, this you don't want to know. Trust me." He swivelled about and went on beyond the trees, to an outcropping of sandstone where Jiao, pedaling, caught up with him.

Boone beckoned him over.

The boy, following Boone's lead, hunkered down in the outcropping.

Boone sighted the rifle in on the tank. "My boy, there's a Jap standing up in the turret." He passed the rifle to Jiao. "Take a look."

The boy steadied the long-barreled weapon and peered through the scope.

"See him?"

"Uh-huh."

Boone took the rifle back and laid it on one of the flat stones. "Here's what I want you to do. I want you to ride your bike down the hill and past that tank, like you're going into town. You're a kid. That tanker's not interested in you. When you get close, you wave to him. He's probably wave back. That's when I'm gonna shoot him."

The boy jerked his face toward Boone.

Boone made a pistol of his hand and fired it at the tank. "Yes, from here. When I hit him, you scramble up one of the treads from the back to the turret and drop this—" He held up the grenade. "—drop this down the hatch. Boom, the three-man tank is a three-dead-man tank."

The boy's face paled.

"You can do this." Boone placed the grenade in Jiao's hand. "See this cord? It's the safety. You pull it. You bang the grenade against the side of the turret to activate the pin, then throw the grenade down the hatch. Eight seconds, boom, so you run like hell."

The boy took hold of the cord. Sweat beaded out on his forehead. "Pull this. Hit the grenade against the tank. Throw it in. Run." He formed the final word 'boom' and released it without a sound.

Boone squeezed the boy's shoulder. He pushed him along. As Jiao rode away, Boone dug into the ammunition pouch. He found a copper-jacketed bullet, pulled the rifle's bolt back, and slipped the bullet into the chamber. Boone shoved the bolt forward and locked it down. After he settled on his belly, he wrapped his left arm through the rifle's webbed sling and brought the barrel down along a stone. Boone sighted once more through the scope. He peered at the tank commander and made the sound of a bullet being fired.

Satisfied, Boone, humming 'Hail, Britannia', lifted his face enough to watch the boy coasting down the hill. When the boy was about ten yards out and had resumed pedaling, Boone moved his eye to the scope.

He sucked in a breath.

He held it.

The tanker's hand went up in a wave, and Boone

squeezed the trigger. Squeezed.

The hand stopped.

A moment and the tanker's body slumped forward.

Through the scope, Boone watched Jiao skitter up on the tank, saw him stumble and catch himself, saw him hesitate, saw him look his way.

Come on, kid, don't stop now.

As if he sensed Boone's thought, Jiao yanked the cord free. He banged the grenade on the tank and flung it down the hatch, leaped off to his bike and raced away.

A report filtered up the hill, the grenade exploding.

Boone pushed himself up. He trotted back toward the truck, waving to the nun to start it rolling. When they came together, Boone pulled himself up onto the passenger seat. "Sister, we're clear all the way to the wharf."

A whistling came from behind, high and arcing down, a sound Boone recognized—a mortar shell. It hit in the truck's wake, throwing up a shower of dirt.

Boone stepped out onto the running board. He stared back, one hand on the stakeside, the other gripping the door frame to keep himself from being thrown off by the rocking, lurching truck. "Sister, the devil's coming. The column's got off the mountain. Put your foot in the carburetor."

She pressed down on the gas pedal. "What about the tank?"

Boone swung back inside the cab. "The crew's dead. Jiao saw to that. When you come up on the tank, swing around it and barrel all the way to the wharf. You've got a ship to catch."

BOONE THREW his hand to the side as the truck neared the end of the dirt street, a signal to the nun to swing the truck crosswise. "We need a roadblock, Sister, and Huizhong is it."

She cramped the wheels and tromped on the brake pedal, throwing the truck into a slide. It swayed to a stop.

Boone laid his hand on the nun's hand. "My guess is we've got less than five minutes to get you and the kids on the junk and out in the estuary, to that steamer. It's that or we're all dead."

She pushed off the seat. The nun dashed to the back of the truck, slapping the boards of the truck bed. "Children. Off now. We must go!"

Hands threw back the canvas, and a gaggle of children scuttled toward her, chattering, jabbering. She caught the first, a girl with close-cropped black hair, under the arms and swung her down. She pointed her toward the wharf. Others jumped down on their own. It became a jumble, the older grabbing the hands of the younger and running.

Boone pulled Jiao aside. He pressed some kitchen matches in his hand. "That store there—" He turned the boy toward what appeared to be a poor man's mercantile. "—find whatever you can inside that will burn and set it afire. Then get out here."

He shoved the boy, and Jiao scampered off the street and into the store.

Boone trotted in the opposite direction, to a warehouse. He flung open the building's double doors and plunged inside, stumbling against bags of rice and stores of fabric, not the greatest for arson. Boone glanced to the side where he saw what he really wanted—barrels, fifty-gallon drums painted with Chinese symbols that translated to 'gasoline.'

He tipped one of the drums on its side. Boone rolled it out the doors. On the way, he snatched up a hammer and a hank of rope and continued rolling the barrel until he had it at the far end of the truck. There Boone wrestled the barrel upright.

He hammered the bung loose. He spun the bung off and stuffed the rope down into the gasoline. Boone let the rope soak for a minute before he pulled it out, taking care to leave one end in the barrel.

Jiao came running up, flames illuminating the windows behind him. "What's next?"

Boone waved for the boy to follow him and ran back into the warehouse. He tipped another barrel on its side. "Roll this out in the street. I'll get another."

The boy put his shoulder into it.

Boone tipped a third barrel over and rolled it, rolled it faster than Jiao and passed him going out the doors. He rolled the barrel to the middle of the truck and set it upright. Boone banged off the bung. Gasoline fumes escaped, the fumes shimmering in the afternoon sun.

He twisted around. Boone stopped the boy's barrel and helped him set it upright where he hammered the bung off.

Boone, breathing hard, leaned on the palms of his hands on the barrel head, his elbows locked. After he caught his breath, he fished in an inside coat pocket. He produced two Havanas, one he handed to the boy. "You ever smoke something like this?"

"Once. I got sick."

"You inhaled. What you want to do is puff on it and you'll be all right." Boone scratched a match on the truck bed. It flamed. He put the flame first to the end of Jiao's cigar, then his own. Boone sucked on his cigar, puffing, pulling in the fire from the match. He flicked the match away and blew out a cloud of smoke. Boone held his stogie up. "Those Cubans, what a great cigar they make."

The blatting sound of motorcycles racing full out came down the street. Boone snapped around.

Two motorcycles burst past the dead tank, a troop truck behind them, the truck flying a Rising Sun flag.

"Oh, damn!" Boone grabbed Jiao and sprinted to the far barrel where he touched his cigar to the gasoline-soaked rope.

The rope caught.

Boone flung his cigar away.

Jiao did the same.

Together they tore off toward the wharf, running hard. At the end, they dove into the harbor as the first barrel exploded. The second went up and the third, then the truck's gas tanks, each explosion sending new sheets of flame high and across to the sides of the street, igniting the buildings.

Boone surfaced, Jiao an arm's length away.

Boone, paddling in place, stared back at the inferno. "Helluva a job, kid. I forgot to ask, do you know how to swim?"

Note: With Clint Boone, I knew I had a character who could carry the stories of the war years. He is, after all, a newspaper man. Boone, as a foreign correspondent, a war correspondent, would move from hot spot to hot spot. His beat is the Pacific. By 1941, the International News Service has pulled him out of China to a safe haven—Hawaii. The war came there on December 7 when the Japanese attacked the American naval fleet in Pearl Harbor. The next day, Congress passed and the President signed a declaration of war.

Pearl
– 1941 –

CLINT BOONE plodded up to the sawhorse barricade and parked his butt on it. "You know how long I've been going?" he asked the policeman there. "Twenty-eight hours and then some."

The cop leaned down on the barricade. "Mister, if you're looking for sympathy, it's not gonna come from me. I've been standing at this place for twenty-four of your twenty-eight hours."

Boone shelled out a Lucky Strike. He lit it, hauled in a lungful of smoke, and blew the smoke out the corner of his mouth. "Why?" he asked.

"Why what?"

"Why standing here?"

The cop jacked his thumb toward a hole in the pavement a quarter block away, all the stores near it dark, closed signs in the windows. "There's a bomb there."

Boone, pinching his cigarette in his lips, grubbed in his jacket pocket for a notepad and pencil. "From yesterday? The thing hasn't gone off yet?"

"Nope."

"You think it's a dud?"

"Dunno. I've just been told to keep everybody away until the Army can send somebody who'll figure something out."

"I guess that's gonna take a while, huh? They're kinda busy." Boone stood. He went to sorting through his wallet for a business card, found one, and stuffed it in the cop's shirt pocket. "I'm INS–International News Service. How about you call my office if anything happens, all right? There's a fiver in it for you."

"Buddy, if something happens, there may not be anyone around here to call you."

"Oh yeah, hadn't thought of that." Boone rescued his card. He put it back in his wallet, touched his forehead in a two-finger salute to the cop, and went on toward a group of people clustered in front of a store, the Kanaloa Apothecary the black lettering on the window said. A speaker over the door blared out the voice of someone reading the war news.

He sidled up beside another cop. This one he knew, one of the few Hawaiians on the force, Akoni Kamaka. "Hey, Kammy."

"Boone."

"What's going on in our fair neighborhood?"

"Lotta fear that the Japs will come back for real."

"Others have been telling me that, too. They say they

don't know whether to stay put or skidaddle up Diamond Head. Did you see the planes?"

"Yesterday?"

"Uh-huh."

"Sure did. I was so close, if I'd had a pineapple in my hand, I could have hit one."

"How's that?"

Kamaka rubbed at the pavement with the sole of his brogan. "Six flew over the beach where my cousin and I were setting up for a luau. I caught a cab to the district station, and I've been on the street ever since. How about you?"

Boone touched his chest, his fingers spread wide. "Me? I hopped a Jeep with some sailors hell bent for the harbor. We saw their ship go up in a ball of fire—the Shaw. There I was and I had the story of a lifetime with four of the Shaw's crewmen. Nobody else did. I've been writing and radioing my stories to San Francisco ever since."

"Really?"

"Well, 'til an hour ago." Boone took a drag on his cigarette and flicked it away. "My editors, they told me they needed stories about the effects of the attack on civilians. I said I wanted to get out to Opana, that the Army's got this new thing out there called radar and I'd heard they saw something. Overruled. So here I am, my friend, using toothpicks to keep my eyelids open."

A new voice boomed over the speaker. Boone and Kamaka looked up along with everyone else crowded in front of the store, most of the faces that Boone could see haggard, one woman dabbing at her eyes with a handkerchief.

"This is John Daley, CBS News, New York," the voice said in stentorian tones. "This just in, a bulletin from Washington, D.C. At four-ten p.m. Eastern time—that's just minutes ago—President Roosevelt signed the Declaration of War passed by Congress only an hour before. The United States is now at war with Japan. Repeat, the United States is now at war with Japan. God help us."

Kamaka crossed himself.

Boone peered at him. "You're Catholic?"

"You aren't?"

"Baptist, sometimes." Boone felt something brush against his backside. He twisted around. "Hey," he called after a boy running away, the boy barefoot and in short pants, the cutoffs frayed, a canvas bag flapping against his side.

Boone slapped his back pocket. "Kammy, he got my wallet."

Kamaka wheeled and raced after the boy, Boone kicking himself in gear to catch up.

"Stop him," Kamaka shouted to the cop at the barricade.

The cop—startled—looked Kamaka's way. He saw the boy and threw himself at him in a flying tackle, missed him and rolled away.

The boy shot under the barricade. He raced on, and, at the edge of the shell crater, he leaped, to get across it. While still in the air, the bomb exploded. The blast wave flung Kamaka and Boone onto their backs, and blew fragments of the boy's body over their heads, plastering the apothecary's window. Dirt and chunks of asphalt rained down.

Boone twisted around. He saw people crouched, staring at the flesh, blood, and shards of bone stuck to the window, some of it sliding down. The woman with the handkerchief turned away. She buried her face in the shoulder of the man beside her.

Boone, too, stared. He breathed out an "ohmigod" and

repeated it— "ohmigod" —as he forced himself to his knees.

Kamaka laid near him on the pavement, pawing at his ear.

"You know the kid?" Boone asked, his own ears ringing from the blast.

"Yeah." Kamaka rolled over onto his elbows. "Shined shoes in a barbershop up the street," he said, his voice a wheeze. "Picked pockets sometimes."

Boone sat back on his butt. He brought out his notepad and pencil. "You ever catch him at it?"

"No."

"He have a name?"

"Hikialani. Hicky."

Boone's pencil slipped. It got away from him as he tried to write. Boone recovered his pencil, just a stub, the point blunt. "Kam, looks like I've got my story. First American civilian killed in the war. A boy, age . . . whaddayah think?"

"Ten."

"—yeah, ten. Kammy, this is gonna rip the hearts out of readers and maybe get me a Pulitzer."

Note: Boone is out to catch up with the five Sullivan brothers from Waterloo, Iowa, serving aboard the USS Juneau deployed near Guadacanal Island in the South Pacific, Guadacanal, occupied by both the American Marines and soldiers of the Japanese Army engaged in a life-and-death fight.

Brothers
– 1942 –

November 7

CLINT BOONE stared at the choppy water below him, the air smelling of salt, wondering how many sharks were down there waiting to snack on him should the rope line break. He shuddered. To live through Shanghai and Pearl Harbor and depart this world as fish food—

"Mister Boone," the chief called out as he continued winching Boone from the battleship South Dakota to the Juneau, a fast anti-aircraft destroyer, "I haven't lost anyone on this kinda transfer so far, well, so far this month. But last month—"

Boone whipped his hand in a circle over his head, for the chief to keep cranking. In the sea bag on his lap, Boone carried a change of clothes, his toilet kit, and, most important, the tools of his trade—reporter's notebooks, a supply of pencils, a four-by-five Speed Graphic, packs of sheet film, packets of flashbulbs, and a box of Havanas. No typewriter. He'd discovered he could honey talk clerks into letting him use theirs.

The bosun's chair on which he rode stopped. It swung there in mid-transfer like a kid hanging from a tree branch, still a fair distance from the Juneau. Concern plowed furrows in Boone's forehead.

"Got a jam here, Mister Boone," the chief called out. He picked up a ballpeen hammer the size of a mallet and whanged away at the winching mechanism.

Something gave. Boone felt it, the chair dipping toward the ocean. He sucked in a breath. Then the movement toward his destination resumed, a steady movement as the chief cranked the winch. When Boone neared the railing, a hand reached out for his sea bag.

"I'll take that for you," a sailor said.

"Thanks."

"Name's Sullivan, George Sullivan. The captain said you want to talk to me and my brothers."

"Yeah, you're famous."

"Not hardly."

Other sailors helped Boone down to the deck where he slapped feeling back into his fanny.

An officer stepped in. "The board seat in that chair kind of hard, Mister Boone?"

"Yeah, but at least it didn't have any splinters." He peered at the bronze oak leaves on the man's collar points. "Lieutenant Commander, you the captain?"

"No, the Ex-O. I've made the wardroom available to you for the next hour, if that's enough time."

"We can start there." Boone reached back for his sea bag. "But I'd like to wander the ship after we talk. I want to see where these fellas work. For the story, of course."

"Of course." The Ex-O nodded to Sullivan. "He's yours, Seaman."

Sullivan stepped off toward the stairway that led up to officers' heaven—the forward superstructure and the wardroom two decks below the pilot house.

"How do you know about us, Mr. Boone?" Sullivan asked as he trotted up the stairs.

"A picture."

They stopped at the top, a few paces short of the wardroom. Boone stuck his hand into his inside jacket pocket and produced a folded newspaper, the New York Journal American, 'An American Paper for the American People' the masthead read.

"This came out the day after this ship was launched—February 15," he said, opening the newspaper to a picture of Sullivan and his four brothers at the launching ceremony. "The Associated Press moved that picture all over the country. Made the five of you famous. Five brothers to serve on the same ship."

Sullivan opened the door to the wardroom and pushed on in. "Mister Boone, we also had the four Rogers brothers assigned to the Juneau—Joe, Jim, Lou, and Pat."

"True, but they've been busted up and sent to other ships. You five, you're still together. I wanna know why." Boone tossed his newspaper to a table and put his hand out to the closest brother. "You're the kid. I recognize you from that picture. All of nineteen, huh?"

The youngest Sullivan shook Boone's hand. "Twenty, sir. I just had a birthday."

"Well, that's excellent. How's your wife and baby back in Waterloo?"

"Fine, sir, got a letter just last week from Kenna. Told me our little Jimmy's walking now, just into everything."

"Must be hard on you not to be there."

"Hard on all of us, sir. But it's the deal we made when

we all joined the Navy after Pearl."

Boone poked a finger toward George Sullivan, who had helped himself to a cup of officer coffee, and Sullivan's younger brother, Frank—second oldest of the five. "Those two, they'd already been in the Navy for some time before you, Matt, and Red decided to sign up."

George brought the pot and a new cup to Boone. "Coffee?"

"Sure. Why not?"

Sullivan poured. "When Frank and I got out of high school, the Depression was still on and the Navy had the only jobs we could get that offered three hots a day and a steady paycheck."

"I guess I can understand that."

"We'd been out for a year and a half before we decided to go back in."

Boone dug a notepad and a pencil out of his sea bag and parked himself on a metal chair at the table to work. He licked his pencil's lead point. "So how's it been out here? Your ship's been through a couple battles, right?"

Frank tilted his head toward George. "He's the only one of us allowed to have his finger on a trigger—a gunner's mate. Brought down six Jap torpedo bombers. The rest of us work below decks."

Boone wrote 'Frank' and underlined the name. "Your job?"

"Damage control and fire suppression. I'm a welder."

"Your brothers?"

"Red—engine room. Matt—munitions. Al, the only safe job—supply clerk. See, he fainted at his own wedding." He laughed, as did the others, and he poked Al's shoulder.

Al, grimacing, rubbed at the punch. "I was nervous, that's all. I never got married before."

"Well, after you came to, we held you up until you

got through your I do's. Ma was so proud." Frank hugged his little brother. "Then you and Kenna present her with a grandbaby, and she's proud of that, too. Pa as well."

Boone looked up at Al. "You give out cigars at the time?"

"Oh, shoot, Mister Boone, I couldn't afford any."

"Well, I've got some in my sea bag. Why don't we do it now?" He unearthed his box of Havanas and held it out, the cover open.

The brothers helped themselves, except for Al. He held back.

Boone scrutinized him.

Al waved a hand. "I don't smoke."

"Oh, hell, take one anyway. I'll shoot a picture of you all with stogies, and I'll send it to your parents. Whaddaya say?"

Nods came. Frank took an extra and put it in Al's fingers while Boone got out his camera. He slammed a film holder in the back and slapped a flashbulb in the gun. That done, he waved the brothers together.

They bunched, all grins and cigars held in various poses.

Boone framed the picture and banged it off, the flash blinding everyone.

Al rubbed at his eyes.

Frank and George lit up. After Frank blew out a lungful of smoke, he came over to Boone packing his camera away. "There's one more story you need to know about."

"What's that?" Boone sat back down, his notepad in front of him.

"Our baby sister, Gen. That's Genevieve." He leaned on Boone's chair and watched him scribble in the name. "When she's old enough, which will be next year, she says she's gonna join the Navy, too. That'll make six of us.

Now that's really got to be a record, wouldn't you say?"

"Interesting, uh-huh." Boone printed the word 'why' and underlined it twice. He gazed up at the brothers. "Still what I want to know is why are all five of you here? Particularly, the kid over there who doesn't smoke. He's got a wife and a baby at home. He could have got a deferment."

George tapped ashes from his cigar into his cup on the serving counter at the side of the wardroom. "It's Gen," he said. He turned back to Boone and rested a hand on the counter. "Her boyfriend, Bill—Bill Ball—he was on the Arizona. When we learned that he had been killed in the attack on Pearl, the five of us marched down to the Navy recruiting office and told the recruiter we had come to avenge the death of our friend. He was desperate for men, so he listened to us until we said he had to guarantee us that we would serve together on the same ship. We didn't get our nickname, the Fighting Sullivans, for nothing growing up. With us, it's like the Three Musketeers, all for one and one for all."

"I heard that didn't work, that appeal to serve on the same ship."

"No, it didn't. I had to write to the Secretary of the Navy. He agreed with us and sent the order down the chain, and here we are."

"Guys, you've all got brass balls."

"Navy brass balls. Of course, I think it helped that Frank and I had already given the Navy eight years between us, most of that time on the same ships together."

Boone went back to his notepad. "And if something should happen to the Juneau?"

George pulled his brothers in, two on each side, his arms around them. "We all go down together."

November 17

BOONE STOOD on the bridge of the South Dakota, tracing with his pencil the route the command ship was traversing from New Caledonia to Guadacanal, three heavy cruisers on the horizon as the battleship's screen. A seaman burst in with a ream of papers on a clipboard. He saluted the admiral lounging in his chair, dragging on his pipe, and passed the clipboard to him.

The admiral returned the salute. After the seaman left, he read the top page, the next page, and the third as well, progressively puffing up more of a storm.

Finally, he swore.

Boone tapped Guadacanal Island on the chart. "Problem, Admiral?"

"Battle report," he said, his briar's stem in the corner of his mouth, clenched in his teeth. "The Sullivan brothers you interviewed ten days ago or so, remember them?"

"Of course. Hell of a story. My editors in San Francisco loved it. Thanks for letting me transmit it."

"You're going to have another story, but this one you can't transmit. I have to embargo it."

Boone swivelled away from the chart.

"The Sullivans' ship, the Juneau—" The admiral rapped the hot ashes out of his pipe into a tin cup. "—the report says it was blown out of the water two days ago. All hands lost."

Boone snapped his pencil. "Jesus Christ, Admiral, Al's wife and baby, and the guys' parents, who's gonna tell 'em?"

The admiral laid the clipboard aside and rubbed his forehead with the heels of his hands. "No one at this time." After some moments, he put a coda on it. "When we do, they'll get telegrams."

"Admiral, you've got to do better than that."

Note: Late in the night of August 1, 1943, 15 PT boats attacked a Japanese convoy in the waters off the Solomon Islands. John Kennedy's boat, one of the 15, sank after the cruiser Amagiri rammed it.

In the South Pacific, Aboard a PT
– 1943 –

CLINT BOONE, kit bag over his shoulder, strolled out of the jungle into a clearing with a beach beyond, the edge of the clearing a dry dock masked from the eyes of enemy pilots by the foliage of overhanging ebony trees. He waved to a crew applying a plywood patch to the hull of a damaged patrol torpedo boat.

One of the men, muscled like a wrestler, shirtless and in cut-off dungerees bleached by the sun, waved back.

"Ho, there," Boone called out, "I'm looking for a Lieutenant Kennedy."

The sailor pounded on the hull, and another man popped up from inside the craft, equally shirtless, deeply tanned like his partner, but slim.

"Jack," the first said and thumbed over his shoulder toward Boone.

The second, polishing a crescent wrench on a rag, peered at Boone.

"I've come for my ride," Boone said. "That damn thing gonna float?"

"We're about to find out." Kennedy beckoned Boone on. "Toss your kit up here and climb aboard. We're going to get this thing back in the water."

Boone slung his kit up to Kennedy, then worked his way up a ladder. After he got himself across the gunwale and onto the deck, the place smelling of marine glue and rubber cement, others working inside the PT departed. They and the outside crew jumped down. They scurried aft of the boat where they swept the sand away from the tracks that would let the dry dock rigging roll down the beach and into the water.

Kennedy helped Boone into the cockpit. There another sailor waited. "My motorman," Kennedy said in making the introduction.

The sailor touched his forehead in a lazy salute.

"Rails clear," someone called out.

"Boys, knock the chocks away," another man called back, his voice raspy, perhaps from too many cigarettes, Boone thought.

A pounding on timbers commenced, followed after some moments by a shout—"Chocks clear!"

The rig, on steel wheels, lurched free of its restraints. It carried the PT downgrade toward the water to the whoops and cheers of the crew on shore, the rig splashing in and slamming to a stop.

But not the PT.

It floated off the rig and into the bay.

Kennedy slicked his fatigue cap on over his thatch of hair before he punched his sunglasses up on the bridge of his nose. "Start the engines," he said.

The motorman mashed three buttons.

The PT's fifteen-hundred-horse Packard motors burred to life, their exhaust burbling up through the water along the sides of the craft.

Kennedy pulled the shift lever into reverse and spun the steering wheel, bringing the boat into a rearward turn to port. As the bow came around, he spun the wheel in the opposite direction and moved the shift lever into drive.

The PT growled its way forward, toward the ocean. When it cleared the breakwater, Kennedy shoved the throttles to full open. The engines bellowed, and the bow pitched up toward the sky. At twenty-seven knots on the gauge—planing speed—the PT rose up on the step. It barreled away, its speed charging up another twenty knots, the air in the cockpit becoming a hurricane.

Kennedy leaned into his motorman and shouted over the racket, "Pappy, go below. I'm going to throw the boat into a turn and see if I can make the patch leak."

The motorman slid down a set of stairway railings and disappeared into the bowels of the boat.

Kennedy nodded toward Boone. "Hang tight!"

Boone gripped a handhold at the side of the cockpit as Kennedy spun the wheel, laying the PT over on its starboard side in so steep a turn that the keel sliced water high into the air, as if the water were snow peeling off the blade of a snowplow at road speed.

Boone's stomach flipped. He fought against throwing up as Kennedy held the turn for a full three-sixty degrees, then laid the craft into a turn in the opposite direction.

Another three-sixty, and Kennedy snapped the PT into a second turn to the starboard.

Boone heaved.

Kennedy held the turn for half a revolution, then righted the boat and hauled the throttles back to idle.

The PT slowed until it wallowed down into the water, waves rolling up against the port side, their peaks breaking off and sliding across the deck.

Kennedy pushed his cap onto the back of his head. "Mister Boone, you look pretty green. Are you all right?"

Boone mopped his face with his handkerchief. "I shouldn'tna had eggs for breakfast."

"It happens to the best of us." Kennedy peered through the open hatch to the forward compartment—the galley and crew quarters. "Pappy?"

"Yeah?"

"Topside."

The motorman trotted up the stairs and took a seat next to where Kennedy stood.

"Well?" Kennedy asked.

"Dry as a bone in the desert."

"No leaks?"

"None that I could see or feel."

"Well, Liebenow will be glad to hear that."

Boone stuffed his handkerchief into his back pocket. "Who's Liebenow?"

"Lieutenant William Liebenow. This is his boat. Ours is down in Honiara for refitting."

"And you're fixing this craft for him?"

Kennedy lounged against the wall of the cockpit, his elbow over the side. "We got tired of waiting for ours. So we gave Bill and his crew the night off last night, so we could borrow his boat and shoot up a Jap convoy coming down the Slot."

Boone shook his head. "Man, you've got one heavy Massachusetts accent."

"Really? No one's ever said that before."

One eyebrow went down on Boone's forehead."

Kennedy grinned. "Just joshing with you. I'm from Boston."

"That explains it. All right, going back to last night, what happened in the Slot?"

"In all the hell out there, someone put a hole the size

of a basketball in our starboard side. We couldn't return Bill's boat like that."

"So you fixed it."

"Right. Damn good patch job, too, for the junk we had to work with." Kennedy pushed himself up. He slapped his motorman's shoulder. "Pappy, it's time we took this boat home."

KENNEDY IDLED the PT into a finger of water—the mouth of a nameless river on Rendova Island. After some minutes of motoring, he guided the boat up to a pier that paralleled the bank. A crew boiled out of nowhere before he could cut the engines and moored the craft to pilings at the side of the pier.

Kennedy, his motorman, and Boone scrambled off while a second crew hauled a camouflage net up and over the boat, hiding the craft from the eyes of enemy pilots.

Kennedy sauntered over to an officer standing on the riverbank, his hands on his hips. Kennedy handed him the ignition key. "There you go, Bill."

"Heard you took a shell last night."

"Something. We patched her up good as new. Well, almost as good as new."

"But not quite?"

"Be happy the patch doesn't leak."

"Jack, if it does and we sink out there tonight, you better pick us up."

Kennedy shrugged. "Afraid that won't happen. We don't have a boat."

"Yes, you do, if you hustle. We got a signal an hour ago that your boat's ready."

"You going to run us down?"

"Better." Liebenow pointed further upriver. "See that seaplane tied up at your pier? The pilot's waiting for you."

Kennedy turned to Boone. "You want to go with?"

"Sure. Why not?"

"It's a two-hour flight and a nine-hour run back. No deep turns, I promise."

Kennedy didn't wait for a response. He hailed a Jeep, empty except for the driver. The three clambered aboard. "Boston Pier," Kennedy said, motioning the driver on.

Boone leaned forward from the backseat. "Boston, huh?"

"There are a lot of us Kennedys there."

"I met a Joe Kennedy from Massachusetts, wore these round, horn-rimmed glasses. This Kennedy was our ambassador to England a couple years back. Know him?"

"A bit."

Boone's face took on that ahh-pshaw look. "Oh, no, he wouldn't happen to be your old man?"

Kennedy laughed.

Boone, too. "Ambassador to England, man, that had to be something. You get much time there with him?"

"Fair amount."

"Any special memories?"

"A couple."

"Mister Kennedy, you gonna tell me?"

"Well, how about this one? I was with him up in the gallery of the House of Commons the day Britain declared war on Germany. That was Three, September, 'Thirty-nine. That same day, the Germans sank the Athenia, and Dad dispatched me to Ireland—to Foynes—where some of the American survivors had been taken, to help make arrangements to get them home. That day I saw what war can do to people."

"You never saw the bombings of London?"

"Yes, but these were Americans. Our people."

"Changed you, huh?"

"You could say that."

The driver stopped under a hand-lettered sign that read BOSTON PIER, THE ONE & ONLY. Kennedy, Boone, and the motorman got out and, with Kennedy in the lead, hiked on to the waiting seaplane, a Navy JRF— to Boone, a civilian, a Grumman Goose. They passed a big-bore gun sitting on crates of ammunition.

Boone stopped. "What the hell is this?"

Kennedy came back to him. "An anti-tank gun."

"You see a lot of tanks out at sea?"

"Mister Boone, this gun fires thirty-seven-millimeter shells, a real killer of a weapon. We're going to mount it on the bow of our boat. Anything we charge, we'll damn well put a hole in it. I'll tell you about it on the plane."

Kennedy stroked the barrel of the gun. He patted it, then wheeled about.

At the plane, Kennedy waved Boone and his motorman aboard. He followed them into the cabin, pulling the door closed behind him. While the trio belted themselves in, the pilot called "Cast off!" to the crew on the pier.

They pulled the rope lines away.

The pilot glanced up in his mirror. "Ready back there, Jack?"

"Let her rip."

He fired his seaplane's engines and motored out into the middle of the channel. When he had a half mile of straight river ahead of him, he pushed the throttles forward.

Kennedy, pitching his voice up to be heard over the roar of the engines, gestured at the pilot. "This is his plane, Mister Boone."

"Yeah, sure."

"No, really. Archie had been flying it for his inter-island cargo and passenger service for a couple years when the Navy came knocking and said they were going to take his seaplane for the duration of the war."

Boone rubbed at the stubble on the side of his face. "They can do that?" he hollered back.

"Emergency war powers. Of course, they have to pay for it, and that gave Archie an opening. He offered the Navy a two-for-one deal—I'll loan you my seaplane at no charge, but you take me with it, and I'm the only one who flies it. It's that, he said, or I'll fight you in court." Kennedy laughed. "So there he is, Mister Boone, Archibald Sidebottom—now Lieutenant Sidebottom—one tough negotiator. If someday I should be in a position where I need someone with his skills, I'm going to remember him."

The seaplane lifted off, water streaming from its hull, and climbed for altitude. Boone felt his stomach sink. He groaned. Glassy-eyed, he wiped his sleeve across his forehead.

"You're not going to throw up, are you?" Kennedy asked.

"Not if I can help it." Still Boone urped. He swallowed—swallowed hard—and mopped his forehead again. Hand shaking, he dug a pencil and notepad from his kit and turned through to a fresh page. "You were gonna tell me about that big gun."

Kennedy leaned forward, his forearms propped on his knees. "The Japs are using shallow-draft barges to move men and material down the Slot. Our torpedoes go under them and our fifty-caliber bullets ping off them. With the anti-tank gun, we can blow holes in them. Hit them below the waterline, Mister Boone, and they will sink."

KENNEDY CHECKED his watch while Sidebottom eyed him in his mirror.

"Before you ask, Jack," Sidebottom said, "Honiara's on

the nose. Going down now."

He pulled back on the throttles, set up his glide speed and held the seaplane's nose high until the hull touched water in the harbor, sending up a spray to both sides of the fuselage. Sidebottom continued on in a high-speed taxi that took the seaplane toward a pier. At the last moment, he hauled the throttles all the way back, the craft gliding, slowing, settling into the water.

Sidebottom jockeyed the port engine's throttle. That brought the seaplane into a turn that carried it close to the pier. "Jack," he called over his shoulder, "throw out a line."

Kennedy went to the door. He opened it and heaved a rope to a sailor on the pier who pulled on it, hand over hand, drawing the seaplane up to the pier. When the hull touched, Kennedy hopped out, followed by Boone and Kennedy's motorman. They marched forward to a PT boat, the number 109 painted on the exterior wall of the cockpit.

A master chief, by the patch on his shirt sleeve, sat on the gunwale, smoking a cigarette. "You Kennedy?" he asked.

Kennedy gave a nod.

The master chief flicked his cigarette away and got to his feet. "Come aboard, Mister Kennedy. Let me show you what my guys have done for you."

Kennedy, the motorman, and Boone made their way up a short gangplank to the deck where they met their host and guide. The master chief stood with his hands in his back pockets. "Mister Kennedy," he said, "I don't know how you got your boat here. The superchargers were shot, and you had all kinds of gunk and crustaceans built up on the hull. Probably the best you could make was thirty-five knots."

Kennedy pushed the toe of his shoe around on the

deck. "Yes, about that."

"We hauled your boat out of the water and scraped down the hull. While I had a crew doing that, I had mechanics in the engine compartment replacing the superchargers on your Packards. They also tuned up the motors. The screws on your drive shafts were not the best, so we replaced them with more efficient units. So, all told, on a test run, fully loaded, we got your boat up to forty-nine knots. That's faster than the company specs."

"How about the torpedoes?"

"Let me show you what you've got." The master chief led Kennedy, Boone, and the motorman back to midships. He put a hand on a new torpedo rack. "Your firing tubes and M-Eights are gone. As you know, the Eights are lousy. Fire one off and you get a flash the enemy sees. If that isn't bad enough, the torpedoes are either duds or they circle back and blow you out of the water. So we gave you the new roll-off launch racks and M-Thirteen torpedoes. No flash, and the thirteens run straight and true. And the best thing, they explode every time." The master chief caressed the torpedo in the rack. "Took two years for the Navy to develop these babies."

"Radar?" Kennedy asked.

"I've requisitioned a unit for you. Who knows when we'll get it. What I'd do is watch for a wrecked PT that's got a radar in it. Rip it out, and we'll install it in your boat for you." The master chief gazed from one end of the PT to the other, his grin suggesting he was pleased with everything. "Mister Kennedy, you're boat's gassed and provisioned, so you're ready to go to war. One last thing. These new drop racks, each is a thousand pounds lighter that the old torpedo tubes. So your boat's two tons lighter than what it was. Running flat out, you might do fifty-one knots, maybe even fifty-two. Time for you to get the hell out of here. The key's in the ignition."

The master chief left the trio and strolled down the gangplank. When he got to the pier, he swung the gangplank away from the PT while, onboard, the motorman cast off the stern line and Boone the bow line.

Kennedy started the Packards. They rumbled while he checked the gauges clustered around the steering wheel. He shot a hand up and shouted to the master chief, "Sir, how do we fire the new torpedoes?"

The master chief waved back. "I guess I forgot to tell you, didn't I? There's a jerk release on the rack. Your torpedo man pulls it, and the torpedo drops in the water and takes off like a scalded dog. Nothing to it."

"I owe you, Master Chief."

"Bring us a case of hooch. That'll keep my guys happy."

Kennedy moved the shift lever into drive. He goosed the throttles, and as the PT motored away from the pier, he gave a last wave to the master chief.

Boone and the motorman made their way into the cockpit, Boone to the chair. "Well, Mister Kennedy, new superchargers, new torpedo systems, a clean bottom, what more could you want?"

"My anti-tank gun. A couple hours hard work and we ought to have that mounted and ready before we go out tomorrow night." Kennedy motioned his motorman in beside him. "Pappy, let's see if the master chief is right about what the One-O-Nine can do."

Kennedy pushed the throttles forward. When the PT hit planing speed, he slammed the throttles all the way to the stops. The motors bellowed and the boat's speed shot up . . . forty, forty-five, fifty knots. And still the speed climbed.

Fifty-one.

Fifty-two.

Fifty-three.

Fifty-four knots.

The PT held that speed.

Kennedy bumped his motorman. "Pappy! With the weight of a full crew, we'll lose a knot or two, but we'll still be the fastest boat in the squadron."

"Jack, we could make us some money on this."

Kennedy bobbed his head.

"How about we set up a race?" Pappy shouted.

Kennedy held tight to the wheel. "With who?"

"Lieutenant Liebenow and his crew. Liebee's a gambler."

Kennedy gave a long face, then a grin and a thumbs-up. He brought the PT onto a compass course of three hundred fifteen degrees for Rendova.

A shadow crossed the boat's bow. Boone saw it and swivelled to look up over his shoulder. "Is that a Jap Zero?"

Kennedy and the motorman also looked, Kennedy's face going hard. "He sees us. Pappy, get on the forward fifties."

The motorman scooped up a helmet. He planted it on his head as he hopped behind the twin anti-aircraft guns. He yanked the safety off.

Kennedy laid the PT into a turn.

Boone brushed against him. "You want me to take the aft guns?"

"Know anything about fifty calibers?"

"I've fired a few rounds."

"You've got to lead the target, you know that."

"Not to worry, I'm an old duck hunter," Boone said as he worked his way to the aft twin fifties.

"That's no damn duck up there!" Kennedy righted the boat as the Zero pushed down into a dive, into its strafing run.

Pappy opened up with his guns as Kennedy banked

away from the Zero's bullets ripping twin paths through the sea.

Boone picked up the Zero on the backside, climbing away. He let off with a burst of gunfire, the bullets arcing, trailing behind the Zero.

"Get him at the top of his turn," Kennedy yelled.

Pappy and Boone both locked onto the Zero a second time, to no effect.

Kennedy steered the PT into a zig-zag pattern. As the Zero went into its dive for a second strafing run, Kennedy brought the boat around for a head-on run at the aircraft.

Pappy laid his gunsight on the Zero. He pulled his triggers back.

The pilot of the Zero jinked away.

Kennedy threw his boat into a turn in the opposite direction, and Boone picked up the Zero climbing away. He laid on his triggers, bullets streaming out of his guns on a straight line into the tail of the Zero, sawing off sections, then a part of a wing.

Boone stopped firing as the Zero stalled. It flipped over on its back and went into a lazy spiral.

"Chalk one up for the civilian," Boone hollered to Kennedy.

BOONE, IN THE SOFT, diffused light of dawn, stood on a pier, counting the PTs straggling in from the sea, four coming up the river.

There should have been five.

He read their numbers on the exterior walls of their cockpits . . . Eighty-Four, One-Fifty-Seven, One-Sixty-Nine, One-Sixty-Two.

No One-O-Nine.

Boone ran to the One-Fifty-Seven—Lieutenant Liebenow's boat—tying up at its pier. "Where's Kennedy!"

Liebenow took off his cap. Using both hands as scrubbers, he rubbed at the exhaustion in his face.

"Where's Kennedy?" Boone repeated.

Liebenow, slump shouldered, stared at him. "I don't know. Mister Boone, he wasn't at the rendezvous point we use after an attack. We searched for him until we ran low on gas."

He grubbed a crumpled envelope out of his shirt pocket and held it up. "Jack's," he said, his voice weary. "He gave it to me to mail home if anything happened to him."

BOONE SAT at a desk under a palm tree, pounding away on an Underwood he had borrowed from the base commander's clerk, working by lamplight.

Liebenow came up behind him. He leaned on the back of Boone's chair and peered over his shoulder. "What are you working on?"

Boone didn't slow his typing. "Personality pieces. Stories on sailors for their hometown papers. It's something to do while my editors decide where they want me to go next."

"Squibs on swabbies, probably not the most exciting assignment you've ever had."

Boone backed up the carriage and x-ed out a word. "I've had worse."

Liebenow punched Boone's shoulder. "How about a scoop?"

"Anytime." He resumed his typing.

"Kennedy's alive."

Boone's fingers stopped. "The hell you say."

"I do say." Liebenow handed him a coconut.

"What's this?"

"Read what's carved on it."

Words. Boone could see them, still he ran his fingers over them, as if he were reading Braille:

NAURO ISL
COMMANDER . . . NATIVE KNOWS
POS'IT . . . HE CAN PILOT . . . 11 ALIVE
NEED SMALL BOAT . . . KENNEDY

"My crew's to pick up Jack in the Ferguson Passage, and he's to guide us through the shallows to Nauro. You want in on this?"

Boone kicked over his chair getting up. "When do you leave?"

"Now."

LIEBENOW, running with lights out except for a single green bulb that illuminated his boat's instrument panel, motored out of the mouth of the river and into the ocean, followed by a second PT, the One-Seventy-One.

Boone glanced at the clock in the instrument panel: twenty-one eighteen. "How far to the Passage?" he asked as Liebenow put the power to his boat's Packard motors.

Liebenow shouted over the noise of the wind in the cockpit. "About sixty miles as you measure distance. An hour and a quarter to get there."

"Man, no moon," Boone shouted back. "It's dark. How you gonna find Kennedy in that channel?"

"He'll find us."

"How's that work?"

"Simple." Liebenow took off his officer's cap. He stuffed it under the instrument panel, to keep the cap from getting blown away. "When Jack sees us or hears us, he's to fire four shots. We'll home in on that." He cast a quick look at Boone. "Our coast watcher up there worked out the plan with Captain Skallett."

Boone grinned. Skallett, the base commander. Most at Rendova called him Skillet. Not the most loved man in the Navy, though Boone felt he had found ways to work around him.

"Boone!"

"Yeah?"

"If you want to grab some sack time, go below. We'll wake you when we get close."

BOONE FELT a hand on his shoulder and pried open an eye. There bending over him was a sailor. "Mister Boone," he said, "we're in the channel. The lieutenant says you should come topside."

Boone pushed himself up on his elbow. "Anything—"

"Not yet."

He swung his feet over the side of the bunk and yawned. "What time is it?"

"Twenty-two forty-five, give or take."

"Thanks." Boone rubbed at the grit of sleep in his eyes. He stretched and got up and followed the sailor up the stairs to the cockpit. Boone gazed around at the silhouettes of a dozen or more sailors lining the perimeter of the boat, both port and starboard, most standing, but several kneeling. He lifted his eyes to the night sky, to the five stars of the Southern Cross, forty degrees up from the southern horizon.

Boone felt the motors rumbling, the boat making slow headway. He rested a hand on the cockpit's wall. "Lieutenant—"

Liebenow, at the wheel, raised a hand. "Keep it. Time to listen."

Boone shrugged. He clambered up on the deck and made his way forward to the twenty-millimeter cannon mounted just short of the bow. "Anything?" he asked in a hushed voice of the gunner standing watch there.

"I thought I saw something," the gunner said, "a couple minutes ago off to the starboard. May just have been a log in the water."

"Mind if I?" Boone motioned at the man's binoculars.

The sailor passed them over the barrel of the cannon.

Boone put the binoculars to his eyes. He scanned the horizon off the bow, turning slowly to port. "Damn, it's dark."

"Yeah."

Three shots went off. A beat, then a fourth. Pistol shots, Boone recognized the sound. Except the last. That, he knew, was a rifle. A Jap rifle? He swung in the direction the shots.

"Muzzle flash," someone shouted. "Thirty degrees starboard."

A sailor waved in that direction.

The engines gunned.

Boone felt the PT turning to a new course, picking up speed. As quickly as it did, the power dropped off.

"Here," came a voice across the water. "I'm over here!"

The engines powered up a second time. The boat rose and glided as the power came off a second time, the glide slowing.

"Man in the water," another sailor called out.

Boone moved to the gunwale. He knelt, the knuckles of one hand on the deck, and scanned ahead. Something appeared to be bobbing in the water. "That you, Mister Kennedy?"

"That you, Mister Boone?"

"Right you are. Whatcha been doin' for the last seven days?" Boone called out as the boat closed the separation.

"Just swimming around, Mister Boone, looking to catch a ride home. How about you?"

"Writing letters to your old man, telling him how you died a hero out here."

Kennedy coughed and spit. "Sea water. Hate the taste of the stuff."

"It is the worst."

"I wasn't in the drink to start with tonight."

"No?"

"A canoe. My pistol only had three bullets. For the fourth, I snatched up the native's rifle. The kick knocked me in the water."

"That's a helluva story."

"True, every word of it."

A pause, the only sound the low rumble of the Packards.

Kennedy spit once more. "Mister Boone, now you find me alive, kind of spoils that dead hero story, doesn't it? You going to throw me a life ring?"

Note: October 20, 1944, General Douglas MacArthur's 6th Army lands on Leyte Island in the Philippines. MacArthur wants to walk ashore, but the beach master won't give him a landing craft to bring him in from the battleship South Dakota.

With Mac
– 1944 –

CLINT BOONE watched as Manfred Ruck—the beach master—whanged down a pair of tens followed by a pair of aces. Ruck then scraped the top of the gasoline barrel with the edge of his last card, the barrel serving as a poker table. "Bullets over dimes, Mister Boone," he said. "Can you beat that?"

Boone, the stub of a cigar parked in the corner of his mouth, slid a pair of jacks out of his hand and onto the barrel.

"Two Johnnies, that's it?"

"And a pair of mop-squeezers." Boone slid the queen of hearts and the queen of clubs in next to the jacks.

"Not good enough." Ruck reached for the pot of six hundred-plus dollars.

Boone held up a finger, stopping Ruck. He flipped his last card in the air, and it came down the queen of spades.

"How about that, good old Calamity Jane for a full house. So, if you don't mind—" Boone raked in the pot. He tapped the bills on the barrelhead, squaring up the cash, and stuffed it in his jacket pocket.

Anger twisted Ruck's face. "Bastard, you're quittin' the game?"

A buck sergeant hustled up. He leaned down to Ruck, "Manny, we've got a problem."

Ruck stared at the new arrival.

"A tank coming off an LCT, it stalled. It's dead out there in the water."

"Cal, this is what you do. You get the Seabees to take a couple cat tractors down there. Tell 'em to tow that damn tank in and get it off to the side where the mechanics can work on it."

The sergeant slapped Ruck's shoulder and trotted away into the night.

Boone flicked his stump of a stogy away. "Your work doesn't stop for a card game, does it?"

"Hell, no. We've landed the Twenty-fourth Corps, so we're secure. Now I've got a dozen shiploads of equipment and supplies to get on the beach. It's gonna take at least two more days. But back to you quittin'."

Boone lit a new cigar. He inhaled a mouthful of smoke and puffed it out as a ring that drifted up and wrapped itself around the lone bug bulb that illuminated the game. "My daddy always told me to stop before Lady Luck turns her back on you."

"But you cleaned me out and my buddies, too. You're not gonna give us a chance to win back a few bucks?"

Boone tapped off his cigar while he turned that thought over in his mind, the ashes falling into the letters F-L-A-M-M-A-B-L-E etched into the barrelhead. Decision made, he brought out the wad he'd won and placed it in the middle. "Ruck, how about just you and me? I'm willing to bet all this on the turn of a card. You game?"

Boone leaned back on the ammunition crate that served as his armless and backless chair. He appraised his opponent.

The beach master picked up his cigarette. He took a drag on it and snorted the smoke out his nose. "I don't have that kinda money. To get that much, I'd have to rob the paymaster."

"Maybe you've got something of value that you could bet."

"Like what?"

Boone scratched at the barrelhead. "A landing craft."

"Go to hell."

"Ruck, what's it gonna cost you? The boat's the Navy's. The Navy crews it and puts the gas in the tank."

"What the hell you want an LC for?"

"A picture. One photograph that will get me a Pulitzer."

"Of what?"

"Of MacArthur wading ashore. Ruck, you refused him a boat. You said you couldn't spring one loose for three days. So he's out there on the deck of that damn battlewagon, smoking up a storm. He's gonna court martial you."

"Can't. He's Army, I'm Navy. Besides, the Secretary of War's my priest." Ruck came forward. He tapped his chest with his thumb. "I'm Uncle Henry Stimson's favorite nephew."

Boone riffled the money. He riffled it again. "You could make a down-payment on a pretty nice house with this after the war."

Ruck appeared to consider that as he rolled his cigarette from one side of his mouth to the other. "High cut wins?"

Boone nodded. He gathered in all the cards and shuffled them and reshuffled them. Then he cut the deck into four separate piles that he reassembled and shuffled one last time.

Other sailors and marines, watching from a respectful distance, edged in, gawking.

Boone pushed the deck to Ruck. "Cut."

Ruck cut the deck a third of the way down and slipped the top part under the bottom part.

Boone squared up the deck. "All right, for the money or the boat, cut."

Ruck tilted his head to the side, as if to see better what he was doing. He began cutting the deck a quarter of the way down, but stopped. He eyed Boone, then cut the deck half way down and turned that portion up.

"He's got the queen of spades, old Dirty Gertie," someone off to the side said.

Ruck, chuckling, rubbed his hands together.

Boone set his cigar aside. "I'd feel good, too, if I'd turned up a queen. Ruck, the odds against me beating that are, shall we say, very big."

He pushed the top card off the remaining pile, then a second card. Boone drummed his fingers on that one. He stopped and snapped the side edge with his thumb. "I think I'll go one more."

He pushed a third card off the pile. This one Boone pulled to himself. He peered at it, then laid it on the barrelhead face up.

Someone to the side whistled. "Did you see that," he said to the sailor next to him, "the king of diamonds."

Ruck drew his hands down his face. "When do you want your boat?"

BOONE, STANDING in the well of a landing craft

bobbing beside the battleship South Dakota, gazed up at a team of sailors lowering a climbing net. "You got the general up there?"

An officer in Army tans came to the railing, the bill of his hat dripping with gold braid.

"General MacArthur?" Boone called up.

"Yes."

"You ready to go ashore?"

"Have been since yesterday. Who the hell are you, and where the hell did you get that boat?"

"Clinton Boone, International News Service. And this landing craft—" He swept his hand around the interior. "—won it in a card game. Well, won the use of it for an hour. So, if you want to go ashore, how about you come on down?"

"Boone you say?"

"That's right."

"Mister Boone, there'll be seven of us—my senior staff and two guards."

"Fine."

The first stepped over the railing and onto the rope netting, followed by another.

Boone decided watching shoes and butts descending was something he could do without, so he went aft, to the landing craft's helm. "Commodore," he said to the sailor manning the wheel, "you ever have a four-star general as a passenger before?"

The sailor rested his forearms on the wheel. "A couple colonels. Mostly I get the grunts and their officers—sergeants and lieutenants. Do I have to salute him? MacArthur?"

"I wouldn't think so. You're the skipper of this craft, so if anyone does any saluting around here, it oughtta be MacArthur saluting you, wouldn't you think?"

The helmsman dipped his head toward his new

passengers now in the well, the last, with a carbine slung across his back, stepping off the climbing net. "Seven, so here we go. Next stop, Red Beach." He pushed the throttle forward, and the landing craft wallowed away from the battleship. It churned toward Leyte Island on the horizon, a half-mile distant.

MacArthur came up. "Sailor, thank you for the transport."

The helmsman held to the wheel with one hand and the throttle with the other, his eyes fixed on the island. "A pleasure, sir."

"A request, sailor."

"What's that, sir?"

MacArthur took his sunglasses off. He polished them with his handkerchief. "Don't run up on the beach. Drop the ramp out a ways. I want to walk in through the water to the beach like the men under my command."

"Walk in through the water, sir?"

"That's right."

"Scuttlebutt is you walk on the water, sir."

"I've heard that, too." MacArthur hooked the bows of his sunglasses over his ears and went forward to where his men lounged, several hanging onto handholds at the side of the LC.

Boone looked up at the helmsman. "Walk on water, I like that. I think I'll use that in my story."

The helmsman, still with his eyes locked on the island growing on the horizon, touched his brow with a one-finger salute.

Boone handed up a cigar. "Enjoy it at your leisure, commodore." He left him and went to MacArthur's party. "General?"

"Yes?"

"I hope you know for us in the news business, this is a photo shoot. We're after good pictures that will be seen back home by everyone across the country."

MacArthur, straddle-legged—braced against the rocking of the landing craft in the sea—jutted his chin out. "Mister Boone, that's what I'm after."

"I figured since there's talk you intend to run for president when this war's over. I can see the headline that goes with the pictures: 'MacArthur Keeps Promise, Returns To The Philippines.'"

MacArthur took his pipe out of his shirt pocket and jammed it in the corner of his mouth. "I like it."

"So on the beach is a crew from Movie Tone News with their motion-picture camera, a couple other reporters with still cameras, and of course, I've got mine." Boone reached inside his kit that he had stowed in a corner of the well and brought out his Speed Graphic four-by-five. He placed a film holder in the back of the camera and moved around to face MacArthur, standing toe-to-toe with him. "Now, General, when the commodore drops the ramp, I go out first, understood? You don't come out until I'm in position to get my picture."

"I can deal with that."

"Thought you could." Boone pointed to MacArthur's pipe. "I think you want to stow that."

MacArthur weighed the pipe in his hand for a moment, then put it back in his shirt pocket.

The LC's diesel motor reversed, slowing the boat. "Stand-by to exit the craft," the helmsman called out. "Water's gonna be up to your knees here. Ramp going down, now."

The helmsman pulled the release, and the ramp splashed into the water.

Boone slung his kit over his shoulder. He strolled forward, down into the warm waters of Leyte Gulf, a short distance off the beach, angling to the side as he went. Finally, he turned back and sighted through his camera's viewfinder at the picture he intended to take when MacArthur and his men slogged into his frame. "All right, General, it's show time!"

MacArthur appeared on the landing craft's ramp, his staff flanking him on either side and a pace or two behind. The group strode down the ramp, into the water, and on toward the beach, the mid-morning sun reflecting in flashes off the splashes.

Boone, from his position, panned his camera with the command party, keeping the seven men in his viewfinder. At what he deemed to be the most dramatic moment— MacArthur leaning forward, striding through the surf toward the beach and the Movie Tone crew's motion picture camera, MacArthur striding toward fame, a demanding look chiseling his features—Boone pressed the shutter release. Only MacArthur was no longer in view. He had disappeared except for his hat floating on the water.

He surfaced, soaked, splashing, spitting water, his thin hair in his face. "Stepped in a goddamn hole!"

MacArthur snatched up his hat. He shook it at the movie crew. "Boone! Take one of my guards and confiscate every goddamn foot of their film. I'll not have anyone see me all wet!"

Note: In 1945, the war in the Pacific raged in the Philippine Islands. Boone finds himself attached to the Army's 24th Division where heat takes down more soldiers than do bullets in the fighting in the abaca fields.

Welcome to Hell
– 1945 –

CLINT BOONE, sweat dribbling down his temples, pushed forward past a line of cat tractors idling, their rain caps popping, dancing on their exhaust stacks, the tractor drivers waiting on what he didn't know. And then he saw it ahead, below a sign that proclaimed 'Welcome to Hell,' a gaggle of mud-caked soldiers and beyond them an officer—a captain by the silver bars on his collar points— and a civilian, the two in a yelling match, the captain bellowing something about the men he'd lost "in that damn sugarcane field."

He shook a fist at a field of green plants twenty feet tall. "I'm through with it! I'm gonna bulldoze the whole damn thing in on the Japs. I'm gonna crush 'em!"

The civilian waved a paper, Boone could see it as he mopped his forehead with his sleeve. "It's not sugarcane. It's Musa textilis!"

"Get the hell out of the way."

"Musa textilis—abaca. The Navy wants as much of it as we can save." The civilian waved his paper once more. "These are orders from Admiral Halsey. You buck him and I'll see to it he throws you in the brig on some god-forsaken rock for the rest of your life. You want that?"

The captain turned back to a ground pounder. "Two of you," he said, jabbing a fist at a lieutenant and the man next to him, "grab that bastard and haul him back to base camp. Pitch him in the stockade."

The two stepped forward but stopped when a jeep rolled up to the head of the column. A colonel slipped off the passenger seat and stalked over to the captain. "Dex, what's the holdup?"

The captain thumbed toward the civilian. "That bastard says we can't bulldoze the field. Says he's got orders from Halsey."

"He has. The lord high admiral's been on the radio, chewing my ass. The Japs have got every field of that stuff on the island, and Halsey wants it, all of it undamaged." He glanced at the column of cat tractors. "Dex, send them back. There's to be no bulldozing, no bombing, no setting of fires. Find another way to get the Japs."

A sergeant sauntered up, a burp gun in the crook of his arm. "Captain."

"Yeah?"

"If you don't mind me askin', how long you been out of the Point?"

"What's that got to do with the price of tea in China?"

"Nuthin'. My question still is, how long have you been outta the Academy?"

"A year if you have to know."

"How long in the islands?"

"Four months."

The sergeant kicked a clod of red clay to the side of

the road. "Captain, I've been here four years. You give me a squad. You let me pick the men, and we'll get this field for you, two days tops."

The captain squared up, his face still red with anger. "How?"

"Now if I was to tell you, you'd just want to argue."

The colonel shook out a cigarette. He lit it. He dragged on it and blew a lungful of smoke to the sky. "Dex, what have you got to lose other than some time. Let him do it."

"Is that an order?"

"A suggestion. Sergeants have been saving our asses since there've been armies."

The captain, after some moments, gave a jerk of his head toward the sergeant.

Boone sidled over to the civilian. "What's all this brouhaha about?"

"Fibers for hawsers."

"Pardon?"

The civilian swept his hand toward the towering green plants that, to Boone, did look a helluva lot like sugarcane. "That's abaca," the civilian said. "The plants grow thicker and taller than sugarcane, and the fibers in them, some of the fibers up to fourteen feet long, and the toughest in the world and impervious to salt water. They're spun into hawsers for tying up heavy ships."

"So?"

"This island is the only place on God's green earth where this plant grows, where it's cultivated."

Boone dug in his pocket for his notepad and pencil. "So that's why the Japs won't give it up."

"And why we must take it, undamaged."

Boone stuck his hand out. "I'm with the International News Service. Who are you?"

"John Angelone, U.S. Department of Agriculture."

BOONE and Angelone sat on cots in the civilian's tent, listening to Les Brown and His Band of Renown playing *Sentimental Journey* on Angelone's shortwave radio, Boone studying the ash on the end of his cigar. "So how the hell did you come to get out here anyway?"

Angelone, stripped down to his shorts and undershirt, leaned his elbow on his knee. "Six years ago—God, that seems a lifetime back—the USDA sent me out to the Philippines to survey the island's agriculture and plant life. It seemed somebody high up wanted to know whether and how much war materiel might be here. These abaca fields and Mindanao's rope-making industry, I came on these in that trip. Never saw the likes of it before." He went to rubbing his knee. "Forgive me, I've aggravated my arthritis hiking all over these islands. Anyway, I didn't know where hawsers were made or even what went into them. Within a year, I was the world's authority."

Boone, sweat circles under the arms of his shirt, resumed smoking. He inhaled and puffed out a series of smoke rings. He watched them drift away. "Were you still here when the Japs invaded, three years ago?"

"Yes."

"And?"

"I was ordered out. 'Evacuate to Hawaii by any means possible.'"

"I sense a story."

Angelone went to massaging his other knee. "We've got pirates in these waters. I got to know some of them. For a price, they hid me aboard one of their boats and smuggled me out to a merchant vessel, the Pacific Queen, bound for—"

A woman's voice cut in at the end of the record.

"This is Tokyo Rose."

Boone looked away. "Here comes the commercial message."

"The war in Europe ended today with victory for the American forces and your allies."

Shouts and cheers went up from neighboring tents.

Someone stuck his head into Angelone's tent. "You listening to Rosie, hey? We beat the Germans, you hear that? Hell, man, we beat the Germans!"

Tokyo Rose came over the radio again. "Boys of the American Pacific Forces, do not think your brothers' win in Europe means you will win here. We know where you are. Boys of the American Army Sixth Battalion, Twenty-fourth Division, you are on Mindanao, trying to take the abaca fields from us. It will not happen. We are coming to strike you down. So, boys of the Sixth, do yourselves a favor, give up. Go home. To encourage you, here is music from your own Glen Miller Orchestra, *I'll Be Seeing You.*"

Boone scratched behind his ear. "Damn. You ever wonder how she gets her stuff."

"Spies."

A burst of light somewhere in the night sky gave an instant illumination inside the tent, then it dimmed, the burst cutting short the cheering and laughter outside.

Angelone looked up. "Fireworks for VE Day?"

Boone went to the tent flap. He poked his head out, and his mouth gaped open at a whistling sound and someone yelling "Incoming!"

Both he and Angelone bolted outside. They ran for a bunker—a trench—and leaped in as a shell exploded, throwing up dirt that showered them and others hunkered down there.

Another shell pounded down and another, then came the sound of a cannon in the distance responding.

More shells inbound—Boone counted six—and a

yell, "Medic!"

Others in the trench hurdled over the side and ran in the direction of the cry. Boone followed them, the group racing toward a blaze that lit the area, a fire in the tent complex that made up the battalion's headquarters.

The eye-stinging smoke and the stench.

The first there pitched burning canvas aside and dragged a shattered body out into the compound. More in the ensuing commotion did the same.

Boone went down on his knees by the first body. He checked the dog tags, then moved on. At the fifth, he stayed. He looked up, his face drawn. "It's the colonel," he said.

THE CAPTAIN paced around the wreckage in the battalion compound in the first light of day, dictating to a clerk: "The battalion commander and his Ex-O are dead. Our company commanders are either dead or wounded except for me, so I have taken command of the battalion until such time as you can send someone of appropriate rank to relieve me. Full status report on the Sixth and its companies to come forthwith. Sign the signal Captain Dexter J. Galt the Third." He clapped his hands twice. "Chop-chop, Corporal. Get that coded and off to General Lawrence at Division."

The corporal peered up from his shorthand. "But our radio was blown up last night."

"Then use my radio at my company HQ."

The corporal saluted and scurried away.

Boone came over, the blood of others on his sleeves and shirt front. "Well, Captain, what're you gonna do now that you've got command?"

Galt set his jaw, his eyes hard, "What I should have done yesterday. Kill Japs." He waved in a claque of lieutenants. "Men, it's up to us to carry the fight to the Japs hiding in the abaca fields. You and I know they're in machinegun nests and spider holes, waiting for us. Get every man jack of your platoons on the line. Pick a field. Surround it. Have the Seabees bulldoze it. While they're at it, you lay down gunfire and hit the Japs with flame throwers. Keep 'em in the field, goddammit. Kill 'em all."

A lieutenant with a three-day growth of beard raised his hand. "Captain, what if some want to surrender?"

Galt turned on his junior officer, a twitch jigging a muscle in his jaw. "What part of your orders don't you understand, Andrews, huh?"

"Um—"

"Let me repeat: Kill. Them. All." He flicked out a finger with each word. "If you can't do it, I'll put someone in charge of your platoon who can. Understood?"

The man mumbled something.

Galt cupped a hand behind his ear. "I can't hear you."

"Yessir," the lieutenant said, casting his gaze to the side.

"Say it louder, mister, and salute, goddammit."

The lieutenant braced. He snapped his right hand to his brow. "Yessir!"

"Good. Now you all go. You finish with one field, move on to the next."

They hustled off to a squad of jeeps and their drivers.

Angelone, standing to the side—ashen—moved in beside Boone. "Captain, you can't do that. You can't destroy the abaca."

"I'll bulldoze and burn every stalk of it to kill the Japs before they can kill us. Kill the Japs, mister, it's the only way to win this goddamn war. Now, if you will excuse me, I have to get out to my companies' HQs and light fires under the butts of the commanders I have to appoint." He marched away toward a waiting jeep.

Boone and Angelone lounged beside one another while a cleanup detail and a detail from Graves Registry went about their work. Boone stuffed his hands in his back pockets. "So, John, whaddaya gonna do now?"

"Radio my report to Halsey."

BOONE, rucksack in hand, and Angelone trotted across an airfield toward a crew gassing up a lone helicopter, a Sikorsky R-4—a two-man craft—the pilot in the seat, studying a map.

"Danny, you lost?" Boone asked.

The pilot stayed with his map, moving his finger along a cluster of hills. "Well, if it isn't our world famous war correspondent. What story are you chasing today, Boone?"

"Halsey."

"You're good, my friend. Chatter has it he's coming to the island." The pilot folded his map and stowed it in a pouch under his seat.

"He is coming." Boone clapped Angelone on the shoulder. "My partner here's been on the radio with Halsey's signalman. The admiral departed his flattop in the back seat of a Hellcat half an hour ago. Should be here in about ten minutes, we're guessing."

The pilot pushed the bill of his fatigue cap up. "I suppose I should practice my salute." He shook his head. "Naw, he's Navy. I'm Army. What do you suppose the Old Man wants?"

"To see the fighting in the abaca fields. You can give him the best view."

The pilot slipped down to the ground. "I fly rescue, Boone. I'm not a tour guide for generals and admirals." He walked back to the helicopter's gas tank as the fuel crew drove away. He spun off the cap and stuck his finger in.

He held it up. "Yup, wet. Full tank. I don't trust ground crews, even when I'm watching them."

Boone came up beside him. "Look, it's important Halsey sees the devastation from the air. It'll give him a better picture. Plus you can put him down on the road because he's gonna want to ream out the field commander. Danny, you can get him to the battle a helluva lot faster than some buck private can driving him in a jeep."

The pilot wheeled around, a Cheshire grin wreathing his face. "Do I get in a picture with The Admiral that you're gonna send to my hometown paper?"

Boone stuck out his hand. "You do what I want. I'll do what you want."

They shook.

Boone started away with Angelone, but he turned around, talking while backpedaling away. "Danny, I love ya. Right now I've got to see a couple other guys, but I'll catch up with ya at the abaca fields."

He swung around with Angelone still beside him and waved to two MPs in a jeep parked in the shade of a banana tree, a family of Macaque monkeys above them, chattering at them.

One of the MPs waved back.

Boone and Angelone continued on, angling toward the MPs. "Mac," Boone called out to the MP in the passenger seat, "I need your help."

The sergeant waved him away. "No thanks."

"Why not?"

"The last time I helped you, you suckered my partner and me into the middle of a bar fight to save your ass from a bunch of plastered marines."

Boone turned his free hand up. "Just because they didn't like the words I put to their corps' song—"

"You were snockered, Boone."

"I admit it. I did have a little too much fermented coconut milk. But this time you can be heroes, I guarantee it."

The sergeant glanced at his driver and partner, a corporal built like a professional wrestler, his biceps straining to burst through the fabric of his rolled-up sleeves. "What do ya think?"

"Hero wouldn't be bad."

The sergeant beckoned Boone in. "So what have you got?"

Boone set his kit on the jeep's fender. "You know Captain Galt?"

"Our little Napoleon? Can't stand the prick."

"Halsey's coming to cashier him for ignoring his orders."

The sergeant came forward in his seat. "The hell you say."

Boone took the paper from Angelone. He passed it to the senior MP who read it and blew his cheeks out when he finished. He handed the paper back. "So you want us there when Halsey's looking for a couple MPs to arrest the tiny tyrant."

"You got it. And you're gonna take John and me along so I can get the story."

The sergeant held up a finger. "There's a price, Boone."

"What's that?"

"You get a picture of me and Willy with The Admiral that you send to our hometown papers."

"You, too?"

"What?"

"Nothing." Boone, snickering, shook his head. "Yah, I guess I can do that."

The sergeant thumbed to the back seat. "Climb aboard.

BOONE directed the driver to the side of a wide spot in the road. Beyond, Galt stood in his jeep, directing the burning of a field, the smoke piling into the sky.

A helicopter—the Sikorsky from Libby Field—circled overhead. It slowed to a hover, then drifted down toward the road, kicking up dust in the final four feet of its descent. When the helicopter touched down, the pilot cut the engine, and the rotor blades spun down to a stop.

A banty-sized man in tans and an officer's hat hopped out of the R-4. He charged toward Galt, yelling something that caused Galt to blanch and clamber down from his jeep.

Boone slipped over the side of the MPs' vehicle. He rescued his Speed Graphic from his rucksack and made his way past the helicopter and up behind Halsey still yelling, still waving a fist.

At the height of the chew-out, Boone moved around to the side and banged off a picture.

Halsey snapped toward the click of the shutter and the man behind the camera. "Boone? What the hell are you doing here?"

"My job, Admiral."

"Your goddamn story won't get past my censors. I'll see to it."

"But my picture will. There's nothing in it that tells the enemy where you are. I shot from a low angle, so all that's behind you is smoke and the sky. No abaca fields." Boone tuned up his smile. "Oh, and when you're finished here, I'd like to get a picture of you with Danny over there—your pilot—and those two MPs walking this way who are gonna slap the manacles on the captain."

A soldier struggled out of a nearby field, a body slung

across his shoulders in a fireman's carry, the soldier clutching an M-1 in his free hand. He laid the body down in the red clay just shy of Galt. "Cap'n," he said, looking up, his face haggard, "this is my sergeant—Sergeant Morris. You sent us out into that damn field yesterday."

Note: From 1945 and the end of the hot war, the world in 1946 went into the start of the cold war. Joseph Stalin's Russia took control, country by country, of everything from Russia's western border to the European democracies. In the United States, the president of a small college in the equally small town of Fulton, Missouri, invited Winston Churchill to journey 4,261 miles by ship, plane, and train from his home at Chartwell, near London, to give a speech at the college.

Riding the rails with Winnie
– 1946 –

BOONE TOSSED his kit up the steps of the Union Pacific's City of Kansas City streamliner to a waiting porter. "They here, yet?"

The porter gave a nod. "'Bout five minutes ago. They got the President's car at the end of the train."

"Elijah, can you get me in?"

"I can try, Mistah Boone. You jus' follow me."

Boone hopped up the steps and moved into the wake of the porter making his way back through two passenger cars to the last car. There he rapped on the door.

"Yes, what is it?" came a voice from the far side.

The porter stuck his head in. "Mistah President," he

asked of one of the two men sharing a couch in the middle of the car, both reading newspapers, "the train's kinda full up. I got this here fella wid me who needs a seat. Kin he ride in yo car?"

Harry Truman turned a page. "Just as long as he doesn't make a nuisance of himself."

Elijah moved inside, with Boone following. He set Boone's kit on the first seat.

Boone slipped him a ten-dollar bill, the porter stammering out a hushed, "I can't take this, Mistah Boone."

But Boone closed the porter's fingers over the money. "Put it in your boy's college fund. He wants to go to Fisk, isn't that what you told me on my last trip?"

"Yassah." The porter bobbed his head. "My boy will appreciate this." He stepped around Boone and made his way out of the car, leaving the reporter in the aisle, shucking himself out of his storm coat.

Boone laid his coat and fedora across his kit. He brushed his fingers through his hair as he went back to Truman and the man seated next to him clutching his own newspaper folded in half, a stout individual with a bulldog face and a stump of a cigar crammed in the corner of his mouth. "I hope you don't mind," Boone said.

Truman looked away from a story in the Kansas City Star about graft in the Independence courthouse. He gave him a campaign smile. "Not at all. Now that you're here, why don't you sit down and join us? Of course, we're catching up on the news for the moment."

Boone settled on the couch across from Truman and his guest. He ran his hand over the fabric. "Pretty plush."

"Pardon?" Truman asked, again engrossed in the crime story.

"Pretty plush, this couch."

"Yes, it's certainly not what I would have ordered."

Truman looked up. He grinned. "I would have been happy with wicker chairs from Montgomery Ward. And you are?"

"Boone. Clinton Boone."

Truman wagged the corner of his newspaper at the man beside him. "Mister Boone, this is—"

"The once prime minister of England, I know." Boone reached his paw across the aisle, and Churchill, after he made a business of laying his paper in his lap, shook hands. "Mister Churchill, if you don't mind me asking, there was talk around the Muehlebach's coffee shop this morning that you lost a bundle to the President last night in a poker game. That true?"

Churchill grunted as he eased back into the couch. He hoisted his paper back up—The London Times, the copy dated February 26.

Truman gave Boone the hairy eyeball. "Fella, I don't think that's appropriate, not when you're a guest in my rail car."

Churchill laid his paper back in his lap. "Now, Mister President, it was bound to come out." He gazed at Boone. "It was forty-one pounds fifty pence . . . thirty-two dollars in your currency. The last time we played, which was in Potsdam, I won, and it was considerably more. Mister Boone, if I may, it would appear the time has come for me to ask you a question."

Boone forced a smile.

"Who are you, really?"

Boone handed Churchill his business card.

Churchill read it and passed it to Truman. "Mister President, this man is one of my colleagues." Churchill collected the card and returned it to Boone. "I was a correspondent at one time for the London Morning Post. That was during the Boer War—Eighteen Ninety-nine."

"I know. I read that somewhere."

"I was a pup back then, Mister Boone. Got caught by the damn Boers and had to escape. Got two books out of the experience, though. You ought to read them." Churchill peered over the tops of his glasses. "Do you intend to use this poker story from last night?"

"I can't think of a reason why." Boone rubbed at an imagined spot on his trouser leg. "No, I'm more interested in what you're going to say in your speech out in Fulton this afternoon, at the college—at Westminster."

"No comment." Churchill winked at Truman.

"So," Boone said, peering up, "I have to come to the speech with the rest of my fellow ink-stained wretches?"

"It would appear so."

It was Boone who now leaned back into the comfort of his couch.

An engine whistle hooted, and the train jerked into a roll that carried it out of the terminal, Boone gazing out at the buildings of downtown Kansas City that in fewer than a dozen blocks gave way to backyards and gardens not yet plowed and the rear of houses beyond them. He saw wash hanging out, sheets billowing in the morning breeze, and in one backyard a tow-headed boy playing with a dog. Boone smiled.

Churchill, rumbling about a story, held his newspaper out for Truman to see. He tapped a photo. "Unbelievable. The people of India are going to present the Aga Khan with two-hundred forty-eight pounds of diamonds—the fat old man's weight in gems—in honor of his sixty years on the throne. Simply unbelievable." Churchill shook his head, his jowls jiggling with the motion. "What did the British people give me after five years as prime minister? Nothing. Just my damn walking papers, as you Americans would say."

Truman folded his newspaper and laid it aside. "Winston, a day will come when they'll regret it. They may even call you back."

"Should they ever, I fear they must first do some hard talking to my Clementine. She's come to like having me at home."

"I'm sure. Now about where we're going, there's one thing you should know about Fulton and the county that surrounds it—Callaway County."

Churchill once more peered over the tops of his glasses, still with his paper in his hands. "And what would that be?"

"Callaway at one time was known as Little Dixie. That's because most who settled there had come from the slave states of the mid-South, brought their slaves with them."

Churchill nodded, or to Boone it appeared to be nodding, but then, he thought, maybe it was just the way the train was rocking.

"Well," said Truman, "back in our Civil War, the county seceded from Missouri and the United States and formed itself into a kingdom—the Kingdom of Callaway."

Churchill collapsed his newspaper, his eyes dancing behind his spectacles. "My heavens. Like England, with a royal family?"

"Winston, I'm sorry. The Callawayans didn't have a royal family. What they had was a militia. Missouri, as you may know, was at that time a Confederate state."

"Yes, yes."

"A Union general by the name of John B. Henderson dispatched six hundred men from Saint Louis to Wellsville in neighboring Montgomery County. From there they were to march on Calloway County." Truman wig-wagged his pointer finger. "You can't keep an advancing army secret, and word got to Fulton."

"I can imagine. How did your Callaway residents respond?"

"By raising an army of six hundred men of their own, and they did it overnight."

"Gracious, gracious, gracious."

"Yes. A Colonel Jefferson Jones led that instant army to the northeastern part of the county where he drilled the men in military tactics out in the open, out where he knew Union spies would see them."

"Bold, indeed."

Truman motioned at the opposite wall, as if it were something in the distance. "Winston, the spies also saw a massive artillery battery in the tree line, something like twenty-eight guns aimed in the direction from which the Union army would come. They high-tailed it back north to Henderson and told him what they had seen. Henderson stopped his march to consider his options."

"Yes?"

"While he dithered, Jones sent an envoy to him with a letter of demands."

"I see." Churchill took his cigar from his mouth and rolled it in his fingers.

Truman removed his glasses. After squinting at them, he polished them with a handkerchief. "The demands boiled down to this: If you don't want a fight, don't invade. Don't harass us. Don't try to arrest us. And recognize that we're a free and independent country with the right to govern ourselves. Do this, and we'll disband our army. We won't attack you."

"Henderson's response?" Churchill asked.

Truman peered through his freshly cleaned glasses. Apparently satisfied, he hooked the bows back over his ears. "He thought about the demands and about that line of cannons that could decimate his army. And he conceded."

Churchill turned toward Truman, surprise lighting his face.

"Yes, that's the way the Kingdom of Callaway came into existence." Truman nudged Churchill's elbow. "Winston, what Henderson never knew, nor his spies, was that those Callawayan cannons up in the woods, they were nothing more than logs painted black and mounted on wagon wheels."

Churchill chortled. "That is amazing, Harry. Simply amazing. Deception on the battlefield, deception to gain an advantage over one's opponent, I do love that."

"I knew you'd enjoy the story."

"Perhaps," Churchill said, puffing up a cloud with his cigar, "perhaps your Kingdom of Callaway is where General Eisenhower got his idea for the phantom army that he had your General Patton train in the south of my country, you remember, for an invasion of the Continent at Calais. That deception tied down two German armies that could have met us at Normandy. What a hell that would have been."

Boone cleared his throat.

Churchill, in response, stared across the aisle at him.

Boone waved away some of the haze of cigar smoke. "Mister Churchill, I know history fascinates you, but may I ask something about today?"

Churchill glanced at Truman and shrugged. "I see no harm in that. Go ahead, Mister Boone."

Boone came forward, his elbows on his knees, his hands clasped together as if in prayer. "You and the President here are two of the most powerful men in the world—"

"Not me, Mister Boone." Churchill tapped the ashes from his cigar into a porcelain ashtray with the seal of the United States on it. "I am now just a lowly member of the House of Commons."

"We could debate that, but to my question. What do you, as formerly one of the most powerful men in the world, think of Joseph Stalin, also one of the most powerful men in the world?"

Churchill took a long draw on his cigar. He held the smoke in for a moment, then expelled it toward the ceiling of the rail car. "He is a butcher, Mister Boone, a murderer of masses of his own people, more than seven hundred thousand in the two years of Nineteen Thirty-seven and Nineteen Thirty-eight alone according to my sources in MI-Six."

"But he was our ally."

"Because we needed him. We needed his armies, Mister Boone, to grind the Germans on the Eastern Front into the mud of the battlefields if we on the Western Front were to save civilized mankind, if we were to save the democracies of the world. That war is over, Mister Boone. We should now take Uncle Joe out behind a barn and shoot him."

"But you'd have to go to war with Russia before you could do that."

"Exactly."

Truman frowned.

Churchill patted the back of Truman's hand. "Not to worry, Harry. I am a realist. I know the difference between what we should do and what we can do. I'm out of office. I can do nothing other than talk, though I can, as you say, gin up a memorable phrase or two."

Boone sensed the train slowing, the clacking of steel wheels over rail joints decreasing in tempo.

The door at the end of the car opened.

The porter leaned in. "Two minutes to Jeff City, Mistah President."

Truman gave a small wave.

Boone pushed himself up. "If you'll excuse me," he said and made his way forward to where his kit, coat, and hat waited for him.

"Leaving us, Mister Boone?" Truman asked.

"Yes. I figure I'm not gonna have time to get a sandwich in Fulton, so I'd better get one here, forward in the dining car."

A PASSEL of men in suits that looked like they had been slept in—reporters, Boone thought—elbowed their way into the dining car, each toting a coat and some carrying cameras. He could hear their grumbling. One pointed at the empty chair at his small table, and Boone jacked his thumb at it.

"Walter Cronkite," the man said as he sat down, "United Press International. You're Clinton Boone, right? I've read you stuff."

"And I've read yours." Boone set his ham and Swiss on rye aside and wiped his lips with a napkin.

Cronkite pulled a menu over. "You talk to Churchill about his speech?"

"Uh-huh, before you got on."

"What'd he say?"

"'No comment.'" Boone put air quotes around the words.

"Same for us." Cronkite waved at a waiter coming away from another table. "I thought sure he'd give us something and we could file early when we get off the train. Now it's going to be a race for the telephones when he finishes his speech. I'm willing to bet the college has only one outside line, so the last man may not get to call his bureau until well after eight o'clock."

A WAITER refilled Boone's coffee cup while Cronkite held a hand over his.

"Walter," Boone said, a wry smile sprucing up his face, "have you ever thought of growing a mustache, a little cookie duster? You'd look good with one."

"My wife would make me shave it off."

"That's too bad. Your voice, Walter, why aren't you in radio? There's money there."

Cronkite toyed with his cup. "I was at one time. In fact, during the war Ed Murrow tried to entice me to join his staff at CBS Radio News, but, Boone, I'm a newspaper man just like you."

"Well, it was a thought." Boone glanced out a window at a sign near the tracks announcing Fulton. The clacking of the steel wheels once more slowed. He stood and shrugged himself into his coat—Cronkite and the other reporters doing the same—as the streamliner glided up beside a slab-sided depot painted the red and green of the MKT Railroad—the Missouri Kansas Texas line.

A conductor stepped into the car. He barked out, "Fulton. Fulton, Missouri. Three-minute stop."

Cronkite pushed out into the aisle behind Boone, and they commenced shuffling toward the end of the car. "Boone, are you going to take in the parade for Churchill and Truman or head up to the college for a front-row seat in the gymnasium?"

Boone poked two fingers down into his suitcoat's inside pocket. "Damn."

"What is it?"

"I'm out of cigars. I should have bummed one from Churchill." He glanced back over his shoulder at Cronkite. "I'm gonna have to go to a drugstore and get a couple. Save me a seat at the college, wouldja?"

BOONE STRODE past a plate glass window embossed with gold lettering proclaiming the store inside to be Saults Drug Store—Prescriptions, Notions & Fountain Drinks. He turned in at the door and made his way to the first counter. "Do you have a phone?" he asked the clerk there.

She pointed back toward the soda fountain. "A pay phone, yes."

He pushed on back, to the far end of the fountain, to a phone booth set in a corner and stepped in. Boone dropped his kit by his feet and fumbled out a nickel. He pressed it into the coin slot. After the phone dinged, he dialed 'O'.

"Operator," came a voice through the receiver.

Boone leaned into the mouthpiece. "Operator, long distance collect to San Francisco, Douglas twenty-five twenty-two."

"San Francisco. Sir, this may take several minutes to connect. Do you wish to wait on the line or would you prefer that I call you back?"

"Call me back." Boone squinted at the number printed beneath the coin slots. "The number here is Essex four-six-one."

"Very well, sir."

Boone placed the receiver back on the hook. He stepped out, leaving his kit in the booth, and went to the tobacco counter. "Any Havanas?" he asked the clerk, this time a man whose unkempt hair and mustache reminded Boone of Charlie Chaplin's little tramp.

The clerk brought up a box from beneath the glass. "I'm afraid the best we carry are Dutch Masters."

"That'll do. Perfectos?"

"Yessir." He opened the box.

Boone helped himself to a fistful and laid a fiver on the counter. While the clerk made change, Boone stripped the wrapping off a cigar. He bit off the blunt end and lit up, taking two good puffs. "Not a Havana, but pretty darn good," he said as he stuffed the other cigars into his inside coat pocket.

He returned to the phone booth only to find a woman inside, talking. Boone rapped on the glass.

She waved him away.

Boone opened the door. "Lady, I'm waiting for a long-distance call from California."

Again she waved him away, still talking into the mouthpiece. "Gladys, there's a man here, very rude. Just doesn't want to wait his turn—"

Boone sucked on his cigar. When he had a good lungful of smoke, he huffed a cloud into the booth.

The woman fanned at it while Boone huffed in a second cloud.

She coughed. She glared at Boone, banged the receiver down on the hook and stormed out, waving the smoke away. "Rude. Absolutely rude," she muttered and pumped on toward the front of the store.

The phone rang.

Boone, eying the woman's legs, picked up the receiver.

"Is this the party placing the collect call to San Francisco?" a voice asked.

Boone turned to the mouthpiece. "Yes, ma'am."

"I have your party on the line."

"Boone?" a male voice asked over the phone.

"Roger-dodger."

"Yes, operator, I know this guy. I'll accept the charges."

"Very good, sir."

A click came, then the man in San Francisco once more. "Boone, whaddaya got for me?"

"An interview with Churchill."

"Is this an exclusive?"

"Would I have anything less, Roger?"

"Excellent. My clocks say it's noon here, two where you are, and three in New York, so your story will make all the evening papers. Boone, you've scooped your buddies out there, so I'm gonna put you in for a bonus. How about ten bucks?"

"Make it twenty-five."

"Fifteen and that's tops. Don't wantcha getting a big head. Hang on now while I get a rewrite man, then you can dictate."

Boone heard a holler away from the phone in San Francisco: "Ned, pick up the line. I've got Boone for you in some podunk town in Missouri."

A click sounded, followed by a new voice. "Packwood here. Boone, let 'er rip."

Boone settled against the wood and glass wall of the phone booth, his smoldering cigar pinched between his thumb and first and second fingers. "Dateline: Fulton, Missouri," he said into the mouthpiece. "Winston Churchill, former prime minister of England, here to deliver a major speech at the appropriately named Westminster College, said the world's democracies, specifically Great Britain and the United States, should execute Joseph Stalin by firing squad if they ever take him prisoner.

"Churchill charged the Russian dictator and wartime ally with crimes against mankind, specifically the murders of seven hundred thousand . . ."

Note: The war starved Americans for new cars. For four years, automobile plants had been producing tanks and other vehicles for the war, artillery guns and shells, even bombers. The first automobiles for civilians trickled off the manufacturing lines in late 1945. Production ramped up the next year and boomed from there on.

A New Car for Boone
– 1947 –

CLINT BOONE stuck his head through the open window of a convertible that had the top up.

"Like it?" a voice asked.

He looked across the front seat to a man who had his head in the opposite window. "Yeah."

"You ready to buy it, or do you want me to tell you about it?"

Boone backed out and patted the door frame. "Sure. I'll give a listen."

The man came around—slim, an Errol Flynn mustache, his suit of a far better quality than Boone's Sears Roebuck. He put out his hand. "Hal Ebersol," he said. "And you are?"

"Clinton Boone." Boone shook the man's hand, noticing grease under the man's fingernails.

Ebersol caught Boone's glance. "When I'm not selling cars or delivering cars or picking them up, I work in the back shop—lube and oil man, sometimes a mechanic."

"So this is your business, huh? Your agency?"

"Open a year now."

Boone returned his attention to the car, an Oldsmobile.

"It's a Ninety-Eight Custom Convertible," Ebersol said. "Just got it in last week, brand new off the rail car. All of a half mile on it." He went to the front where he reached his fingers in under the nose of the hood. Ebersol pulled the release. He pushed the hood up and jammed a support rod under it to hold the hood there. "Look at that motor, the biggest Straight-Eight you could ever want. Cadillac builds it for us."

"What'll it do on the road?"

Ebersol rubbed his hands together. "Guess."

"Ninety, maybe?"

"Catch this. I took a two-door coupe version of this car out to a track outside the city. A hundred and ten on the straight-away."

Boone, smiling, massaged his chin. "I'd say that's enough."

"Absolutely, considering most country roads in the state are speed limited at forty-five. You ever drive an automatic?"

"Floor shift only."

"Mister Boone, you're in for a treat." Ebersol closed the hood. He took out a handkerchief and polished his fingerprints away. "Once you're in drive, this does all the shifting for you. You just work the gas and the brake pedals. We call it a Hydra-Matic."

"Really."

"Uh-huh. During the war, when Olds wasn't building cars, they put that transmission in Stuart tanks, so you know it's rugged, not about to give you any problems. You might like to know I drove Stuarts in the war."

"Pretty light, weren't they?"

"They were scout tanks—fast as a scared deer. As long as we didn't drive into an ambush, it was pretty hard for the Germans to hit us."

He beckoned to a young woman working an adding machine and recording numbers at a desk.

She came over.

"My wife and accountant, Mister Boone. This is Cindy." Ebersol opened the driver's door, and she slipped in behind the steering wheel. "Mister Boone, Cindy's going to show you how the top works."

She reached up to the top of the windshield and unbuckled two toggles.

"In most convertibles you've ever been in," he said, "you have to stand up, then wrestle with the top to get it to go back and down into the boot. The wrestling, most women can't do that."

He motioned at a button on the dash. She touched the button, and a motor whirred up, retracting the canvas top and folding it down into the boot.

"When it starts to rain," Ebersol said. Again Cindy Ebersol touched the button. The top, in response, rose up. It came forward and settled in place.

Ebersol spread his hands wide. "Impressed?"

"How much?"

"Do you have a car to trade in?"

Boone shook his head. "I've never owned one. When I've needed a car, I've borrowed one or took a taxi."

"No trade-in, huh?" Ebersol gazed at the rear fender, as if he were making some mental calculations. A speck of dust caught his attention. He whisked it away. "All right," he said as he pocketed his handkerchief, "I can let you drive this beauty out of the showroom today, right now—

without my wife—for twenty-three hundred dollars. And some tax. The governor has to get his, you know."

Boone pulled out a roll, the outside bill a Ben Franklin. "Mister Ebersol—Hal—I know what your markup is. I'll give you two thousand cash right now, and you swallow the tax. It's that or I go down the street to the Hudson agency. They've got a convertible that I hear is a helluva car."

Ebersol hesitated. He glanced at his wife back at her desk.

She nodded.

BOONE AIMED his new Oldsmobile into a parking slot in front of the Kansas City office of United Press International. There at the curb stood a fellow newsman, Walter Cronkite, lighting a cigarette. "Some car," Cronkite said when he looked up.

Boone laid his arm across the back of the passenger seat. "Get in. I'll take you for a ride."

Cronkite did as he was invited to do. Once inside, he ran his hand across the dashboard. "So what's the story here?"

"Well," said Boone as he backed out of the slot, "I had all my wartime pay still in the bank, so I thought the time had come to spend it. A good chunk of it, anyway."

He squared up the car, then sped away at twenty-five miles an hour, the city speed limit, an elbow out the window and the top down.

Cronkite settled back into the comfort of the seat. "All I've got is a Ford, a pre-war job."

Boone glanced at his passenger. "And a wife and three kids. You're probably buying a house, too, so I don't expect you have much left over from your paycheck for smokes, let alone a better car."

He slowed and turned north onto a county road. As the Olds rolled out into the countryside, Boone kicked up the speed, a cornfield coming into tassel on one side of the pavement and a pasture with Ayrshire dairy cattle grazing in it on the other. "When Truman built these roads for Jackson County, he built them to last, so . . . let's see if this little old Oldsmobile will do what the salesman said it would."

Boone stepped down on the accelerator. The wind in the car became a tornado, swirling around, whipping Boone's and Cronkite's hair every which way as the speedometer shot past seventy, past seventy-five, past eighty, Boone keeping the pressure on the gas pedal.

A motorcycle swung out from a patch of hickory trees, lights flashing and its siren screaming.

Boone looked up at the image in his mirror. He grimaced and took his foot off the accelerator.

The motorcycle cop moved out into the passing lane, waving for Boone to pull over.

Boone idled down. He eased the Oldsmobile off onto the shoulder, gravel crunching under the car's tires.

The motorcycle, back behind Boone again, rolled off, too.

Both stopped.

Boone sat there, waiting for what he knew was coming. He drummed his thumbs on the steering wheel.

Cronkite glanced at him. "Glad I'm not the one driving."

The cop, clad in sheriff's tans, strolled up, a hand on the butt of his holstered gun. "Do you know how fast you were goin', fella?"

Boone hazarded a look at the officer. "Can I ask you a question?"

"What's that?"

"How long have you been a cop?"

"Five years. What's that got to do with anything?"

Boone narrowed his eyes. "So, you weren't in the war then?"

"No."

Boone looked to Cronkite. "This guy's a damn shirker. Can you believe that, Walt?" He turned back to the cop. "Cronkite here was in England and Europe, and I was in China and the South Pacific. And you wanna ticket us for doing a little over the limit?"

The cop leaned down into Boone's face. "A little over? Fella, you were flyin'! Eighty-five plus. This is gonna cost you big time."

He took out his summons book. "License."

Boone handed his on.

The cop scrutinized it. "You get this with, what, fifty cents and a Wheaties box top?"

"No, I took the test."

"How many times?"

"Just once. Passed it on the first try."

"Uh-huh." The cop read off the license: "Clinton R. Boone, Two Twenty-six Osage Street, Mission, Kansas." He gave Boone a cold stare as he handed the license back. "Mister Boone, you are now in Missouri, my state, in my county. I tell you I can't wait to get you in front of the judge. In fact, how about you follow me back to the courthouse, and we'll do just that?"

BOONE SLOGGED down the courthouse steps, his hands shoved deep in his pockets, Cronkite walking beside him, his arm around Boone's shoulders. "It's not too bad, Boone. It only cost you forty-five dollars and another twenty for that shirker remark. Want me to drive?"

Boone stopped at the sidewalk. He took out a cigar and a book of matches.

Cronkite motioned at Boone's car just ahead of them, nosed in at the curb. "You've got an electric cigar lighter in your new car. Did you know that?"

Boone stared at his matches. He put them back in his pocket and went on to the car and got in.

Cronkite slipped in from the other side. He pushed the lighter in. While he waited for it to get hot, he took out a cigarette and rapped the end of it against the back of his hand, packing the tobacco tighter.

The lighter clicked.

Cronkite pulled it out. He touched the glowing end to his cigarette. After he got a good burn going, he passed the lighter to Boone who pressed it to the end of his cigar. He puffed and, as he blew the smoke toward the sky, Boone shook the lighter like one would a match, to put the fire out.

He pitched the lighter over the side of the car.

Cronkite stared at him. "What'd you do that for?"

"Huh?"

"Why'd you throw the lighter away?"

Boone jerked his face in the direction the lighter had gone. "Ohmigod. That's what I've always done with a dead match after I've lit my cigar."

He got out and searched the pavement for the lighter with no success. Boone wondered, as he stood there rubbing at the short hair on the back of his neck, as he remembered the sound of the lighter dinging off something, could it have been the rusting pickup parked next to him? Could the lighter have bounced off, hit the pavement, and maybe rolled under his car?

Boone got down on his knees.

He peered under the Oldsmobile. There the lighter was. He reached for it, touched it, but the lighter rolled a couple inches away.

Boone laid flat on his belly. He reached again,

stretching his arm and hand until he felt the lighter with the tips of his fingers. Boone worked his fingers, drawing the lighter into his palm. "Got it," he announced to no one other than himself as he scooched his way out and up. He peered down at the grit of the street on the front of his suit. Boone went to brushing the grit away, all the time puffing on his Havana.

Once more he got into his car. Boone returned the lighter to its socket. "Some days, Walter, start out all sunshine. You know it's really gonna be terrific, and then it just turns to horse shit."

"And that's the way it is."

Boone snapped toward Cronkite. "What?"

"I said that's the way it is, the way things work out."

Boone punched his finger into Cronkite's lapel. "Walter, that line—that's the way it is—hang onto that line. Someday, if you ever get back into radio and get a news show like Lowell Thomas', you can use that line to end your show . . . and that's the way it is, August Seventeenth, Nineteen Forty-seven."

"Maybe." Cronkite peered at his wristwatch, at the time. "Oh, man, I've got to get back to the city. I've got an appointment with the mayor in twenty minutes."

"Not to worry." Boone started the Oldsmobile's motor, the Straight-Eight burbling up into a rumble. He checked for traffic, saw a Greyhound and, after it passed, backed out. Boone straightened up the car and whipped it around in a U-turn that headed him and Cronkite west for Kansas City.

The motorcycle cop, coming out of a café with a half a sandwich in his hand, hopped into the traffic lane. He held his sandwich up.

Boone stopped. He leaned out around his windshield's corner post, the better to see the officer. "Now what?"

The cop laid his sandwich on the hood of Boone's car. He brought his summons book out of his back pocket and opened it to a fresh page. "Mister Boone, I gather you must enjoy collecting traffic tickets."

"What?"

"That U-turn."

"So?"

"That's illegal."

"Since when?"

"Since January, when the common council passed an ordinance outlawing it inside the town limits."

Boone blew up a cloud of cigar smoke. "The hell you say. I live on the other side of the river in Kansas. How'm I supposed to know that?"

The cop took a pencil from the band on his cap. He scratched Boone's name and license information from the previous ticket onto the new one. "I suppose, if you like, we could go back in the courthouse and you can tell it to the judge, though you're not likely to get much sympathy."

"Why's that?"

"He just hates Kansans."

Boone, smoldering, stubbed out his cigar. He flicked it into the street.

The cop looked up from his book. "Oh, sir, now I've gotta write you up for littering."

Note: The Soviets stopped highway, rail, and river travel to Berlin a number of times between February and early June of 1948. On June 24, they made the blockade total. Boone, transferred by the INS to Europe, found himself in the middle of the Berlin Airlift in which American, British, and French pilots were flying 5,000 tons of food and coal to the city each day to feed and, in the coming winter, keep warm more than two million people.

The Candy Bomber
– 1948 –

ARCHIE SIDEBOTTOM, at the controls of an airfreighter hauling twenty-five hundred gallons of bottled milk to Berlin, glanced back at the man in the jump seat—Clint Boone. "Buckle up, buddy. It's about to get hairy."

Boone looked up from his notes.

Sidebottom nodded to the side. "See off there to my port?"

Boone peered out a window to his left.

"See that Russian fighter out there? That damn Yak-Three? See the red tail on it?"

"Got 'im."

"That bastard's buzzed me on the last four flights.

Today, I'm gonna get him." Sidebottom banked his four-engined behemoth to the side and rolled out on a course that put the Russian dead on his nose.

Boone leaned an arm against the back of the pilot's seat. "You're gonna ram him?"

"If that's what it takes to get rid of him. Thirty seconds."

"Archie—"

"If I had a cannon, Boone, I'd blast him out of the sky. All that's left is to play chicken. Twenty seconds."

"Arch, the German kids waiting for this milk—"

"Ten seconds."

Boone, straining, fought the impulse to duck as the Russian fighter hurtled in. It jinked away at the last moment, jinked into a climbing turn, the wash from its propeller buffeting the airfreighter, rattling the thousands of bottles of milk in their wire crates in the cargo bay.

Boone blew out his cheeks. "Jesus, Archie—"

"Score one for the good guys." Sidebottom banked his aircraft back on course for Berlin's Tempelhof Airport. He squeezed the transmit button on his microphone. "Tempelhof Tower, Navy Skymaster Four-Seven-Niner-Bravo, fifteen miles out."

"Seven-Niner-Bravo, Tempelhof Tower, two birds ahead of you. Altimeter three-zero-point-two-one. Clear with a seven-knot breeze from the north. Call five out."

"Roger, Seven-Niner-Bravo." Sidebottom throttled the engines back to half. He dipped his brow for his co-pilot to lower the landing gear.

Boone heard the motors running the wheels out and down. He felt the ssshunk of the gear locking into place.

"Three green lights," the co-pilot said to Sidebottom.

"Half flaps, Ronnie."

The co-pilot pulled a control handle down to its second detent.

Boone sensed the increasing drag and felt the plane hop as the flaps extended down beneath the wings, down into the slipstream.

Sidebottom pushed the nose of the airfreighter down, to keep it on the glide path to the airport. He pressed the transmit button again. "Tee Tower, Seven-Niner-Bravo five out."

"Seven-Niner-Bravo, departing Army Skymaster on the runway. You're cleared to land after he takes off. He's rolling."

"Roger, Seven-Niner-Bravo." Sidebottom motioned ahead to a crowd of people—mostly children—clustered on a mountain of rubble close to the near end of the runway. "Boone, that's who we're doing this for."

"I see 'em. I'm gonna go talk to them after you shut down—for my story. How much time have I got?"

"Full flaps," Sidebottom said to his co-pilot.

The co-pilot pushed the flap handle the rest of the way down at the same time Sidebottom eased the throttles back, the airfreighter whistling over the crowd, the plane's tires screeching as they touched the runway and spun up to speed. Sidebottom hauled the throttles back to idle. "Brakes, Ronnie."

The co-pilot stepped hard on the brake pedals. As the aircraft slowed, Sidebottom herded it off onto a taxiway, to a ramp where a string of other airfreighters stood nose-to-tail, unloading, their engines silent.

Boone moved his finger along the line, counting— eight, all Douglas C-Fifty-four Skymasters.

Sidebottom idled his up behind the last and shut his engines down. He hooked his elbow over the back of the seat. "Boone, you've got thirty minutes. That's all it takes to offload. If you're not back—"

"I get left behind. I get it." Boone, out of his seat, pushed through the cockpit door to the cargo bay, the cargo doors already open. The August heat swept in.

BOONE SIDLED up beside a man in G.I. tans winding the mechanical drive in an eight-millimeter camera. "Whatcha filming?"

"The kids over there beyond the fence, those watching the planes come in." The man folded the winding key back against the side of his camera. "You?"

"I thought maybe I'd talk to them. Could be a story there." Boone grubbed a notepad out of a side pouch on his rucksack. "I'm with the INS."

"Not heard of that."

"International News Service." Boone paged into his notepad. "When Stalin laid down this blockade, my boss told me to catch the first MATS flight I could and get the story." He got out his pencil. "Your name, Lieutenant?"

"Gail Halvorsen."

"S-o-n or s-e-n?"

"E-n."

"From where?"

"Salt Lake City." Halvorsen adjusted the f-stop setting on his camera.

Boone scratched down the name and hometown. "I know why I'm here. How about you?"

"Army pilot flying for Operation Vittles."

"They give you a DC-Three or a Skymaster?"

"I started with a Three. Two weeks ago, they switched me up to a Skymaster. Heck of a freight hauler, that aircraft."

Boone tucked his pad and pencil in his shirt pocket, and dug into his rucksack for his Leica. "Mind if I take a picture of you filming those kids? I'll see that it gets to the Tribune back there in Salt Lake."

"Fire away." Halvorsen brought his movie camera's

viewfinder up to his eye. Boone watched him frame his shot of the rag-tag collection of German children, some in shoes, most barefoot, the children turned away, focused on a cargo plane inbound for a landing. He watched Halvorsen film the group as they waved to the pilot— shot his own picture at that moment—then followed Halvorsen as he panned up to the airfreighter, catching it as it passed overhead, swivelling to follow and film the aircraft as it touched down on the runway.

Done, Halvorsen again twisted the winding key, winding the motor once more as he strolled to the fence, Boone moving along with him. "*Guten Tag*," Halvorsen said. "Anyone speak English?"

Several hands went up.

He slipped his camera into its carrying case slung from his shoulder. "My friend here and I would like to talk to you."

One pointed up at the next aircraft coming in. "You pilot? You fly?"

A smile bowed Halvorsen's lips. "Yes. Why are you all out here?"

The questioner, in short pants and his sleeves rolled above his elbows, shrugged. "It's something to do."

Halvorsen took a pack of Wrigley's Doublemint from his shirt pocket. While he pulled out a stick of gum and peeled its wrapper away, Boone saw something Halvorsen didn't—the children inching forward, their eyes on the gum.

Boone nudged Halvorsen. "Think maybe you oughtta give that away?"

Halvorsen looked up. Startled, he passed the stick through the fence.

The talker tore off a small piece of gum. Others crowded around him did the same until there was nothing left.

Halvorsen gave over the rest of his pack, and he and Boone watched as others who had missed out on the first stick divvied up the remainder.

"You know, the next time I fly over, I could drop some more," Halvorsen said.

Eyes, expectant, zeroed in on the pilot. "How will we know it's you?" the talker asked.

Halvorsen rubbed a hand back over his buzz cut. "Well, I guess I could wiggle my wings."

"Uncle Wiggly Wings," someone said. "*Oheim Wacheln Flugel.*" Others clustered near him laughed.

Halvorsen touched his chest. "*Oheim Wacheln Flugel, ja. Vielleicht morgen.*"

Some children grinned while others clapped their hands.

"What'd you say?" Boone asked from the side of his mouth.

"Maybe I'll fly tomorrow. I'm not on the schedule, but I can ask."

Boone took a bill from his wallet. He folded the bill into Halvorsen's hand. "Buy a bunch of candy bars at the PX for me and drop them with whatever you drop. We might as well make us some good friends here."

Halvorsen gazed at the money before he pocketed it. "Sure, why not. I've got to catch a flight back to base. How about you?"

"Maybe later for me."

Halvorsen backed away. He waved to the children behind the fence as he did. "*Morgen, aus der himmel. Kaugummi.*"

Tomorrow, out of the sky. Chewing gum.

Boone shook his head. He beckoned to the talker, beckoned him to the fence. "Kid, I'd like to get a souvenir. You think you could help me?"

The boy—maybe fifteen, maybe sixteen, Boone

thought—stared at him.

"Souvenir. *Andenken.* Something I can take home, back to the States."

The boy waggled a finger. "What kind of *andenken?*"

"A German rifle. I can pay. And, of course, I'll pay you a finder's fee. *A finder's gebuehr.*"

"How much?"

This guy's a negotiator, Boone thought. Just the person I need. "Five Deutsche marks. New currency."

The boy huddled with a girl smaller than he. A friend. Maybe a sister, Boone thought. Turning back, the boy shook his head. "Must be fifteen."

"Sorry, too much. I might consider going up to seven."

"No, thirteen."

"All right, eight."

"Twelve."

"Nine."

"Eleven."

"Kid, let's split the difference. What's your name?"

"Hans. Hans Fredrick. Ten marks, yes. I take you to the man who has what you want."

"But you don't know what I want."

"You said a rifle."

"A Gewehr Forty-three."

"The man may have one." The boy motioned to his left. "There's a break in the fence by those trees. See—"

The rumble of a Skymaster's engines, the freighter landing, drowned out the boy, but Boone saw him and the girl run toward the trees. He double-timed it after them. When he caught up, the boy pulled up a section of the chain-link.

Boone crawled under. Once on the other side, he slapped the dust out of the knees of his trousers. "So, where do we meet this man?"

"Not far." The boy set off at a fast walk toward the

nearest set of houses, the girl with him, most of the houses bombed-out or wrecked by tank fire.

Had to be the Russians. Boone knew it. They had captured the city. Eisenhower had given it to them.

"Your English, it's good," he said when he again caught up.

"My sister and I, we were born in America."

"Really?"

"*Ja*, our father was a diplomat in your capital until he was called back here, seven years ago."

"Where is he now?" Boone glanced at the boy without breaking the pace when the boy didn't answer.

"Dead?" Boone asked.

"*Ja.* The Russians killed our mother, too."

"Who do you live with then?"

"Our grandparents. Their house damaged, so we live in the cellar, Opa, Oma, and Tanten Amelie and Frieda."

The trio ducked through an alley to a second rank of houses, most as ruined as those in the first rank.

"Six of you living in a cellar?" Boone asked, huffing from the strain of keeping the pace set by the talker and his sister. "Do your grandparents or your aunts work, have jobs?"

"Opa, he used to get a pension. No more."

"Then how do you live? What do you do for food?"

"I steal. I'm very good at it. Never caught. Not once. This way." The boy pointed to another alley. Half way through it, he and his sister jogged down a set of steps. At a basement door, he knocked.

"*Ja!*" came a voice from inside—a man's voice.

"Hans Fredrick. *Eines kunden haben.*"

I have a customer.

Boone heard the shuffling of feet beyond the door, then the door opened. In the doorway stood a squat, rotund man wearing an eye patch, a Luger shoved in his belt.

"*Ja?*"

"*Diese mann wuenscht ankaufen un Gewehr vierzig drei.*"

This man wants to buy a Gewehr Forty-three.

The man hooked a pair of wire-rimmed glasses over his ears. He studied Boone. "*Amerikaner?*"

The boy gave a firm nod.

"*Geld gute?*"

"*Ja.*"

The man looked up the steps. "*Haben sie nachgefolgt?*"

Anyone follow you?

"*Nein.*"

The man waved the trio in and closed the door behind them.

In the dim light, Boone made out stacks of wooden crates. He recognized the markings on some, but those with Cyrillic lettering threw him. If there was to be another war, he'd have to learn Russian and he knew it. The man, he concluded, was a black marketeer, an arms dealer willing to sell to anyone who had the cash. Boone wondered where he got his stuff.

The man waddled down one row. He picked up a crate and toted it back to a table. There he pried the top off the crate.

Boone peered inside. Gewehr Forty-threes. Twenty to a crate. Never issued. He tilted his head toward the rifles. "May I?"

The man said nothing, so Boone lifted a rifle out. He checked the firing chamber—empty—then jammed the butt into his shoulder. Boone sighted along the barrel at a scrap of paper tacked to a far wall and squeezed the trigger twice. Two clicks. Satisfied, he laid the rifle across the open crate. "How much?"

The boy repeated the question in German.

The man patted the gun. "*Einhundert marks. Neuen devisen.*"

One hundred marks. New currency.

Thirty dollars and change in American money. Not bad, Boone thought. Not worth haggling over. "I need a clip of five bullets—tracers," he said.

The man reached for a box of ammunition.

Damn, the old pirate knows English.

The man took out five shells, each with a red-tipped bullet. He handed them to Boone and a clip to load the shells into. "Five marks, please."

BOONE GALLOPED over to the portable stairs leading up to the cargo bay of an Army Skymaster, his rucksack on his back and a hunting case concealing a long gun in one hand. He popped his other hand up to the crewman standing in the doorway, a sergeant by the chevrons on his sleeve—the aircraft's loadmaster. "Can I hitch a ride back to Wiesbaden?"

"You can if you hustle yer butt up here. The captain's startin' the engines."

The first of the freighter's four motors whirred up. It fired, stuttered, then smoothed out in a low idle.

As Boone clambered up the stairs, the second motor fired.

The loadmaster stepped back. "Whatcha got in the case there, bud?"

"War souvenir."

A gaggle of workers on the tarmac rolled the stairs away. After they disappeared, the loadmaster slammed the clamshell doors shut and locked them, darkening the interior. One light on the forward bulkhead glowed. Someone in a jump seat beneath the light held up two fingers to Boone, then pointed to an empty seat next to himself.

Boone made the trek forward, shucking his rucksack. When he got to the bulkhead, he dropped into the seat and dropped the rucksack to the floor, the aircraft already rambling out to the departure runway. Boone slapped the knee of the man next to him. "So, Lieutenant, thought you'd be gone by now."

Halvorsen rubbed at his five-o'clock shadow. "I had a few more things I wanted to film. How about you?"

"I bought me a souvenir." Boone patted the gun case in his lap. "I've got a couple Jap guns at home. Thought I should have one from the Krauts."

A speaker above the light crackled, the crackling followed by a tinny voice. "Everybody back there in the bay, buckle up. We're on the active, about to take off."

Boone snugged himself into a shoulder harness and seat belt. He glanced at Halvorsen doing the same. "So, you figure out how you're gonna make the candy drop?"

The engines came up in a full-throated roar, shaking the walls, floor, seats, and Boone and Halvorsen as the empty airfreighter rattled down the runway. Boone pressed the tips of his fingers into his ears. After liftoff and climb-out, the engines settled back at a lesser power setting, the sound a high thrum.

Boone took his fingers away from his ears. "So I was asking," he said, pitching up his voice, leaning into Halvorsen to make himself heard over the noise in the aircraft.

Halvorsen pitched up his own voice. "The idea that came to me is to attach my gum and your Clark bars to parachutes and throw them out of my window."

"Parachutes?"

Halvorsen brought out a handkerchief to which he had tied four strings, one on each corner. He drew the ends of the strings together. "I wrap these around whatever I want to drop and out the window it goes."

Boone reached for the handkerchief. He examined it. He turned the small parachute inside out. "Why not just throw the candy out the window?"

"Boone, I'm at a hundred feet, coming in at ninety-five knots, the kids won't see a pack of gum or a candy bar falling through the sky—well, maybe a candy bar—but white parachutes like this one they'll see."

"HAVE YOU ever met our base commander?" the mess sergeant asked as he piled pancakes on Boone's tray. "He's always raising hell with us for something. Wecker the wrecker."

Boone gazed at a pan of sausage patties. "Can't say I've had the pleasure."

The sergeant forked on three patties. "If it's not one thing, it's another. There's a speck of something on a pot. We can't get his brand of coffee. A server's not wearing a freshly pressed shirt. You want some scrambled eggs?"

"Sure."

"Collins has got that for you." The sergeant leaned on his spoon. "Wecker, someday I'd like to—"

Boone moved to the next server who scooped on scrambled eggs. A third added a glop of hot cereal. "Coffee?" asked the fourth.

Boone held out his tray. "The works. Coffee, milk, juice if you've got it."

"O.J., that's rare around here, but the sarge managed to get us twenty gallons in this morning." He set a glass of the golden stuff, a half-pint of milk, and a mug of coffee on Boone's tray.

Boone turned away. Ahead of him stood a colonel talking to another officer. Boone looked back at the sergeant. He tilted his head toward the colonel and got a nod in return.

Boone winked. He stepped up behind the colonel and upset his tray, spilling breakfast onto the back of the man's shirt.

The colonel wheeled around. "What the hell—"

Boone winced. "I'm sorry, sir, I didn't see you."

The sergeant raced around with a cleanup rag. He raked at the mess on the base commander's shirt.

The colonel swatted him. "Get the hell away from me, soldier. And get someone out here to mop up the damn floor."

The sergeant scurried away. As he did, the colonel—Wecker by the nameplate above his shirt pocket—braced himself in front of Boone. "Who the hell are you, soldier?"

"Not a soldier. A war correspondent, Colonel. INS. And I'm sorry for this."

"Sorry don't feed the bulldog." Wecker pushed his face into Boone's face. "I'm gonna bust you out of here back to the States. Report to my office at O-Nine Hundred, after I get myself into a fresh uniform."

He stormed away.

The sergeant hustled in with a scoop and a bucket. He came up to Boone. "Nice job, fella."

"It was kind of an accident."

The sergeant gave Boone a thumbs-up. "Sure enough. Now buddy, if I was you, I'd get my fanny off this base before Wecker can throw you in the stockade."

"But breakfast—"

The sergeant turned to a compatriot on the serving line. "Collins?"

"Yeah?"

"Fix up one to go for this guy."

"You got it."

The sergeant crouched down and set to scooping up

the mess. "Buddy, give Collins a couple minutes, okay?"

"Can do," Boone said. He went in search of the wash pile. There he stacked his tray, then peeled away to a table where Archie Sidebottom sat with his crew, sucking down coffee. Boone slid onto an open seat.

Sidebottom raised his cup to him. "Saw what you did to our base commander. I expect somebody's running to the welding shop to make up a medal for you."

"Archie, it was an accident."

"Oh yes, it sure was. If I believed that, you could sell me the London Bridge."

"Ooo, now there's a thought, but the Brits might miss it. Can I ride out with you on your first flight?"

"Sure, let's go." Sidebottom pushed up and headed for the wash pile with his tray.

Boone cut away, but turned back. "I've gotta get my stuff. I'll meet you at your plane."

BOONE, LOOKING like a baggage porter humping along with his duffel under one arm, rucksack in that hand, and a lunch pail and his encased long gun in the other, hauled up to the stairway at the side of a Skymaster.

The crew chief in the doorway waved Boone up. "You do cut it close, mister. Another minute and we'da been outta here."

He took Boone's duffel and shuffled forward to the bulkhead at the front of the cargo bay, making his way past pallet after pallet stacked high with sacks of flour, Boone following. He stowed Boone's gear, then pounded on the door to the cockpit.

"Yeah," came Sidebottom's voice from beyond.

"Your passenger's here."

"Send him in and button up. It's time to go."

"Roger dodger." The chief opened the door for Boone.

Boone clapped him on the shoulder. "Thanks for your help."

"Oh, I've got something for you." The chief excavated in his pocket. After a moment, he brought out a medal that looked like a miniature fried egg, the medal suspended from a green ribbon. He pinned it to Boone's shirt. "From the mess crew. They said it's for valor in the face of the enemy."

Boone brushed his fingertips over the faux medal. "I'm rarely without words—"

The chief pushed Boone through to the jump seat, Sidebottom glancing up in his mirror. "Boone, strap yourself in."

Boone snugged a safety belt across his lap.

"Ronnie, fire number one."

The co-pilot pressed a button over his head. He held the button in as the far port engine spun up and the first of its cylinders ignited.

"Fire number two."

A voice came through the cockpit's speaker. "Seven-Niner-Bravo, Ground Control, hurry it up. The aircraft ahead of you is moving."

Sidebottom squeezed the transmit button on his microphone. "Roger, Ground." He leaned into his co-pilot. "Fire four, then three. I'm releasing the brakes."

Boone felt the aircraft roll.

At the end of the taxiway, Sidebottom turned the airfreighter into the wind and ran through his checklist, checking controls and gauges. The co-pilot changed the radio frequency from Ground Control to the Tower.

Sidebottom again pressed his transmit button. "Wiesbaden Tower, Navy Skymaster Four-Seven-Niner-Bravo, ready to go."

"Seven-Niner-Bravo, take the active. You're cleared for departure. At three thousand feet, turn right to a heading of zero-five-two degrees and contact Radar Control."

"Roger, Tower, cleared for takeoff." Sidebottom read back the rest of the departure instruction as he trundled the airfreighter out onto the runway. He shoved the four throttles to the top of the control quadrant.

The burst of power pressed Boone back into his seat. He watched the ballet ahead of him, Sidebottom's and the co-pilot's hands pushing this control forward, pulling that one back, snapping one switch up and another down. At three thousand feet, Boone felt through the slight compression of his spine the aircraft bank around to a new heading.

The co-pilot spun the radio dial to a different frequency.

Sidebottom pressed his transmit button. "Radar Control, Navy Skymaster Four-Seven-Niner-Bravo with you at three thousand on a heading of zero-five-two degrees."

"Seven-Niner-Bravo, I have you on the screen. We've got showers and a lot of scud today. Stay below the clouds. Traffic inbound for Wiesbaden will be above you at nine thousand."

"Roger, Radar Control." Sidebottom laid his microphone aside. He looked up in his mirror. "So, Boone, what are you up to, today?"

Boone pulled himself forward. "Four behind you is an Army Skymaster. The pilot's gonna drop chewing gum and candy bars to the German kids at Templehof. I'm gonna shoot a picture of it that's gonna win me a Pulitzer."

SIDEBOTTOM pointed through the windshield. "They're out there."

Boone rose up from the jump seat. "Yup, I see them."

Sidebottom raised his microphone. "Templehof Tower, Seven-Niner-Bravo on final. I have a passenger who needs a Jeep and a driver."

"Seven-Niner-Bravo, we can arrange that. You're cleared for landing."

"Roger that." Sidebottom wagged a finger at the flaps control. "Ronnie, let it all hang out. Full flaps."

BOONE DROPPED to the tarmac. He turned back in time to catch his rucksack thrown down to him by the crew chief. "Chief, thanks."

"Getcher picture and get back here in thirty—"

"Or you'll leave without me, I know." Boone swivelled away to a Jeep idling up beside him. He slid onto the passenger seat. "Corporal, get me to the approach end of the runway."

"Yessir."

Boone glanced at the driver. "You're a woman?"

"Last time I checked, sir."

She let out on the clutch and guided her vehicle toward a perimeter road, shifting the transmission up through the gears.

"If I may ask," Boone said, "shouldn't you be in a WAC uniform?"

"No sir. President Truman made all us WACs regular Army on Twelve June. The WAC uniform is only for dress. In the motor pool, I wear the same fatigues as the men. I'm a mechanic."

The wind messed with Boone's hair. "Tell me, how'd I rate you?"

"I'm also a driver. But, sir, I'm a mechanic first and a darn sight better than most of the men I work with."

"And surely modest."

She slowed for a gasoline tanker turning off the road

in front of her. "Sir?"

"Nothing." Boone zipped open the main body of his rucksack. He took out a big press camera, a Speed Graphic four-by-five. "A mechanic, you say? That explains the grease under your fingernails."

"You noticed, sir."

"Can you pick up your speed? In eight minutes, I have to be in position to shoot a picture of an incoming flight."

The driver stepped down on the accelerator, closing the distance between her Jeep and a caravan of trucks loaded down with what Boone couldn't tell for all the tarp covers. She swung out into the passing lane, shooting past the caravan as an inbound caravan of empties loomed up. Boone gripped the grab bar on the dash, his knuckles going white, his eyes dialing open to dish size. She cut back into her lane as the lead inbound truck came abreast and shot by, the driver hauling down on his air horn.

Boone pried his fingers off the grab bar. "Where'd you learn to drive, soldier?"

"The Indianapolis Speedway. Same place I learned to be a mechanic."

"You wouldn't happen to be related to the wild-man pilot I'm flying with, Archie Sidebottom?"

She glanced at Boone. "He's my cousin."

"Figures."

"You'll never get me up in an airplane, sir. Archie's tried. Scares the umph out of me."

"Really? What's your name?"

"Jean Heitsman."

"Tell you what, Jean, after I get my picture, I want to get a picture of you. I think you could be a helluva story." Boone motioned ahead toward the fence and the mountain of rubble beyond, the mountain covered with children and an adult here and there. "See where that fence is pulled up? I gotta get out there."

Heitsman slowed the Jeep. As she rolled it off onto the dirt, Boone hopped out. He scrambled under the fence and raced like a greyhound chasing a rabbit to a position on the mountain that put children ahead of him. Boone slammed a new film holder into the back of his camera. He set up his shot and held his position until a Skymaster came lumbering down final approach, its pilot rolling the aircraft from side to side, waggling its wings.

Good old Uncle Wiggly Wings, Boone thought.

Out of the window came a half-dozen miniature parachutes.

Boone pressed the shutter release on his camera.

SIDEBOTTOM picked up his microphone. "Radar Control, Seven-Niner-Bravo level at nine thousand, outbound for Wiesbaden."

"Roger, Seven-Niner. How about a pilot report?"

Sidebottom made a three-sixty as best he could while maintaining level flight, looking out his aircraft's windows—first down out his window, then up out his window, continuing above out the top of the windshield, and down to his right and out his co-pilot's window. "Control, we've got scud below at about four thousand, pretty clear at nine, clouds above but breaking up to the southwest. I can see sunshine."

"Got it, Seven-Niner. Keep an eye out for the red-tailed bandit. Other pilots have seen him in the neighborhood."

"Roger, Radar." Sidebottom glanced up in his mirror. "Boone, you get your picture of the candy bomber?"

Boone stared out the co-pilot's window. "Yeah, got the picture. By the way, I met your cousin Jean."

"She's here?"

"In the motor pool. A mechanic and driver." He brought his gaze to Sidebottom, to the back of the pilot's right ear from his vantage point in the jump seat. "Got a helluva story with her, Arch: WAC Mechanic Learned Her Trade at the Indy Five Hundred."

Sidebottom laughed. "She sure did. Drove the cars on the track after she worked on them. One day, I saw her hit a hundred twenty miles an hour. Boone, I could never do that, not with another car only a half an arm's length away. She's crazy."

"Says the same of you." Boone swivelled back to the co-pilot's window. "Archie, do you see out there what I see?"

Sidebottom leaned toward his co-pilot. He looked past him. He scanned the sky beyond and swore.

Boone shot out of his seat, back to the cargo bay. He returned, zippering open his hunting case. Boone took out his rifle and slammed a magazine with the clip of five cartridges into the gun's magwell. "You wanted to shoot him out of the sky? Let me do it for you."

Sidebottom craned around. "With what? That?"

"Why not? Can you make him make a run at us?"

Sidebottom thumbed his co-pilot out of his seat. Boone slipped in. He slid the co-pilot's window open as Sidebottom leaned the airfreighter to the starboard. Sidebottom rolled out with the Russian on his nose, the Russian responding, banking toward the airfreighter.

Boone stuck his rifle out into the hurricane of wind. "You've gotta make him pull up on my side, Arch."

"You know our closing speed?"

"I'm guessing five hundred fifty."

"Damn good guess. You'll never hit him."

"Arch, I'm the old duck hunter, remember?" Boone fixed his aim sixty degrees up.

Sidebottom skittered his aircraft ever so slightly to

the port and down, enough that the Russian jinked up and to his port, Boone squeezing off five shots, the tracers streaking out, one ripping through the Yak-Three's wing, through the gas tank.

The aircraft exploded.

Sidebottom banked back on course as the remnants of the Yak spiraled away. "Boone, nobody's gonna believe this."

Boone pitched his rifle out the window. "Believe what? Something happen here?"

Note: With the war over and the car companies turning out trainload after trainload of new cars, people were buying again.

Cars, Cars, Cars
– 1949 –

DAD BOUGHT a new Chevrolet from Kefler's, a four-door. He was so proud of it.

When he got it home, he took us all for a ride, my brother between him and my mother in the front seat, me in the back seat.

Dad stopped when he got to an intersection. After the traffic cleared, he put his hand on my brother's knee, which was where the nob would be on the floor-mounted shift lever in our old car. Dad shifted the transmission from third gear to first.

Only it didn't work.

Our new car had three-on-the-tree, the shift lever mounted on the steering column.

Three-on-the-tree, you had to get used to it.

It took Dad a couple days before he quit reaching for my brother's knee.

One Sunday, Uncle Nate came over to show off his new car. He gave us the grand tour. When he slipped behind the steering wheel, he said, "Look at this."

He touched a button on the dash.

Uncle Nate was a smoker. He'd never owned a Zippo or a Ronson in his life. A match was just fine, taken out of the little box he carried in his shirt pocket. Scratch the match on the side of the box and Uncle Nate had instant fire.

"This," he said, a huge smile wrapping itself across his face as he again touched the button on the dash, "this is an electric cigarette lighter. You push it in. When it gets hot, it pops out and you light your cigarette."

We all piled inside, and off we went for a ride. It was summer, so we had all the windows rolled down. Air conditioning? In our town, we only had that in The Phantom Movie Theater. No one had air conditioning in their home and certainly not in their car.

Out of habit, Nate stuck a cigarette in the corner of his mouth, all the time talking to my dad in the front passenger seat. He hit the lighter. After a minute or so, it got hot and popped out, and Nate put the glowing end to the end of his cigarette.

Still talking, he puffed away to get a good burn going.

Uncle Nate then did as he did when he lit his cigarette with a match. He shook the lighter to extinguish the flame, then pitched the lighter out the window.

When he realized what he had done, he glanced at my dad. "Oh damn," he said, "that's the third lighter I've thrown away."

Note: Over the river and through the woods to Grandmother's house we go . . . for Thanksgiving.

Football for Shorty
– 1950 –

THERE ARE traditions that even a 10-year-old knows. For one, Thanksgiving is always at Grandma's. The families of my dad's brothers and one sister are always there, which means all the cousins are there. Some of whom I see only once a year—here.

Now Grandma doesn't have a television set, so there's no football game to watch after we stuff ourselves. The aunts and my mom head for the kitchen to pack away the leftovers and wash and dry the dishes, and the uncles and my dad drift off to the living room to lounge on the couches and in the overstuffed chairs and talk and talk . . . and eventually fall asleep.

They always do. It's tradition.

Also a tradition, the cousins and my brother and I race outside for a pick-up game of football, tag so the littlest can play. The oldest cousin, in college, and my brother, in high school, draft the players, the biggest first, the littlest next apportioned to the two teams, leaving the in-betweeners left begging—the 8-, 9- and 10-year-olds . .

. Please, please, please, pick me, pick me.

Each finally get drafted. I go to Marcus' team because my brother doesn't want me. And all us 'tweeners know we'll never get to touch the football. We're too small.

But this one year, Marcus gets the ball from his center and dances around in the backfield, looking for a receiver. All his regulars are tied up by other big teens, so he sees me, the only one in the open, and he throws the ball to me!

I catch it, and my brother tears after me. But I dodge him and race off with the football through the lilac bushes where he's too big to go, and I head for the goal line—my dad's and Uncle Arthur's cars—and score. My brother howls at me and Marcus about me being out of bounds, but Marcus says we never established foul lines, so as long as I stayed on the lawn, I was okay. And, since he was the oldest and the biggest, his argument carried the day . . . and I got the touchdown.

Note: My dad was a believer in the values of 4-H, so it's no surprise that he got my brother and me involved as soon as we were eligible to join. That was at the age of 10.

Hang on
– 1951 –

THE COUNTY FAIR brought it all back, the memory of that day in the summer of 1951. I was 11 and a member of the Mukwonago 4-H Club.

That year my project was beef. I had raised a steer, a wild one it turned out. He was a free ranger before anyone thought up the terms free-range chickens, free-range pigs, and free-range cattle.

He also was a kicker and a runner. And he outweighed me by 650 pounds.

When I was breaking him to lead, he is the one who led, dragging me at the end of his halter rope up and down our farm's lane until he wore out the both of us.

Still, came the day we took him to the fair. I don't know how Dad and I got him in the truck, probably with Dad pulling him step by resisting step up the loading chute and me whacking the steer across the rump with a board to keep him moving.

What I do remember is getting him off the truck at the fairgrounds. I had a tight grip on my steer's halter rope and was turning him toward the chute. He must have seen freedom out there because he bolted and dragged me down the chute after him. When he hit the ground, he shifted into high gear and hauled me through the parking lot with me screaming "Help! Somebody help me!"

He took a right at the end and raced past the beef barn and on into the carnival's midway, something he'd never seen before. The crowds and the noise scared him, so he stampeded on wild-eyed with people scattering, leaping to get out of our way.

The stop, when it came, was instant. He crashed into a fence and fell in an exhausted heap with me tumbling over on top of him, still holding onto the halter rope.

My dad ran up. "You alright, son?" he asked.

Surely I lied and said yes.

He smiled as he took the halter rope from me. "Son, you sure showed him who's boss. You took him on a tour of the entire fairgrounds, didn'tcha?"

Note: After a year of fiddling with a decision of whether to make a run for president of the United States, Dwight Eisenhower couldn't put it off any longer. In May, he sent out the word that he would announce his candidacy for the Republican nomination at a rally on June 4 in his hometown of Abilene, Kansas.

The Marksmen
– 1952 –

JAMES EARLY sat at a table in the window of the Brass Nickel, soaking up the warmth of the morning sun and coffee from his cup.

"Days like this," he said to the man across from him—John Silver Fox, his chief deputy—"I'd just as soon sneak off and go fishing."

Silver Fox cut a bite from his wedge of rhubarb pie. "When's the last time you did that, chief?"

"Come to think of it, never. But I could find some cattle work that needs doing out at the ranch." Early stared out the window at a Chevy Suburban with a state license plate pulling into a parking place in front of the café. A tall man in a cattleman's hat and a suit that looked like it had come straight from the pressers slipped out and unrolled himself to his full height. "Oh Lord."

"Trouble?"

"It's Lawrence Hickman. Whenever he comes around, he's peddling a job nobody else wants."

"Chief, maybe we can sneak out the back."

"Too late. He sees us." Early waved to Hickman, motioned for him to come in.

The bell over the front door jingled.

"Hicky," Early called out, "you caught Big John and me loafing."

Hickman came up and took the third chair at the table, the one facing directly to the window. "Maybe I can change that for you."

Early waggled a finger at the man behind the counter. When he got Roddy Dodge's attention—Dodge, the Nickel's new short-order cook—he held up his cup and motioned to himself and Hickman. He got a nod in return. "So, Hicky," Early said, "what brings you away from Topeka and your desk at the KBI?"

"You've heard Ike is going to run."

"Yup."

Dodge slipped a mug of coffee in front of Hickman and proceeded to refill Early's cup.

"A wedge of rhubarb pie, fresh baked?" Early asked the new tablemate.

"I could be talked into it."

Early looked up to Dodge. "Pie for the gentleman and put it and his coffee on my tab."

After Dodge departed, Early folded his hands over his cup. "About Ike."

"Next month—June—he's going to announce in Abilene. The governor's asked me to put together a security detail."

"Hicky, that's a job for the Secret Service and the State Police."

Hickman stirred sugar into his coffee with Early's knife that he'd appropriated. "I agree. The Secret Service will be around Ike like ticks on a dog, and the State Police and city police will be on the ground. I need a detail on the high roofs with rifles and walkie-talkies. Jimmy, you can pick your own men."

EARLY, his feet on a stack of wanted posters on his desk, fiddled with a dart while keeping his desk phone's receiver pressed to his ear. "Ronnie," he said into the mouthpiece, "Big John's had to beg off the roof detail I've been asked to put together."

"How's that?" came Ronnie Galt's bass voice through the receiver, Galt, the sheriff of Dickinson County, Abilene its county seat.

"Family emergency at the rez. So my niece is gonna take his place, be my spotter and backup."

Galt didn't respond. In the silence, Early heard someone reading the livestock market report. Galt, he thought, must have tuned his office radio to the Abilene station, KABI.

"Ronnie, you still there or did you hike down the hall to the flusher?"

"I'm here, Cactus. Really? Your niece?"

"She's the top shooter on K-State's rifle team."

"I thought that gal was cross-eyed."

"That's her cousin from out in Wakeeney. This is Laney I'm talking about."

"I'm with ya, but shootin' at paper targets an' shootin' at a real person, that's two different things. So who else you got?"

"Daniel Plemmons." Early pegged his dart at a picture of Adlai Stevenson thumbtacked to his bulletin board, Stevenson, the governor of Illinois expected to get the Democratic nomination for the presidency.

The dart nicked the governor's left ear. Early wondered what he could get with the next dart.

"Plemmons?" Galt said. "That cowboy? I thought he'd be on the State Police ground detail."

"Not when Daniel can showboat. Nobody better with a sniper rifle."

"Well, why the hell then do you want me?"

Early hauled his feet down to the floor "Ronnie, the Secret Service thinks there's someone local who's got it in for Ike. You know everybody."

"Maybe, but I'm too fat to climb up to the roof of anything higher than my chicken coop. Tell you what, I'll loan you a couple of my deputies for the high job and I'll be your ground co-ordinator, keep you all from shootin' one another."

"Two?"

"Like you an' Laney, a shooter and a spotter. You'll like my shooter. He's real handy with a thirty-ought-six. Plus Melvin's got no fear of heights."

"How's that?"

"He was a paratrooper in the last war, jumped out of perfectly good airplanes."

Early drummed his fingertips on his desk. He stopped and rubbed his chin, considering his choices. "Ronnie, can you have your boys meet us at Fort Riley, at the shooting range?"

"When?"

"Tomorrow morning. Eight o'clock."

TWO MEN, reminiscent of Mutt and Jeff in the Sunday comics, strolled away from a Studebaker pickup, Jeff with a deer rifle slung over his shoulder and Mutt clutching high-power binoculars. They came to Early and a young woman sorting through paper targets at his Jeep. "You the man in charge?" the tall one asked, looking at Early.

"I am if you fellas are from Abilene." Early reached out his hand.

The tall one glommed onto it. "Name's Melvin Knox. I go by Mel. And my partner's Gardner Wilson."

"You the former paratrooper?"

"Both of us."

Early drew the young woman at his side into the conversation. "This is my niece, Laney Early."

Knox snatched off his cowboy hat, a Windcutter. "Yes, ma'am. I've seen you shoot at the collegiate regionals at Wichita State. I'd hate to come up against you."

Early studied him. "Wichita State?"

"Yes, sir. Gardner and I are from down that way. We got our degrees there on the G.I. Bill."

Before Knox could say more, a bullet-nosed Ford cruised in and slid to a stop on the far side of Early's Jeep. A state patrolman stepped out, the patrolman wearing silvered aviator glasses.

"That," said Early, nodding to the new arrival, "completes our detail. Daniel Plemmons, the trooper in our district. You boys ever met him?"

"Not had the pleasure."

Early waved Plemmons over. "Daniel, I'd like you to meet Mel Knox—the tall one—and his spotter, Gardner Wilson. They're both deputies from Dickinson County."

Plemmons touched an index finger to his eyebrow in salute. "Your sheriff says good things about the two of you."

Knox gave an uneasy smile.

Plemmons eyed Knox's thirty-ought-six. "That's a fair piece."

"Well, I always thought so. It's a Winchester."

"Jimmy, you shooting with that relic you brought back from the war?"

"Got a new scope for it, an eight-power the Marines used in the South Pacific."

Plemmons glanced at Laney. "Sis, how about you?"

Laney fetched a gun case from the backseat of the Jeep. She laid the case on the hood and unzipped it. "A Mosin-Nagant with a four-power scope. My coach recommended the rifle and qualified me on it."

"Damn, that is a good one. You know, though, you and your uncle and Knox here could do a whole helluva lot better than what you have." Plemmons went to the trunk of his car. After a moment, he returned toting a rifle with an extra-long barrel and a telescope of a kind Early had never seen before. Plemmons rested the gun's stock against his hip.

Early whistled. "You steal that, Daniel?"

"Uh-uh. Friends at Quantico, they let me 'borrow' four of these for field testing, flew them out for me. This little darlin' fires standard thirty-ought-six bullets at a range of up to a half-mile with an accuracy that will blow your mind thanks to this." He caressed the scope. "This part—it's an adjustable ranging telescope, three to nine power—this part is totally experimental. What say to a demonstration?"

Early gave Laney a fistful of paper targets and a walkie-talkie.

She trotted away, to mount the targets at fifty and a hundred yards.

Plemmons leaned into Knox. "Most hunters can't see a mule deer clear enough at the distance to the farther target to identify it let alone make the kill shot, right?"

"I can."

"Really? Show me."

Knox and Wilson sauntered to the shooting berm, talking softly, Knox gesturing about how he intended to set up the shot. He laid down behind the berm and settled his rifle across it. Wilson knelt at his shoulder. They continued talking, as a golfer and his caddie might, while Knox adjusted the gun sight for the distance. He tossed a handful of grass in the air. The partners watched the grass drift with the breeze, then considered the allowance for the windage Knox needed to make. He settled in, squinted along the sight, and squeezed the trigger.

Wilson studied the target through his binoculars. He shook his head.

"First ring, high and to the left," Laney called back over her radio.

Plemmons, on the far side of Knox, bumped the shooter's shoulder with the toe of his boot. "You wounded him. With the weapon I've got, I can do a Robin Hood, put two bullets dead in the center of the target, but you wouldn't believe it unless you went down range and dug out the lead." He took a target from Early and, with a pencil, x'd the corners of a triangle inside the center ring, the x's less than an inch apart. Plemmons handed the paper back to Early.

While Early talked it through with Laney on the radio, Plemmons got down in the prone firing position. He pushed his aviator glasses up onto the top of his head and sighted through the scope, his fingers on the magnification ring. "Adjusting the magnification locks in both your range and the drop of the bullet to the target."

He twiddled with the ring. "Now me as the shooter, I'm all set. All I have to do is keep the crosshairs on the target and squeeze the trigger. Jimmy, with your scope you make a guess at the drop of the bullet, then you aim high to hit your target, right?"

Plemmons didn't wait for an answer. He estimated the windage in the same way Knox had, and, after a moment of steadying himself—holding his breath—he squeezed off a round. "That's the top of the triangle," he said, glancing back at Knox. He ejected the spent cartridge. That jacked a new cartridge into the firing chamber. Plemmons again put his eye to the scope. "Next. The lower left corner."

He moved the crosshairs to the new point, Early and Wilson watching the target through their binoculars. Plemmons squeezed off a second round. He ejected the shell and once more adjusted his aim. "Now the third, the lower right corner."

He sucked in a breath, held it, and squeezed the trigger one more time.

Laney's voice crackled through Early's walkie-talkie. "He made the triangle."

Early gave Plemmons a prickly look. He took his place at the berm, sighted in on the triangle with his Springfield, and blew out the center.

Plemmons gazed at the target through Early's binoculars. "I have to say, Jimmy, that's pretty good. Can you do it at five hundred yards? At a thousand?"

THE HEAD of the Secret Service detail glanced up from his notes at the sight of Early and his colleagues, all in gray slickers and carrying weapons cases and binoculars, lazing their way into the back of meeting room in Abilene's Sunflower Hotel.

The man looked at Sheriff Galt seated beside him, Galt paring his fingernails with a pen knife. "Who are they?" he asked in a growl.

"The marksmen the KBI sent us." Galt polished his nails on his pant leg. "The one with the mustache, that's James Early, Riley County sheriff."

"I thought you said KBI."

"Well, that, too. It's complicated." Galt stuffed his knife in his back pocket. "Kind of a rag-tag collection, don't they look like? But they're the best at what they do."

"If you say. Just as long as they follow orders."

"Oops."

"Oops, what?"

Galt looked away, toward a city map taped to the wall.

The man stared at Early.

Early sensed eyes upon him and returned the stare. The Secret Service man beckoned him forward. "Mister Early," he said, "this security briefing started a half an hour ago. Where've you been?"

Early peeled off his cattleman's hat. He shook the rain from it. "Walking the town, figuring out the best places for us to be."

"I've already made those assignments."

Early pushed a wet fingertip along the tabletop that separated the Secret Service man and Galt from the other lawmen in the room. "Begging your pardon, sir. My group's on assignment here for the governor, to provide rooftop security and to, if necessary, kill anyone who might be a threat to General Eisenhower. Your name is, sir?"

The man laid his wallet open on the table, revealing his shield and identity card. "Alton Miller, senior agent in charge."

Early closed the wallet. "Well, Mister Miller, I've been directed to work with you. You know that. But, as for assignments and orders, we make our own."

Miller's face took on the appearance of a storm cloud about to erupt. "I'll take this up with Eisenhower when his train gets in."

"Better work fast, sir. Ike's train gets in at two. You'll have fifteen minutes to get him from the depot to the theater and the marquee where he's to make his speech. By then, Mister Miller, we'll have been in place for more than an hour, studying the crowd as it grows. Anyone suspicious, we'll have spotted them long before you do. A question, if I may."

"Am I gonna like this?"

"I don't know."

"Go ahead."

"How long have you worked for the general?"

Miller picked up his wallet. "Two weeks come Wednesday."

"Ten days. I worked for him for four years in the war. Who do you think he's gonna defer to?"

Galt sliced his way in. He hustled Early toward the side of the room and the map where he bent down until his forehead touched Early's. "Cactus," he growled sotto voce, "you're lyin' about workin' for Ike."

"I was in his army."

"As a corporal, a gawddamn lowly two striper."

"Mister Miller doesn't know that. And he's not about to ask."

"You willing to bet your badge on that?"

Miller elbowed in. "I don't know what your little party is here and I don't care. But, Mister Early, I do care where you plan to be. Show me on the map."

Early stabbed the theater next door to the hotel, the courthouse two blocks south and across the street, and the Midland grain elevator four blocks east with a direct line of sight to the theater. "The elevator is the key. It's the highest point in the town."

Miller pawed at a sideburn. "How about north on Buckeye?"

"That's all residential. Your ground team—your city and state cops—they're gonna have to cover that."

KNOX LED the way to the Alamo Saloon on Southeast Fifth. "I didn't think that Secret Service fella was ever gonna let us out of there to get lunch."

"This place any good?" Early asked as he, Laney, and the others stepped inside, the aroma of frying steaks smothered with onions greeting them.

"The best. Steaks two fingers thick, chuck wagon stew, cornbread, cattle-trail coffee."

"Pardon?"

"Cattle-trail coffee. Coffee so thick, sheriff, you can patch saddle leather with it. We cut our coffee in strips like jerky and chew it."

"I prefer mine in liquid form."

"Weak-water stuff, huh?"

Early gazed over the tables and booths. "A bit crowded."

"Well, what did you expect with Ike coming to town?" Knox looked across the way. "Big table over there with a rancher I know at it. Looks like he's finishing up."

Knox waved to the man, gestured at the table and back to the quartet clustered around him. He got a high sign in return.

Knox again led out. "Mister Rumsford," he said as he got closer, "can we join you?"

"You can have the table. I'm done here."

Knox stood his gun case in the corner. Early and the others followed suit. As each took a chair, Knox made the introductions, minus titles.

Rumsford, a ragged mustache beneath his nose and a three-day growth of beard on his chin and cheeks, dipped his brow toward the gun cases.

"Hunting rifles," Early said before Knox could respond. "Mel here's invited us to shoot some coyotes with him after the big festivities uptown."

Rumsford looked at the hand-lettered 'Ike for President' sign over the cash register. "Quite something, isn't it?"

"You see all the flags they got up there on the theater marquee where Eisenhower's to speak? There and at the railroad station and the route from the station to the theater? I've never seen so many flags."

"Yup, well, I'm gonna try to get down front so I don't miss anything." Rumsford pushed back from the table. "Nice to meet you all. But if you'll excuse me, I better git."

The rancher made his way toward the door. After he paid his bill and went outside, Knox leaned across the table to Early. "What was all that stuff about shootin' coyotes?"

"Mel, I wasn't about to let you say why we're really here. The fewer people who know, the better."

"CACTUS," came the Dickinson sheriff's voice over Early's walkie-talkie, "you there?"

Early laid his binoculars aside after a scan of the crowd filling Buckeye Street, people jostling for positions to better see Eisenhower when he came to the podium on the theater's marquee. Early on the roof, two stories above, pressed the transmit button on his walkie-talkie. "Go ahead, Ronnie."

"I know the threat."

"Say what?"

"Cactus, I know the threat."

"Who?"

"Zebulon Rumsford, an old rancher from south of town. His sister just told me. She keeps house for him. She's real panicked."

"Rumsford? We met a rancher named Rumsford at lunch."

"Scruffy fellow, droopy mustache worse'n yers?"

"Yeah." Early glanced at Laney. "Said he was gonna get a spot down front. I haven't seen him. Does the sister know where he's likely to be?"

"No, but after Rums left a couple hours ago, she went to his gun cabinet and found his Springfield rifle and his forty-five revolver gone. I've got a guess, though."

"Ronnie, this is no time to keep secrets."

"Cactus, it's no secret. Rums got an uncle edgin' up on eighty-six, lives in a house a block from where you are, north on the opposite side of the street. Damn good sightlines from the second floor and the attic there to where Ike's gonna be."

Early and Laney both snatched up their binoculars. They turned and scanned the houses in the next bock. Early pressed the transmit button on his radio. "Which house, Ronnie?"

"White two-story. You see it?"

"Got it."

"Anyone pokin' a rifle through an open window?"

"Not that I can see." Early glanced from his binoculars to Laney.

She shook her head.

"Cactus," Galt called back, "I got Dickie Eisenhower and a deputy. We're rammin' through the crowd to bust our way in. If Rums there, we'll get the bastard."

Early aimed his binoculars down to the herd of people in the street, to a fat man parting them like Moses parting the Red Sea, only the fat man held up a revolver, not a shepherd's staff. Two men came behind him, the city police chief Dickie Eisenhower and a deputy.

They broke free and ran for the house where they clattered up the steps and inside.

Early, watching, rolled the knurled focus knob on his binoculars. He zeroed in on the open front door, then moved his binocs from window to window, worked his way up, across the second floor, and up again to a half window under the eave in the attic.

His radio crackled. "Cactus," came Galt's voice, "not a damn soul here. We've checked everywhere, even the root cellar."

Galt came out on the front porch, his handie-talkie pressed to his ear. He flopped down on the steps, winded.

"Ronnie," Early said into his radio, "why's this fella got it in for Ike?"

"Rums' boy, Sim, the boy was killed in the war, on D-Day. Normandy. Just nineteen. Rums blamed Ike for the death of his one and only child. If that wasn't enough, Rums' wife got so grief stricken that she drowned herself in the pond out behind the buildings on the ranch. Cactus, Rums could be anywhere or maybe nowhere."

The crowd broke out in applause. Early leaned over the edge of the roof. He peered down to the marquee, to Eisenhower stepping through a window to a podium, multiple flags of the United States and Kansas to either side. Miller and another Secret Service agent flanked Eisenhower.

The governor of Kansas, Edward Arn, also at the podium, tapped the microphone. He tapped it again and, looking at the crowd, said into the mic, "Is this thing on? Can you hear me?"

A smattering of applause came from some of the people below.

Arn slicked up the sides of his cowboy hat. "Ladies and gentlemen, fellow Kansans," he said, "you know why we're here, to welcome home one of our favorite sons, Dwight Eisenhower."

Raucous applause and cheering filled the Abilene air. Someone whistled.

Arn waved for silence, then pointed off across the way. "Ike grew up just five blocks from here, over on Southeast Fourth Street, attended school here—grade school and high school—and, after graduation, worked at the Belle Springs Creamery for two years on the night shift so his brother Edgar could go to college. Ike's chance at college came in Nineteen and Eleven when he got appointed to West Point. In all the years that followed, Ike's never forgot this is home."

More applause and shouts of "Hey, Ike!"

Arn pulled Eisenhower in front of the microphone.

Eisenhower gave a warm smile to the crowd. He removed his hat. The breeze and the mist coming down from the slate gray clouds overhead played with Eisenhower's thinning hair. He placed his speech on the podium, looked up, and waved to the crowd. "Governor Arn, my fellow Kansans," he said into the microphone.

The applause grew louder, drowning out his words.

"My fellow Kansans," he said again, raising his voice.

Still the applause continued.

Early ditched his cattleman's hat for his slicker's rain hood. "Eisenhower's gonna catch his death if he doesn't put his hat back on," he said to Laney pulling up her own rain hood.

Eisenhower again waved to the crowd, blinking like a mystified owl through his glasses.

The applause faded.

"My fellow Kansans," he said once more, "we are experiencing today a Kansas shower, but I assure you there's not half the water here as there was in the English Channel eight years ago today."

Applause interrupted. When it again faded, Eisenhower once more gazed out over the crowd. "If the Kansas wheat can use this rain," he said, "it's okay by me."

Early stared off toward the roof of the courthouse to his right where he had posted Knox and Wilson, and then toward the top of the Midland Grain Elevator's tallest silo straight ahead, a thousand yards up to the Union-Pacific's tracks where Plemmons was to be. "Melvin? Daniel? You there?" he said into his radio.

Knox came back in the affirmative, but nothing from Plemmons.

"Daniel?" Early repeated.

Laney peered through her binoculars at the top of the grain silo. "He's there, Unc, but I think he's having trouble with his handie-talkie. He's waving it at us and pointing down. I think he's going down for another radio."

Early swore. He clicked his transmitter button three times. "Daniel, Daniel," he barked into his talkie, "stay up there! Stay up there! We'll get a radio to you. . . . Melvin."

"Go, sheriff."

"Give your rifle to Wilson and get over to the grain silo. There's a second radio in Plemmons' car. Get it up to him."

"Roger that."

"I can't see him," Laney said. "Wait a minute, he's back. He's crouched down at the sandbag, scoping the crowd. My God, there's a muzzle flash. He's shooting!"

Early shoved his talkie to Laney. He grabbed up his rifle and dialed in the scope on the top of the silo. Early squinted at the image in the crosshairs. "That's not Daniel."

A flash lit up his scope.

When the burst of light faded from his eye, Early

moved the crosshairs up an inch from the opposing rifle's gunsight. He squeezed the trigger, and the image dropped.

"Did I get him?" Early asked Laney as he ejected the spent shell.

She scanned the roof line. "You hit the sandbag. I can see sand running out. Wait a minute. Wait a minute. He's back."

Early re-sighted on the target. He squeezed the trigger again. Again the image dropped behind the sandbag Plemmons had set out as a gun rest. "What do you see, Laney?"

"I can see Knox coming up on top of the silo."

Knox's voice came through Early's radio. "Sheriff, I've found Plemmons. He's tied up like a steer in a roping contest. Looks to be out cold."

Early pulled the talkie back to himself. He pressed the transmit button. "Someone was firing this way."

"I know. I heard the shots."

Early peered over the ledge to the marquee. "Ike's still going on, so the shooter didn't hit anybody."

"I can see him this side of the sandbag. He'd not movin'."

Knox came forward. He put his fingertips on the man's neck. "Sheriff, it's Rumsford. He's dead."

EISENHOWER, Arn, and the others stepped back inside the theater, speech over, Eisenhower wiping the rain off his glasses.

Galt intercepted them. He latched onto Eisenhower's arm. "Ike, you came within a cat's whisker of bein' killed out there."

"What do you mean?"

"Zeb Rumsford, you remember him?"

"Yes, he was in my high school class. That was forty-three years ago."

"He was gunnin' for you. Took two shots at you before that fella over there—" Galt motioned to Early slouched in a chair, holding his sniper rifle by the barrel, the butt of the gun's stock on the floor. "—he killed 'im."

"I didn't hear any gunfire."

"Rums was a thousand yards away, on top of Midland's tallest grain silo. His shots came during applause. My colleague there—the sheriff of Riley County—was two stories above you. As you can see, he's got a silencer."

Eisenhower came over to Early, his hand out. "You have my gratitude. This is going to get into the papers, sheriff."

Early grimaced.

"Do you have a problem with that?"

"General, I'd just as soon this be forgotten."

"I don't know that that can be done."

"Look, if you make me famous for this, you're painting a target on my chest. I don't need that. I've got a little girl to look after. She's only two."

Eisenhower massaged his chin. "I can't put a lid on this, but I can have a talk with the news boys."

EISENHOWER stood behind a table in the Sunflower Hotel's meeting room, a half a dozen reporters and photographers on the other side of the table.

Eisenhower rested his knuckles on his hips. "Boys, all of what I am about to tell you is off the record. This afternoon, while I was speaking, someone made an attempt on my life. Why isn't important. What is important is that someone in my security detail killed the assassin."

A reporter for the Associated Press raised his hand.

Eisenhower pointed to him.

"Ike, who saved your life?"

"No comment."

"You aren't going to tell us, even off the record?"

"That's right."

"We'll get it from someone else."

Eisenhower wagged his finger at the reporter. "Robert, if you do—if any of you do—I will personally call your editor and see to it that you're out of a job."

"You can't do that."

"Do you want to try me?"

The reporter looked away.

"I didn't think so. I know you all have stories to file, so I won't hold you up any longer."

The claque of reporters and photographers, grumbling, rose as one and trapesed out of the room. One photographer held back. He snapped a flash photo Eisenhower talking to Arn, then followed the others out.

Early, still in his slicker, lounged at the back of the room with his niece, Plemmons, Knox, Galt, and Miller, the head of Eisenhower's Secret Service detail. Early laid his hand on Galt's shoulder. "Ronnie, I know who I'm voting for."

Note: Trains, as vital as they are to commerce, well . . .

Dead Ahead
– 1953 –

BOB HATCHER and Bob Lewinsky—called the Bobsy Twins by the Soo Line's dispatchers—strolled along beside a seventy-one-car freight train on a side track, heading toward the front, toward the lead diesel of a three-engine unit, the engineer and fireman ready for a new day.

"Hear from Al?" Lewinsky asked—Alvin Douglas, the crew's conductor.

"Yah, he's sick. Don't let on to the other crew. We'll cover for him."

Hatcher and Douglas had been teamed for the past ten years, from the days when steam was king on the road. Lewinsky had joined them only a year ago, the kid then twenty-one and fresh out of the Army.

Hatcher waved at the men climbing down the ladder from the lead diesel. "You gas it up for us?" he hollered.

"Gas, oil, checked under the hood, even washed the windshield," the first to hit the cinders called back, the engineer for the crew that had driven the train all the previous night. "Give the dispatcher a holler. Yer ready to go."

The departing men, all toting lunch boxes, trudged off across the tracks to a parking lot and their pickups.

Hatcher climbed the ladder of the diesel, the diesel and its twins thrumming at idle. The air in the cab smelled of fuel oil and cigarette smoke. He took down the conductor's clipboard and signed in. After he forged Douglas' signature, Lewinsky also signed the duty sheet. Hatcher then motioned him to the seat on the right side of the cab. "Lew, you drive today. Do a good job of it, I'll recommend you for the next opening that comes down for a full-fledged engineer."

Lewinsky slid his lunch box under the seat. He settled himself before the instrument panel where he pulled over the engineer's checklist. He ran the checks of all the gauges and controls in front of him and to the side, twenty-six in all. Lewinsky initialed the list and set it aside. "Ready to go," he said, bringing his hand to the throttle.

Hatcher reached overhead for the microphone clipped next to the radio. He pressed the transmit button. "Dispatch," he said into the mic, "Hatch with you. Soo F-Thirty six-D ready to roll out for the mainline."

"Hold where you are, Bobsy One," a voice came back. "The Dominion's running behind. It should pass you in a minute, then you're cleared to go."

"Roger dodger—"

"—You old codger," the dispatcher came back, laughing.

Hatcher pressed the transmit button again. "Look who's talking. Ronnie, you're less than a year from retirement. They've got a Mickey Mouse watch waiting for you."

A passenger train thundered by on the mainline hardly an arm's length away, the Dominion southeast-bound for Chicago, the air concussions and the noise shaking Hatcher and Lewinsky's engine and them with it.

The dispatcher came back after the noise subsided. "You're cleared to go, Old Dog. The switch to the mainline is open."

"Lew's driving today," Hatcher said into his mic.

"The kid, huh?"

"I'm gettin' him ready to be an engineer."

"Bobsy Two," the dispatcher said over the radio, "none of Hatch's bad habits, now, ya hear?"

Hatcher tilted his brow at the throttle.

Lewinsky pushed forward on the lever, and the train rolled forward.

Lewinsky touched a button on the panel, setting his engine's bell to ringing, a warning to everyone within earshot that Thirty six-D was moving.

Hatcher leaned out the fireman's window. He watched the railcars behind, each in turn snap through the switch. When the last cleared, he slapped Lewinsky's shoulder.

Lewinsky pushed the throttle further forward, bringing the generator motors up to six hundred rpm. The train picked up speed.

"No more than forty five now," Hatcher said over the rising noise level in the cab. "When you get the high ball, you're okay to go for sixty."

Lewinsky gazed out the windshield, a hand on the throttle and a foot on the plate in the floor—the dead man's switch. "What about that school up ahead?"

"Foxworth? Do the usual, sound yer horn and watch for any kids scooting across the tracks."

Hatcher went back to the conductor's seat. There he pulled out a file and paged through it, glancing down bills of lading to see what he was hauling today—hopper cars of corn and wheat, war ordnance from the Badger Works, reefer cars packed with cheese. He shook the file. "Lew, most of this stuff is bound for the West Coast. Up in Minneapolis, they'll switch it to the NP for Tacoma."

"Yup, and that ordnance, I bet that goes from Sea-Tac by boat to Korea."

Hatcher returned the folder to the conductor's file drawer. "How come you never got there?"

Lewinski looked over his shoulder. "Uncle Sam wanted me in Germany, in case the Ruskies came screaming through the Fulda Gap. In my year and a half there, I never figured out how we were supposed to stop 'em."

Hatcher motioned at the windshield. "Keep your eyes ahead, soldier."

Lewinsky turned back. He blanched and hit the horn. "A kid on the tracks!"

A girl, crossing to the school, froze deer-in-the-headlights still, looking at the train.

Hatcher jumped forward. He slammed the panic button, dumping air, engaging the emergency brakes, locking up the wheels the full length of the train, steel screeching on steel, the train propelled by fifteen hundred tons of freight and rolling stock but slowing.

A boy shot up the embankment. He threw himself at the girl and both flew clear as the first engine slid by.

"Holy shit." Hatcher raked a hand down his face.

Lewinsky glanced across at the senior engineer shoving open the fireman's window. "Let 'er go or stop?" he asked.

Hatcher leaned out. He saw the kids running toward the school. "Stop, gawddammit. I'm gonna hike back there and yell at those kids."

"NOOO!"

Hatcher whipped around. He looked where Lewinsky stared, ashen.

A woman, at a grade crossing half the length of a football field away, stood in the middle of the tracks.

"Get outta there, lady! Get outta there."

She crossed herself and dropped to her knees.

"Hatch, we're gonna hit!"

A purse—red—spun out to the side, off over the weeds, the wheels of the train still locked up, speed still playing off, the wheels' howl still deafening. A hundred yards more, then two hundred yards.

And the train stopped.

The only sound remaining, the thrum of the diesels' generators at idle.

Hatcher took down his microphone. He pressed the transmit button. "Dispatch, Thirty six-D. Dead stop. We hit someone," he said into the mic, his voice unearthly hollow.

The thrum the only answer.

Seconds passed. Ten, maybe fifteen. To Hatcher it seemed an eternity before the radio came alive.

"Bobsy One—Hatch—ohmigod. A car or truck?"

"A person. A woman."

"Ohmigod, Hatch. Hatch, where are you?"

"The grade crossing beyond the Foxworth school. Call the sheriff's department and an ambulance. She's gonna be dead."

"I'm on it. I'll start the paperwork for you, too."

"There's always that, isn't there?" He shoved the microphone back into its clip.

Lewinsky, green now, burst from his seat into the head in the nose of the diesel. He retched into the toilet. "How do you take it?" he asked after he washed his mouth clean with water from a jug by the head's steel sink.

"I've been here before. Three times." Hatcher gathered up a tarp he kept stowed to the side of the fireman's seat. He tucked the tarp under his arm and climbed down the ladder to the gravel.

Lewinsky, wobbling, followed him down. "Hatch, I killed her."

"It's cold comfort, Lew, but you didn't."

"Yes, I did."

"Lew, it was a damn suicide. She wanted us to hit her."

"But still—"

"No 'but still.' Enough of that. Let's get back to the crossing."

They walked away from the three engines. Once clear of their thrum, all they heard was the crunch of gravel beneath their shoes and the warbling of a redwing perched on a fence post beyond the railroad's right-of-way.

"Lew, listen," Hatcher said, "you gotta learn to shut these things out or they'll eat you alive."

"How do you do that, man?"

"Some of my buddies, Lew, they drink. I guess I do, too. I've been something of a regular at the Ace High since the first one, twenty years ago."

"What was that?"

"The accident? A low-boy. It high centered on a grade crossing. Destroyed the low-boy, the dozer on it, the tractor and the guy in the cab. Dragged the whole damn mess a half a mile."

They cleared the train and kept walking.

"Mind if I ask you something?" Lewinsky said.

"Go ahead."

"You a Jesus man?"

"Not hardly. The nuns beat that outta me in parochial school."

As they continued on, they saw it ahead, a misshapen lump on the gravel between the tracks.

Hatcher stopped. "This is gonna be bad, Lew."

Lewinsky stopped beside him. "That why you've got the tarp?"

"Yah. Ever since the first, I've always carried a tarp in the cab."

"Hatch, if it's all right with you, maybe I'll hang back."

Hatcher touched the kid's shoulder and went on, moving with a slow, rolling gait. When he came up to the body—the head and torso a mash of tissue, fabric, blood, and bone—Hatcher shook out the tarpaulin. He draped it over what had fifteen minutes before been a living being.

Done, he mopped his sleeve under an eye that had teared up.

The purse—the red purse—he remembered it. The sheriff would want it. Hatcher side-hopped down the embankment to the weeds. He swatted his way through to the fence line. There the purse laid among the burdock, a blood smear across the plastic. Hatcher picked the purse up by the strap, one end torn free. He carried it with him back to the crossing.

On the west side, he saw a Crosley—blue and rust— parked on the shoulder of the county road. That was an awful car, he knew well. He had owned one for a month before he unloaded it on his brother-in-law. But that car, that one, blue and rust, it looked familiar.

He went to it and peered in through the driver's window. "What's that?" he heard himself saying.

Hatcher opened the door. He reached in for a sheet of paper on the seat. He read down the page, something about a husband buried at the Peekland Cemetery . . . married eleven years . . . the loneliness . . . frustration with a continually sick child . . . getting by on county welfare, the shame of it all. . . . And a name, Shelby Dodds, and the words, "Sweetpea, I'm going home to be with Daddy. Do not forget me."

He folded the paper. Hatcher turned away, his shoulders sagging. It came back to him in a flood—Shelby Dodds. The prettiest girl. His son had dated her when the two were in high school, Shelby Wills then. She had married his boy's best friend, George Dodds. Dodds had died, what, a year ago? Two? He couldn't be sure.

He leaned against the car. "Lordy, Lordy, Lordy, this is one you didn't have to take. What are you tryin' to do, get me into the church house?"

His head dipped forward until his chin rested on his chest. "I'll make you a deal, God," he whispered. "If You never let this happen again—"

Hatcher's hand holding the paper rose. It moved in the sign of the cross as he murmured a prayer burned into his memory more than half a lifetime ago, not the 'Our Father,' but the prayer for the dead.

Note: Roy Rogers made it big, first in the movies (1935-1951), then on radio (1944-1955) and television (1951-1957). For 10 years, he was the most popular Western star in the country. What kid in the early 1950s didn't watch Roy and Dale—Roy and his wife, Dale Evans—on their Double R Bar Ranch on Saturday mornings?

Old Roy and the Cincinnati Kid
– 1954 –

HE WAS a city kid, frustrated because he couldn't have a horse.

"If we got you a horse," his dad said, "where would you keep him?"

"In the garage," the kid said.

"Oh, I don't think your mother would go for that. It would poop on the car. And speaking of poop, what would you do with all those piles a horse produces?"

"Umm, fertilize the garden?"

Dad narrowed his eyes. "Do you know how small our garden is?"

"Well, maybe I could start a business and sell it around the neighborhood, to other people who have gardens."

That stopped Dad. The thought of his son becoming an entrepreneur . . . life lessons and all. But still, there was that ordinance in Cincinnati that said no livestock within the city limits. So he put that out on the floor, figuring that would be the end of this discussion.

"But a horse isn't livestock," the kid said. "It's a pet. Like a dog. We've got lots of dogs on our street. And each one has a license tag on its collar, so it's legal."

Oh boy, my son the lawyer, Dad thought, and he's only ten.

This was not to be the end of the discussion.

The kid squared his shoulders. "Roy Rogers has a horse."

"Ah, so that's it. You want to be a cowboy."

"Yeah, I already have the holster set with two guns."

Indeed he did. He had begged for it for most of a year, so there it was under the Christmas tree, a Roy Rogers-signed set of six shooters—cap guns. The only thing that could have been worse, his mother had concluded after the first week, would have been to have given him a snare drum.

"Did you know," asked Dad, "that old Roy didn't have a horse when he was your age?"

The kid became bug-eyed.

"When he was growing up upriver from here, he had a mule," Dad said. "Actually, it was his father's. They used it to work the farm outside Duck Run. And he wasn't Roy Rogers. He was Leonard Slye. The name and the horse didn't come until he got to Hollywood as an old man of twenty-four. Maybe, son, you should wait until you're twenty-four."

Note: On to high school.

Meet Bessie Bursack
– 1955 –

I WAS a country school kid for all of three months, attending a one-room school in Johnstown in the spring of '54. Dad had bought a farm on Rock Prairie, a mile from the school. We moved there in March.

That fall, I climbed aboard a big yellow bus for the eight-mile ride to Janesville High School. Like all the other ninth grade boys who had attended a country school in the Janesville district, I wore blue jeans, well-washed farm work pants.

We got teased a lot because of our trousers. The city guys wore dress pants. They felt they were oh so much better than us and let us know it.

Our English teacher, Bessie Bursack, sided with us. "Let me teach you some insults from William Shakespeare you can use on them," she said.

One that I remember is 'You poor, base, rascally, cheating lack-linen mate!' It's from *Henry IV Part 2*.

And this from *Troilus and Cressida*, 'Thou sodden-witted lord! Thou hast no more brain than I have in mine elbows.'

Jerry Peterson

But my favorite of all those she taught us is from *King Lear*, 'Thou art a boil, a plague sore.'

To be truthful, the insults didn't get us far. We drew some gaping mouths and blank stares, but then the city guys found other ways to come at us.

Miss Bursack knew it, too. She took us aside one more time. "Look," she said, "I've seen your grades from your country schools. You're all smart. Beat the city kids in the classroom. They'll know it and back off."

Bless her. She was right.

Note: The Janesville/Beloit rivalry.

Duking it out in the Parking Lot
– 1956 –

I DIDN'T know rivalries could be bloody affairs until I got to high school.

The realization came the night we played an away football game in Beloit, against Memorial High School's Purple Knights.

It was Memorial's homecoming.

We won.

I no longer remember the score, but we in the stands were subjected to a lot of hooting and hollering as we made our way down and out to our buses.

We underclassmen figured that was the end of it until our buses rolled into the parking lot behind our school. We were all going inside, to the J-Room for a sock hop.

A herd of cars were there. Angry Memorial students boiled out of them and charged our buses. We had to fight our way out and through the lot to get to the safety of the doors being held open for us by teachers.

Lots of knuckles bruised, lips torn and bleeding, and eyes that would be swollen shut and black by morning.

Our big guys at the dance gloried in their injuries. The admiring looks they got from the girls, the flirting, to them it made it all worth it.

Of course, we undersized underclassmen, we had run through the mob before anyone could catch us and pound us into the pavement. We weren't getting any attention from the girls, not even from the girls in our own classes.

Johnny Deihl grabbed my elbow. "Hey," he said, "we're not gonna get no lovin' this way. Come with me."

He hustled me out to the parking lot, tame now. The police had run off the Beloit hoods.

Johnny ripped my shirt.

I wasn't going to take that from a friend, so I ripped his.

He grabbed up a fistful of parking lot grim and smeared me with it.

I did the same to him.

We then went at each other's hair.

"I get it," I said. "All we need now is some blood. You want me to bust you in the mouth?"

"Hell, no." Johnny brought out a small bottle. "Fake blood. I never go to a Beloit game without it."

He dabbed some around the corner of my mouth, and I dripped a little under his nose.

We went back inside, each with an arm around the other's shoulders.

Deb Anderson came up to Johnny. She touched a finger to the side of his nose. "Are you all right?" she asked.

"Yeah," he said, "but you should have seen the other guy. Big Beloit kid. I sure kicked his—"

She put a finger on his lips, and together they rocked out onto the dance floor.

Betts Miller, who was with Deb, stood next to me. "You look awful," she said.

"It's not too bad," I said. I kind of shuffled in place, uneasy, not knowing what to do.

When a slow dance came, she took my hand. Betts led me out on the dance floor, danced real close to me.

"I'm feeling better," I said to her.

The lights dimmed, and she gazed up at me. And she kissed me.

"Yes," I breathed into her ear, "I'm feeling much better now."

Note: I was now seventeen and bold enough to date.

And They Were Such Nice Shoes
– 1957 –

SEAFOOD in Wisconsin was fish.

On Friday night.

And then only if you were Catholic.

Still, I wanted to impress her, so I took her all the way to Milwaukee—the big city if, as for me, home was Janesville. Milwaukee where they, indeed, had a seafood restaurant. Cap'n Dan's.

It was on the lake shore.

Great view of the iron ore boats plying the waters of Lake Michigan, bound for Gary, Indiana, and the sailboats just . . . well, I never knew where they were going, maybe back into the harbor after having drifted with the breeze past Breakwater Lighthouse.

"And what would you like?" the waiter asked.

She put her menu down. "The smoked trout," she said.

Well, she was Catholic, so I figured she knew what she was doing, and me, a Lutheran, I just followed her lead and ordered the same.

He took our drinks order next—iced tea for her, milk for me—then asked, "Would you like an appetizer?"

I must have appeared to be lost because she touched my hand and said to him, "Shrimp, please, for both of us. With cocktail sauce."

That came quickly, two plates of these curved things with tails on them. When I picked one up to try it, I discovered it had kind of a clear plastic armor-plating on it.

"You have to peel them," she said and demonstrated. She got hers clean and those little dangly legs picked off, then dabbed it in what looked to me to be ketchup and ate it. At the last moment, she pulled off the tail.

Now that I knew what to do, I found those little fellows pretty darn good. So good I put down a bucketful.

The waiter came. He cleared away our dishes of debris and set our plates with the main course in front of us.

I looked down at it, and it looked up at me, a fish with its head still on and one glassy eye staring up. My stomach lurched.

I kicked over my chair, getting away from the table to make a run for the bathroom, but it all came up in a gushing retch, all over the waiter's shoes. Nice shoes, too.

We hurried out of there, she taking my wallet to pay the bill. And outside, she said, "I'm driving," which was all right with me. I was green and sick and rode all the way home with my head out the window.

Note: I advanced a year. I'm now graduating from high school.

The Hot Seat
– 1958 –

IT WAS our last chance to party what with summer jobs and college ahead. Graduation was going to break up 'the crew' as we liked to call ourselves, so when Ernie said, "Hey, we got two hours before we gotta be in our caps 'n' gowns. How about a last swim?"

Sure, we said yes. Fred had the beer—Pabst.

Well, actually we all did. It was darn hot, and it seemed like a stupid idea to let the stuff cook in the trunk until after we got our diplomas.

So Ernie wheeled his top-down Ford off the highway and onto the gravel road that led to the old quarry, the turn setting the pine-tree air freshener suspended from his mirror to swinging like a metronome.

One of the guys ported a couple empties over the side as we roared down the road, and Bob jacked open replacements. One he handed to Ernie and the other he kept for himself. Was it his third or fourth? I couldn't keep track of his. Heck, I couldn't keep track of mine.

Jerry Peterson

Ernie slammed on the brakes. He threw the car into a slide, and when it stopped, he stared at a chain across the road. "Who the hell put that there?"

The road into the quarry had never been chained.

Never.

But it was now.

Bob waved his bottle. Oh, for a magical sword that we might cleave that impediment in two.

Ernie stared at him. "You swallow a dictionary or somethin'?"

"Just beer. We kin walk in, I guess."

So we did. We kicked off our shoes and socks and pants and peeled off our shirts as we went along, making bets on who could throw his trousers the farthest. Ernie won with that outfielder arm of his.

Our shorts went last, after we made our way across the riprap to the water's edge. Then we sloshed our way in. Oh, I tell you, that water was a relief. The races, the hollering, the seeing who could dunk who, we never saw them coming until Rosemary Holland called out, "We've got something here." And she did, and the Deahl sisters, and Betts Miller.

They held up this collection of clothes and shoes— our clothes and shoes—Betts waving my pants at me.

Now you don't joke with Bob, not after he's had four beers or was it five? He dove under and came up with a fistful of mud and rocks and pitched the mess at them, and they ran . . . with our clothes.

Hardly a minute later, we heard Rosemary's Chevy peel away.

Ernie, red faced with anger, dope-slapped Bob, the thwack echoing off the quarry's walls. "What the heck you do that for, Bobber-dobber? They got our clothes, man!"

Fred, jay nekid as the rest of us, splashed his way out of the water. "I don't know about you, but I'm gonna catch hell from my dad if I'm late. My cousin lives over the hill. I'll get some clothes from him."

"You goin' barefoot?" I asked.

"How the heck else am I gonna get there?"

Ernie sloshed up to the shore. "I kin drive ya, drive us all."

"They got your keys, man."

"I got one hid under the fender."

So out we went, ooching and ouching across the riprap and up the road to Ernie's car. Fred, the first in the back seat, came up swatting at his fanny, squalling "I been branded!"

Those Naugahyde seats baking in the sun, they're like fire, so we ripped the rugs up off the floor and used them for seat covers.

Ernie barreled us out of there and onto the highway, and this siren went off behind us. Fred punched Ernie. "You can outrun 'im!"

"The hell I can." With that, Ernie stepped his bare foot over onto the brake pedal.

We waited a long time after he stopped, none of us daring to look over our shoulders. Then we heard it, the crunching of gravel under boots, and there he was, Deputy Baxter leaning on Ernie's door. "You boys lose something back there?" he asked.

That's when we saw him bring up that damn Polaroid camera.

"Sheriff's got a new rule, boys," he said, looking all of us over. "We gotta take a picture of every traffic stop. Now step out here and smile."

Note: Come with me to the city of dreams.

Me & Hollywood
– 1959 –

TRUE STORY.

I made it in Hollywood . . . if you define 'made it' as I got there.

Did that in 1959, and perhaps could have made it in television . . . if you define 'made it' here as getting a role in a TV series . . . had I taken one more step.

During the summer of '59, I joined up with two Frenchmen who wanted to drive from Wisconsin, where they were working, to California before they headed back to France. They had a car. I just had to pay for part of the gasoline.

I was about as loose as one could be, being 19 and between my freshman and sophomore years in college.

We left with a letter of introduction to a ranch family in Montana the French guys' employer knew. And we stayed and worked on that ranch for a week before heading on.

This ranch was so far from the nearest town that the rancher had to fly there to pick up the mail and buy groceries. One day, I rode in the co-pilot's seat of the family's Cessna 172 on one of those flights.

My two fellow travelers were an interesting pair. One was kind and caring and conscientious to the nth degree. He played everything safe, and he was a good driver. In contrast, his partner must have been related to Evel Kenievil. Speed limits and stop signs meant nothing to him. One night when he was driving in the mountains, I thought sure he was going to kill the three of us.

An absolutely harrowing drive.

When I complained—the complaining building to a shouting match—he refused to relinquish the wheel to me or his partner. So in a huff, I said when we get to California, I'm getting out.

He and his partner dropped me at the bus station in Sacramento where I bought a ticket to L.A., and they went on to San Francisco.

I knew one person in the City of Angels, Cindy Harmon from North Prairie. Cindy's parents and my parents were long-time good friends . . . and so were Cindy and I.

When she got there some months before me, she interviewed with Frontier Airlines and got hired as a stewardess. When I arrived in the city, Cindy was in the company's training program.

The Greyhound made a stop in Hollywood before going on downtown to the main terminal. So, for no other reason than it was Hollywood, I got off . . . and discovered to my good fortune that there was a YMCA next door.

I checked in and got a room.

On my second morning there, while I was standing at the mirror shaving, two guys came out of the showers and up to the next mirrors to shave, too. Being young dudes, we struck up a conversation . . . who are you and what are you doing here.

"We're actors," said the shorter of the two, the guy

with dark hair. His partner was blonde and taller by six inches . . . and didn't talk much. "We're working in a new western series for television, a show called *Laramie*."

It was to air that fall on NBC.

Said the talkative one, "You ought to come out to where we're shooting in the Hollywood Hills."

I demurred, said I had to find a paying job.

Now if either had said maybe we can get you on as an extra . . . but they didn't.

After I got home and went back to college, one evening in October I tuned into *Laramie*, and there were the two guys from the Y . . . Robert Fuller and John Smith. The stars of the show.

Prior to *Laramie*, their work in theater, television, and the movies was hit and miss. They were learning their craft. And most of the time they were broke. That's why they were living at the Y. I expect that within a year of landing on *Laramie*, both Fuller and Smith bought sizable homes with swimming pools in the backyard.

Smith would work another ten years in Hollywood, and then his career fizzled.

Not so for Fuller. He worked a half a century in Hollywood before retiring and starting a horse ranch in Texas.

He preferred to work in Westerns, and his final role—and a recurring one at that—was as Wade Harper on *Walker, Texas Ranger* . . . Harper, the great, great grandson of Jess Harper, Fuller's character on *Laramie* three decades before.

Had I gone out to the *Laramie* set, could I have made it, at least for a little while? Probably. I knew how to ride a horse. Fuller, who had grown up in Florida, and Smith, who had grown up in California—Hollywood, actually—had to learn on the job.

I probably would have been cast as the seventh

cowboy on the right, truly as an extra with no lines of dialogue.

As the seventh cowboy on the right, I would have had something in common with another actor who was closer to my age, Bruce Dern.

He had studied acting with Lee Stasberg in New York City.

Dern wanted to work on Broadway. One day Strasberg told him you've learned everything you can from me. You ought to go west. All the other young actors are, to get into television. "Westerns are big," Strasberg said. "You'll likely be cast as the seventh cowboy on the right. Just be sure you're the best damn seventh cowboy on the right, and you'll make it."

Dern got to Hollywood in 1960 and was cast in small roles in television's *Route 66* and the movie *Wild River*.

In 1962, he was cast, finally, as the seventh cowboy on the right in the then new television western series, *Stoney Burke*. Actually, Dern was hired as a secondary lead and appeared in 17 of the show's 32 episodes.

Over the years, he would appear in 80 movies and a list of television shows as long as your arm, winning a bucketful of awards, but never an Oscar or an Emmy.

At age 84, Dern is still working.

Note: I step on stage . . . for real.

Theater Stories
– 1960 –

MY TASTE for grease paint came first when I was in high school.

I was cast in two musicals, *Oklahoma* and *South Pacific*, minor rolls that put me in the chorus for both shows. Lots of singing and some stage movement that we called dance.

Between *Oklahoma* and *South Pacific* I tried out for and won a role in a comedy, *The Torch-Bearer*, an old spoof of community theater—amateur theater.

Scenery fell down. Actors missed cues and forgot lines. False mustaches fell off. Props weren't where they were supposed to be. Actors tripped over scenery braces. Just everything that could go wrong in a stage production, playwright George Kelly included in his 1922 script.

Unwittingly, Danny Wilson playing Huxley Hossenfrosse and I were offstage at one moment, waiting for our entrance. We were talking, not paying a lot of attention to the play when we thought we heard our cue. We rushed on only to discover we were five minutes early.

We couldn't rush off, so we stayed onstage. We drank tea to pass the time, nibbled on cucumber sandwiches, always in character, and made pretend conversation until our real cue came up.

In the final show of my senior year, the director cast me in the lead in *George Washington Slept Here*, a comedy written by Moss Hart and George S. Kaufman.

Of all the actors in the original Broadway production, back in 1940, only one is vaguely remembered, Percy Kilbride. A superb character actor, Kilbride made his fame playing Pa Kettle in the Ma and Pa Kettle comedy films of the '40s and '50s, ten films in all.

Warner Brothers signed Jack Benny to play the lead in the 1942 film version of *George Washington Slept Here*. Screenwriter Everett Freeman, as he reworked Hart and Kaufman's script, reworked the role of lead Bill Fuller to give Benny more of the laughs.

It was at Milton College that I was introduced to the plays of William Shakespeare. In high school, in one of my English classes, we read Shakespeare's old war horse, *Julius Caesar*—read and discussed, but not acted. There's a difference.

At Milton, I acted in two Shakespeare plays, *Twelfth Night* and *The Tempest*.

In *Twelfth Night*, I played Sir Andrew Aguecheek.

It was here that the director, Prof Herb Crouch, told us about the raked stage, something we students had never heard of.

A raked stage is slanted toward the audience, the theory and reality being that the audience could better see the actors higher on the stage, those behind the actors who were down front.

Lord help you if you were playing a jester in a show on a raked stage. You're juggling three oranges and you drop one. It's going to roll out into the audience before you can catch up with it.

"We had that kind of stage when I was a student here," Prof Crouch told us. "The only way we could be sure the scenery wouldn't slide away into the audience was to nail it to the floor.

"One show we did," he said, "required a set change, so, during the act break, while the curtain was closed, we were all on stage, pulling up nails, shifting out the old set and hauling in the new and hammering it down.

"Can you imagine what the audience thought was going on?"

We could. And, like Prof Crouch, we were glad the college tore out the raked stage and replaced it with a flat floor.

Note: Every college student faces the same question, what the heck am I going to do after I graduate?

A Degree that Prepared Me to do Nothing
– 1961 –

I GRADUATED from high school respectably, number 38 in a class of 364 students. It was enough that the admissions officer at nearby Milton College said he wanted me. He offered me a scholarship—free tuition—if I would come study at his college.

Free tuition. That got my attention.

I picked up a second scholarship that bought my books.

Going to Milton College only six miles from home, I could be a commuter, so no dorm expense.

And if I carried my lunch, I didn't have to buy food at the cafeteria. As a matter of principle I didn't want to do that. The college had farmed out the cafeteria to a private company—the Profit Company. Believe me, that really was the name of the outfit. It irritated me that a private company could stick it to the students.

Anyway, in the fall there I was standing in the registration line, waiting for my turn to sign up for classes. Someone came working his way along the line, asking each student in turn, "Can you sing? "Can you sing?"

When he got to me, I said yes.

He said, "I want you in the choir."

That was my audition. I sang for Bernie Westland for four years.

I majored in speech, English, and social studies at Milton College, and discovered I also had enough hours in history courses that I could claim a history minor. I was set to get a B.A., a Bachelor's of Arts degree.

The realization came at the beginning of my senior year that I was going to graduate equipped to do absolutely nothing.

I looked around for options. I had always enjoyed being a student, so I figured maybe I could be a teacher. I made an appointment to talk to Herb Hadow, the college's one-man education department.

Mister Hadow set me up for a couple courses I needed to get a teaching license. One of them was educational psych.

On the first day of that class, the prof teaching it told all of us students with the straightest of faces that psychology had nothing to offer education. He then proceeded to teach us experimental psychology for a semester. Fascinating stuff.

Mister Hadow also set me up to do the required six weeks of student teaching. He got me into the English department at Edgerton High School.

Came the day, he took me over, introduced me to my supervising teacher, and left, saying he'd check in on me from time to time.

My supervising teacher talked me through the job and what she was teaching. The next day, I sat in on her classroom. At the end of the day, as she was packing up, she said, "Mister Peterson, tomorrow, you're on your own. You know my routine. You know what to do. You teach. You make the lesson plans. You make the homework assignments and check them. You write the tests. You administer them and grade them. At the end of it all, you issue the quarterly grades. Any problems, come see me in the teachers' room."

I didn't have any problems. I never went to see her, although she, like Mister Hadow, occasionally stopped in on my classes. So did the principal.

That was it. I graduated with an education minor and secured a teaching certificate, issued by the State Department of Education, that said I was qualified to teach English, speech, drama, and social studies at the high school level.

I was equipped for a job.

Note: I graduated from Milton College in the spring with a teaching degree and a job. Returning public school teachers at that time had to sign their contracts by April 1. After that date, superintendents were free to go hunting for teachers to fill any vacancies they had. I bagged my job in early May. I would be teaching English and speech at Adams-Friendship High School up in the central part of the state.

A Place on the Lake
– 1962 –

I ARRIVED a couple days early in Friendship for my first teaching job, arrived without a place to stay.

"I've got a house on the lake," Missus French told me during a break in our new teacher get-acquainted meeting. "It's available for rent. Everything's included. Would you like to see it?"

Would I? She might as well have set a steak dinner in front of a starving man. Sure, I'd like to see it. A house and not an apartment, and fully furnished, terrific because I didn't even own a beanbag chair.

So I followed Missus French out to the lake.

The house was on a point, no other houses close by, so lots of elbow room.

In the walk-around of the grounds, she showed me the boat that came with the place, a rubber dingy with oars, the dingy blistered with patches, so much so it looked like it had the pox. The lake was small. A county ordinance prohibited motorized craft, and that was fine with me. I didn't waterski, nor did I have any desire to listen to Johnson outboards scream across the water.

"You can paddle out to the middle of the lake and fish," she said, "or just catch some rays, work on your tan."

Fish? That requires patience I don't have, but after a hard week of teaching I could see myself on a Saturday pottering around on the lake, my Sony transistor in the bow tuned to the Badgers football game, just me and whoever else might be out in their rowboats.

"How much?" I asked.

She named a price that she knew fit my income.

"Deal," I said. "I'll take it. When can I move in?"

"This afternoon," she said.

No contract, as I recall. Not even a handshake. Just a verbal agreement between two teachers who would be working together in the same building for the next nine months.

A house on the lake, a bed, a living room with a couch and coffee table, a well-equipped kitchen where I could cook, and a boat. What could be better?

The test came the third Saturday in September, an ideal fall day—warm, bright sun, no wind. After putting down a couple hot dogs fresh off the grill, I launched the SS Rubber Ducky. Did I mention the house's boat was yellow?

I paddled out to the middle of the lake and there, after dialing in the Wisconsin Rapids radio station, I leaned back against one gunwale and dangled my feet over the other, into the water. Pure comfort, lulling . . . and I fell asleep.

I woke to the game announcer yelling, "Holy moley, Wisconsin wins! Wisconsin wins!"

I jerked to the side, toward the radio, and felt pain. The sun had fried me.

At the same moment, a nearby fisherman, wild-eyed—he must have heard the end of the game, too—whipped up on his rod, his lure snagging the Rubber Ducky. He ripped a swatch out of the Duck's bottom, sending the Duck, my radio, and me to the bottom of Friendship Lake.

It wasn't until the next day when I got the Sunday newspaper that I learned what I had slept through out there on the water. With twenty seconds to go, Minnesota quarterback Sandy Stephens, assured of a win, threw a pass, going for a second touchdown, but Jim Nettles, our defensive end, intercepted on our two-yard line, then ran the ball back ninety-eight yards for Wisconsin's second touchdown and the victory. We got to keep Paul Bunyan's Axe for another year. And I got to salvage the Duck—drag it back to shore and buy a new radio—me with my sunburn slathered with calamine lotion.

Note: Year Two, teaching at Adams-Friendship High School.

Afternoon at the Movies
– 1963 –

THERE IT WAS, a panoramic view of the Arabian Desert, the sun shimmering on the sand, heat waves rising. Then, in the far distance, a lone rider on a camel comes plodding this way . . . toward me and the audience around me. As the rider comes closer, the music swells, the theme of the movie *Lawrence of Arabia*, the music as rich and dramatic as the scene on the wide screen before us.

We were there, a carload of my students and me.

The movie had come out the year before, in 1962, in December.

Over the months that passed, audiences grew as word of mouth spread, as people who saw the movie told their friends, "You've got to see this one." The seven Oscars the movie won, including an Oscar for Best Picture, also helped draw people in.

Why we didn't go sooner I don't know. This was in an era when there wasn't a rush to pack the theaters on the first weekend of a movie's release.

You remember that I'm teaching at Adams-Friendship High School at this time. I'm now in my second year.

You should know that Adams County was once the poorest county in Wisconsin. It lost its title to Menomenee when the Legislature created that county in 1959.

Poorest county or second poorest, few high school kids had ever been outside of the county. I thought I could change that . . . at least a little.

I was the high school's theater director, so soon after I got to Adams-Friendship I had a cadre of students who were excited about plays, musicals, and movies. So I traded my Desoto convertible for a nine-passenger Chevy Corvair Greenbrier, and, with the support of parents, we set out to go to a show somewhere at least once a month.

Charlie—one of my students—said we could make the van a ten-passenger vehicle if I let him ride in the back over the engine, on the cargo floor. He'd throw a blanket and pillows back there for comfort.

We had a rule. We would never leave out any student who wanted to go but felt he or she couldn't because they didn't have money for eats and a show ticket. The rest of us would chip in to cover that student's expenses.

The first play we went to was in Minneapolis, Tennessee Williams' *The Glass Menagerie* being presented at the new Guthrie Theater by the Guthrie's repertory company.

We walked in early, to see the place, and my students' eyes bugged out. Down front was a stage unlike anything they had seen before—a thrust stage. Ours back at the high school was the traditional proscenium stage cut into the wall of the gymnasium. Our seats, hard folding chairs. The Guthrie's, well-padded theater seats.

That stage, I said pointing to it, the theater's founder, Sir Tyrone Guthrie, wanted it to look like the stage in Shakespeare's Globe Theater.

We opened the program book that I had purchased to the center spread. It showed The Globe on one side and The Guthrie on the other. The difference between the two, I said, is the audience area around the stage. Where we have seats here, The Globe didn't have any. The audience—the groundlings—stood for the whole performance which might be a couple hours to three and a half hours long.

Charlie ran his hand over the fabric of one of the seats. "This is pretty plush," he said. "We've got it good."

And we did. We saw Hal Holbrook play Jim O'Connor, the gentleman caller. Holbrook was not yet the star he would become.

We shot down to Milwaukee for *Camelot* playing at the Pabst Theater. The musical had opened on Broadway three years before and won four Tonys.

What we didn't know then was that the show, when it premiered in Toronto, ran long . . . four and a half hours, the final curtain coming down at twelve-forty in the morning. Playwright and lyricist Alan Lerner said that only the Wagner opera *Tristan and Isolde* equaled *Camelot* as a bladder endurance contest.

Lerner, Frederick Loewe—Lerner's partner and composer—and director Moss Hart cut *Camelot* to two hours.

We went to see the road show and got the cheapest seats we could, up in the fifth balcony, the seats with no knee room and so narrow that we were almost sitting on each other's laps.

Robert Goulet played and sang his Broadway role of Sir Lancelot.

Another time we went up to Stevens Point State University for a college production of *Teahouse of the August Moon*, a post-World War II play set in Okinawa. It had won a Pulitzer Prize for Drama back in 1953.

Stevens Point's theater was on the second floor of an academic building.

In one scene, several characters drive on stage in an Army Jeep. Most theater companies would find a way to fake that scene, but the Stevens Point Players used a real Jeep. We wondered how did they get that into the theater? When we left, walking down the double-wide staircase to the lobby and out the double doors to where we had left my van, Charlie had figured it out. They drove the Jeep, he said, through the doors, up the stairs, and down the hall to a backstage entrance. Had to be double doors there, too, he said.

There weren't.

I had talked to the director during the intermission. He told me they had driven the Jeep through the double doors at the top of the stairs into the auditorium where they had laid planks across the rows of seats. They drove the Jeep over the seats and down to the stage.

"I don't believe that," Charlie said.

I just raised my hands palms outward, feigning innocence.

We returned to Milwaukee on another weekend for the Milwaukee's Rep's presentation of Bertolt Brecht and Kurt Weill's *Threepenny Opera*. We came away singing The Ballad of Mac the Knife and what we called the hamburger song. In the opera, it's The Cannon Song, a duet between Mac and Police Chief Tiger Brown, old Army buddies who sing about war and how their troops would chop the enemy into "beefsteak tartare."

A fair number of my theater students ended up going to college as a consequence of having tasted life outside of

Adams County if only for brief periods of time. They got their degrees and settled elsewhere.

I expect most are like me today, still going to theaters to see plays, musicals, and movies. Some may even be community theater actors. And perhaps one followed me and became the director of a high school theater program.

Note: Like many teachers, when summer came I went to summer school. For me, that was the University of Wisconsin in 1963 and Marquette University in '64 and '65. The summer of '64, though, had more.
2,007 words

I Played Summer Stock with Harrison Ford
– 1964 –

THE NEXT TIME you see Harry—that's what we all called him at the Belfry Theater—tell him I asked you to say hello for me.

But, wait, I have to work up to this story. You need some background.

When I began poking around the University of Wisconsin for a master's degree program, the last thing I wanted was a major in education. I wanted substance.

I was the theater director at Adams-Friendship. During my first year there, I produced six shows, so something in theater seemed appropriate. I discovered UW was the national hub for the arts council movement and community theater, the hub created by Robert Gard who launched the Wisconsin Idea Theater back in 1945.

I tapped into all this and that summer attended a number of community theater conferences around the country. Directing in a professional community theater looked interesting. The premier professional community theater at that time was in Pittsburgh—The Pittsburgh Playhouse. Three stages under one roof. They could and did everything from small shows to big, splashy Broadway musicals.

The more I learned about these theaters, the more I wanted to apply for a job with one, but I was under contract to return to Adams-Friendship for a second year.

It was also while bopping around the country at conferences that I learned that one of the most highly respected directors in these theaters was Father John Walsh in Milwaukee, at Marquette University's Teatro Maria.

So I left UW's graduate school for Marquette's the next summer. There I took classes in oral interpretation and television production.

The year before, Father Walsh had built an outdoor theater at the end of an alley near the campus. The stage was a triple-decker thrust stage patterned after the Stratford Festival Theater in Canada which was patterned after Shakespeare's Globe Theater.

This became Teatro Maria's summer home.

By the time we summer school students rolled onto campus, Father Walsh had already cast his first show of the season, Shakespeare's *Julius Caesar*. It was well into rehearsals.

After I settled into the dorm, I went over to the theater and introduced myself to Father Walsh. "I'd like to be in your company," I said.

We talked a bit, then he made his decision. "There are lots of crowd scenes," he said. "I can always use more people. But you won't have any lines."

That was fine by me. I just wanted to see how this man worked. So I became a spear carrier—well, an infantryman toting an M-16. This production of *Julius Caesar* was in modern dress.

I played nine different characters in nine different scenes. Run off stage at the end of a scene, change costumes in less than half a minute, and run back on stage as a part of a new crowd before the lights go up.

There were war scenes in *Julius Caesar*. Twice a night I was shot, died both times.

Father Walsh selected Marc Connelly's *Green Pastures* for the next show. Again he inserted me into the crowd scenes, only this time he gave me a couple lines.

Connelly drew on Roark Bradford's collection of stories titled "Ol' Man Adam an' His Chillun" in writing his script. The play won a Pulitzer Prize for Drama in 1930.

Green Pastures presents a series of Old Testament stories as seen through the eyes of a young black child. It originally used an all-black cast. Walsh decided it would be wrong to do that. Most of his actors were white, as were most of the students at Marquette. Walsh's actors would have to do the play in blackface. That, he said, would be an insult to the black community of Milwaukee.

So we did it in normal stage makeup. And we dropped the black dialect. There is a heavenly choir in the show. For this, Walsh reached out to one of the black churches. They loaned us their choir, and their choir rocked the house every night.

Since the stories are seen through the eyes of a child, Walsh sent several of his stage crew to the city's Bible bookstores to buy kids' coloring books that portrayed stories of the Bible. He used a style he found in one of those books, a style he particularly liked, in designing the set pieces for the play. That brought lots of color to the stage and the look that Walsh envisioned.

The hazard of outdoor theater is sometimes it rains. One night when The Lord was hurling lightning bolts at the sinners down on the Earth—He above us on the third stage, we below him on the first—a real lightning bolt exploded in the sky. With it came thunder and an instant downpour—a deluge. Father Walsh raced out on the stage and called off the rest of the show. "Keep your tickets and come back tomorrow night," he shouted to the audience scurrying for what shelter they could find in Teatro Maria's alley.

Summer school ended. I was pumped after having been in two of Father Walsh's shows, so I went home to Janesville with half the summer remaining, wanting to do more theater. For that, I went over to The Belfry, between Delavan where I would be teaching in the fall and Lake Geneva.

The Belfry was a summer theater with an indoor stage, so shows were never canceled because of weather. The resident company of actors lived in a barrack behind the theater. During the days, they built and painted sets, made costumes, and rehearsed whatever show was coming up next. In the evenings, they presented the play or musical that was up in the rotation.

This theater was the first summer stock theater in Wisconsin, so it had a long history. Paul Newman was a cast member in 1949, Del Close in 1953, Gary Burghoff in 1962, and Harrison Ford in 1964. All were college students at the time or recent graduates.

Newman and Ford you know. Close became a film and television actor of note, a writer and a teacher. He spent a lot of years directing for improv companies around the country and teaching improvisation, most notably at Second City in Chicago.

Burghoff grew up in Delavan and graduated from Delavan-Darien High School where I would be teaching.

After his summer with The Belfry, he went to New York City. Burghoff didn't do well there, finally giving up in 1967. He came home, but not until after he auditioned for the role of Ned Brown in the planned Off-Broadway production of Charles Schulz's *You're a Good Man, Ned Brown.*

The director, Clark Gesler, telephoned Burghoff in Delavan and said you've got the role if you're willing to come back. He did and played Ned Brown for 1,597 performances.

From there, Burghoff went to California and the role of Radar O'Reilly in the film version of M*A*S*H. In the television series, he played Radar for eight years.

At The Belfry, I found the director, Allen Buzzell, and used the same line with him that I had used with Father Walsh—"I'd like to be in your company."

He told me I was a little late, that the season was half over. "Besides," he said, "I have all the actors I need."

We talked some more. I told him I would be teaching at the high school, that I would be running the theater program.

Finally, he said, "All right, you're in. But I can't pay you."

That was fine with me. I would be at home, commuting in for rehearsals and performances. I wouldn't be an expense to the theater and, other than gasoline for my car, no expense for me.

Buzzell was rehearsing the musical *Little Mary Sunshine* in which he had cast Harry Ford as Captain Big Jim Warrington, the male lead.

I was not introduced around, so I didn't meet him or any of the other actors.

After ten minutes together, Buzzell said, "Come back next week when we start rehearsing *The Fantasticks*. You're The Mute."

What luck. I had seen *The Fantasticks* the previous summer at The Isthmus Playhouse in Madison. A great show. Minimum scenery, requiring a lot of imagination of the actors and the audience.

And a lot of imagination for The Mute. I had to pantomime, among other things, building a brick wall to separate the young lovers from one another.

It turned out to be a good thing that I didn't have any lines. On the day of the opening night, I had to call Buzzell from the dentist's office. "I'm having my wisdom teeth pulled," I said, "but I'll be there in time for the show."

I was.

With all the wadding in my cheeks where my wisdom teeth had been, I looked like a chipmunk.

"How you doing?" Allen asked when he saw me at the makeup table.

I peered at his image in the mirror and mumbled something to him that neither he nor I understood.

I made it through the performance without spitting blood on anyone, but I did have to change the wadding between acts.

Allen did one neat thing for my character. The Mute is usually made up as a pantomimist—white face with painted-on features. He said he wanted me as a sad-faced clown. "You figure it out," he said.

It took a couple tries at the makeup table to get it right. We were blessed with a superb show photographer. The close-up he took of me in makeup he enlarged and had it framed. It's on the wall in my office today.

Harry? Allen cast him as El Gallo, again the male lead, a role Harry had played in Ripon College's production of *The Fantasticks*.

Harry had attended Ripon for four years. He quit before graduation when Allen hired him to be in The Belfry's summer company.

I was in one more show at The Belfry, *Once Upon a Mattress*, the musical adaptation of the old Hans Christian Andersen fairy tale, *The Princess and the Pea*. Allen cast me as The Jester.

The show opened Off-Broadway in 1959 and moved to a Broadway theater—the Alvin—the same year. A struggling 26-year-old actress, comedian, and singer, Carol Burnette, was cast in the lead as Princess Winifred. Her performance made her a star.

I had my brief moment. We actors moved the scenery and furniture, resetting the stage between scenes with the lights up and the audience watching. Allen choreographed all the movements. We were to stay in character, he said.

As The Jester, I got to bring the king's throne onstage for one of the scenes. After I positioned it on the platform, I stepped back and studied the throne, giving the impression that I wanted everything to look just right. I saw a speck of dust on the arm of the throne and, drawing a handkerchief from my sleeve, whipped the speck away. I made a show of it to laughter, then applause as I, the court jester, danced off stage.

After the performance, after the curtain call, Allen came to me, boiling with anger. "Don't you ever, ever mess with my show again," he burred.

I did.

Every night.

To laughter and applause.

Allen gave up on his threat to do me bodily harm.

I left the company after the final performance. It was time for new teacher orientation at the high school.

Others were leaving, too, for jobs elsewhere. Allen was short of actors.

For the last show, the musical *Damn Yankees*, he had to cast himself as The Commissioner. Again Allen cast Harry in the lead, this time as the baseball player Joe Hardy—"Shoeless Joe from Hannibal, Mo." Joe and The Commissioner have one scene together. In a newspaper story a couple decades ago, Allen said because of that scene he got to trade lines with Harrison Ford.

Had I stayed with the company, it's likely Allen would have cast me as The Commissioner, and then today I could say I once traded lines with Harrison 'Harry' Ford.

Note: Wisconsin Farm Bureau owned a special place up in Door County called The Clearing, created a half-century before by a prominent landscape architect, Jens Jensen. It was both a retreat and a folk school of sorts, in the summer offering all kinds of classes. The main mission, though, was to preserve this magical land of quiet where one could go for a period of time to escape the noise of daily living.

The Clearing
– 1965 –

HE HAD WALKED the retreat's path in Wisconsin's Door County every evening for a week, at the end of the path a cliff that overlooked Green Bay.

A great place, if he went at the right time, to watch the sky where it met the watery horizon to the west go from a fiery gold, to a mellow orange as the sun slid from sight, to pink, to early nighttime purple, the water sometimes placid, sometimes wild.

All of it inspiring for a poet who needed to get away from the drag of teaching at a mountain college, where the only open water one could enjoy was a koi pond behind the president's house.

He meandered along, lost in his thoughts—woolgathering as the old phrase has it—another hundred yards and . . . something crept into his consciousness, something whispering this isn't your path.

He gazed around.

The trees, they were different. No longer pines, but tulip trees and in bloom. The trillium that fringed the path, gone. In their place, psychedelically colored poppies and bachelor buttons, and mushrooms of a species he'd never seen before, a wee person there, wrestling with one, breaking it off.

He knuckled his eyes, not believing—a wee person? He knew the tales of fairies and leprechauns, but they were just that, tales in literature and stories told around ancient fires, stories passed down from his Irish ancestors. When he opened his eyes, the wee person was gone, if he or she or it had ever been there. And the mushroom, too. Just a stump left where it had been. He touched the stump. This was real.

A swirl in the grass swished away. He followed it, trotting to keep up, the grass and the swirl ending at a pile of soil. The wee person scrambled up with his mushroom and disappeared down the other side, down a hole that looked to be an abandoned badger's den.

He knelt and peered into the hole, into nothingness. When he looked up, a ramshackle cottage, weathered gray with some shingles missing, laid ahead in a clearing.

That something in his consciousness, it whispered to him don't go there, but he did, drawn by a power he'd not felt before.

He stood at the door, wondering whether to knock. Seemed only polite.

"One mo," rumbled a voice from within.

One long mo.

When the door at last squalled open, he startled.

There stood an old man clutching a stirring spoon, a chef's hat tipped forward over one eyebrow and a red-striped apron tied up under his arms. His beard and build suggested he could be related to Santa Claus.

"Who were you expecting," the man asked, "the wicked witch? She's not lived here for years."

The man waved him in. "Name's Nicholas Lickety. Don't get many visitors. In fact, you're the first in some time. What's your name?"

"Donald Jay."

Lickety turned back. He thrust his arms out. "Donald Jay what?"

"Just Donald Jay."

"Seems I should know you, Donald Jay. Follow me to the galley. I'm cooking."

Jay straggled along, his head swivelling as he took in each room in succession, his mouth agape. The interior was nothing like the exterior. This was bright, welcoming, comfortable, something that might be featured in Southern Living magazine rather than WWM—Witches & Warlocks Monthly.

Aromas enticed him on, rosemary and thyme and a hint of chili pepper. He drifted into the kitchen where he found Lickety at a butcher-block counter, chopping away at a pile of vegetables.

"Making a stew for tonight," he said.

The wee person from the mushroom patch peered around a canister. He tipped his duffer's cap to the stranger and grinned, revealing a mouthful of teeth, jagged like a piranha's, then he dragged his mushroom out to where Lickety worked with the speed of a demon.

Lickety stopped. He examined the mushroom. "Oh, Simon, this is an excellent specimen. Should I sauté it and we can have it for supper, or should I put it in the stew for tomorrow's noon meal?" He leaned down to the wee person, the better to hear the response.

Lickety nodded. "Yes, I agree. We'll sauté it." He swept the vegetable chunks into a heap and scooped them over into a pot that he carried to the kitchen's cooking range. "Donald Jay, have you met my harvester?" He tilted his head toward the wee person. "Simon Thimbleful here is in charge of tending the wild things that grow in the nearby meadows and woods and gathering them in when the time is right."

"I did see him outside. I just never expected—"

Lickety stirred the mass in the pot. "No, most can't see Simon or his clan. Only special people."

"Special? What makes them special?"

"They're poets."

"And you know this how?"

"You've heard of the Lord of the Dance?"

"Of course."

Lickety squared up in front of his guest. "I'm the Lord of Poetry."

"I thought that was Calliope's job."

"Hers was to be the muse for epic poetry. Her sisters Euterpe, Thalia, Erato, and Polyhymnia oversaw lyric, pastoral, love, and sacred poetry respectively. That all changed when the sisters retired at the end of the Greek Age. Their jobs were consolidated, for the purpose of efficiency, and assigned to me."

"You don't look old enough."

Lickety laughed, laughed hard, his head snapping back, spilling his chef's hat to the floor. He snatched up his hat and scrambled getting it back in place over a knot of hair that to Jay looked to be something like a horn.

Lickety forced a smile. "Mister Donald Jay of Aldershot, West Virginia—Aldershot College, yes, I know about you, a lot about you—next February

Fourteenth I will be two thousand six hundred seventy-eight years old. Don't you find that interesting, February Fourteenth? A century ago, I took it on myself to convince one Joyce Clyde Hall, then a resident of Kansas City, Kansas, selling picture postcards there, that he should create the first mass-produced Valentine and place a love poem in it . . . Roses are red/violets are blue, that sort of thing. That was Nineteen Fifteen. You know the company."

Jay tugged at his earlobe. "As it happens, I do."

"Yes, of course, you do. Your mother wrote verses for Hallmark Cards, didn't she? Eight hundred forty-six verses or was it forty-seven? It's in my files somewhere." Lickety went back to the cooking range, bumping the top of his hat with the heel of his hand one more time to shift it into its proper place over his right eyebrow. He turned the flame down under the stewing pot. When satisfied with the level, he lifted a domed cover away from a cake. He looked to Jay. "Made this yesterday. Would you like to try it?"

"I don't know. I've read the stories, the lore of what happens when one eats with fairies."

Lickety parked a hand on his hip. "My dear young man, those are just that—stories. The cake, would you like to try it?"

Jay looked away, then back. "Maybe. I guess it won't hurt. I did skip supper."

"If I do say so myself, I'm something of a master baker. This is a chocolate/raspberry/orange marmalade swirl cake." Lickety cut three wedges, two normal sized and one mini, that for his harvester who tucked a tiny bandana into his shirt collar for a bib.

Lickety set the plates on the table. He gave Jay a fork and reserved one for himself. Thumbleful produced his own small eating utensil from his vest pocket.

Lickety wove his fingers together. "I'm sorry I can't offer you coffee with your cake, and you do have a taste for those brews they serve at Starbucks. But what we do have are herbal teas that we make ourselves. Today it's lamb's wort tea, quite good."

Jay gave a nod.

Lickety reached for a ceramic pot in the shape of a gnome on the back of the cooking range. He filled a mug for his guest and one for himself, then tipped a dollop into a miniature cup for Thimbleful.

Jay sampled the tea . . . and hacked up.

Lickety grimaced. "A bit strong is it? Stir in some bee spit."

He passed a honey pot to Jay, who drizzled some of the sweetness into his tea.

Jay sampled his tea again. "Tolerable," he wheezed and cut a bite of cake with his fork.

A tine snagged on something.

Jay picked at it . . . a bit of parchment paper, folded.

He unfolded the paper, brushing cake crumbs away as he did. He perused the paper and glanced up, puzzled.

Lickety, his hands cupped around his mug of tea, leaned back in his chair. "I forgot to tell you. This cake is a fortune cake. That paper you have, that's your fortune."

"But it's blank. There's nothing on it."

"Hold it over your tea."

With an eyebrow arched, Jay held the parchment in the steam wafting up from his mug of honey-sweet lamb's wort. A letter appeared, then two, then words. "It says," he said, " 'Today you must relaunch yourself on your life's journey. It is your Homeric destiny.' "

Jay rubbed at the hair on the back of his neck. "I don't get it."

Lickety took the parchment. He turned it and held it before his visitor. "You're a fair poet, Mister Donald Jay of

Aldershot, West Virginia, an academic. You write in experimental forms appreciated by at best, what, six of your colleagues? Mister Donald Jay, become a great poet, one who will be read by the generations. Write an epic poem in which you share with everyone your adventures and what you learned from them, what you learned about the world, about life, and about yourself. But you can't do that until you kick yourself in the pants and get out the door. You can't go back to that college."

Lickety laid the parchment aside. He brought a leather-bound book out of his apron pocket and slid it across the table. "My gift to you, a journal. Open it."

Jay laid the front cover back, revealing a black inner cover, embossed on it in gold script PROPERTY OF MISTER DONALD JAY OF ALDERSHOT, WEST VIRGINIA, A POET OF THE AGES.

Lickety aimed his index finger at the door. "Go. I've given you your title, now earn it. Your journey begins out there."

Jay, hesitant, pushed back from the table. Thimbleful scurried ahead of him. Before Jay could reach for the latch, Thimbleful tipped his head at the door, and it opened. It swung outward.

Jay stepped onto the threshold. As he did, the clearing and the woods beyond evaporated, replaced by a turquoise sky shot through with pulsing strands of a luminescent material.

He swivelled back to Lickety, but there was nothing from where he had come, no comfortable rooms, no kitchen, no fortune cake, no wee harvester, no Lord of Poetry. Just more turquoise sky and those pulsing strands.

A puff of wind unbalanced him, and he fell backwards, tumbling.

A voice came to him as he rolled through the air. Lickety's voice.

"Where do you want to start?" the voice asked. "Wish it and it shall be so."

Note: I get my wings . . . advanced wings. Professional wings.

Up, Up and Away
– 1966 –

THIS WAS the year I passed the flight test for my commercial pilot's license. I could now fly for pay.

But back to the test. At the completion, my flight examiner, Russell 'Van' Van Galder, said my aerobatics were adequate, "but let me show you what I really want."

Van was an old-time pilot with tens of thousands of hours of flight time. He got his license back in 1934, soloing in a Curtis Pusher after only four hours of instruction. He probably flew an A-1. Two seats side-by-side, dual controls. You sat out in the open air, forward of the wings, the engine and propeller behind you. You can see the Pushers on YouTube.

Van bent the Cessna One-Fifty we were flying through the smoothest series of maneuvers I'd ever experienced. He put my instructors to shame, and I had thought they were really good.

The upshot was that I went back to practicing flight maneuvers—everything from the basic stuff to figure eights and chandelles. I ever practiced short field landings and slow flight, making the One-Fifty hang on the edge of a stall for minutes instead of seconds.

Did I do Immelmann turns? An Immelmann is a half loop with a half roll. I don't remember. I do remember that I didn't do spins or hammerhead stalls. Both of those are advanced aerobatics. Two pilots I've flown with had flipped our aircraft into a spin. Scared the be-jeesus out of me because I wasn't expecting it.

One time I got caught in a cloud. I became disoriented. Without realizing what I was doing, I pulled the nose of the aircraft up. The aircraft stalled. It flipped into a spin, and I corkscrewed out through the bottom of the cloud. In the clear, when I could see what was going on, I did everything we pilots are taught to do to stop a spin and recover to normal flight. Emergency over, I got the shakes. I sweat.

Looking back now, I wish I had taken a couple hours of flight training with Van and learned those advanced maneuvers.

The absolute greatest fun for me came when I challenged another young pilot flying out of Rock County to a short-field landing contest. It was the end of the day. The air was calm. There wasn't a whisper of wind. We were coming in on Runway 32. One hundred feet in, if you were really good, you could make the turnoff onto Runway 36 and taxi to Hodge Aero, the base for both of us.

A Cessna One-Fifty needs four hundred forty-five feet for a normal landing.

My colleague, first in the pattern, overshot. He came in a tad hot and missed the turnoff.

I came in behind him. On the final approach to landing, I ran the flaps out full and slow-flighted in— forty-eight miles an hour—hanging on the edge of a stall until I touched down on the first foot of concrete, the

stall warning horn blaring. I stepped hard on the brakes—
I stood on them—to play off the little speed I had and
made the turn off.

Van would have been proud.

Note: This story of the Vietnam war starts in 2018, long after the war was over but not in the least bit forgotten.

Carl
– 1967 –

THE SUNDAY before Memorial Day 2018, Pastor Jamie asked all to stand who had someone who was at one time but no longer living, to share the names so they could be included in the morning prayer.

I was one of those who stood. So was my wife Marge. She shared the names of her first husband, Don Smith and four of her six brothers—Al, Bob, Jim, and Jack White.

Next Jamie pointed to me.

"Carl Hallberg," I said, my voice breaking. "One of my students. Vietnam."

I sat down and wept.

I GRADUATED from college, an education major, in May of 1962 and landed my first teaching job within a month. I would be teaching English and speech at Adams-Friendship High School up in the central part of the state. The state, of course, Wisconsin.

The Vietnam war was heating up, so I figured I'd better beat the draft. I went down to the recruiting office where I talked with an Army sergeant. "I'd like to get into the warrant officer program," I said. "I want to fly helicopters."

He looked me over. "Do you wear glasses?"

The answer was obvious—a new pair that rested on the bridge of my nose.

"Yes," I said.

"Forget it." 'It' meaning the warrant officer program. Said he, "You have to have twenty/twenty uncorrected vision."

I walked out.

A year later, the Army, now desperate for helicopter pilots, dropped the vision requirement.

Before that, however, my friendly county draft board sent me a notice: "You have been selected to serve . . ."

This was the summer of 1963. I had signed a contract to teach a second year at Adams-Friendship. I took the letter to Mister Sardeson, my superintendent of schools, and asked him what I should do.

"We'd kind of like to keep you here," he said. "Why don't I write a letter to your draft board and ask them to reclassify you as vital personnel, to grant you a deferment?"

He did.

They did.

And I continued teaching.

Advance now to April of 1964. Mister Sardeson offered me a contract for a third year. But I had heard the principal of Edgerton High School, where I had done my student teaching, was moving over to Delavan-Darien High School—a much larger school—to be that school's new principal.

This was a man I really liked, an administrator whom I held in high regard. Kind, caring, thoughtful, and fair to the nth degree.

I drove down to see him, said I wanted to work for him.

He needed a teacher of English and theater, he said, and laid a contract in front of me.

I signed it.

But I would not get to work for him. Mister Dennis died that summer. I instead worked for his replacement. But that's a story for another time.

It was there at Delevan-Darien that I met Carl. He was a junior and in my class. No genius as a student, but witty and a lot of fun. He was interested in theater and worked backstage in every production I directed.

My last show was George Bernard Shaw's *Saint Joan*. One evening, the cast and crew and I were sitting on the stage, batting around ideas for how we might promote the show, to build attendance. Finally, I threw out my thought. "Why don't we bomb Delevan?" I said.

Carl lit up. "Yeah, let's do that."

When the Army wouldn't have me for the warrant officer program, I drove out to the Rock County Airport and signed up for flying lessons. I learned to fly fixed-wing airplanes as a civilian. Paid my own way.

I told the group I now had a private pilot's license, that we could bomb Delevan with show leaflets.

All agreed.

Someone designed the leaflets and got them printed, then on the designated Saturday afternoon, I rented a Cessna Skyhawk.

Carl and I flew over Delevan at five hundred feet, Carl in the co-pilot's seat pitching handful after handful of leaflets out his window, laughing hysterically as he did. One would think he'd never had so much fun.

Every one of us who has been a teacher has had a student who would do anything for us, a student who was a joy, a student we came to love as if he were our son or she, our daughter. At Delevan-Darien, that student for me was Carl.

He and I both graduated that May. I went on to get my commercial pilot's license and flew charter for Hodge Aero.

Carl? He wasn't interested in college. He probably figured the Army was going to get him, so why not sign up?

He became an infantryman, a grunt, a ground pounder in Company B, Fifth Battalion, Seventh Cavalry, First Cavalry Division.

Carl landed in Vietnam on February 18, 1967.

Three months later to the day, he was dead. A ground casualty. Killed by an explosive device, his service record says. I'm guessing the explosive device was a land mine that he stepped on or tripped when he and his squad were on patrol somewhere in Quang Ngai Province.

Quang Ngai was one of the worst places to be, a Vietcong hot bed, the site of the Bien Hoa massacre the year before Carl got there and the My Lai massacre the year after Carl was killed.

The Vietnam war was a civil war, for us a damnable war, one in which we should never have been involved.

It killed my student.

That morning in church, after I said, my voice breaking, "Carl Hallberg. One of my students. Vietnam," I cried for fifteen minutes.

I'm crying now as I type these words.

Note: This is the year of the Earthrise photo taken by the Apollo 8 astronauts, the earth rising above the moon's surface. Dramatic. A scene never viewed before by anyone. It's also the first year of manned space flight where people—the three men of Apollo 8—spent Christmas in space. The astronauts commemorated it by reading the Creation story from the Bible to all of us listening on Earth. They were flying. I was, too, but at a lower altitude.

The Fat Boy vs. the Electric Motor
– 1968 –

I WALKED into work—it was summertime, a Friday—and Art told me today I'd be flying one of the Ryan brothers out to Minnesota, to inspect a highway job.

"Check out the Apache. Make sure everything's ready to go," he said.

The Apache, one of the two twin-engine aircraft we flew, is a chunky bird, not very fast but comfortable. It carries a pilot and three passengers about anywhere you want to go.

We got out there, to Pipestone, in under two hours and landed, not at an airport, but on a stretch of U.S. 30 being rebuilt by the Ryan Brothers.

It's not legal to land on a highway, but since that section of road was not yet open to the public, technically it wasn't a highway. Still I didn't want to stay there, so I let Bob out and said I'd fly over to the Pipestone airport and wait there. "What time do you want me back?"

He glanced at his watch. "Six o'clock." he said.

The airport was about ten miles away, a short hop. Turned out it was an unattended grass strip. If you needed gas, you called a telephone number in town for someone to come out.

I didn't need gas.

I broke out my sack lunch and chowed down.

Lunch finished, I decided to crawl under the wing of the Apache and sleep for a couple hours, but someone flew in in a Citabria rigged out as a spray plane.

I had never seen a Citabria up close. It's a tandem two-seater aircraft, kind of like the old Piper Cub, except this sporty little dude is intended to fly aerobatics if you like to do that sort of thing. But a spray plane to put down insecticides and herbicides on crops?

The big Stearmans were more commonly used for that and the new Cessna Ag Wagons and the Piper Pawnees.

Citabrias are small. They don't haul much, but compared to the other spray planes and dusters, they're cheap.

I strolled over and introduced myself to the pilot, Joe Swindler. I said I'd long admired the Citabrias, but I'd never been up in one.

He said if I didn't mind sitting on the floor behind the front seat, he'd be glad to give me a ride. So away we went. I would get my opportunity to fly a Citabria as pilot-in-command thirty-two years later.

A bit before six, I flew over to the job site. Bob was waiting along with two hefty fellows who, like Bob, looked as if they could play on the front line of a professional football team. Beside them was a cart with the biggest electric motor on it that I'd ever seen.

I got out and looked over the crew.

"The motor goes with us," Bob said. "Where's the cargo hatch?"

"Oh, wait, stop," I said. "I don't think the Apache can carry all of us and the motor, too. Too much weight."

Bob and I decided to work out the weight-and-balance problem right there. I wasn't worried about balancing the load. It was all this beef and iron.

Bob whipped out his mechanical pencil and, right there on the wing of the plane, he started to write down the numbers. "How much do you weigh?" he asked me.

Of the four, I was the lightweight. One eighty.

He put down his weight, two ten. His buddies, two forty and two fifty-five. Then he estimated the weight of the motor at one hundred pounds even. He drew a line, totaled the numbers and came up with a load of nine hundred eighty-five pounds, almost half a ton.

I got out the aircraft manual and looked up the load specification, then added in the weight of the fuel on board. "Bob," I said, "we can carry nine hundred four pounds. You can't take the motor."

The motor needed repairs. That's why Bob wanted to fly it back to Janesville. It was Friday. His two big employees wanted to go home, to be with their families for the weekend.

Bob mulled over the numbers, then made his decision. He looked at his biggest guy. "Virgil," he said, "the motor goes. You stay behind."

Note: July 16, the first moon landing. I landed, too, me far from the moon in Kentucky, at Hopkinsville, and then in Wisconsin, at Fort Atkinson, up the road from my home base at the Rock County Airport.

One Unhappy Passenger
– 1969 –

THE ASSIGNMENT was to pick up four passengers at the Fort Atkinson airstrip the next morning at 7:00 and fly them to Hopkinsville, Kentucky.

Easy enough.

This time I got the Skymaster, a six-passenger twin-engine Cessna. New, clean, and fast.

The four men worked for Thomas Electric, and they were going down to the factory in Kentucky.

An argument ensued when I stepped out to see who wanted to sit where. One would go in the back row, two in the middle, and one up front in the co-pilot's seat next to me, they decided.

One, however, insisted that he didn't want to fly at all, that he would drive.

The senior executive—the decider—stared at him. "Well, why didn't you tell me yesterday?" he said. "You could have driven all night and been down there to meet us. Now you don't have time. Get in."

Grumbling, Ned did. Next to me.

The flight over southern Wisconsin and the full length of Illinois was uneventful. Clear, sunshine, ideal weather. It all went to hell in the view of my unhappy passenger when we neared the Ohio River. My route was to bring us over Evansville, Indiana, on the Ohio, and go due south from there to Hopkinsville.

The river generates its own weather system. Every time I've flown into the area, the weather's been stinko.

This day, there was fog over the Ohio and clouds above. There was no flying through the stuff, so I hauled back on the control wheel and brought the Skymaster up into a climb, aiming to fly over the clouds. I glanced at my passenger. His eyes were bugged out, and he was clutching both sides of the seat for security. When I got us two miles up, I picked my way through the cloud tops, then set up my descent for Hopkinsville. Ned didn't let go of the seat until we were on the ground.

For the return flight, four hours later, Ned took the third row, waaay in the back. He didn't want to see where we were going, but I could hear him moaning back there as the Skymaster climbed for altitude to get us over the clouds that still clogged the Ohio River Valley. Once north of the river, again in the clear, I took us down to eighty-five hundred feet. The day had heated up, so we had tremendous thermals, lots of them—columns of hot air rising up from dark areas of the ground. For the next two hours, we rode the thermals up and down as if they elevators.

A lot of moaning came from the back and snarls from the other passengers for Ned to shut up.

Relief finally arrived when Fort Atkinson hoved into view. I landed the Skymaster and taxied up to where the men had left their cars. As usual, I was the first out, to help my passengers get out. Three were appreciative for the flight, down to Hopkinsville and back in a day compared to three days if they had driven.

Then came Ned, absolutely ghost white and wobbling. Said he to me, "Peterson, if I never see you again, it'll be too soon."

Note: I worked for Kansas Farm Bureau for a decade, first as associate director of the communications department, then as the director. As a part of my job, I created radio programs that aired on 22 stations around the state. So I joined the Kansas Broadcasters Association and the National Farm Broadcasters Association.

The stories in this decade are not necessarily in the order in which they happened. Most I can tag to a specific year, but several I'm not just sure. Now to the first story. In the mid-1960s, Westminster College bought a church designed by Christopher Wren that had been blasted and burned by the German Air Force in the bombing of London a quarter century earlier. The college had the church shipped over in pieces and rebuilt on the campus, a $10-million project, mighty big for a pretty small school.

Christopher Wren's Last Laugh
– 1970 –

"YOU HAVE got to see this," he said.

He: William Dunn, Callaway County (Missouri) District Court judge.

Me: A radio reporter with a network in the next state

west. I had just finished interviewing Dunn on the work he'd pioneered, sentencing scofflaws to what was to become known as community service rather than fining them or jailing them for their minor offences.

"This?" I asked.

"Out at the college. It's completely restored. Just amazing. We're real proud of it."

"Yes, but I don't know what 'it' is."

"Fella, don't you read the newspapers? The Christopher Wren church."

I packed away my tape recorder. "English," I said. "This could be interesting. My mother's family traces back to the land of the Tudors and the Windsors."

The judge, of a Southern cast—a big bellied man who this day wore a white suit—motioned to a black boy to come to him, the boy tinkering with a scale to the side of the judge's bench in the courtroom. He handed the boy a mitt full of keys. "Gaby, wouldja run down and start my Cadillac for me? And while you're at it, put the top down and the windows, too. It's a nice day out there."

The boy—about ten, I guessed—grinned like he'd been given a cone with three scoops of strawberry ice cream on it. He bobbed his head and ran out.

Dunn swung his attention back to me. "Gabriel's my right-hand man around here. Keeps my car washed and polished, fetches the mail, does little chores for me." He thumbed at the scale. "We got us a group of those TOPS women—Take Off Pounds Sensibly. They meet up here in the evening once a week. Sometimes I have Gabe set the scale to read a couple pounds low and other times a couple pounds high. Just drives those biddies batty at the weigh-in, how they lost a couple pounds one week and gained three the next."

I could see it with my mind's eye. I laughed with the judge.

He hefted himself out of the chair he'd been using at the defense table. He collected his Panama hat, and together we sauntered out of the courtroom and down the marble stairs to the main floor, then the exit to the square. Beyond on the street, in the shade of a catalpa tree rich in bloom, bees buzzing in and out, working the blossom clusters for their pollen, there it was, a white Cadillac, a 'Fifty-nine, the kind with the big tailfins and the four torpedo taillights. The boy was there, hunched against the steering wheel, wiping down the dash and the instrument panel with a tacky cloth.

"Love this season," the judge said as he put on his hat. "Smell that catalpa tree." He leaned a hand on the driver's door and there touched the arm of his helper. "Gabe, we're goin' out to the college. You wanna drive today?"

The boy looked up at Dunn. "Judge, you know I'm not old enough."

"Gabriel, you are one honest man. I suppose you want to be paid a day's wages, huh?"

"That's the way it works, judge." The boy folded his dusting cloth as he got out. He held the door open for Dunn.

Dunn hefted himself in, then gave the boy a bill. I couldn't see the denomination. "You tell your momma," Dunn said, "she's to put half that in the bank for ya, for your university fund, all right?" He stared up at me. "You gonna get in or you gonna walk?

WE MADE the turn onto the college grounds. Several blocks on, it loomed up in the windshield, a church built of Portland stone, the stone a brilliant white in the sun. "The thing's from London," the judge said, "first built back almost nine hundred years ago. Came to serve the neighborhood that grew up around it. Aldermanbury. I had to memorize that name."

He hoisted a hand to the driver of a car approaching him and got a salute in return. "Somewhere in the Fifteenth century, by royal charter, the church became the home of the Worshipful Company of Haberdashers— shopkeepers who sold men's clothes. If Harry Truman knows that, he's gotta love it 'cause he and a buddy were partners in a haberdashery over in Kansas City after WW-One."

Dunn drifted his Cadillac across the opposing lane into a parking space on the wrong side of the street. He ran the left front tire of his car up on the sidewalk. "That church, when it was a wooden structure, burned to the ground in Sixteen and Sixty-six—" He pumped the numbers out on his fingers: one-six-six-six. "—in the Great Fire of London. Leveled just about everything north of the Thames. Rebuilding churches got to be pretty low on the totem pole, so it was five years before the city authorities got around to hiring someone to rebuild Saint Mary's of Aldermanbury as this church was known and fifty others. Christopher Wren got the contract."

Dunn slid his bulk out of the car. "When we get inside, remind me there's a special story about that I should tell you."

I, too, got out. When I came around to the sidewalk, I tapped my shoe against Dunn's tire.

He glanced at it. "Oh, that? That's the way I park. Everybody knows it."

"You could get a ticket."

"Son, you forget, I'm the judge." He turned to the church, sweeping his hand up toward the steeple. "This church, the college got it to make it a memorial to Winston Churchill who spoke here after the war, his Iron Curtain speech, you probably know about that. What you don't know is I was in the college gymnasium for that speech, just a young pup of a lawyer at the time. I've got it all locked up here—" He touched his forehead. "— memorized that speech and just about every word Churchill said that day."

We started up the steps. "When we got this church, it was a burned-out hulk, a remnant of the bombing of London in WW-Two. The people of Aldermanbury were tickled to be shed of it. We had the walls dismantled stone by stone, everything marked, brought the whole mess over here and put it back together on a new foundation. The roof, that we had to build new, too."

Dunn opened the heavy oak door, and we stepped inside, the judge removing his hat and organ music welling up to greet us. Dunn waved to the organist. "Don't stop on our account, Darlene. Wonderful music. You gonna play that piece Sunday?"

"Yes," came the voice of the young woman at the keyboard.

"What is it?"

She rested her hands on the bench seat. "Bach's Toccata and Fugue in D Minor. I'm going to play it when everybody comes in. So, judge, plan to get here early if you want a good seat."

"I'll do that, Darlene. You go ahead and rehearse now. I'm just showing this young fella around."

She nodded and resumed somewhere in the middle of the piece. I recognized it, that music, from seeing Vincent Price play it on a pipe organ a couple months earlier in a new horror movie, *The Abominable Dr. Phibes.* Scared the bejesus out of me when Price as Phibes turned to the camera, and he had only half a face.

I followed Dunn up into the balcony which he said was new. The old church didn't have one. We made our way down front where we looked out over the seating area below, the organ keyboard, the pulpit with its intricate carvings—everything at the front of the church.

He nudged the side of my shoe. "You were supposed to remind me of something."

I leaned on the railing, entranced by the candelabra chandeliers that must light the church at night. "A story," I said.

"Yes, that's right." Dunn settled in a seat and laid his hat in another. "Wren designed the roof in such a way that the walls supported it. He didn't need columns inside the church which was the usual method for holding a roof up in a structure like this. When a committee from the council came to inspect the church, they were horrified—no columns. They said the roof's gonna fall, you've gotta put columns in there. Wren told them the columns weren't needed. 'You want to be paid?' someone asked. 'Then you put in the columns.' Well, you can guess that Wren wanted to be paid. He had the columns built and installed, ten of 'em like you see out there in the main part of the church. Now look at the tops of the columns."

I did. Each appeared to be about two fingers short of the roof.

"That's right," Dunn said. "Those columns don't support anything, but you can't see that from the floor. So Wren got paid . . . and had the last laugh on the council."

He slapped his hands together in glee.

Note: My press card made it possible for me to meet a goodly number of prominent people over the years that I was a radio and newspaper reporter. Here's a sampling.

Well Known Folk
– 1971-78 –

MIND IF I drop a few names?
     That's okay?
     Excellent.
     Richard Nixon.
     Dan Rather.
     Lowell Thomas.
     Bill Curtis.
     Art Linkletter.
     Charles Kuralt.
     William Simon.
     Earl Butts.

EARL BUTTS?
     You have to be as old as me to remember Earl. He was the dean of the College of Agriculture at Purdue (1957-1967), a great storyteller, and one of the General Motors Speakers Bureau's top public speakers for more

than a decade before GM discontinued the bureau.

I met Earl several years after Richard Nixon named him to his Cabinet as Secretary of Agriculture.

Earl had been President Eisenhower's Assistant Secretary of Agriculture and had headed the U.S. delegation to the United Nations' Food and Agriculture Organization meeting in Rome in 1954.

I was in the battery of farm broadcasters who interviewed Earl when he came to Kansas City for an event in 1974 and a short time later to Kansas State University. He learned my name at the first press conference and remembered me at the second. Sure made me feel like I was king of the hill.

Earl, as a storyteller, could rip off dirty stories and racist jokes with the best of those who grew up in the very, very white Midwest of the 1920s and '30s. And that triggered his fall from grace.

After the 1976 Republican National Convention adjourned, Earl, Pat Boone, Sonny Bono, and John Dean hopped a commercial flight to California. Dean had been President Nixon's White House counsel and had served time in jail for his participation in the Watergate cover-up.

Earl told a racist joke to his seatmates in answer to a question Boone had asked.

Dean used a line from that joke in a Rolling Stone story, attributing the line to "an unnamed Cabinet officer." A New York Times reporter figured out who that Cabinet officer was and wrote his own story. The Associated Press picked it up and sent the story, with the full joke uncensored, around the country. About every daily newspaper ran it, but not before the editors cleaned up the story. However, the editors at the Madison Capital Times and the Toledo Blade were tougher souls. They ran the story uncensored.

Of those who censored the joke, the editors of the San Diego Evening Tribune offered to send the full uncensored story to anyone who requested it. More than three thousand readers did.

The uproar it created in the White House was such that Earl decided it was best to resign and go back home to Indiana.

His troubles, though, were not over. A couple years later, he was jailed for tax evasion.

<u>Bill Simon</u>, secretary of the Treasury (1974-1977)

SIMON MADE his first fortune as a bond trader on Wall Street and his second, estimated at $300 million, buying and selling companies after his years of government service.

To that government service, in 1973 President Nixon appointed Simon Deputy Secretary of the Treasury. Concurrently, Simon served as the first administrator of the Federal Energy Office where he created and ran the Federal Energy Administration, becoming, in effect, the country's first energy czar. In his spare moments, he also ran the President's Oil Policy Committee and served on the President's Energy Resources Council.

In 1974, Nixon named Simon to the post of Secretary of the Treasury.

Three months later, Nixon resigned and his successor, President Ford, asked Simon to stay on.

I was working on a radio story in 1975. I no longer remember the subject, but it had something to do with inflation which was shooting up at the time. Simon had strong views on that, so I got the telephone number for his office and called him, figuring I'd get his secretary who would route me to someone else, who would route me to someone else, who would connect me with some lowly soul in the Treasury's P.R. department.

Who picked up?

Not Simon's secretary, but Simon himself.

It was well into the evening, and we talked for half

an hour with my tape recorder running. I asked maybe three question, and he expounded.

I ginned a good story out of that conversation.

A couple months later, I was working late. My studio phone rang, and I picked up.

It was Bill Simon.

Now I'm a radio reporter/farm broadcaster in Kansas. I didn't have a national audience, yet here it was, the Secretary of the Treasury calling me.

He just wanted to talk over some issue that had come up. Maybe he thought I would be a good sounding board. Simon talked and I listened, occasionally asking a question here and there for clarification.

And, darned if a month later, he called again. Both of us worked late, and he knew that.

I didn't record those two calls. I sensed what Simon wanted to discuss was not intended to be reported.

Lowell Thomas, world traveler and radio newscaster (CBS, 1930-1976)

IF YOU ever watched the movie *Lawrence of Arabia*— the 1962 film collected seven Oscars—you saw an American war correspondent traveling with British Army Lieutenant T.E. Lawrence in the Sinai Desert, Lawrence leading an Arab army against a Turkish army of the Ottoman Empire. This was 1918, during World War I.

In the movie, Arthur Kennedy played the correspondent, Jackson Bentley. In real life, the correspondent was Lowell Thomas.

Thomas made his first fortune touring the world during 1919-1920, narrating on stage the film footage he had shot of Lawrence in the desert war. An estimated 4 million people saw his show.

Thomas followed that by writing the first of his two books about Lawrence, *With Lawrence in Arabia*. It came out in 1924.

Thomas was a prolific writer, writing 57 books in 54 years, many of them travelogues.

His last two books, though, were autobiographies, *Good Evening Everybody: From Cripple Creek to Samarkand* and *So Long Until Tomorrow*.

That phrase, "Good evening, everybody," was Thomas' sign-on for his daily radio news and commentary program; "So long until tomorrow," his sign-off.

In 1976, shortly after the publisher William Morrow brought out Thomas' first autobiography, the Kansas State

Broadcasters Association secured Thomas as its convention banquet speaker. We met in Dodge City, and I was there.

Thomas regaled us for more than an hour.

The next morning after breakfast, he was walking with some of us in the hallway of the convention hotel. He said he needed to find a ride to Wichita, to the airport, to catch his flight back to New York City. I said I'd be glad to take him.

For the next several hours, as we rolled eastward along Highway 400, Thomas told me about working on his second autobiography—it came out the next year—and getting ready to go skiing on Alaska's Kahiltna Glacier with his son who was then the lieutenant governor of Alaska.

Going skiing on a glacier? At age 84? Yup.

Thomas topped that the next year when he married his second wife, Marianna Munn. They took a 50,000-mile honeymoon trip, revisiting many of the places in the world that had brought Thomas great joy, great memories . . . and great stories.

Charles Kuralt, television newsman and anchor (CBS, 1957-1997)

KURALT JOINED CBS News as a writer two years after he graduated from college.

Between college and CBS, Kuralt worked as a reporter for the Charlotte News in Charlotte, North Carolina. There he wrote a column titled "Charles Kuralt's People" that won him an Ernie Pyle Award. That recognition got him the job in New York.

Kuralt moved in front of the camera two years later, hosting the network's "Eyewitness to History" series. CBS then made him a network correspondent, and he traveled the world, reporting the news from hot spots. In time, he became the network's chief Latin America correspondent, then its chief West Coast correspondent, and next he covered the Vietnam war.

Kuralt grew tired of all this, tired of trying to beat NBC and ABC reporters to the best hard news stories of the day. He asked for a break, proposing that he travel the backroads of our country in search of human-interest stories, people stories, the kinds of stories that became the network's "On the Road" series. It aired on *The CBS Evening News with Walter Cronkite* for 25 years. The series is back. CBS brought it back in 2011 with Steve Hartman doing the job Kuralt had done.

Concurrently with Kuralt reporting his people stories from the backroads of America, in 1979 he started and hosted *CBS News Sunday Morning*, an assignment he continued until 1994 when he retired.

Kuralt first came to Kansas when he was trekking across the country, climbing each state's highest mountain for "On the Road."

Climbing Kansas' highest mountain was really just a stroll up a hill. You see, Mount Sunflower, near the Colorado border, at 4,390 feet above sea level rises only 100 feet above the surrounding pasture land.

Ed and Cindy Harold own the mountain and the ranch that surrounds it. At the top, Kuralt found a picnic table, a sunflower sculpture made from railroad spikes, and a plaque that stated "On this site in 1897, nothing happened."

He had fun with it all, and it made for one sweet story.

I met Kuralt a couple years later when we had him speak at our state broadcasters convention. I interviewed him for my own radio series. At the end, Kuralt said, "If you come across any story ideas you think I could use, send them to me," and he gave me his card.

I sent him two ideas in the next year. One he selected. He came out with his film crew and spent several days at the Barbed Wire Festival hosted by the Kansas Barbed Wire Museum in Rush County. The museum is home to the world's largest collection of barbed wire . . . barbed wire, that stuff ranchers use to keep cattle in their pastures.

The festival draws several thousand barbed wire collectors ever year. Most of the collectors are—you guessed it—old ranchers, guys with stories to tell. Kuralt's kind of people.

Then, of course, there was all that barbed wire, samples of more than 2,400 different kinds. Kuralt didn't know there was a museum for that stuff.

He also didn't know there was a Post Rock Museum

just down the road. I should have mentioned it to him.

Nor did he know there was a Tractor Seat Museum in the next county to the north. I forgot to tell him about that, too.

Or that there was a National Agricultural Center (museum) and Hall of Fame a few miles outside of Kansas City.

But I got my own radio stories on each of those.

<u>Art Linkletter</u>, radio and television personality (1934-1967)

JOHN GUDEL created the first radio game show, *People Are Funny*, launching it on the NBC network in 1942. Art Baker was the host. The show was broadcast live from Hollywood. A year later, Art Linkletter took over the show. As a young man, he was, as Steve Martin would say, a wild and crazy guy, announcing after he had sent some poor soul out on a particularly outrageous stunt, "Aren't we devils?"

He delighted in those stunts Gudel built into the show for contestants that would have the audience howling with laughter. In one, a contestant was required to register himself and a trained seal at Hollywood's Knickerbocker Hotel, explaining to the desk clerk that the seal was his girlfriend.

Some of the stunts went over years. In one, Linkletter announced he would give $1,000 to the first person to find one of twelve balls floating off the California coast. Two years passed before someone claimed the prize, the someone from the Marshall Islands more than five thousand miles away, where one of the balls had washed ashore.

The games and stunts continued when Linkletter and the show moved to NBC Television in 1954, becoming the first game show on TV. The radio show ran concurrent with the television show, both going until 1960 when NBC discontinued them.

Cranking back, in 1945 Guedel created the first radio variety/talk show—*House Party*. He sold it to CBS with Linkletter as the host. The show moved to ABC for a year, then back to CBS where it remained for the next six years.

Guedel then sold a primetime version of *House Party* to ABC Television in 1950. Two years later, it moved to CBS as *Art Linkletter's House Party*. There it became a daytime staple, running for 17 years.

Linkletter created one of the show's most popular segments, "Kids Say the Darndest Things." Linkletter bused in school children between the ages of five and ten and interviewed them in front of the camera. Often he would ask, "What did your mom or dad tell you you shouldn't say?" And they would say it, to the delight of Linkletter and the studio audience.

Over the years, he interviewed 23,000 children, give or take a couple. Linkletter spun two bestselling books out of it, *Kids Say the Darndest Things* (1957) and *Kids Still Say the Darndest Things* (1961). Charles Schulz of Peanuts fame illustrated the book covers.

Bill Cosby brought that segment back as a half-hour show on CBS in 1995 where it ran for five year. Steve Harvey brought it back one more time in 2016 as *Little Big Shots*, this time for NBC. Harvey was booted from the show in 2019 and replaced by Melissa McCarthy.

But back to Linkletter. He and Walt Disney were close friends, so close that Disney gave Linkletter the opportunity to buy into the new theme park he was building—Disneyland. Linkletter passed. He thought the park would never survive. But when Disney had it finished and was getting ready to open the park to the public, Linkletter offered to host ABC Television's coverage of the grand opening. His work spurred so much attendance that Disney offered Linkletter the park's camera and film concession. Linkletter this time jumped at it.

He made a small fortune from the concession over the ten years he held the contract.

Linkletter made a bigger fortune with the hula hoop, as an investor and promoter.

Tragedy struck in 1969. Linkletter's daughter Diane, then 20, jumped to her death from her sixth-floor kitchen window. She was a drug user. She had been for several years. Linkletter believed she was tripping on LSD, believed that's why she killed herself. It tore him up.

Some months later, we had Linkletter as our banquet speaker at the National Farm Broadcasters Association's convention in Kansas City. He entertained everybody as we knew he would.

When it was over, I asked him if he would sit for an interview.

"Yes, of course," he said.

We went to another room where no one would interrupt us.

There I could see it in Linkletter's face, a weariness and pain. So I asked, "How do you handle it, your daughter's death?"

He poured out the story, all of it over the next half-hour, and how it now had pushed him into going on a national drug awareness campaign to tell parents what they needed to do to keep their children from using drugs.

If Linkletter were alive today, he would be disappointed that the problem still exists.

<u>Bill Kurtis</u>, television reporter, producer, narrator, and news anchor (1966-present)

I HAD long wanted to interview Kurtis. He is, after all, a Kansan.

You know Kurtis now as the announcer and scorekeeper for the NPR comedy quiz show *Wait, Wait, Don't Tell Me.* When I knew him, he was a correspondent for CBS Television News.

Kurtis broke into television way back in the 1960's while attending law school at Washburn University in Topeka. He worked part-time for WIBW as a reporter. One day—June 6, 1966—while studying for the bar exam, Kurtis shot out of the classroom over to the station, to anchor the evening news for a friend who had taken the night off.

Darned if a tornado didn't come roaring up to Topeka from the southwest just as the evening news show ended. Fifteen seconds after a confirmed spotting by a station cameraman out in the field, Kurtis broke into whatever was on at 7 o'clock. He reported an apartment building had been destroyed, concluding his news break with these words, "For God's sake, take cover."

The tornado killed sixteen people as it tore through the city.

Kurtis went back on the air where he stayed for the next twenty-four hours, anchoring the station's coverage of the tornado and its aftermath.

His on-air work was such that, three months later,

Chicago CBS television station WBBM hired Kurtis as a field reporter and news anchor.

Kurtis hopped between WBBM and the network for the next twenty-two years, occasionally taking breaks to host documentaries for PBS.

In 1988, he formed his own company to produce documentaries. It churned out more than 500 documentary series that aired variously on PBS, A&E, the History Channel, and CNBC, usually with Kurtis as the on-screen host.

Kurtis now frequently hosts the Decades cable channel's daily news magazine *Through the Decades* and has since 2015 when the channel was created.

Over his career, Kurtis has racked up two Peabody Awards and a slug of Emmys.

I caught up with him in 1970, or maybe it was 1971. Kurtis had come back to Topeka to speak at an event at his alma mater, Washburn University. During a break, he and I strolled around the university's plaza, talking, with my tape recorder running. I no longer remember what we talked about, but Kurtis was as kind and charming as he is in front of a camera. And that voice. In earlier years, we would call it a radio voice, deep and resonate. When you hear it coming through your television set, you know it's Kurtis without having to look at the screen.

One last story. Those who know the *Little House on the Prairie* books and the old television series of the same name know that the Ingalls family moved to Kansas at one time—southeast Kansas near present-day Independence.

Kurtis' father bought the site of the Ingalls' cabin and barn, and the surrounding ranchland, when he, as a brigadier general, retired from the Marine Corps.

When the senior Kurtis died, Bill and his sister Jean inherited the ranch and the Ingalls home site. To preserve the site—particularly the cabin—Bill and Jean started a non-profit museum. To give visitors more to see, they bought other buildings that dated back to the 1870's and moved them to the site—the one-room schoolhouse where their grandmother had taught, the tiny Wayside, Kansas, post office, a homesteader's farmhouse, and several farm buildings from the period.

Kurtis also bought more land, creating a larger buffer so no one could ever build a tacky roadside attraction near the site.

Kurtis didn't have to do any of this. I'd like to walk around the site with him, just as he and I walked around the Washburn plaza, and let him talk about why he did.

Richard Nixon, president (1969-1974)
Dan Rather, television news reporter and anchor
(CBS, 1962-2006)

THESE TWO go together.

Kansas State University has a lecture series through which it invites prominent Americans to come to the campus and talk to the students. In 1973, the committee in charge of the series selected Richard Nixon, then in his fifth year as President of the United States.

Nixon's staff accepted on the President's behalf because Kansas, they felt, was a rock-solid Republican state. He could come here knowing there was little chance that the campus streets would be clogged with anti-Nixon protestors. The President was in trouble. The Watergate story had broken. His popularity was dropping through the floorboards.

I applied to be a part of the press corps, and whoever was in charge of the appropriate office in the White House sent me a name badge.

Nineteen Seventy-three, compared to today on security matters, was an innocent time. No metal detectors anywhere. Nothing at the doors of the Field House where Nixon was to speak. Sixteen thousand students, faculty members, and guests flowed in unimpeded, filling the place to the rafters.

I did have to show my White House-issued name badge to a Secret Service agent who then waved me into the area down front roped off for reporters. When he didn't ask to look inside my camera bag, it occurred to me that anyone who wanted to get Nixon, and could cobble together a press badge, could easily have toted in a weapon.

The audience was polite and attentive, and gave the President a standing ovation when he finished. Nixon then was hustled out a back door to a helicopter that flew him to Salina where Air Force One was waiting on the tarmac.

No press conference.

No chance to ask the President a question.

For me, no story.

Then I spotted Dan Rather, at the time CBS's White House correspondent and a thorn in the President's paw. He was packing up his equipment, and he was alone. The Field House by then was almost empty, so I wandered over, introduced myself, and said, "How about an interview?"

"Sure, I've got a couple minutes," he said.

I whipped out my tape recorder. We rambled on for maybe a minute about nothing I felt would make a story, my microphone in Rather's face. When I noticed that he was about to glance at his watch, I asked the question I wanted to ask: "What's it like being a correspondent for one of the big three networks?"

Said Rather, "It's hell on marriages for those of us who do this."

He had just gone through a divorce.

I didn't know that.

And he wanted to talk.

Note: As I said in introducing the stories for this decade, some are out of order. This is one. It really belongs to1976, our nation's Bicentennial year. The celebrations that year, they were many, but one involved more people than any other.

Eastward, Ho!
– 1979 –

I HAVE one regret.

I didn't join the Bicentennial Wagon Train traveling the old trails from Los Angeles to Valley Forge. That train was one of seven that traversed the country that year. It came up the Gila and Santa Fe Trails into Kansas.

I was working for Kansas Farm Bureau at the time. I knew a lot of ranchers who would have loaned me a couple horses and a saddle for the trip. Tie a sleeping bag behind the saddle and whatever other gear I might need, like changes of socks and underwear, on the spare horse, and I'd have been set to survive out on the trail for the final two thousand miles.

Thinking back on it, my boss likely would have given me six months off to do the trip. I was a department head—communications—and I had a good staff who could have covered for me, probably would have been glad to if it meant getting me out of their business for half a year. But I had no one to do radio for me. That was exclusively my territory in the department, and I hadn't trained anyone to be a backup. I suppose I could have suspended the service for the duration . . .

And I was married. Would Sallie have let me go?

Then there was my work with our church. I was an elder and I occasionally taught a Sunday school class. And I was the vice-president for education of our Manhattan Toastmasters Club.

And, and, and . . . too many ands.

Had I joined the train, I would have been an outrider. The outrider's job each day was to grab a fistful of Rededication Scrolls and ride off to a community some distance from the train. Working with the people there, the outrider whipped up enthusiasm for the mission of the train—getting signatures on those scrolls. "Pledge of Rededication" was written across the top of each scroll in large letters. Underneath was an excerpt from the Declaration of Independence, and then a promise that signers were recommitting themselves to the principles of the Founding Fathers, something important in our county's 200th year.

By the time the seven trains, trains from every corner of the country, rolled into Valley Forge on July 3rd—300 wagons and 5,000 drivers and riders—22 million people had signed those scrolls in every state in the Union, including Alaska and Hawaii. If the scrolls had been rolled out flat and stacked, the stack would have risen 214 feet. That's the height of a 20-story building.

Twenty-two million people. No one other Bicentennial project touched so many.

Note: Okay, one more Farm Bureau story. I couldn't get it in the 1970s' portion of this anthology, so it's here, leading off the 1980s.

Me and Al Hirt and the Hotel Dux
– 1980 –

IT'S AMAZING how one forgets things. Somewhere near the end of my tenure with Kansas Farm Bureau—I'm guessing it was in January of either 1977 or '78—our national organization, the American Farm Bureau, hired me to work in the press room at the AFB's national convention in New Orleans

Actually, I did double duty. I did both my job as communications director for my full-time employer, Kansas Farm Bureau, and in my spare hours did whatever my part-time and temporary employer, AFB, wanted me to do to help news reporters and farm broadcasters covering the convention get the stories they wanted.

Looking back, it all was a mistake. Instead of working eight- to 10-hour days, I was working 12- to 14-hour days. By Day Four of the convention, I was bleary-eyed. Still that evening—a Friday evening—I wanted to get one more story, a feature story for my own radio network. I wanted to cut an interview with jazz trumpeter Al Hirt. He had a club a couple blocks away on Bourbon Street.

I called.

The club manager said yes, come on over. I could catch Hirt during the break after his first set.

Now you need a bit of background.

I got hooked on the music of Herb Alpert & The Tijuana Brass back in the 1960s, when I was working for Michigan Farm Bureau. I bought Alpert's album "Whipped Cream & Other Delights" just for the cover, as a lot of other young guys did. The music happened to be good, too. The album sold 6 million copies.

Alpert, when he was about to play "Whipped Cream" in a concert, would tell the audience, "Sorry we can't play the cover for you."

You should check out the cover. Just google the album.

Next came Al Hirt, the Round Mound of Sound, with "Java" and the album "Honey in the Horn," both million sellers. Hirt played a sweet trumpet.

He was a deft musician. When Hirt played the theme song for the 1960s television show, *The Green Hornet*, his fingers were a blur as he triple-tongued his way through the piece. Same when he played "Yakety Trumpet," his version of Boots Randolph's "Yakety Sax."

By the time I got to New Orleans, Hirt had recorded 39 albums. That's a lot of music. All of it good, and some of it spectacular.

I WALKED to Hirt's club and went in, not feeling well. I got there in time for his last number before his first break. I sat at a table and listened and watched him play. A big-bellied man and heavy, he was sweating profusely, his trumpet in one hand, a handkerchief in the other, the handkerchief for mopping the sweat from his face.

The number ended and the manager guided me back to Hirt's dressing room. I explained what I wanted and brought out my tape recorder. Hirt and I talked for a while—a good interview—he perspiring and me getting progressively more cold, growing pale. Finally, Hirt, staring at me, said, "You don't look too good, fella."

To which I said I didn't feel good.

"Fella," he said, "you gotta get to a hospital."

I don't remember whether Hirt or his club manager took me out to the street and hailed a cab. Whoever it was got in an argument with the cabby about which hospital to go to. In exasperation, Hirt or his manager yelled, "Take him to Hotel Dux."

The proper name is Hotel Dieu—it's French—but at that time most New Orleans residents pronounced it Hotel Ducks.

Turns out it was a Catholic charity hospital known for its exceptional care, and it wasn't too far away.

I staggered into the E.R. Whoever was at the desk took one look at me and called for a couple orderlies to put me on a gurney and roll me out into the hallway, to the end of a line of some 25 or 26 others waiting to see a doctor. Remember, this was a Friday night.

In New Orleans.

Gunshot wounds.

Stabbings.

All kinds of stuff.

It was two hours before a doctor saw me. I didn't mind. Most of the time, I slept.

After he checked my temperature, my lungs and my breathing, he said I had pneumonia and told an orderly to take me upstairs. "Get this guy a room."

I don't remember much of the next two days other than this little nun, who must have been 85—Sister Mary Francis. She asked if I'd like to see my minister.

Jerry Peterson

I said he was four states away.

"Then how about me?" she asked.

I agreed.

She was retired, but not without a job. Sister Mary Francis spent her days at the hospital, going from room to room, visiting with patients. She was a friend to everyone who wanted a friend.

She was one of God's angels, a sweet, sweet person.

On my last day, as I was getting ready to leave, Sister Mary Francis came in. "Is there any last thing I can do for you?" she asked.

I glanced at the flowers several people from the convention had sent. "Sister," I said, "there are probably some patients here who don't have any flowers. How about picking a couple and giving my flowers to them, a couple people you think the flowers would help?"

She offered that sweet smile of hers and said she would do that for me.

ONE last story.

A couple days into my stay, when I could finally track, I called home to my wife Sallie and told her what had happened and where I was. The convention was over. All the Farm Bureau people had left.

"I'll come get you," she said.

The drive from Manhattan, Kansas, to New Orleans is, in round figures, a thousand miles. Roughly a 20-hour drive.

I did not know until Sallie arrived that she had recruited a friend of ours to come with her, Roscoe Swan, a major in the Army at Fort Riley and the post's inspector general.

Roscoe was nervous and in a hurry to get back on the road. "I won't relax until we get out of Louisiana and

Mississippi," he said. "I was scared to death coming down here, me a black man with a white woman. At least now you'll be in the car with us."

The segregated South, it was an awful and all too recent memory.

Note: By 1980, Farm Bureau and I had parted company. I was now a journalist, working for newspapers, first for the Douglas County News-Press in Castle Rock, Colorado, then Beckley Newspapers in Beckley, West Virginia.
680 words

Millionaires, You Can't Throw a Stick without Hitting One
– 1981 –

IT WAS A FLUKE that I ended up in Beckley-By-God-West-Virginia, me a flatlander from Wisconsin.

Beckley is in the mountains of the southern part of the state, in coal country. Of course, West Virginia's mountains are not like the mountains of the far West. They're worn down, kind of nubby, but they are steep enough and close enough together that in some of the hollows you don't see the sun for most of the day, the exception being the hour or two at midday when the sun is directly overhead.

But back to the fluke.

Raleigh General Hospital in Beckley was looking for a dietitian for its new neonatal unit. My wife Sallie applied and was invited to come up for an interview. We were living in eastern Kentucky at the time.

I went along and, while she was at the hospital, I went over to the newspaper office, to see whether they might be hiring for its reporting staff. They were.

I got a job.

Sallie didn't.

She ended up working in Dayton, Ohio, as the dietitian for the state mental hospital there.

She moved north.

I moved south.

We got a house for Sallie, and I lived in a motel . . . initially.

All I wanted in Beckley was an apartment, preferably furnished. So I found a real estate agent who took me around. We got into one residential area where all the houses were small and 40 to 50 years old. "You have a millionaire living there," she said, pointing to one humble place, "and there. And there," she continued, pointing to several neighboring houses. "They're all coal men who made it big but never wanted to live anywhere but the house that had always been home. In fact," she said, "in Beckley you have more millionaires per square mile than in any other city in the country."

I was impressed.

Beckley, though, was not the first West Virginia city of coal millionaires. That was Bramwell, down in Mercer County, just a tad north of the Virginia state line. Its wealth came out of the Pocahontas Coalfield that stretched 40 miles to the north. By 1910, 13 coal barons—men who made millions mining in the Pocahontas and shipping the coal to Europe—lived in Bramwell. They all built mansions, most of the houses still standing and restored to their glory looks of the 19-teens. Per capita, the small town had more millionaires than even Beckley would have 80 years later, more millionaires per capita than any other city in the country at the time. Its high school sports teams were known as The Millionaires.

A lot of that coal money went into the Bank of Bramwell, making it by the 1920s the wealthiest bank in America. Chicagoans who wanted to build skyscrapers in the early twentieth century came to the Bank of Bramwell for financing.

The town was never very large. At its peak, it had 1,690 residents. That was 1920. Today, Bramwell has a couple fewer than 350 residents.

When I worked for Beckley Newspapers, the population was just a smidge under a thousand.

A lot of pride in that town. The day I learned that Bramwell hosted an annual Christmas candlelight house walk, I scheduled myself to be there. Eleven of the mansions were on the tour, and I got to see them all as well as the Bramwell Presbyterian Church where the walk started, that church built over three years—1890 to '93—and paid for by I.T. Mann.

Mann came to Bramwell in 1890. Thirty-five years later, his wealth from coal and investments exceeded $80 million. In today's money, that would be $14.25 billion.

He lost it all in the crash of 1929, as did several other Bramwell millionaires.

The people who bought the mansions in the 1960s, '70s, and '80s got them for the proverbial song. They then sunk their paychecks and savings into restoring them.

To these homeowners, it all paid off in 1984 when the Town of Bramwell was named to the National Register of Historic Places.

Note: Here they come again.

I Meet an Ambassador
– 1982 –

NEWSPAPERS attract some strong people.

Unusual and memorable people, too.

I expect reporters who work in television say the same thing.

In Beckley, we had a fellow who would come in once a month to brief us on what was going on in the universe. His business card read: Ambassador to the World.

As I recall, nobody knew his name. In fact, we didn't know anything about him, other than what his card said.

The newest reporter on staff always drew the assignment to talk with him.

Perhaps at other newspapers the Ambassador to the World would have been given the bum's rush, but we enjoyed him. We knew we would come away with a good story we could entertain our fellow reporters with over lunch.

Another man I cannot call strange. He was, though, unusual.

Beckley Newspapers was as white as could be. We didn't have one black employee in the entire organization, although the city had a significant black population.

That population wasn't covered by the newspaper. Black businesses, black organizations, not even black engagements and weddings could get space in our pages.

The attitude of Beckley's business and community leadership was very southern.

I thought this was wrong and suggested to our managing editor that we ought to be reaching out, that we ought to be covering the black community. If that suggestion went anywhere, it went in the wastebasket.

Then I met a black man about my age, a community organizer who was assembling a boycott of a local company, to force them to hire a certain number of black employees. I thought this was a business story that we should cover, so I went after it.

At the end of the interview, I asked the organizer, "Have you thought of putting together a boycott of the newspaper, to get blacks on staff?"

"Yes," he said, "but you don't pay enough to make it worth getting jobs there for our people."

He was right. Reporters' wages were and are notoriously low except for those few who work at, say, the New York Times or the Wall Street Journal. One reporter at our newspaper with a young family qualified for food stamps, although he never applied. I would have qualified, too, had not Sallie been working. Same for two other reporters. Their wives worked at the newspaper, one as a photographer, the other as a reporter.

So a fair question is why do we in journalism do it? Why do we work for poverty wages?

It comes down to this: We like the job.

We like talking to people and then writing stories that other people read, stories that sometimes bring changes in the community. And some of us enjoy being crusaders, investigative reporters who turn up corruption and cronyism and put a hot light on it with our reporting.

But I've detoured.

No, I haven't.

I was telling you about our wages. They were so poor that we reporters would jockey for any assignment that came with a free meal. The best in Beckley always was the annual meeting of the chamber of commerce. The chamber would bring in a top speaker that gave us a feature story for the newspaper, and the dinner, of course, gave the lucky reporter a steak, something none of us could afford at home.

Was taking a free meal ethical? No.

Today, most newspapers give reporters' expense accounts with orders that the reporters must buy their own game tickets, concert tickets, movie tickets, meals—whatever—so we can never be beholden to the business, organization, governmental unit, office holder, or candidate we're covering.

MEMEORABLE people. There were a lot over the decade that I worked for newspapers, but let me tell you about one. The mayor of Glasgow.

That's Glasgow, West Virginia, not Glasgow, Scotland.

It's downriver from Montgomery where I was the newspaper editor.

Glasgow's Main Street businesses were closing their doors and moving closer to Charleston, in order to get the metro traffic they needed to survive. Each business lost to the town cost jobs and a loss of property and business taxes.

Glasgow's town government was hurting.

I was sitting with the mayor one afternoon, and he spilled out his grief. "What I'm thinking of doing," he said, "is—we have the Kanawha River going up the south side of our town—I'm thinking of taxing every barge tow that goes by. The towboat captains are gonna raise hell, but we have to get the money somewhere so we can maintain our services."

I didn't report that conversation. Had the mayor put a proposal before the town council, I would have.

A couple weeks later, he had a new thought. Actually an old thought. U.S. 60 ran along the north side of Glasgow. "My dad put a speed trap there in the Nineteen-thirties," the mayor said. "I can do the same thing."

And then he had a better thought.

He drove to Charleston, to the state capitol, and walked into the governor's office. He laid it out for Arch Moore . . . give me some money for my town or I'll set up a speed trap on 60 and see to it that you get all the blame when the truckers and car drivers complain.

Every West Virginia governor had a slush fund.

Moore thought about the headlines that would paint him as the miser who wanted to keep a small town broke.

Bad business in an election year.

The mayor came away with the money he wanted.

Note: I've met a lot of authors over the years. The first was Kentuckian Jesse Stuart.

Me & Jesse
– 1983 –

I READ Jesse Stuart's *The Thread That Runs So True* when I was in the eighth grade and attending a one-room country school very much like the one-room school where Jesse taught when he was a young man.

The story made an impression on me.

Never did I think that one day I would meet Stuart. But I did.

It was 1975. I was visiting my wife's parents in eastern Kentucky, in Carter County, about forty miles away from W-Hollow in neighboring Greenup County where Stuart lived on the farm he bought after he was first married.

I called him, said I, too, was a writer and I'd like to get acquainted.

He said come on over.

Stuart was 69.

What I didn't know at the time was that he was wearing out, tiring of strangers calling and stopping in to see him. Shortly after our conversation, Stuart had his telephone unlisted.

We had a great time together. I had attended a country school as he had, he for eight years, me for only three months. We both had been teachers. And we both were writers.

After a long talk in the front room of the old log home, he said, "Would you like to see my library, where I write?"

Absolutely.

The library was a couple steps away in another room, the walls lined with shelves and the shelves full of books and piles of manuscripts. Those piles were stories, essays, and poems that Stuart had written but had not yet published.

There, too, were all the books he had published up to that time, just short of 60 . . . collections of poetry, collections of essays, biographies, five volumes of his autobiography, novels for adults and children, and 11 collections of short stories.

A lot of those short stories—460 in all—he first sold to magazines such as The Saturday Evening Post. Those stories paid the bills for Stuart and his family in his early writing years.

He also sold hundreds of poems and articles as well.

At the time we visited, most of Stuart's books were out of print. You couldn't get them. Later that year, he and friends created the Jesse Stuart Foundation and assigned his literary estate to it, all his books and unpublished manuscripts. The foundation would become a publishing house and, as I'm writing this—July 2018—it has reprinted more than 30 of Stuart's books. The foundation's goal is to reprint all of them, then edit those piles of manuscripts and publish them as well.

After Stuart died, the foundation began holding annual symposiums in which scholars analyzed Stuart's works and discussed their importance, often presenting research papers that would be published and circulated in literary circles.

The symposiums didn't interest me, but the Stuart Weekends did. I attended the second which included tours of all the sites in Greenup County that were important to Stuart, ending at the cemetery where he's buried.

The guide on our bus was Stuart's sister, Glinnis. The stories she told were vastly entertaining and insightful.

The bus ground its way up to the head of W-Hollow where Glinnis pointed to the rock at the edge of a field where Stuart wrote the first line of a sonnet: "I am a farmer singing at the plow." Dutton published that sonnet and 702 more that Stuart composed in a collection it titled *Man with a Bull-Tongue Plow*. That was 1934. Stuart was 28, a farmer and a high school English teacher. Irish poet George William Russell called that collection the greatest work of poetry to come out of America since Walt Whitman's *Leaves of Grass*.

Those sonnets are a joy to read.

We stopped at another place where Stuart wrote. His typewriter was there, and Glinnis told us about how, when money would become tight, her brother would sit at that typewriter and pound out story after story and poem after poem long into the night and mail them off to magazine editors, crossing his fingers in the hope that they would buy them. They usually did, and in the return mail, there were the checks.

Stuart also wrote a mountain of letters on that and other typewriters, at least 30,000 letters, and one estimate places it at 50,000. Sometimes he would write 40 letters a day. Stuart believed anyone who wrote to him deserved a response.

Some of his letters dealt with the practical matters in life. In one, he raised hell with the power company for misplacing his check for $8.51, payment for a previous month's electric bill. Ever the poet, Stuart wrote that letter in the form of a poem.

It was here at this stop that Glinnis told us of their grandfather who had two families, one on each side of a mountain. Neither family knew of the other until the old man died. The problem became where to bury him, Glinnis said. The wives compromised and planted the old man at the top of the mountain, midway between the two families.

We all laughed.

True story, she said.

On the way to the cemetery, she had the driver pull over to the side of the road, near a set of railroad tracks that passed between two steep hills. "One winter when we were kids," she said, "we had a blizzard that filled in between those hills. No trains ran for two weeks while the men of the area shoveled out the railroad tracks."

Stuart never used that story, but I did a decade later, incorporating it in a story I titled "The Christmas Gift."

The tour ended at the Plum Grove cemetery where Stuart and Naomi, his wife, are buried.

For a man who travelled the world—a Guggenheim Fellowship in 1937 allowed Stuart to tour 25 nations in Europe; in 1960, he took on a year-long assignment as a visiting professor at the American University in Cairo, teaching what he loved most, poetry; two years later, the State Department sent him on a world lecture tour, talking about the value of education and hard work in societies that were changing from an agricultural to an industrial base . . . 372 talks in Iran, Pakistan, the Philippines, Korea, India, Thailand, and other counties. In Iran alone, Stuart, ever the sightseer, rolled up 2,500 miles while there to give 10 talks—he always hurried home to

Greenup County, to W-Hollow, to family and friends and his typewriter.

Note: A newspaper story.

Johnny B and the Grandson of Devil Anse
– 1984 –

JOHN BLANKENSHIP and I were desk mates or, rather, desk neighbors. He had the desk next to mine.

He came to Beckley Newspapers from The Bluefield Telegraph where he had a reputation as a fine feature writer and columnist. I came from The Douglas County News-Press in Colorado where my reputation mirrored his.

We both also liked the police beat, and we were sharp-eyed photographers. We knew how to get a winning picture on the first take.

But when it came to stories, John had the edge. He had grown up in West Virginia. He'd lived all his life there. He knew everybody in the southern part of the state who was worth knowing, including Harve Hatfield, Devil Anse Hatfield's grandson.

The Hatfield-McCoy feud? You surely have heard parts of that story

The West Virginia Hatfields and the Kentucky

McCoys lived on opposite sides of the Tug Fork River. They fought over who killed whom in the Civil War, who owned a hog, a court judgement upholding Devil Anse's claim on several thousand acres of McCoy timber land, a claim that eventually made the Hatfields wealthy and left the McCoys struggling to survive on a three-hundred-acre farm. And there were more killings, arrests for the killings, killers sent to prison and one hanged.

Just how many were killed over the twenty-eight years of the feud has been debated for multiple decades by those trying to make an accurate count. But these things are sure. Nine Hatfields were sent to prison for various murders of McCoy men, seven for life. One Hatfield man was executed—hanged.

Additionally, while there are a lot of descendants from the various branches of the Hatfield family, of Devil Anse's nine sons, only one presented him with a grandson.

One.

Grandson.

Harve.

He lived outside of Oak Hill, ten miles north of Beckley.

John told me he intended to interview Harve.

I said I'd like to go along, that I'd be his photographer.

No, said John, this was solo.

But we did drive together up to Oak Hill. He dropped me at the courthouse where I said I'd get my own stories, and he went on to Harve Hatfield's house.

Here's the strange thing. John never talked about that interview. I don't know if he got anything. I don't recall that he wrote a story. If he did, I never read it.

I did top John once.

Jay Rockefeller was our governor at the time. One morning when I was driving into work, I saw a sign in front of Wally Smith's Super Fine Market that read HAVE LUNCH WITH JAY TODAY.

Jay?

Jay Rockefeller's coming to Beckley? And we can have lunch with him?

I wheeled in.

I talked to Wally.

He said, "Yeah, sure, you can have lunch with Jay. Be here at eleven o'clock."

I was.

There a table was waiting, a table set for two—white linen tablecloth, fine china, wine glasses.

Wow, me and the governor!

Wally waved over the meat department manager spiffed up in a sport jacket and bow tie.

"Jerry," Wally said, "this is Jay. Jay Martinelli. You're gonna have lunch with him today."

The thing was a play on the name, a promotion for the store.

"You have no idea how much talk this has created," Wally said, grinning like it was him about to sit down to lunch with the governor.

I had Wally take a picture of me across the table from Jay, the two of us clicking our wine glasses together.

And I turned our time and that photo into a business story that ran in the next day's paper.

Later in the year, when I was interviewing the governor on some issue, I told him about having lunch with Jay.

Jay Rockerfeller rocked back in laughter.

"The next time I'm in Beckley, I've got to stop in on Wally," he said. "I'll take him to lunch."

Note: The telephone rings.

Being the Editor is a Hazardous Business
– 1985 –

THIS IS a really really short story and the gospel truth.

I'm now the editor of The Montgomery Herald in Montgomery, West Virginia, a small town not far from the state capital.

Like all newspapers, we ran the police blotter—who was arrested for what the previous day or, for us, the previous week. The Herald was a weekly paper, out on Wednesdays.

We ran the blotter because our readers always wanted to know whether any of their neighbors were in trouble with the law. It gave them great grist for gossip. For us, the material was easy to get. Just go down to the cop shop. The arrest reports were there, all a matter of public record.

The phone rang one Thursday morning.

My office manager answered it. She listened a moment, then handed the phone to me. "You'd better take it," Rosella said.

I did. "Peterson here," I said into the mouthpiece.

A man's voice came back laced with anger. "You the editor?" he asked.

"Uh-huh."

"You have it in the paper that I was arrested for being drunk and disorderly and aggravated battery at the high school football game Friday."

That caused me to pause. "Were you?" I asked.

"Was I what?"

"Arrested."

"Yes, but I didn't do those things. You convicted me in the newspaper."

"No, we didn't. We just reported you were arrested for certain charges. It's public record."

"Look, you got my neighbors to jabbering because of what you put in that paper of yours," he said, his voice getting louder. "I'm an old man. I'm a cripple. You know what I oughtta do? I oughtta teach you a lesson. I'm gonna come down to your office and wrap my cane around your head."

He hung up.

Gingerly, I did the same.

And locked the front door.

Note: The telephone rings.

Names in the News
– 1986 –

ONE NAME.

John Hey.

John was a district court judge running for a position on the State Supreme Court.

I was a member of the Montgomery Rotary Club, and Judge Hey had been invited to speak to us.

Terrific. The Supreme Court race was hot and Hey was involved in a bit of a scandal, so here was my opportunity to get a big story on the judge, the scandal, and his positions on the issues that were likely to come before the court for my newspaper, for The Herald's readers.

The scandal. The judge had used court funds to pay a nanny for taking care of his young children. Hey maintained that freed him to do the court's work, thus it was a legitimate expense.

The first thing he said to us Rotarians after the club president introduced him is that he wouldn't take any questions about the nanny business. "I've said all I intend to on that," he said.

Hey filled his twenty minutes with lots of great stuff. I took extensive notes, writing down some of his better statements and zingers word for word.

I shot the photos I needed, then went back to the office and wrote the story.

It ran in the Wednesday paper.

Thursday morning, the judge called.

"You don't know how to spell my last name, do you," he said. "It's H-E-Y, not H-A-Y."

I'm a farm kid. I spelled the name the way I was used to. In doing so, I violated one of the principles of good reporting: Always ask the person how she or he spells their name, even if it's as simple as Joe Smith.

"I'm not complaining," the judge said, "but you did it sixty-three times."

I apologized and said I'd run a correction next week.

He said I didn't have to do that, but I did . . . as a matter of principle.

Thursday morning the next week, John called again. He thanked me for the correction, then added, "I'm always happy when I can get two stories for one."

Note: I had lived and worked in the mid-South for a half dozen years before I met my first real author from the region.

Say Hello to Lee Smith
– 1987 –

LEE SMITH grew up in Grundy, Virginia—serious coal country—a short distance north of where I was the editor of the Richlands News-Press.

When we met—she came to my town to teach several writers workshops for high school students—she had brought out her fifth novel, *Family Linen*. The only place in the area where you could buy it in those pre-Amazon days was in Grundy, at the library. Lee had arranged with her publisher that it be a fundraiser for the library—her hometown library.

She was now a force among the writers of the mid-South, a splendid writer and storyteller, a delightful individual whom everybody loved who met her or read her books. But she had yet to have a bestseller, so she supported her writing habit by teaching at North Carolina State University.

Lee wouldn't have a bestseller until she brought out her eleventh novel in 2003, *The Last Girls*.

We sat in the high school library after those workshops, talking, and out of that conversation came a good story for my newspaper.

Over the next several years, we would be together at writers conferences and when her book promotions brought her into the area. We've corresponded a couple times. And I've read a number of her novels. Like her fans, I've thoroughly enjoyed them.

Lee would be pleased that I'm now writing my big mid-South novel, about the beginnings of the air mail service in Tennessee.

The good news is that, at age 75, Lee is still writing. She writes every day.

Said she in her memoir, *Dimestore: A Writer's Life*, "Suddenly, lots of things of my own life occurred to me for the first time as stories: my great-granddaddy's 'other family' in West Virginia; Hardware Breeding, who married his wife Beulah, four times; how my Uncle Vern taught my daddy to drink good liquor in a Richmond hotel; how I got saved at the tent revival; John Hardin's hanging in the courthouse square; how Petey Chaney rode the flood; the time Mike Holland and I went to the serpent handling-church in Jolo; the murder Daddy saw when he was a boy, out riding his little pony—and never told...

"I started to write these stories down (in high school and college). Many years later, I'm still at it. And it's a funny thing: Though I have spent most of my working life in universities, though I live in piedmont North Carolina now and eat pasta and drive a Subaru, the stories that present themselves to me as worth telling are often those somehow connected to that place (Grundy) and those people (family and friends). The mountains that used to imprison me have become my chosen stalking ground."

You've not read one of Lee's novels? You should. She has thirteen out . . . plus four collections of short stories.

Note: Fifty years ago, on Halloween Eve, Orson Welles and his Mercury Theater players stepped up to the microphones in a CBS studio and began Welles' dramatization of H.G. Wells' *The War of the Worlds*. The broadcast frightened thousands of people who thought the broadcast was a real radio news report, that the Martians had landed in New Jersey and were coming for them.

Boo
– 1988 –

LEONARD WELLES Findley and his girlfriend stood on the front stoop, punching the doorbell and punching it again until the door creaked open.

Findley whispered to his girl, "Sounds like the *Inner Sanctum.*"

She gave him a perplexed look.

"It's an old radio show," he said.

Still the perplexed look.

Just too young, he thought. She, like him, was of the television generation. For her, radio was for listening to N.W.A.'s *Gangsta Gangsta* when her Sony Discman was busted. For him, it was Bobby McFerrin and *Don't Worry, Be Happy* and Old-Time Radio on WPR on Sunday nights.

An elderly woman with a killer smile and hair that appeared to have been styled by a tornado looked out on them. "Welcome to Orson Welles' boyhood home," she said and waved them in. "Do you youngsters know who Mister Welles was?"

Findley shifted the weight of his backpack slung over his shoulder as he made his way through the door. "Yes, he was my grandfather."

The woman's eyebrows shot up, but not the girlfriend's. She frowned.

"Really?" the woman said. She leaned in toward Findley. "Yes, now that I look more closely, I do see Mister Welles' face in yours when he was about your age. And the hairstyle with that one curl tipping down on your forehead. Did you know your grandfather well?"

He shook his head. "He never acknowledged me or my mother. She was his love child. Illegitimate, I'm afraid."

"And your name is?"

"Lenny. Lenny Welles Findley."

She picked up a book from a side table in the entryway, a biography of Orson Welles. "Illegitimate. That would explain why we have no record of you."

He raised a finger. "I do have my birth certificate and my mother's, if you'd like to see them."

"I'm the curator here. Yes, I would."

Findley set his backpack down. He grubbed out a manila folder and handed it to the woman.

She flipped the folder open, adjusted her glasses, and read . . . Leonard Welles Findley. Birth date: August three, Nineteen Sixty-four. Birth place: St. Helena's Hospital, Phoenix, Arizona. Father, yes. Mother: Diedra Welles Mortenson.

She shuffled that certificate to the back and scanned the next . . . Diedra Welles Mortenson. Birth date:

February fourteen, Nineteen Forty. Birth place: Los Angeles General Hospital, Los Angeles, California. Mother: Cynthia Marie Mortenson. Father: George Orson Welles.

Both were stamped as certified copies provided by the respective Departments of Licenses and Certificates of each state.

"Remarkable. Truly remarkable." She rubbed a twitch away from the side of her nose before she passed the folder back to Findley. "Do you know what's going on here today?"

Findley returned the folder to his backpack and brought out a tape recorder no larger than a box of Marlboros. "The historical marker out front?"

"Yes, we're dedicating it today. It was fifty years ago tonight that Orson made his famous *War of the Worlds* broadcast."

He showed his recorder. "I'm a graduate student at the UW in Madison. I was hoping there might be some people here who heard that broadcast. I'd like to interview them for my thesis project. It's an oral history— how people reacted."

A young woman in a business suit, a clipboard in her hand, bustled in. "Doty," she said to the grand dame, "WTMJ is here. Is it all right if they set up? And I just got a call from the governor's office. Governor Thompson is on the way. He should be here in five minutes."

The curator gave a nod, and her assistant dashed back outside.

Alone again with her guests, the curator took Findley by the elbow. "We weren't able to get any of Orson's family here today. It's such a shame, don't you think?"

"Indeed."

The curator lit up, as if a spotlight had been turned on her. "I've just had a thunderbolt of an idea. Tell me,

Mister Findley, would you like to come up on the stage we have set up by the marker and say a few words?"

THE GOVERNOR waved to the crowd as the applause went up. He returned to his chair, the October afternoon warming all gathered before the stage and around the Orson Welles Boyhood Home historical marker.

The curator hurried to the microphone. She gazed at Thompson. "Governor, it was so good of you to be here for this dedication. Now I have a surprise for you and everyone here." She motioned to the side of the stage where Findley and his girlfriend stood. The curator beckoned to him.

Findley hopped up on the stage and came to the microphone.

The curator wrapped her arm around his shoulders, grinning like someone who had just been served an oversized portion of cherries jubilee. "Governor," she said, looking to him and then to the audience, "by dint of good fortune, as if Orson himself were gazing down upon us, we have with us the great man's grandson, Leonard Welles Findley. He has agreed to grace us with a few words."

She swept away.

Findley squared himself in front of the microphone, his backpack hanging by a single strap from his shoulder. He ran the fingers of one hand back through his hair while, with the other hand, he clung to the lectern.

"Fans of my grandfather," he said into the microphone with some hesitancy, "I did not know my grandfather until his final days. He had kept my mother and me at more than arm's length. But on one of his final nights at the hospital three years ago, I dressed as an orderly and sneaked into his room. We talked for hours. He knew he was dying, and I got the sense he wanted to make his peace."

Findley stopped and, with all eyes fixed on him, he cleared his throat. "Forgive me if I get a little choked up. I told my grandfather I was a student at the University of Wisconsin, that I was studying theater history. That was like a shot of whiskey to him. He warmed and said that made me the only one in his family to be in his home state. 'After I die,' he said, 'would you do something special for me? Would you spread a portion of my ashes at my boyhood home in Kenosha?'"

Findley swung his backpack around. He set it beside the microphone, and from the pack, he brought out a silver urn engraved with Welles' name and his birth and death dates. Findley held the urn up. "With the permission of Governor Thompson whom I voted for and Miz Doty Sparks, the curator here, today I'm going to fulfill my grandfather's wish."

The WTMJ cameraman sharpened the focus of his lens, bringing it in tight on Findley and the urn he held next to his face.

THE PHONE rang. Findley, at the sink, shook water from his hands as he went to answer it. He pressed the receiver to his ear.

A voice came through. "Is this Orson Welles' grandson?"

Findley pulled the receiver away. He squinted at it, then put it back to his ear. "Before I answer that," he said into the mouthpiece, "who is this?"

"Cedric Norton. I'm with the Tonight Show. Johnny saw the tape of you spreading Orson Welles' ashes at that Wisconsin house. He wants you on his show tomorrow night."

A smile tugged at the corners of Findley's mouth.

"Mister Findley? Mister Leonard Welles Findley? Are you still there?"

"Yes."

"Mister Findley, I'm authorized to send a corporate jet to pick you up. Can you be with us?"

"Absolutely."

"And we'll pay you an appearance fee. Mister Findley, after I work out the flight schedule, I'll call you back."

Findley huffed on his fingernails, then polished them on the front of his shirt. "I look forward to your call."

Findley's girlfriend hurried out of the bedroom, fidgeting with a paperback as he hung up. "Lenny, I listened in on the extension. They're going to find you out."

"No, they won't. I'm too good for this not to be true."

FINDLEY ROCKED on the balls of his feet, waiting. Then he heard it, Johnny Carson reading from his cue card. "Ladies and gentleman, my next guest is a young man from Wisconsin, a graduate student. He is the great Orson Welles' grandson, and what a story he has to tell. Please welcome Leonard Welles Findley."

A stagehand gave Findley a push. He stumbled forward, out through an opening in the curtain and onto the stage, the lighting blinding him. He worked his way toward Carson, Carson standing, leading the applause. When Findley got close enough, Carson reached for his hand and guided him around in front of his desk to 'the couch.'

The applause died when Findley sat down.

Carson leaned forward, his elbows on his desk. "Tell me, Leonard . . . do you mind if I call you Leonard?"

Findley smiled. "You can call me Lenny if you'd like, as long as I can call you Johnny."

"Tell me, Mister Findley–" Carson swung to the audience and raised his eyebrows. After the audience laughed, he came back to Findley. "Lenny, it must be something to be Orson Welles' grandson. He was such a great actor and director and raconteur. I think I had him on my show six times."

"It was seven," Findley said.

"Seven, really? All right so yesterday, fifty years to the day of Orson's broadcast of *The War of the Worlds*, you were there in Kenosha, spreading his ashes at his boyhood home. What was that like for you with your state's governor there and a television film crew?"

Findley laughed. "It was a hoot. But as my grandfather would say—well, the man who is not my grandfather would say—boo. None of this is true. All of this was an elaborate Halloween joke just to get on your show."

Carson leaned back, his hands open, palms up. "The spreading of his ashes?"

"They weren't his ashes."

One eyebrow rose on Carson's forehead while the other went down. He drummed his pencil on his desk, then burst out laughing and threw his pencil over his shoulder. "Oh, that is funny. Lenny, you had me going there for a minute."

Carson turned to the audience, gesturing to Findley. "Ladies and gentlemen, Leonard Welles Findley, the grandson of the great Orson Welles!"

Note: One could title this story "The Joy of Cats." One could. But I won't.

The Longest Two Hours
– 1989 –

ONE SHOULD never move cats without the proper equipment.

Never!

This all happened back before you could buy a cat carrier at Walmart. Sallie and I were moving from Jonesborough, Tennessee, to Knoxville down the highway a couple hours drive.

We loaded a twenty-six-foot U-Haul truck with everything except a mattress we kept back, to sleep on that last night in our old house. We packed that behemoth tight.

Our cats—Cat One and Cat Two, so named by me when a veterinarian's assistant insisted we had to have names for our cats for her records—our cats wandered the house, looking lost. Nothing they had known in the two years we'd had them was there.

Then they wandered outside, I guess following the scent trail. That led them to the truck. They peered up, the back door still open, and there was home. They scrambled up inside, found the couch, and settled in for the night.

The next morning, after breakfast and loading the mattress and our overnight kits, I put the two cats in orange crates and stacked them in the center of the seat. The cats were to ride next to me while I drove.

These were silent cats for as long as we had them, but now they became yowlers, angry at being imprisoned. They would reach a claw out through an air hole and snag me. I wasn't twenty miles down the road when I ran out of my supply of band aids, so I released the cats. I gave them the run of the cab, figuring they'd sit on a box and watch out the window, that, like a dog, they would become fascinated with all of the life passing them by and be content.

Noooo.

They developed a game. Drop to the floor. Explore for a moment, then claw your way up my pant leg and arm and sit on my shoulder. From that vantage point, watch the traffic . . . for maybe fifteen seconds. Then down over the back of the seat. Crawl under, burrowing through the tools and other stuff I had packed there, to my pant leg, then up and repeat the circuit.

For two hours.

The longest two hours of my life.

Until we got to Knoxville, to the new house and, for them, freedom.

Note: How many people do you know who have brushed up against the space program?

Me and NASA
– 1990 –

I'VE ALWAYS been fascinated by space, space flight, colonizing the moon . . . going there to see if it really was made of green cheese as adults told me when I was a little kid.

We know that green cheese tale is not true, of course.

How many of us watched the manned moon landings of 1969, '71, and '72? Two in each of those years.

One of my neighbors, Moore Malpress, an old farmer, didn't believe any of it. Said he after that first landing, "Ah, they can put anything on television."

There was a good movie—*Capricorn One*—in 1977 in which the first Mars landing is, well, it's staged. It's all a government hoax. Moore, had he seen that movie, would have loved it. To him it indeed would have been proof that "they can put anything on television." It's believable, I suppose, if you pump up whatever it is with enough special effects.

But back to me. In high school, I discovered Robert Heinlein, a superb science fiction writer who in time would be called the dean of sci-fi writers. I read every one of his novels that we had in our library. Heinlein led me to Isaac Asimov, Ray Bradbury, and Arthur C. Clarke.

Clarke, in my opinion, was the better writer of the four. With Stanley Kubrick, he co-wrote the screenplay for the 1968 movie, *2001: A Space Odyssey.* A year before NASA astronaut Neil Armstrong stepped off the lunar lander Eagle onto the surface of the moon, we in the movie theater were going back to the moon to investigate a curious discovery thought to have affected human evolution.

And then, of course, there was HAL, the rogue computer that took control of the flight to Jupiter.

I've brushed up against NASA five times for real, first in 1970 when I was working for Kansas Farm Bureau. That year, the American Farm Bureau held its convention in Houston.

For reasons I can't remember, I drove the roughly eight hundred miles there. It turned out to be a good thing because, when the convention was over, I decided to do a little more driving, out to NASA's Houston Space Center, to see if I could find an interesting story.

The Houston complex is huge. I turned in at the main gate where the guard on duty asked me who I was there to see.

I said I didn't know, that I was a farm broadcaster and I'd like to talk with someone about what NASA was doing in the field of agriculture.

He dialed up the P.R. department. Someone there said send the guy up. The guard then gave me a building number and a room number in that building . . . and off I went.

The P.R. person made some calls while I drove over. When I got to his office, he took me to another floor and introduced me to three men working in satellite imagery.

They showed me several of the agricultural applications, how NASA and Department of Agriculture scientists could estimate crop production from satellite pictures, could figure out the health of a particular crop in an image—crop diseases, insect infestations, the effects of too much rain and the shortage of rain. Then they switched to satellite images of rivers and lakes. "We can identify water pollution from space," one said. "By changing the colors, we can tell you what the pollution is in that image and the magnitude—how serious it is."

All the images and their updates are plotted by longitude and latitude, so, if a researcher wants to know what's going on in, say, a particular section of your state, the NASA people can call up the images for that section in a couple minutes.

After a half an hour, I thanked my hosts and headed for the door. I didn't get there. One of the three asked me what I knew about the space shuttle program.

Nothing, I said.

"Would you like to see the sketches?"

This was one year into the development of the shuttle, I learned. The first wouldn't be built for another six years, and it wouldn't fly for another five.

I expect someone in the P.R. office suggested my hosts in satellite imagery turn me onto the shuttle program, for a story in a farm publication. Spread the word of what NASA was doing. Help build public support for the budget to pay for it.

The sketches were artists' renditions, the craft blasting off and in flight, to me this was the stuff of Robert Heinlein.

Hang onto this. We'll return to the shuttle in a bit.

A couple years later—1973 or '74—a U-2 spy plane flying for NASA landed at the Salina airport where it was to stay for a couple days. On a lark, I drove over to shoot some pictures of this storied aircraft and find out what it was doing there. Turned out the pilot, using the jet's belly cameras, was taking high-altitude photos of cropland. Sound familiar?

The crew gave me a NASA phone number to call for more information. I followed up and thought I had the makings of a story that TV Guide would be interested in. In the 1970s, the editors of TV Guide loved space stuff. An editor I contacted said yes, send on what you have.

When I finished the story, I read it and concluded it just wasn't very good. I put the story and my photos in my desk drawer.

My third brush with NASA came in 1980. I was living south of Denver, outside of Sedalia, Colorado, a town so small that all it had was a tavern north of the main street and an abandoned business building south of the main street. That was it, other than the Denver-Rio Grande railroad tracks on which the town fronted.

That business building wasn't exactly abandoned. It contained a storefront and a man about my age had moved in. He had rented it for a home and a workspace. He was an artist . . . and a promoter. He created a chili cook-off that drew in teams from along Colorado's Front Range and judges from the Denver television stations. It got a lot of attention, a lot of coverage for a town with only two buildings.

The artist-slash-community promoter and I became friends. One day, I asked him what he'd been doing before he came to Sedalia.

"I worked for NASA," he said. "I designed the gloves for the astronauts' space suits."

I SAID we'd return to the shuttle.

Crank forward to 1986. I was now the editor of the Montgomery Herald in Montgomery, West Virginia.

That January, on the Twenty-eighth, the space shuttle Challenger blew up 73 seconds after blast-off, killing all aboard including Christa MacAuliffe, who was to have been the first teacher in space.

Later in the year, someone at West Virginia Tech—the university in our town—decided that the school should do something to memorialize MacAuliff. Plant a tree, another someone said. So that became it.

Tech's president contacted NASA and said he'd like Jon McBride to be here, to be a part of the ceremony.

McBride, a West Virginian 100 percent—born in Charleston, grew up in Beckley, got his bachelor's degree in aeronautical engineering from WVU—had piloted the Challenger on its sixth flight, two years before.

NASA executives agreed and dispatched Jon to Montgomery.

After the ceremony, we walked the campus, talking about space flight, his experiences, and the Challenger disaster. That was his spacecraft. He had been scheduled to fly it again, but that wouldn't happen now. The remaining three shuttles were grounded for three years.

In time, Jon would get another chance to fly. In 1988, NASA selected him to command the crew of STS-35, the tenth flight of the space shuttle Columbia, to go up in March of 1990.

In May of 1989, Jon decided to retire from the space program. He left NASA to become president and CEO of the Flying Eagle Corporation in Lewisburg, West Virginia.

Now he's fully retired and living in Florida, near the Kennedy Space Center where he's a regular with NASA's "Lunch with an Astronaut" program, lunching and talking with visitors to the center.

IN 1990, I drove down to Huntsville, Alabama, to interview former University of Tennessee Space Institute graduate and Tennessee astronaut Henry Hartsfield for the University of Tennessee's College of Engineering alumni publication. Henry had been named to the college's Board of Advisors.

Henry was then NASA's Deputy Manager for Operations, assigned to the Space Station Projects Office at the Marshall Space Flight Center. He was responsible for the design, planning, and management of the space station, everything including assembling a budget and selling Congress on funding it.

He showed me the design of the station, the first unit that would fly in eight years and the final component 13 years later. I spun a fascinating story out our time together.

A sidebar to that story focused on Henry's flight aboard the space shuttle Columbia in 1982 that brought him, as the pilot, over the Knoxville World's Fair. From space, he broadcast his greetings to the fair goers.

I failed to ask how clearly he could see the fairgrounds from 200 miles up. Henry did say he could see the city.

Even if he were able to make out the structures on the fairgrounds, he wouldn't have been able to fully appreciate the Tennessee Amphitheater. What he would have seen looking down from space was two white blobs. From the ground, from Cumberland Avenue that passed over the middle of the fairgrounds, Henry would have seen the twin tents that roofed the amphitheater, tents that looked then, and still do, like gigantic breasts. They gave rise to the amphitheater's nickname: The Dolly Parton.

Note: Every story begins somewhere. A lot of mine began in 1989 when, at the age of 49, I became a graduate student at the University of Tennessee.

In the Beginning
– 1991 –

I GUARANTEE that, if you are an author, someone at every book event you do will ask you where do you get your ideas?

For me, many have come from newspapers, from stories others wrote, stories that beg to be retold with greater detail and depth, with information and thoughts slipped in that weren't known. The fiction elements.

But the idea for the first long story I wrote at the University of Tennessee came from a book, a book written by a fellow prince of the news trade, Vic Weals, from his book *Last Train to Elkmont*.

Elkmont is a town high up in the Great Smoky Mountains, far enough up that I've never driven there.

I've spent a fair amount of time in and around Townsend, the last big community before you get to Elkmont, so I've set a number of my "Wings over the Mountains" stories there.

Vic had been a reporter for the Knoxville Journal for 39 years, interviewing old timers in the Smokies about their families and putting their stories in his Tennessee Travels column.

The story of Vic's that grabbed me—retold in chapter 13 in the book—he titled "If a lumberjack had wings."

It centered on one John Williams who, back in 1923, wanted to learn to fly. So Williams took lessons at the Knoxville airport, then bought a Jenny biplane crated up and had it shipped into the mountains on two railroad flatcars. He and friends assembled the aircraft at Townsend. For three days he flew passengers for money from a cow pasture outside of town.

At the end of summer, he had his old flight instructor fly the Jenny up to Elkmont where Williams lived with his wife and 13-year-old son. The flight instructor—Frank Andre—told Williams not to try to fly the Jenny out of the narrow mountain valley until he first put an additional coat of dope on the fabric that covered the airplane's fuselage and wings, to tighten the fabric and make it waterproof.

Williams didn't. One Sunday morning, he attempted to take off from Elkmont's island airstrip and crashed into a boulder at the end of the field.

That was the end of the Jenny and the end of John Williams' passion for flying.

In my story, I have two brothers—Ben and Harold Wright—buy a Jenny in a crate and have it shipped up to Townsend where they and friends assembled . . . etcetera, etcetera.

Mine was not a newspaper story. It was a you-are-there story. You're with Ben and Harold as they argue over whether they should buy an airplane, about who should get the first flight, about what might come after.

You are there as Harold watches Ben, at the controls of the Jenny on the first flight, waddle down the pasture, as he watches Ben lift off, as he watches him just barely clear a boulder at the end of the field, as he watches him then crash into the trees beyond.

It was an exciting tale.

A fellow student in a short story writing class we were taking liked the story so much that he convinced the editor of a new literary journal that he should run it in the journal's premier issue.

I titled the story "The Other Wright Brothers."

Note: I met Thelma Dykeman, Tennessee's premier novelist and short story writer, at the University of Tennessee/Knoxville. She was teaching in the English department, teaching The Art of the Short Story. I signed up. All of us wrote stories that semester, a new one every week, and we workshopped them in Miss Dykeman's class. I had always wanted to write a ghost story. That class gave me the opportunity. Here it is. If Miss Dykeman were alive today, I think she would be pleased to know I've written more than 600 short stories to date, among them 82 for this collection.

The Medallion
– 1992 –

"THEY SAY dogs know, that dogs can tell," the old man said, his words hardly more than a whisper.

The fellow on the next stool, a student—disheveled—rubbed at the sand in his eyes. "You talking to me?"

"I said dogs can tell."

"I heard what you said. Are you talking to me?"

The old man's words were mumbly, but they had a certain insistence about them. The student glanced at his watch: seven forty-eight. He had an eight o'clock class—

thermodynamics—the last class of what had been a powerfully long day, a day that had started before sunup, had started at five a.m. The student, stocky, with a shock of brown hair shaved at the temples, had come from Martin Marietta several hours earlier, where he worked a day job in the quality control lab, a job that forced him to take night classes at the UT if he wanted to finish his engineering degree. He sat there in the lunchroom under Gilbert Hall, studying his half-empty styrofoam cup, this stranger on the next stool. Styrofoam, now there's an engineering wonder—chemical engineering, wasn't it?

Where did that thought come from?

The old man patted the student's arm, then dug his fingers in. "Dogs can tell."

"Hey, take it easy." The student twisted but couldn't pull his arm out of the old man's vice-like hold. He stared at the man, stared into his face, stared into his eyes. Could he be some spooky old professor who should have been retired a couple decades back?

Surely not. The senior professors he knew had silvery gray hair, well styled, while this man's hair was stark white and shaggy. And his face was ashen, lines carved in it like furrows in a newly plowed field. The skin under his chin, it flapped as he rambled on about dogs.

Everything about him said ancient, the ill-fitting sweater that smelled of what, stale cigar smoke? Singed flesh? Faded brown, coming out at the elbows. Baggy trousers patched below one knee.

Everything except the man's shoes. The student gaped at them—high-end Adidas—sneakers. A gift from his grandson? Or maybe they were his grandson's.

The vice grip relaxed. The student recovered his arm and stared at the man's hand so powerful, the skin as smooth as a teenager's.

"Dogs," the old man said. "I should have paid more attention."

"What dogs? What are you talking about?"

"Last night. I should have paid more attention."

"Paid more attention to what?"

"My dog."

"Oh sure, everyone oughtta listen to his dog. Fella, you've gotta excuse me. I've gotta get to class." The student swirled the last dregs of coffee in his cup and tossed them back. As he rose, that vicelike grip again bit into his arm. It hauled him back down onto the stool.

"Perkins Hall is haunted, you know," the old man said, his voice husky, feverish.

"Aw, come on, it's Halloween I know. You're gonna make me late for class."

"Where's your class?"

"In Perkins. Where else?"

"I wouldn't go if I were you. No, I wouldn't go." The old man squeezed the student's arm.

Three people—students by their book bags—rose from a table in the far corner of the room. They hefted their bags to their shoulders and made their way toward the door where they chucked their cups and wadded napkins into a trash can.

"Night, Ray," one of them called to the counterman checking the day's receipts.

"Ya all come back," the counterman sang out. "Tomorrow, I'll put new grounds in the coffeepot for ya."

The old man watched the departing students in the mirror above the counter.

"Let's go over there." He gestured toward the vacated table and pushed his companion along by the elbow. "You've got to be warned."

The student twisted, yet again he couldn't break free from that death grip. "Can't you let go of my arm, man?"

The old man shoved him into an empty chair, then slipped into the chair beside him.

"Yeah, well—" The student tried to laugh. "You're really gonna tell me this story, aren'tcha?"

"Yesssss." The old man stretched the word, gave it the sound of a snake hungering for a meal. He wagged a finger in the student's face. "I'm like you. I heard the stories, and like you, I didn't believe them. I told everybody, hell, old buildings creak and groan. That's normal. That's not spooks. And Perkins Hall is old."

The student glanced to the side for an escape, but the old man skooched his chair around, blocking the way. "Last night," he went on, "I was working late, running a program on bridge design. Few people are in Perkins after eleven. Even the janitors have gone home by that hour, so I brought my dog to keep me company."

"I didn't know you could bring pets in the building."

"It's amazing what you can do when the dean's not around. You, you're interrupting me." The old man paused to arrange his thoughts. "I was working in the computer lab—third floor. You know the one?"

The student shook his head.

"Took a solid hour to set up the problem, to punch in all the codes. Finally, I turned the problem over to the computer.

"My dog—he's a black Lab, you know. I call him Smoky. Smoky, he put his head on my lap, and I rubbed his ears while the computer worked away at the problem. It had been running a couple minutes when the door opened and then closed, the door behind me. Smoky growled.

" 'Come on now,' I said to Smoky, 'it's just probably Denver. You know Denver. You saw him earlier.' But Old Smoke continued to growl, low and defensive. I ignored it because at that moment the solution came up on the screen. And I tell you, the numbers were fantastic.

"I called over my shoulder, 'Den, why are you still here?' Denver Catron, he's another graduate student. We'd worked together earlier in the evening. I thought he'd gone home.

"But Den didn't answer.

"Smoke continued to growl, so I turned around, and nobody was there. Who the heck is playing tricks at this time of night, I wondered.

"Then I heard footsteps—moving away, down the hall—and something else, like something being dragged.

" 'Company,' I said to Smoke, 'let's check 'em out.'

"I pushed my chair back, and the two of us went to the lab door. Just as I turned the knob, I heard the stairwell door swing open at the far end of the hall. Smoky and I stepped out, and we heard a shhh-thump, shhh-thump, shhh-thump on the stairs, going down.

" 'Hey, wait!' I called out, but no one answered. Just the rhythmic shhh-thump, shhh-thump, shhh-thump going down toward the second floor.

" 'Come on, Smoke!' I shouted. The two of us, we broke into a run. We slid at the end of the hall to make the turn to the stairwell. Below, I heard the second-floor stairwell door open, and now there were feet running down the hall below us, in the opposite direction, away from Smoky and me. I took the steps four at a time and leaped the railing to the second-floor landing.

"At the far end of the hall, I heard a key rattling in a door lock. Someone threw a door open, and, as Smoky and I burst into the hall, I heard something being flung through the air and glass shattering."

The old man sucked in his breath. "Ahead I saw the door to Doctor Epson's office open. Smoky and I raced for it. 'Doctor Epson, is that you?' I called out. 'You all right?'

"We were twenty feet from his office, ten, then five. Smoky and I burst in."

The old man glanced over the student's shoulder, to see if the counterman was listening. "It was black as a villain's heart in there. I fumbled for the light switch and found one on the wall, next to the doorjamb. I slammed the switch up, and light flooded the room—an empty room. There was no one there."

He pushed his foot forward on the linoleum and then back. "Something crunched under my shoe, friend, as I stepped toward the desk. I looked down. The floor was littered with all kinds of junk and papers. Everything that had been on Doctor Epson's desk and in his glass-front bookcase was on the floor. Looked like a hurricane had gone through.

"I leaned back against the wall, my chest heaving as my lungs sucked for air. Finally, finally, I gasped out, 'If anyone's behind the desk, gawddammit, show yourself. You can't get out.'

"All I heard was me breathing and Smoky panting. I said to Smoke, 'Come on. If he won't come out, we'll have to go back there and get him.' "He put his hand on the student's knee. He gripped it. "Friend, we picked our way through the debris of books and old test papers, and I leaned over the desk as Smoky came around the side. No one was there, just more books on the floor, some thumb drives and—who threw the rough draft of my dissertation around the office? Pages and charts from my third chapter were everywhere.

"I reached down, friend, to salvage the pages." He aimed his pointer finger at the floor between the student's feet. "A medallion winked up at me through the mess, one that Doctor Epson had received last year for being the advisor to the region's top student civil engineering chapter.

"When I retrieved the medallion, I heard something above me, whispering through the air." The old man twisted around and looked up. "A black plastic trash bag glided left, then right, seesawing down through the air like a falling leaf.

"A bell dinged in the hallway. Smoky spun around— the elevator's bell, signaling that the elevator had arrived on our floor. Shhhhhh-shump!" He pulled the fingertips of his hands apart, then rammed them back together. "The door opened and closed. I heard the motor whir. So I grabbed the medallion, and we ran out of the office, to the elevator. I saw the light flash on behind the number three.

" 'Come on, Smoke,' I said, 'let's take the stairs!'

"We ran down a side hallway, and I flung open the stairwell door. Smoky and I took the steps three at a time. I stopped him at the top landing. 'Quiet. Listen,' I whispered.

"Nothing. Nothing but graveyard silence."

The old man rested his forearms on his thighs. "Friend, I got down on my hands and knees, and I pushed open the stairwell door. Smoke and I, we started through the doorway, but something caught at my pant leg. I yanked, yanked hard and something ripped, and my leg came free. I reached back. I felt a tear in my trouser leg. My knee stuck out through it." He gripped the patch below his knee, showed the sewing job.

"Smoky and me, we crept down the side hallway. When we got near the corner, I heard a low growling beside me. I turned, and the hair on the back of Smoky's neck bristled. He stood there, stiff legged.

"Slowly, cautiously, friend, ever so cautiously, I leaned out 'til I could see around the corner. And there was nothing there. The hall was empty.

He leaned back in his chair. " 'It's okay,' I said to no one in particular, 'we're alone.' "

He came forward again. "Only when I stood up did I realize, friend, that something was wrong. I glanced back around the corner. The computer lab where I had been working was dark, but I hadn't turned the light out, I know I hadn't. I edged around the corner, and a light snapped on in the lab.

"I knelt in front of Smoky and pulled his face to mine. 'Someone's playing one hellaciously elaborate game with us, Smoke,' I said. 'Let's go see who the dumbhead is.'

"The clicking of keys on a computer keyboard came from the room. Whoever it was, I knew he was one fast typist, and that ruled out Den. Well, we strolled down to the door like we owned the building, and again that low growl welled up beside me. I glanced down at Smoke. The hair on his neck and the full length of his back stood on end. 'Cut that out,' I said. 'It's just another student in there.' "

He rapped on the student's knee. "I opened the door and called out, 'Hey, fella, who're you to be working so late?' But whoever it was didn't answer. He just kept typing.

" 'Hey, didn't you hear me?' I asked as I went down the aisle toward the computer where someone sat hammering away at the keyboard. But still he didn't answer. I thought, 'This guy's really into whatever he's working on.'

"When I came up behind him, I put my hand on his shoulder and shook him. I leaned down. 'You supposed to be here this late?' I asked.

"The man swung around. He glared at me, his eyes a fiery red, and I felt Epson's medallion turn white hot in my hand. I leapt back. I dropped the medallion. When it hit the carpet, it burned a hole right through it. I glanced up at the computer, and whoever had been there was gone. But a message blinked on the screen, friend, a message blinked on the screen.

"I forced myself into the chair, and I read it." The old man spread his hands as if to show what was in front of him. "I read it, friend, the message: 'I rule the night at Perkins Hall, not you.'

"I learned in close, trying to see behind the electric words. But all I saw in the screen was my reflection, an image that at that moment fascinated me. I became lost in it.

"Then, friend, as if someone had rammed an icicle into my gut, I sucked in wind. 'Smoke,' I said, 'my hair. It's white!' " He raked his hands back through his hair. " 'Smoke,' I said, 'my hair's always been as black as yours.' You see, friend, I'm only twenty-six. But when I turned to Smoky, he was white as an Alaskan winter."

The tension washed from the ancient's body. He slumped in his chair.

During the telling of the story, other students, by twos and threes and some alone, had drifted out of the lunchroom. The place emptied, except for Ray at the sink, washing dishes, impervious to his last guests.

Silent seconds slipped away from eternity's mantle clock.

The student arched an eyebrow. "Old man, are you pulling my leg?"

The old man looked over to the counterman. "Ray, would you let my dog in? Smoky, he's just outside the door."

The counterman came away from the sink, wiping his hands on his apron. "You promise to keep him out of my kitchen? The health inspector would raise hell if he knew I let a dog in here." He went to the front door and pushed it open. "Come on, old Touser. Your master wants to see you."

A white dog shambled in. After it spied the old man, the dog went to him, sat down and laid its head on the old man's lap.

The student motioned at the dog. "This doesn't prove anything. That dog's an albino. I've seen albinos."

Anger flashed across the old man's face. "Then look at this."

He held up his right hand, the palm out. There seared into the flesh, a reddish black mark the size of a dime. "Epson's medallion did that."

"Oh come on—"

"Give me your hand!"

The student couldn't stop himself.

The old man pushed himself up. He grabbed the student by the wrist and yanked him from his chair. He slapped something into the student's open hand. "Here! Epson's medallion."

He curled the student's fingers closed over the medal.

The student screamed.

He threw the medallion down and watched it scorch the lunchroom's linoleum.

Note: The Soviet Union came apart in 1991, leaving the surviving government of Russia essentially broke. If you need money, what do you do? You have a sale.

Junk Sale
– 1993 –

TUBBY SMITH, occupying a bar stool at the Nevermind Tap, turned a page in the Janesville Gazette. He nudged his compatriot, Ott Fleming. "Ott, would ya look at this."

Fleming gazed into his beer.

Tubby nudged him again. "Hey, look at this.

"What?"

"This." He stabbed a finger at a story on the world news page.

Fleming leaned in. He read the headline and raised an eyebrow. "A Russian junk sale?"

"Yeah, space junk. They want to sell a moon lander and a rover they never used and a whole bunch of other stuff. Think about it."

"Think about what?"

"Ott, are you dumb or what? We've got us a genuine astronaut right here in Wisconsin, Deke Slayton. Old three-fingers Deke flew in space as a part of the Apollo-Soyuz mission back in 'Seventy-five. He worked with the

Jerry Peterson

Ruskies, man."

"So?"

Tubby closed his newspaper. "Up there in Sparta, in Deke's hometown, they're gonna build a Deke Slayton museum. We could buy this stuff, Ott. We could buy this stuff for the museum. They're already set to get a bunch of stuff from NASA."

Tubby dug out his wallet. He dumped out a bunch of bills and change and counted it. "The newspaper story said that New York auction house, they've set an opening bid of five million dollars. I've got twenty-three dollars and eighty-six cents here. That's a start, man. How much have you got?"

"Enough for another beer."

Tubby swatted Fleming in the shoulder. "Be serious here, man."

"I am serious. Look, maybe you could talk Ruthie here into lettin' you put a collection jar out on the bar. In a couple months, you might have two, three hundred dollars, maybe enough to buy a poster or a Russian space glove."

Tubby went back to his own beer. "That's not much."

"But it's somethin'. Maybe they could have Deke's space glove shake hands with the Russian space glove. Make quite a picture, wouldn't it?"

"Yeah. Yeah, maybe it would. But it would be a whole lot better to get that eight-wheeled Russian moon buggy and have a dummy in Deke's space suit leaning against it."

Note: The Rose Bowl, the Wisconsin Badgers vs. the University of California Los Angeles Bruins.

Game of a Lifetime
– 1994 –

TUBBY SMITH taped a PROPERTY OF T.H. SMITH sign, SIT HERE AT YOUR OWN RISK, to a bar stool at the Nevermind Tap. He stepped back and admired it. "Think I paid for this stool with all the beers I've bought in the past year, wouldn'tcha say, Ruthie?"

She only shook her head while she filled a pilsner glass with Leinenkugel Canoe Paddler, a commercial playing on the television set above the bar that all ignored. "Hey, Virgil," she called out and slid the beer down the bar to the waiting patron.

The picture on the TV changed to that of a football field, the voice of a sportscaster coming out of the set: "This is Keith Jackson back with you. We're well into the fourth quarter here at the Rose Bowl, Wisconsin leading, but not by much, only five points, fourteen to nine."

Tubby and the others in this retreat from domestic harmony or disharmony looked up at the set, the two teams lined up against one another.

"Wisconsin has the football," Jackson said. "There's

the snap from center Cory Raymer. The quarterback, Darrel Bevell, has the ball. He's dancing around, looking for a receiver to his right."

"Come on, Cory!" someone yelled.

"No one's open," Jackson rambled on. "He's running now, running to his left, running for daylight. Whoa Nellie! Bevell lays a lick on a Bruins tackler and gallops on by him, the crowd going wild."

Someone threw a bowl of Cheetos in the air as others at the bar hooted and hollered, drowning out the TV. Tubby jumped up. He knocked over his beer as he did, whooping, doing his version of the north woodsmen's stomp, waving a hand above his head.

Ruthie-the-bartender cranked the volume up on the television, Jackson bellowing, "Oh Mother, that kid's never run with a football in all his life and look what he did. Unbelievable! All right, now, they're lined up for the point after. There's the snap. John Hall kicks it. It's going, going, gone straight through the uprights. Wisconsin now leads the Bruins twenty-one to nine."

Tubby brushed his hair back as he sat back down. "The game's not over yet, Ruthie, but I think we're gonna take it. First time for us bein' back in Pasadena in thirty-two years. How about another beer?"

She threw him a bar rag that slapped him in the side of the face. "Clean up your mess first," she said.

He did, watching the screen and the kickoff, UCLA's run back to the Wisconsin twelve, a pitchout to halfback Ricky Davis and his run for a touchdown.

Tubby moaned. He put his head down on his arm on the bar.

"And there's the point after," Jackson said over the television. "The game tightens in the final minutes. Wisconsin twenty-one, UCLA sixteen. This Bruins team came into the Rose Bowl as the odds-on favorite. Their quarterback's dangerous. He's already passed for two hundred eighty-eight yards in this game."

Tubby pulled his jacket over his head rather than watch the next kickoff. Wisconsin received, only to give the ball over after four plays, having been backed up to their eighteen yard line.

"Twenty seconds to go," Jackson announced.

Tubby lifted a portion of his jacket that had covered one eye.

"There's the snap," Jackson called. "UCLA quarterback Wayne Cook breaks into a run. Holey-moley, Archie Bunker, look at that. He's brought down on the Wisconsin fifteen, after a gain of only three yards. The Bruins go into a quick set, but there's the final gun. Wisconsin wins. Wisconsin wins! Their first win in four appearances in the Rose Bowl."

Tubby hollered out his yahoo. He flung his jacket away as he swivelled away from the bar only to be doused in beer by the bartender, Ruthie.

"If I had a pitcher of Gatorade," she said, "I would have doused you with that. But all I had was Pabst."

Tubby licked the beer dripping from his mustache. "Not bad, Ruthie. It's sure not Leinenkugel's, but it's not bad. Now I suppose you want me to mop the floor."

Note: Michael Jordan quit the Chicago Bulls in 1993, after nine years with the team, three of those years in which he helped the Bulls win the NBA championship. He quit. A lot of fans thought it wasn't worth the time to watch basketball anymore.

Michael is Back
– 1995 –

TUBBY SMITH leaned against his bar mate at the Nevermind, Conner Brown, the two popping back beer nuts as they watched ESPN's SportsCenter, Suzy Kolber in the anchor chair.

Tubby winked at Conner. "Suzy's some looker, don'tcha think? But she could do with a push-up bra."

Ruthie-the-bartender slapped a wet rag on the bar in front of Tubby, startling him. "You are one sexist pig, Tub."

"Hey, it's you who said you wouldn't mind getting in bed with Suzy's co-anchor, Keith Olbermann, you an old married woman."

"Oh, shut yer trap or I'll get Eddie out here to bounce you out the door."

Tubby waved his hand in front of Ruthie. "Shh-shh-shh. Look up on the screen. They've got a picture of

Michael Jordan up there."

Kolber's voice came through the set: "This announcement in in just the last few minutes. His Airness is back. Michael Jordan has come out of retirement to rejoin the Chicago Bulls."

Whistles came from several at the bar.

Tubby bumped Conner's shoulder. "Hey, we've got reason to watch b-ball again."

Conner looked down into his beer. "I kinda liked watching him play minor league baseball. I liked watching him miss catches and strike out."

"What?"

"Yeah, King MJ needed to be knocked down a peg or three. He got rich, rich, and richer playing basketball, but he never did a thing for us blacks."

Elbow on the bar, Tubby propped the side of his head against his knuckles. "Are you some kind of racist or something? He was great for the Bulls and all of us who watched him. He'll be great again."

Conner looked up from his beer. "Name me one thing he's done for us people in the black community. He's never once demonstrated with us, never once picked up a picket sign. He's never spoke out for better pay or fair treatment for us. He never even went into south Chicago to help his people there—my people—get out of the damn slums, get us something better than the cinderblock apartments at Cabrini Green."

Tubby stared at Conner. "You're bitter, man."

"You would be, too, if you were black." He slid a bill onto the bar. He pushed it to Ruthie. "Apply it to my tab, babe. I'm goin' home."

Tubby gazed after him as he left.

Ruthie sidled over. "Tub, I'll bet back in the 'Seventies you watched *All in the Family*, you and Archie Bunker."

"Yeah, I did," he said, his gaze following Conner turn up the sidewalk and move past the Nevermind's plate glass window. "Liked it, too. Those were the days."

Note: The weather can really ruin your day.

Nobody Hits a Hummer
– 1996 –

TUBBY SMITH pushed into The Nevermind Tap and up to the bar. There, as he wiped a glaze of mist from his glasses with his handkerchief, he parked himself on his regular stool.

The bartender came over, Dwight who sometimes subbed for Ruthie. He slapped a coaster on the bar. "The usual?" he asked.

"Not a Leinie. Not tonight. Make it a Dirty Momma."

Dwight pulled up the ingredients—brandy, coffee liqueur, and half-and-half, that from the underbar fridge—and set about pouring them over ice. "How's the weather out there?"

"Soup. Froggy foggy soup. I had to drive with my head out the window. Thank God, there were no nuts out there."

The bartender set the finished drink on the coaster. "Well, you've got that Hummer. You're safe."

Tubby sipped his Dirty Momma. "Better be. I just got it out of the shop. Last week, I got rammed in the rear coming here."

"Oh, so that's why we didn't see you." Dwight picked a pilsner glass out of the sink and stripped off the water. With a clean towel, he polished the glass dry.

Tubby bent over his drink, stirring what remained with his finger. "I bought that big honker of a beast, figuring the wife and me would be safe in it. But that car is an accident magnet. Deer run into it. I've been sideswiped by a school bus. Little old ladies step off the curb in front of me. But tonight, thank you very much, everybody's home."

"Seems like. You're the only one who's been in in the last hour."

Tubby tossed his drink back and banged the glass on the bar. "Hit me again. I'm gonna be here a while. I came to watch the Badgers whip Purdue on your monster TV."

The bartender took the glass back. He dropped it in the sink and set out a fresh one, put some ice in it. As he reached for the brandy, a deliveryman in a Miller's jacket and ball cap slammed the front door open. He hauled off his gloves. "Who's got the Hummer out there?"

Tubby raised a finger.

"Sorry, buddy, we got freezing stuff with this fog. My beer truck, when I was turning in, I slid . . . right into your car. Crushed one of your fenders."

Tubby motioned to Dwight, beckoning him in close. "Skip my drink," he said. "Just gimme the bottle."

Note: When I was in graduate school at the University of Tennessee and a member of the Knoxville Writers Guild, we talked a lot about Cormac McCarthy. He grew up in Knoxville, and at this time he was making his way as a novelist, although some of his stuff was hard to read. He won a National Book Award for his 1992 novel *All the Pretty Horses* and, eventually, in 2007, the Pulitzer Prize for Fiction for his novel *The Road*. McCarthy was and is a minimalist, writing with an economy of words and a focus on surface description. The story you're about to read is an experiment on my part, a challenge to see whether I could write in the minimalist style McCarthy exemplifies.

The Diary
– 1997 –

HE STOPPED at Hardee's for breakfast, went through the drive-up lane for a sausage, egg, and cheese biscuit and white milk—why the restaurant chain never stocked chocolate milk was beyond him—and drove on. He ate in the car while rolling up the miles, heading for Champaign to see his younger brother, steering with his knees when he had to twist the cap off the milk chug.

A semi passed by in the opposing lane, throwing slush from last night's snow up on his windshield. He flicked on the wipers.

He had a date to see his brother, to spend the weekend doing the bars that lined the main drag in Campustown. They hadn't been together since Christmas, a sad time because their parents had died in a car crash the month before.

Finished with breakfast, he crumpled his sandwich's wrapper and tossed it over his shoulder into the backseat where it fell among a litter of balled-up napkins, pizza boxes, and Pepsi cups.

A sign came up at the side of the highway: five miles to his exit. Time to call, he told himself, and brought up speed dial for his brother on his cell. Seven rings and no answer. Where the hell are you, Siddy? he wondered. You pull an all-nighter and you're not home yet?

He followed another car onto the exit, a Buick of recent vintage. Somebody else headed for the university? Very likely, he thought.

A mile into the city, he cut away from the Buick. He veered off onto the first of a rat's maze of side streets that led eventually to the two-bedroom rancher where his brother lived, where he had lived when he had gone to the U of I, a house their parents had bought for them so they wouldn't have the expense of a dorm and the cafeteria.

Twenty-three thirty-five AS Lane, there is was. Nobody knew what the A-S stood for. His father, a life-long Democrat, told anyone who would listen that it was Adlai Stevenson Drive. He had a sign made up that proclaimed that and staked it up on the berm next to the driveway.

Parked beside the house was his brother's Yugo. He got it for a buck when his Dodge Dart gave up the ghost.

The Yugo ran . . . sometimes. When it didn't, he called his brother to bring his tool box and fix it. He hadn't called about the car this time.

He parked behind the Yugo, slung his backpack over his shoulder, and meandered to the front door. No need to knock. He had his own key, so he let himself in.

Siddy, he hollered, you decent?

No answer.

He closed the door and worked his way inside, stepping over discarded hiker boots and an abandoned parka. He moved past a brick-and-board bookcase and the godawful purple- and green-striped futon that Siddy had found behind a dorm after move-out day last spring. From the front room, he went to the kitchen.

No Siddy.

Not in the bathroom, either. He stopped there, annoyed by water dripping in the sink. He twisted the handle hard on the cold water faucet. His brother never seemed to do that. Next trip he'd have to bring a pipe wrench, get into the guts of the faucet, and replace the worn washers.

He went onto the first bedroom. There was Siddy asleep with his back to him. He shook his brother's shoulder.

Siddy?

No answer.

He pulled on his brother's shoulder, rolled him over. He wasn't breathing.

Siddy?

He laid the back of his hand on his brother's forehead.

Cold.

He touched his fingers to his brother's carotid.

Cold, also, and no pulse.

Omigod—

He dropped his backpack and tapped nine-one-one into his cell.

Emergency Center, a voice said.

This is Hugh Warrington at twenty-three thirty-five AS Lane. My brother's dead. What should I do?

Stay where you are, she said as if this were routine. I'll dispatch an officer and the EMTs.

He clicked off. Maybe he shouldn't have. If he had kept the call going, he would have someone to talk to while waiting.

He gazed around the room. There on a makeshift desk by his brother's computer, a computer Siddy had built himself—the kid was an electronics wizard—was his brother's diary.

He picked it up. He paged into it, to yesterday's date. I am so hungry, Siddy had written in block letters, the letters a bit squiggly. He had never learned cursive. I haven't eaten for three days. Will this ever end? I am so broke. I have no money.

But he had a job, at Perkins. And at Christmas he had said the tips were good. He could keep up with his college expenses, except for a doctor's bill back in the fall when he had come down with walking pneumonia.

He paged back, stopping at an entry that read Fired, the entry two Mondays before. Fired, it said, for stealing food. I had to, it said. I am only sorry I got caught.

When had money gotten so tight for him? He had never complained. He had never asked for help.

Back at Christmas, now that he thought about it, his brother looked thin, thinner than usual, like he had been losing weight. Now, as he laid there in the bed, he looked like a stick figure.

The diary—he stuffed it in his backpack—the police don't need to see this.

———

THERE WAS the funeral followed by a struggle to make sense of the incomprehensible, a struggle that went on day after day when he wasn't working. After three months, he gave up on the struggle. He just shelved it. He made a daytrip up north to where his parents had been buried. There, alone in the cemetery, he dug a hole between the two graves and inserted the urn that held his brother's ashes. If there was anything to feel good about it was here. It was now. His parents were together with their son.

Except for Uncle Glenn in Milwaukee—his dad's brother, a bachelor—there was no one else. On his mother's side, all were dead.

If he didn't have children, he was the end of the family line. And one day, he, too, would be planted here.

Depressing.

On the drive back home, he decided to get on with his life, to quit his job and move to Chicago, to start over. To dwell endlessly on all this stuff, one could go crazy.

And crazy he didn't want to be.

YOU NEVER talk about your brother, she said as she picked at her broccoli salad.

He looked up from the steak he was cutting. Where did that question come from? It had been five years since Siddy had died. She came into his life only a year ago, so she never knew him.

Siddy would have been wild over her. She was a beauty. Slender, long legs. Her face and figure got her modeling job after modeling job. Some of the assignments took her to Europe.

That's where they had met, in Paris where she was on a shoot and he was in the city, checking into a possible acquisition for his employer. And now they were living together in a condo in the east Marina Tower—the East Corncob some Chicagoans called it—talking about maybe getting married.

My brother? he asked.

Yes, you've got his gee-dee high school graduation picture on the mantle. When I get tired of it and hide it, you find it and drag it out again. But you won't talk about him.

What's there to talk about? He died.

When?

Five years ago.

Of what?

Do you want the God's honest truth?

Yes.

He stared at her salad, at the tiny bit on her fork. How much have you eaten? he asked.

Enough.

Three bites? I've eaten half my steak, all of my salad, and I'm looking forward to the peach pie I brought home from Trader Joe's. Are you anorexic?

What?

Anorexia nervosa.

I'm just being careful what I eat.

So you don't gain weight.

Yes, and maybe lose some. Marta took me aside at the agency the other day and told me if I want to advance in this business I have to lose fifteen pounds.

Lose fifteen pounds? You're six feet tall, a hundred and thirty pounds. That would take you down to one fifteen. You're starving yourself to death.

But if I want to get the cover of Vogue, if I want to snag a contract to be the spokesperson for an international beauty products line, I've got to do it.

He laid his knife and fork aside. And his napkin as well. Then you'll do it without me, Babe. You wanted to know how Siddy died. He died of starvation. I can't watch you do the same thing. I can't take that again.

He left the table.

In the front hallway, he placed his key on the Melange Cooper credenza—a three-thousand-dollar purchase—and walked out of the condo.

Note: I like detective stories. Meet The Fish.

The Fish and the Case of the Big Beefers
– 1998 –

THE FISH—Hymie Wallerstein of Wallerstein & Crooke Discrete Investigations—occupied his usual spot, the back booth in The Pagoda, putting down his third jelly-filled mint snickerdoodle cupcake and eavesdropping, the latter a habit.

An ugly habit.

A voice that sounded like a slow-turning sander ground through from the booth behind him. "They won't pay up."

They? When people talked about 'they,' The Fish always wondered who 'they' were.

"Da brodders?" another voice asked, this one wheezy, "At dat donut joint?"

The Fish knew of only one—the Donut Shack, operated by the Smith Brothers, Tom, Dick, and Wendell.

"I say we get 'um tonight," the sander said.

The grunts of a couple heavyweights pushing themselves off bench seats came next, followed by the sound of size fourteens slapping up the aisle, toward the cash register.

He didn't owe the Smith Brothers anything, but thought he ought to check it out. So The Fish laid a fin on the table and scribbled a note at the bottom of the check: "Whatever's left is your tip."

Note finished, he departed by the back door.

Sweet Sue came by. She picked up the cash and the check, and, as she read The Fish's note and did the calculation—a twelve-cent tip—she said something awful under her breath.

THE FISH preferred to do his checking at night, figuring if the big beefers were going 'to get' the brothers, they'd do it in the dark. So he sat parked across the street from The Shack in his dollar Lincoln—he had bought the old girl with her suicide doors for a buck from Sid Abramovitz's wrecking yard, to save her from the crusher. The Fish fiddled with the tuner, settling on a Public Radio station and Peter Van De Graaff's all-night classical music show . . . some German orchestra playing the overture from *Der Fledermaus.*

A car cruised into the alley next to The Shack, the car's lights going out.

The Fish pressed the button on the side of his Rollex knock-off. That illuminated the time . . . two thirty-one. He punched off the radio, ran his window down, and heard car doors open and close. In the dim light from the lone bulb above The Shack's alley door, he saw someone with a pry bar break in.

The Fish slipped out of his car. He trotted across the street, checking his blaster to make sure he had rammed a full magazine into the pistol grip. At the alley door, The Fish skinned inside, into the bakery. He inhaled the heavenly aromas of rising dough and sweet frosting . . . and something else, something putrid.

Gasoline.

A match flamed up.

"Drop the match," The Fish bellowed, "and I'll fill ya full a holes."

The light snuffed out. In the dark, someone whammed into him, The Fish's gun going off, hitting something above. He felt himself going over, felt himself falling into something soft, felt, as he laid there, something wet drizzle onto his forehead.

The door from the store side slammed open, and an overhead light came on. "What's going on in here?" someone hollered.

"Wendell?"

"Fish?"

"I'm over here in your flour bin."

A small guy came up in his baker whites, a baseball bat in his hand. "What the—"

"Wendy, a couple a hoods was tryin' to set fire to yer place."

"And you thought you'd help out by jumping in my flour? You know how much you ruined?"

The Fish pulled himself out of the bin. He looked like a ghost, a ghost with chocolate syrup half covering his face. "Think yer brothers would mind if I billed ya for gettin' my suit cleaned?"

Note: Get out the Windex. It's time you cleaned your crystal ball.

2024 — Return to the Moon
– 1999 –

LEM PILOT Ross Stonewell touched the transmit button on the side of his helmet. "Nashville Control," he said, "Space Trax One on the moon at Base Taurus-Littrow. I can see the rover right where the old Apollo Seventeen crew left it."

"Roger, LEM."

"You suppose the key's still in the ignition?"

"Our Freedom of Information request got us Seventeen's complete flight record. We found a note in it that indicates the key's there. LEM crew, Auntie Mae says you're cleared to exit the lander. Get out the spare batteries and explore."

Stonewell and his co-pilot, Claire Holms, unbuckled their seat belts and shoulder harnesses.

Holms kicked the release that both opened the hatch outward and lowered a ladder to the surface of the moon.

She moved toward the hatch, but Stonewell put his hand out. "Sweetie," he said, "never you forget who's the commander of this flight. I go first."

He skinned out through the hatch and onto the ladder. There he hopped down three rungs at a time. At the bottom, standing in the dust of eons, Stonewell caught the tool bag that Holms tossed to him. While she climbed down, he helped himself to the two lithium-ion batteries strapped to a leg of the lander and bounced off toward the rover last used fifty-two years ago.

At the rover, he lifted both seats back. That exposed the cases that contained the expired batteries. Stonewell tried the latches on first one case, then the other, and found them frozen.

"This calls for my Doctor Who sonic screwdriver," he said to Holms watching from beyond his shoulder. Stonewell rustled in his tool bag. He brought out a ballpeen hammer and whanged first one latch, then the other on the first case, breaking off both latches. The front panel fell away. He did the same surgery on the second battery case.

Stonewell pulled the dead battery out the passenger's side case. He slammed a new one in and tossed the dead battery on the pile of junk left behind by the Apollo Seventeen crew. He threw away the old battery from the driver's side as well and shoved in the remaining new one.

"Claire," he said to his second, "the panel that holds the battery in here, jam it in place and I'll duct tape it. Gimme my trusty ballpeen and duct tape, and I can fix anything."

Stonewell produced a roll of silver tape from his tool bag. He tore off two lengths and slapped them across the ends of the panel and along the sides of the case while his partner kept a gloved hand on the panel so it wouldn't move. Again, with his partner's help, he did the same to the panel for the case beneath the passenger's seat.

He motioned at the ignition. "Pard, they did leave a key. How about you turn it and let's see if this here antique's gonna work."

She went around to the driver's side. There Holms climbed aboard and twisted the key. The needles on both battery meters snapped to the top of the green.

She gave a thumbs-up.

Stonewell settled himself in the passenger seat. "Claire, I forgot my driver's license. You brought yours, didn't you?"

"It's in the LEM," she said.

"Just like a woman."

That drew a death stare from Holms. After some moments, she turned away from him. "Where to, El Hefe?"

"I saw something a couple miles off to the west on our first fly-over that I want to see up close. Something rounded, not like the rocks and boulders we've got around here. Just looked out of place."

"Okey-dokey."

Stonewell waved off toward the horizon "See that pinnacle? The map showed a pass next to it. You ought to be able to drive up out of this basin, through that pass and down into the next crater."

Holms pushed forward on the T-lever. The rover responded, creeping away. She pushed the T-lever further forward, boosting the speed of the car to a spritely six miles an hour. "You know," she said. "driving this thing on Earth is nothing like driving up here in such low gravity. This is some dune buggy."

The car bounced over a handful of small rocks, startling Stonewell. He cinched down his seatbelt. "Sweetie, just don't tip us over or break an axle. It can be one ding-dang darling of a long walk back to the lander."

"You worried, Mother?"

"If I was, kiddo, I wouldn't let you drive."

STONEWELL and Holms sat at the top of the ridge, gazing downslope into the next crater.

"Is that what I think it is?" she asked.

"Get us down there and we'll check it out."

Holms eased forward on the T-lever, inching the rover into a pokey two miles an hour as she guided it down and through a litter of boulders that separated her from the target. Fifteen minutes in and she drew up beside it.

Stonewell stared at the humped form. "Damn, it's a VW Beetle. Where the hell did that come from?"

"Looks like it's been here a long time, Chief. See how thick the dust layer is on it."

Stonewell dismounted. He swept away the dust on the driver's side of the windshield and peered in.

Holms went around to the back of the car. "Boss Man, see anything in there?"

"Yeah."

"A little green man, maybe?"

"No. A metal plate on the driver's seat. I can see writing on it." Stonewell opened the door. He brought the plate out into the full light of the sun. By the color, the plate appeared to be bronze. "Damn, Claire, this is a garble. I think maybe it's German."

Stonewell knelt at the back of the car. "That figures, my capitan. The license plate here, TX-forty four-fifty one. TX, that's Karl Marx Stad. That was a state in old East Germany."

"You know Duetsch?"

"Yah." She pushed up.

He handed her the plate.

Holms ran her hand over the lettering. She sucked in a breath. "Alpha Dog, are you ready for this?"

"Am I gonna like it?"

"I don't know. It says 'Kommandant Klaus Von Richter and Haupt Hannah Meuller were here, Seven September Sixty-one dash Nine September Sixty-one. Flight inspired by United States President J.F. Kennedy. If you have found this, you have found history.' My God."

She looked up at Stonewell, her mouth agape. "Do you suppose this was their moon rover?"

Stonewell put his hand on top of the car. "If it is, how the hell did they get it up here, and why the hell don't we know anything about it? Claire, it's time we called home."

Note: The assignment in one of my writers groups was to write a short short story in the first person. Perhaps you've been stopped for speeding, and you've had to explain yourself to the cop who's standing beside your car, tapping his ticket book on the edge of your rolled-down window. We were given thirty seconds to come up with an idea, so most of us around the table cast back in our lives for something, a real incident we could hang a story on. For me,my incident happened in Arizona.

I Only Tried to Help
– 2000 –

OFFICER, I know what it looks like, but I wasn't trying to jack the guy's car. And who would want to jack an old Yugo anyway. Now if it were a Lexus—

But back to what happened. I was filling my truck with gas, and he was at a pump at the next island. He had just finished. He was driving off, and I saw this gasoline pouring out of the filler pipe of his car because he hadn't put the gas cap on. He had set the cap on the roof, Sir, and forgot it. I saw it slide off as he drove away.

I do mean gas was pouring out of his car. It was a torrent, splashing everywhere. I could see that if his tailpipe dragging on the concrete sparked, it could ignite the whole thing.

Sir, I just couldn't let that happen, not in good conscience. I couldn't let him turn himself into a crispy critter, so I raced after him.

I caught up with him before he got to the street. I'm there beating on his window to make him stop, but he wouldn't. He glared at me as he clung to his steering wheel like it was a life preserver. In that glare of his, I saw fear, Officer. Maybe he was afraid of me because he didn't know me. I was a stranger. Anyway, I did what seemed right. I ripped his door open and hauled him out before his car could catch fire. It became an awful fight right there on the tarmac, me trying to save him and him trying I guess to get away. We were wrestling there, rolling around, pounding on one another . . . and that's when you drove up.

Honest Injun, Sir, that's what happened.

What? You're an Arapaho?

I'm being disrespectful?

I thought with your hawk nose and your deep tan you were an Iraqi refugee who got on with sheriff's department.

Follow you to the station? What about this guy here I was trying to save from becoming a human torch? Aren't you at least gonna ticket him for public endangerment?

Endangering who? Himself. Me. The whole frickin' truckstop if his car had blown up! Really. And destruction of personal property—he tore my new work jacket. I paid forty-three ninety-five for this two days ago back in Wisconsin at the F&F Boutique.

What's the F&F Boutique? What rock have you been living under, Sir? Farm & Fleet. Everybody knows that.

The backseat of your cruiser?

What?

Now?

Note: It's back to my writers group. This time the assignment was to build a short short story around the prompt a tough day at the office or on the job for either you or a fictional character.

No Sympathy
– 2001 –

HE SWUNG into the Nevermind on crutches, a cast on one leg and a patch bandage covering an ear, and hoisted himself up on a stool.

Dwight, the man behind the bar, stared at the new arrival. "Tubby, what the hell happened to you?"

"I gotta have a beer first," he said. "Make it a Spotted Cow."

"Draft or bottle?"

"Heck fire, man, I don't come here for something I can buy at the Jiffy Mart."

Dwight took down a pilsner glass from the overhead rack. He slipped the glass under the tap and hauled back on its handle. "So what happened that you've got this cast and bandage and those crutches?"

"Would you believe it, Dwight buddy, I fell off the garden house I'm building for my wife."

Jerry Peterson

The bartender raked off the overflowing head before he passed the glass across to his patron. "Fell off that house, huh?"

Tubby sucked down half his Cow. As he set his glass back on the bar, he licked flecks of foam from his mustache. "Man, I needed that. Yeah, today I was shingling, doing fine until that Gladys, that gal who works at the post office—you know her, she's built like, ummff—anyway, she's my neighbor. She comes out in her bikini, I guess to work on her tan, and she gives me this little wave."

Tubby downed the rest of his Cow. "Well, I was twisting around to get a better look as I wave back, and that's when I slipped. I'm up there flailing my arms like a turkey trying to fly, trying to get my balance back, and my nailer in my hand goes off like a machinegun, firing a half-dozen roofing nails into my foot."

Dwight leaned on the bar, a bar rag in his hand, hooked by the story.

"I'm really yowling now," Tubby said, punching the line with his fist. "I trip on the eave as I'm throwing my nailer away and go over the edge and down eight feet, falling onto my wheelbarrow on my shin. I hear this cracking, and I know what that means. I end up on the ground on my back like some turtle, grasping my leg, howling, and she comes running. Thank God, she's got her cell."

"Her cell." Dwight said, bunching up his bar rag. "In that skimpy outfit, where'd she have it?"

"I don't know, man. Anyway, she calls nine-one-one for me, and they dispatch an ambulance."

Dwight, now with his elbows parked on the bar, leaned in even closer. "Tub, the EMTs don't come in a snap of your fingers. Whaddja do while waiting?"

340

"Cried a lot, I guess. Then she sees my ear's bleeding—I banged it or scraped it somehow—and she puts this hankie on it. She holds it there. She's real close, an' I'm getting this one helluva view." Tubby cupped his hands in front of his chest. "And that's when the ambulance crew arrives. My crew. You know I'm a volunteer EMT with the fire department."

"Your crew, huh? Well, that's good," Dwight said.

"No, that's bad."

"Why's that, Tub?"

"They have this great big hoo-haa at the mess I'm in. I'm there in pain, bleeding, sprawled on the ground. No sympathy, man." Tubby slammed his fist on the bar, upsetting a bowl of beer nuts. "My God, Dwight, I gotta have another Cow. Make it two, no, make it three. My pain pill's wearing off."

Note: What anthology would be complete without a wedding story? I remember one wedding where, during the rehearsal, Reverend Al Simone, the pastor of my family's home church in Mukwonago, said to the bride, "This is where I ask your father if he brought the dowry, the six goats and two cows." All he got was a perplexed stare. To which he said, "I'm sorry, dear. No dowry, no wedding." And then Al smiled. Everyone got the joke, and the tension of the rehearsal was broken.

The wedding
– 2002 –

ETHYL FLIGHT, the wedding planner—consultant, she preferred to be called—her nostrils flaring, paced the porch of New Berlin's First Lutheran Church. She threw up her hands. "Whoever would let a bride go out in a car without a full tank of gas?"

Gail Willoby—the bride's mother—peered at her watch. "She didn't run out of gas. Her car broke down. She'll be here."

"But the wedding—my wedding—I've planned this wedding for months. I'll not have some silly bride ruin it by being late."

"Missus Flight, she called. The Triple A's on the way with a tow truck."

light grasped Willoby's arm. She sank her fingernails deep in the woman's flesh. "You've got to help me."

"Me? How?"

"Stand in for your daughter. We've got to get this thing going. Reverend Bjorstein's got a funeral here, right here in this very church in forty-nine and a half minutes."

The bride's mother pried the wedding planner's fingers away, one by one. "Missus Flight, I'm sure the dead man won't mind if the reverend holds the funeral back a little."

"Is that supposed to be funny? Is it? Missus Willoby, I don't allow people to be funny at my weddings." She shot to the door and fired a look inside. "Have you seen the groom? Has anyone seen the groom?"

"I sent my husband looking for him."

"I have the bridesmaids and the groomsmen ready to go." She came back to the bride's mother. "Have you seen the best man?"

"He's missing, too?"

She latched onto Missus Willoby's arm again. "Maybe I can get the groom's father to stand in for his kid. We've got to get this thing going." She dragged Missus Willoby to the door. "See there? Reverend Bjorstein's up front. Pacing like that, he's wearing a trench in the carpet. I'm going to signal the organist to start playing the wedding march."

"We don't have an organist. We have a pianist— Bunny Martin."

"I fired her. Whoever heard of a wedding without organ music? It just isn't done, certainly not at my weddings."

"But she's my daughter's best friend."

"Missus Willoby, she took it like a trouper. Now get your daughter's bouquet and stand at the end of the aisle.

And smile. I'm going to get the groom's father to go in for the groom." She pushed the mom inside.

"I don't think this is legal."

"Reverend Bjorstein won't notice the substitutions. He's almost blind, for Heaven's sake."

CARRIE WILLOBY, in her Saturday casuals—short shorts and halter top, her hair in curlers—paced beside her Kia Soul fresh from the body shop, dents removed and a new "I WANT YOU, BABE," Music Machine paint job on it.

She tapped redial while taking a drag on the toke pinched in her lips.

"Triple A," a woman's voice answered through the speaker in Willoby's cell.

She removed the toke. She held it in her fingers as she lifted her cell to her ear. "Lady, I'm still waiting for my tow truck. It's late. I'm late. Where the H-E-double L is it?"

"Please, ma'am, who is this, and where are you?"

Two quick WUP-WUPS interrupted, short bursts on a police siren. A sheriff's department patrol car, its lights flashing, rolled off onto the shoulder of the highway and up behind Willoby's car.

She cringed. She flicked her toke away into the weeds. Now it was only the stash in the glove box that worried her.

"Trouble, miss?" the deputy asked as he stepped out.

"Yes, but I've got a call in for a tow truck."

Just then a tow truck came barreling down the hill in the opposite lane, its hazard lights blazing. The truck slowed. When it got abreast of Willoby, it stopped.

The driver leaned out his window. "You called?"

"Yes."

He threw his truck into reverse and whipped it around into the northbound lane, braking short of the Kia's front bumper.

"Okey dokey, sweets, what's the prob?" the driver asked as he climbed down from the wrecker. He, tattooed from the back of his hands to his shoulders, the rest of his torso masked by a 'Here's to you' Pabst Blue Ribbon muscle shirt, went to a control panel. He pulled on a lever. The wheel lift unfolded out from the back of the truck and down to the ground. A pull on a second lever and the lift slid under the car's front wheels.

"The motor quit," Willoby said, glancing back at the deputy strolling her way. "It won't start. I've tried."

"Yah, that happens." The driver knelt by one the Kia's wheels. He strapped it to the lift, then went after the other. "If the boss man had come out—old Poppa Bopper—he'd take a peek under the hood, diagnosticate yer problem for ya, and get ya goin'."

He hopped back to the control panel. There he pushed a lever that hauled the lift closer to the truck, then a second that hoisted it and the Kia's front wheels clear of the ground. "Yup, sweets, I'm no mechanic. I just hook 'em up and haul 'em away. The Kia dealer in town for ya?"

She, uneasy, looked up at the deputy now standing beside her, his hand resting on the butt of his gun. "Driver," she said, looking back to the wrecker, "what's your name?"

"Nails."

"Nails, can you take me to church? I'm late for my wedding."

"Gettin' married today, huh? Which church?"

"First Lutheran."

"Know where that is, sweets. Why don'tcha ride up front with me? I can move some trash around, make space."

"No thanks. I have to change and comb my hair out. I can do that in my car on the way."

"Whatever rings your bell."

He slid behind the steering wheel in the truck's cab while she slipped around the deputy and into the backseat of her car.

Nails raced away, the car in tow.

Willoby watched the deputy through the rear window, the deputy growing smaller by the second. She let out a long breath, then scrunched around to the side, to her wedding dress laid out on the seat and seatback. She couldn't step into the thing in so small a space, so she wriggled it over her head. As she did, the car jolted. Willoby glanced out the window at the blur of scenery going by and wondered how fast they were going. Eighty, maybe? To her, it felt more like ninety, maybe ninety-five.

HAL GARDNER leaned against his best man, Carson Bolt, his arm around Bolt's shoulders, both disheveled in their tuxedos and each clutching a can of Miller High Life.

Gardner waved his can at his car in the ditch, a Volkswagen Beetle with a Rolls-Royce hood and grill. "I don't think we're gonna get to my weddin', do you?" he said, his words slurred.

Bolt threw back another slug. He belched. "We could call someone."

"We could if you hadn'tna challenged me to that cellphone throwin' contest." Gardner held up his beer. "How many of these have we had?"

"Dunno. We started with two six-packs at breakfast, an' one of 'um's gone an' mostta the second."

"Damn, I think I'm gonna throw up." Gardner took a step down into the ditch and heaved. He raked the slobber from his lips with his sleeve.

Two quick WUP-WUPS interrupted. An unmarked car, lights flashing in its grill, rolled off the freeway and onto the shoulder, up to Bolt.

A man in civilian clothes—a charcoal-gray suit, white shirt and tie—stepped out. "Looks like you're in a bad way," he said.

Bolt motioned with his can at Gardner. "Not as bad as my frien' there. That's his car in the ditch. We were on the way to a wedding when a turkey flew out in front of us, the biggest turkey you ever seen."

"Whose wedding, if you don't mind me asking?"

"His." Again Bolt wagged his Miller's can at Gardner still in the ditch, now bent down, his hands on his knees.

"Who is he?" the civilian asked.

"Hal Gardner."

He studied Bolt. "Your friend wouldn't happen to be marrying Carrie Willoby, would he?"

"Uh-huh."

"How about that." The civilian chuckled. "My wife and I are on our way to the same wedding. What say we give you a ride?"

Bolt flung his can away. "I'm for that." He slid down into the ditch and hauled Gardner back up. "Hal, these kind people want to give us a ride to the church. Is that good or what?"

"Yeah, tha's good."

Bolt, with the civilian's help, poured Gardner into the backseat.

"By the way," the civilian said with his hand on Gardner's shoulder, "did Carrie ever mention to you that she has an uncle who's the sheriff in this county?"

Gardner shook his head.

"She does. It's me." He went to the trunk and came back with a breathalyzer. "Breathe into this contraption for me, would you?"

Gardner did.

The sheriff put on his glasses, the better to see the reading. "Whoa there," he said, "a two point eight. That's close to a record. Tell you what, I'm gonna give you a wedding present—a ticket. Monday morning, you get to visit with the county judge."

Gardner waved his hand. "Can't. Honeymoon. We'll be in . . . where are we goin', Carse?"

"Cancun."

"Yeah, Cancun."

"Huh-uh." The sheriff squeezed Gardner's shoulder. "I'm gonna give you another wedding present. Stainless steel, made-in-the-USA, handcuffs. After the wedding, you and your drunk buddy here, you're gonna be my guests in our five-star jail."

MISSUS FLIGHT raced down the steps to Carrie Willoby backing out of her car, her car hanging from the rear of the tow truck. "Thank God, you're here," she said.

She grabbed Carrie by the shoulders and gave her the once-over. "Oh, my, your hair's a mess and your dress, it's all twisted, but we can't wait any longer. Do you know where your groom is?"

"He's not here?"

The unmarked sheriff's car rolled in and up to the steps, up behind the Kia. The sheriff stepped out. He opened the back door and helped the handcuffed Hal

Gardner stumble out and stand. Gardner leaned against the car.

"Missus Flight," the sheriff said, "I do believe I have something that belongs to this wedding."

Carrie ran to Garner. She hugged him. He ended up leaning on her. "I've missed you, babe," she said into his ear. "I've had such a rotten morning."

The sheriff extricated Gardner. He opened one of the cuffs that bound the young man and snapped the cuff on his own wrist. "Carrie, hon, your about-to-be husband has had a rotten morning, too—public intox, DUI, violating the open-container law, causing an accident on a public highway, endangering the safety of others, and probably three or four more charges before all of this is over. But first, hon, he's gonna get married to you."

"Uncle Steve, handcuffed like that?"

"Hon, I'm not gonna let this guy get away from you or from me."

A county cruiser turned into the far end of the church's horseshoe drive. It pulled up, boxing in the tow truck and the Kia hooked to it.

The deputy, once out of his cruiser, beckoned to the sheriff.

He came over with Gardner in tow.

"Sheriff," the deputy said, "I think the bride over there is a pothead."

"You sure?"

"Ninety percent. She smelled of marijuana when I stopped on Eighty-Three to lend assistance to her. Her car was dead at the side of the road. The tow truck driver hooked up to her car and got her car and her out of there before I could get Harlow out."

The sheriff looked over his shoulder to Carrie, wringing her hands and pacing. "Do it," he said.

The deputy opened the backdoor of his cruiser. He brought out a German shepherd on a leash and led the dog—Harlow, the name on the dog's Kevlar vest—to the Kia.

Harlow walked around the car, sniffing. At the car's front passenger door, he barked once and sat down.

The deputy opened the door, then the glove box. He held up a fistful of baggies. "We've got a hit."

The sheriff again looked at his niece. "Robert, do your duty."

"You want me to arrest her? Here?"

"And cuff her."

"You sure you want to do this, sheriff?"

"Yup. After you hook her up, you and Harlow walk her down the aisle. I'll have this yahoo waiting." The sheriff shook the jewelry that bound Gardner to him. "They're gonna get married."

"And afterwards?"

"It's off to jail. They can honeymoon in adjoining cells. Won't this all make great pictures for their wedding book?"

Note: Most people I know don't care for winter. Then there are us Norskis, Swedes. And Finns.

North to Alaska
– 2003 –

HE KNEW it was his lucky day when he found that twenty-dollar bill in the Sears parking lot, and he knew what to do with it.

Invest it.

He slopped his way through the slush, across the street to the Kwik Trip. "What can I get for twenty bucks?" he asked the clerk.

"The lottery's got a new scratch-off game," she said. "Hit It Big. Scratch off six numbers and you could win two hundred thousand dollars."

He looked at his bill, at the first six numbers on it, considered them, then ran a finger down the list of winning numbers next to the Hit It Big game. There they were, not the first six numbers on his twenty, but the last six numbers, the seventh set of numbers down the Hit It Big's list, his lucky number seven.

He inserted his twenty into the machine.

After a moment, it burped out a ticket.

One lonely ticket.

With a dime he found beside the lottery machine, he scratched off the first number. A four.

Then a seven, a two, an eight, a one, and another four.

He threw his ticket into the air. "I'm a winner!"

The clerk hustled around. She snatched up his ticket and proceeded to check the numbers on it against the numbers on the winners' list. She whistled. "Dicky Bob," she said, "you're gonna get two hundred thousand dollars. Well, a hundred thousand after the tax man takes his cut."

A hundred thousand dollars. That had to be one huge pile of twenty-dollar bills, he thought. He'd never seen that much money.

He, too, whistled. "Know what I'm gonna do with this?" he asked. "I'm gonna get myself out of this puny Wisconsin winter weather and go up to where it really snows. I'm gonna go to Alaska, buy me a dog team and a sled and run the Iditarod. Ten days to cover a thousand miles of ice and snow. Man, that's my idea of heaven."

Note: All of us who write books, who have books out there for readers to buy, get the same question: Where did your main character come from? Did you base her or him on someone real? Perhaps yourself? Our characters do have stories.

Welcome to the World,
James Early
– 2004 –

JAMES EARLY was not born.

He stepped into the world—my world—fully formed in 2004 . . . 5-foot-2—5-4 in his boots—37 years old, a ragged mustache. And he was a lawman, a sheriff. The sheriff of Riley County, Kansas.

In Early's world, though, it was not 2004. It was 1952. He was driving a john boat up Poyntz Avenue—Main Street in Manhattan, Kansas—during the Great Manhattan Flood. The Big Blue River had backed up into the city, its muddy waters reaching the second floors of business buildings. Early and the coroner—the coroner driving a Chris Craft, a rich man's boat—had just found a body floating in an alley next to the Wareham Hotel.

Early would not have come along at all had it not been for a small group of mystery writers and fans in Manhattan who decided that there was a need for a conference for mystery writers who set their stories in small towns. In 2003, they announced that they would host the first conference of its kind—the Great Manhattan Mystery Conclave, that it would take place in September of 2004.

To provide an incentive for new writers to come, the organizers said the conclave would sponsor a short story contest, that the best stories entered would be published in an anthology the following year.

That got my attention. I was looking for an opportunity to get published. Yes, I had been published in a handful of literary journals by 2004, but I wanted wider exposure.

To me, this could be it.

Of the genres, mystery is number two in sales. Romance is number one.

As a long-time fan of mysteries, I figured I surely could write a short one. You just need a body and a detective, and from there the story would take care of itself.

The rules said the story must be set in or around Manhattan.

I had lived and worked in Manhattan for Kansas Farm Bureau for the better part of a decade, so I knew the area and portions of its history well. I figured that ought to give me a leg up on the competition. I believe it did.

I needed a spectacular event from Manhattan's past in which to place my mystery. I remembered seeing pictures of the flood of 1952. What better place to have a murder than where all the police are up to their elbows in a higher priority business—disaster relief. No one would have time to go looking for a killer . . . except one man, the sheriff, directed to do so by the city police chief who had no time to deal with this.

Thus was born my story, "Dead Pool."

The detective to me was a natural. As a newspaper reporter, I had worked with a number of sheriffs and chiefs of police, and, frankly, I liked the sheriffs better. They had bigger territories for which they were responsible. And they were elected, not appointed or hired. They had to have the support of the residents of their counties.

Those I knew were straight-arrow honest. That's what I wanted in my sheriff, but I also wanted a man who would be driven to do what's right even when it conflicts with the law.

It's that quality that dictated the end of "Dead Pool" and the end of the second short mystery I entered, "Big Dam Foolishness." And it's those endings that set these two stories apart from most short mysteries.

Contest Judge Nancy Pickard, a top writer of mysteries set in Kansas, selected both stories for the anthology. I'm the only writer to have two stories in the book.

You can read them in my own anthology, *The James Early Reader.*

Note: What did you get for Christmas?

I received the perfect gift for a writer . . . a box of story cubes.

Says the promo line on the cover, let your imagination roll wild.

Story Cubes contains nine cubes, and there's a picture or image on every surface of each cube.

Nine cubes.

Fifty-four images.

Ten million possible combinations . . . maybe more.

So you can't get writer's block with this game.

What you do is chuck the cubes out onto a table or your desk, then look at the nine images that roll face up and compose a story around them.

In one of the several variations of the game, you pick a title, then roll the cubes and create a story that works with the title.

You must use all the nine images in your story.

So now it's demonstration time. I'm going to roll the cubes for you, then see whether I can create a story titled "My Worst New Year's Eve Ever."

Here we go—rattle, rattle, rattle—annnnnd here come the cubes. Face up as they stop we have the world, a star, a cellphone, a lightbulb, a barefoot footprint, a fish, a turtle, a bridge over a stream, and a rainbow.

Ooo, this is one tough set of writing cues.

My Worst New Year's Eve Ever . . . Really, Ever
– 2005 –

I MASHED 9-1-1 into my phone.

"Rock County Com Center," came back a weary voice, "what's your emergency?"

I stared at a green light hovering on the horizon. A star? The place where I stood smelled of burnt eggs. "I think I need the police."

"Where?" the com tech asked. "My screen shows you're on a cellphone."

"Oh, yeah, the bridge over Turtle Creek, down by Shopiere."

"Gotcha. I can have a sheriff's car there in three minutes. What's your emergency?"

"This is gonna sound strange."

"Buddy, tonight it's one strange world. I've had three calls in the last hour about aliens snatching people at a biker bar."

"Really?"

"Would I make this up? There's a full moon somewhere. It's the only explanation."

"What I've got could be serious."

"All right, lay it on me, man."

"I, ahh, I found a set of barefoot footprints in the snow—seven toes on one foot, nine on the other, I swear. They go up on this bridge to a pile of clothes like none I've ever seen before. I think maybe someone jumped."

I peered over the railing. There below, a dead fish floated on the water . . . and a shadow. What the h-e-double—

Something smacked me in the back of the head, igniting a burst of colors as I went down, a <u>rainbow</u> of colors, but before the <u>lightbulb</u> in my brain went fzzzt, I heard a high-pitched voice saying, "He measures sixteen-point-five-four kumquitz precisely. Our other specimens are larger, much larger. Shall I throw this one back?"

Note: The Samuel L. Jackson movie, *Snakes on a Plane*, is not the inspiration for this story. That was a dreadful film, a box office flop that deserved to be. No, the inspiration is my cousin Eldon who, in this story, is known as Tiny.

Snakes Alive
– 2006 –

"IT HAPPENED before the days of air-conditioning," he said to the bartender over his second beer. "It was spring like this and it was hot."

"How hot?" the bartender asked while he polished a pilsner glass.

"Hot enough you could fry ants on the sidewalk with a magnifying glass."

"Oh, Tiny, you're exaggeratin' a mite, wouldn'tcha say?"

"Well, maybe a mite." The guy, balding and what was left of his fringe going from gray to white, took a swallow from his stein, the Budweiser stein he always brought from home. "Anyway, all the teachers could do to provide some relief for us and themselves was to throw up the windows an' hope for a breeze."

The bartender set the clean glass on the back bar. "Did it work?"

"Some. But for me, an open window was an opportunity I couldn't resist."

"How's that?"

Tiny rubbed his thumb along the rim of his stein. "Walking to school that morning, I decided to catch me a couple grass snakes to put in the center drawer of my English teacher's desk. I'd do it during the lunch hour. I had her for fifth period, and I knew she'd open that drawer. I could just see the eyebrows shoot up off her face.

"Anyway, there were a lot of snakes out, so I caught me a bagful and smuggled 'em into the school. Hid 'em in my locker."

The bartender washed another glass, all the time listening.

"Come lunchtime—" Tiny sniggered a little. "—I went to my locker and got my surprise. I took it to Missus Millard's room and, just as I was about to dump that bag of snakes in the drawer, I heard the girls outside, laughing and carrying on. And I thought, why not."

The bartender quit washing. He propped himself on the palm of his hand on the bar, the knuckles of his other hand tucked into his waist.

Tiny swizzled his beer with his finger, his eyes glistening. "There I was with this bag full of fun, so I went to the window and leaned out—"

The bartender stared at him. "You didn't."

"I sure did. There, two stories below me, was this knot of girls laughing and carrying on over their sandwiches and Twinkies. I upended my bag. I rained snakes on 'em." He hooted and pounded on the bar at the memory.

"The screams," he said between snorts. "And, oh, how they ran."

"You get away with it?"

Tiny sobered up. "What?"

"Didja get away with it?"

"Oh, hell, no. Mister Hotz's office was right below Missus Millard's classroom. He must've seen that shower of twisting serpents because he was up the stairs and standing in the doorway before I could turn around. He did that 'come here to me' with those bent, ink-stained fingers of his, and I got to be the janitor's assistant, scrubbing floors and washing blackboards for the rest of the year."

Note: I always thought writers who said their characters talked to them were a bit strange. And then James Early, who was in my first two mystery short stories, whispered to me there's more here than you told. There's a book.

How James Early Got His First Book
– 2007 –

THAT WHISPERING came in 2005, after a woman had been murdered in my hometown. The police knew who did it—the woman's husband—but they couldn't prove it . . . until the man confessed to his father a half-year later.

The father called the police. He told them of his son's confession and where they could find the murder weapon.

It was a fascinating story, verging on the unbelievable, so I decided to fictionalize it.

I jacked the story back to 1949, moved it to Kansas, and changed the names of those involved. No one who knew of the original crime who read *Early's Fall* recognized it.

A novel needs a far larger cast of characters than a short story.

In "Dead Pool," the cast was James Early and Doc Grafton, Early's close friend and the county coroner, plus a handful of minor players.

In "Big Dam Foolishness," I gave Early a chief deputy, Hutch Tolliver. Early needed someone of size on his staff so nobody would mess with him, and Hutch had size. He was 6-foot-4. When he wore his 10-gallon hat, Tolliver looked to be almost 7 feet tall.

I filled out the central cast in *Early's Fall*, giving Early a wife and a best friend, Mose Dickerson, a fellow lawman, a constable. Like Early, Dickerson was a small man. And, like Early, he had absolutely no fear although he wasn't the brightest penny in the cash drawer.

With a cast and a story line, I invested a year in writing and polishing the novel.

Of course, this was not the first novel I had written. I had written nine others and had racked up 165 rejections for them from agents and editors.

I wasn't ready to send out query letters for *Early's Fall*. I don't know why. Perhaps I was afraid of getting rejection number 166. Anyway, the organizers of Love Is Murder/Dark & Stormy Nights, a mystery writers conference in Chicago, announced that unpublished writers who registered for the conference could get a critique of 20 pages of their novel by a published mystery writer. And the service was free.

I signed up and sent in my pages. The organizers assigned them to Tom Keevers who had six crime novels out at the time, all published by Five Star.

At the appointed time, we sat down together. Tom started into my 20 pages, saying a lot of good things about them. At one point, he looked up and stopped. He saw a tall guy down the hall. Excuse me, Tom said, and shot down the hall to talk to the man. I didn't know who he was. I later learned it was John Helfers. John had placed

Tom's novels with Five Star. Tom told John about my manuscript and said you have to acquire it.

Six months later, after John's readers had reviewed the manuscript and recommended publication, he did.

He placed it with Five Star, and I got a contract and a check—an advance against royalties.

Two years later, after maneuvering the manuscript through all the publication processes, Five Star brought out *Early's Fall.*

Kirkus gave it a starred review. A friend and fellow mystery writer, Mike Hayes, published by Poison Pen Press, told me he didn't get a starred review until his third book.

When I look back at James Early's journey to publication—and mine, too—we both were fortunate. Lucky.

We owe debts to two men who saw what could be and acted on it, Tom Keevers and John Helfers. I've told them so, so many times.

Note: I'm a Damon Runyon fan, doubly so because Runyon was born in Manhattan, Kansas, where I worked for the better part of a decade. While I was there, other Runyon fans were trying to determine which house had once belonged to his parents. They eventually did and went to work securing a historical marker. Being a Runyon fan and a writer, I knew at some time I would have to see if I could write a story in his style. Here it is.

A Holiday to Celebrate
– 2008 –

MAX 'THE UNDERTAKER' Slotnick organized it, the Valentine's Day party to end all Valentine's Day parties.

"Come as your favorite hood, or moll if you are of the feminine persuasion," the invitations read. They also gave time and place, plus a request for an RSVP.

Well, nobody says no to The Undertaker. Max runs the Heavenly Rest Funeral Home and has for twenty-seven years. He's been known to supply his own customers when business gets slow. They've never been able to prove that down at the central police station, so Jewels Wellington, the chief of detectives, tends to watch Max rather closely, hoping to make a case.

Came the appointed day, or rather evening, we all drive up in rented Hudsons, Pierce-Arrows, Cords, Packards, and Lincolns, all circa 1927-dash-32. But the best was Max. His sons, Max Junior and Antoine, they drive up in this 1929 Duesenberg J double-cowl Phaeton, stretched and fitted with a glassed-in and curtained box for carrying occupied caskets behind the second cowled section, a straight-eight under the hood—three-hundred twenty supercharged horses straining to gallop free.

Well, they drive right into the garage at Wessex and Thirty-second Street, right up to the buffet table that has this centerpiece ice sculpture of Al Capone holding his favorite machine gun, angels with haloes to either side, all set amidst a bed of red roses. They get out—Max Junior and Antoine—and open the back. They roll out two mahogany caskets with brass fittings and, when they open the lids, up sit Max and his lady, she in a Ma Barker hat.

Cheers all around. And champagne toasts. And chocolates to die for. Eddie 'Greasy Thumb' Randolph brought them in a violin case, the chocolates he said he 'purchased' from a favorite bon-bon store owned by, who else, The Undertaker.

Great joke that gets lots of laughs from Max.

The meal, what can I tell you—Porterhouse steaks as thick as your fist, shrimp and scallops for those watching their waistlines, baked potatoes the size of bowling balls, Panera bread slathered with Shullsburg Creamery butter, wedges of Goda cheese, flagons of Pilsner beer and, for dessert, Cherries Jubilee.

Just as the waiters are about to set fire to the dessert, a squad of fellas in Chicago police uniforms of the 1920s roll in this table on which resides a giant, multi-layered cake, a message piped on it in red frosting: *Remember the Valentine's Day Massacre.*

The fellas in police uniforms snap to attention, and on a signal from no one knows who, they blow their whistles. Out of the top of the cake pops not some hot blonde cookie in pasties, but Jewels Wellington, and he's carrying a goddamn-for-real tommy gun with which he sprays off the longest round.

We're all diving under tables and chairs and cars, praying we're not next in line for Max's services, when Wellington lets off with a cackle and hollers, "Gotcha, suckers. No bullets, not even blanks. Just a string of firecrackers I saved from my own favorite holiday, the Fourth of July."

Note: Madison's Overture Center, a multi-theater, cultural arts complex that cost $205 million, opened in 2004. The heart of the Center is a 2,251-seat concert hall. Huge. Absolutely huge. Said one farm boy who attended an event there, you sure could stack a lot of hay in here.

This is Culture?
– 2009 –

"WHAT LEVEL?" the traffic director asked, a trim young woman standing outside the elevator.

I held our tickets out to her.

"The balcony, yes," she said and ushered us aboard. "This is the elevator you need."

I squared around to the exit door. "Does it go all the way up?"

"All the way up to the balcony, that's right."

Actually, I was about to find out that, in this hall, the balcony is the second balcony. The first balcony, well, they call that the mezzanine. Why?

Ahh, there's a mystery for you.

Anyway, the light snapped on behind the 'B', and the door slid open. Marge and I got off and strolled down the hall to a door that, indeed, opened to where it should— the balcony.

There I showed our tickets to an usher.

"The eleventh row," he said and pointed up to the row beneath the row beneath the ceiling.

Twenty-two really steep steps away.

Marge looked at them, dismay filling her eyes. "Don't you have an elevator up there?"

The usher shook his head. "We're waiting for someone to win the Power Ball and give us the money so we can put in an escalator."

That was the end of the sympathy and of help, too, so we trudged up the mountain, panting and wheezing the higher we got, our lungs straining, our legs wobbling.

We made it after what seemed like a half an hour and flopped down in our seats, exhausted and winded, wishing we were on a jetliner and the oxygen masks would drop down. The atmosphere is really thin up there.

Others stumbled in, as bushed as we were, and the concert started. Maestro John DeMain, conductor of the Madison Symphony, walked out onto the stage to applause from the audience. He took the podium and turned to all two thousand of us and bowed. When he came up, he pointed his baton to us up in the heights. I swear he pointed to Marge. I prefer to believe it was his way of recognizing her for her efforts in scaling Mount Overture, to be there for an afternoon of classical music.

First up, Prokofiev's *The Love of Three Oranges*, not the whole opera, just a six-movement suite.

The music is a bit strange, as is the opera for which Prokofiev composed the music. The light's dimmed in the upper reaches of the balcony, so I turned to the program notes and worked hard to stifle my urge to laugh as I read. The opera premiered in Chicago in 1921, and the critics savaged it. Wrote the critic for the Tribune: "After intensive study and close observation at rehearsal and performance, I detected the beginnings of two tunes...

For the rest of it, Mr. Prokofiev might well have loaded up a shotgun with several thousand notes of varying length and discharged them against the side of a blank wall."

The opera flopped in New York, too. No fans. Only a confused audience and angry critics. Wrote the composer: "It was as though a pack of dogs had broken loose and were tearing my trousers to shreds."

The first movement, weird. It sounded like each section of the orchestra was playing from a different composition, the movement titled—appropriately, Marge concluded—*The Ridiculous Fellows.*

All was not a loss. When the orchestra went into the third movement titled *March*, Marge said to me, "I've heard this before."

Said I, drawing on a note in the program and my own memory, "You have. It's the theme music for the old radio show, 'This is Your FBI.' "

The concert came in three parts. Part 2 was Tchaikovsky's *Concerto for D Major*, featuring guest violist Gil Shaham.

Shaham wowed the audience with his skill and showmanship, winning a standing ovation that continued until he agreed to an encore, a duet with the orchestra's first-chair violinist.

That, too, drew a standing ovation.

Intermission followed.

The couple to my left and the woman behind me broke out the eats, a bag of prunes for the couple and a plate of cheese, crackers, and grapes for the woman behind me.

All I had was a stale food bar I found in my coat pocket. I left it there.

Part 3, Rachmaninoff's *Symphony No.3 in A Major.*

The program notes warned us that this wasn't the audience's favorite *Rhapsody*, but a shorter and lesser work that had gained some popularity in recent years.

Symphony had its moments, enough to get a standing ovation for the orchestra. Or maybe the audience just wanted to get out of the hall and across the street for sushi and sake or a burger and a beer.

When Marge and I got down to the lobby, she said, "Well, we've done that. I've heard the Madison Symphony. We don't have to do that again."

I took that to mean 'next time get tickets for seats by the door.'

Note: I watched the 2010 Tim Burton/Johnny Depp film *Alice in Wonderland*, a dark, dark, dark picture as one expects from director Burton. A darn good movie and a darn good story. Audiences flocked to it in such numbers that it became the fifth highest grossing film of all time. Of course, I also remember watching Walt Disney's 1951 animated version of *Alice*. The best part of that movie for me was the Mad Hatter's and March Hare's Merry Unbirthday Party. If you've not seen that scene, call it up on You Tube.

Happy Un-birthday
– 2010 –

SHE STARED at the calendar and decided she'd had enough.

No more birthdays.

Sixty.

That was it, and she told her sister so. "No more birthday parties. I'll cut you out of my will if you ever throw another one for me."

Sis took that as a challenge. Big number 61 was a month away when she remembered the raucous unbirthday party scene in the old Disney movie, the Mad Hatter and the March Hare singing and spilled tea on everyone, well, on the Dormouse who could barely keep awake.

She drafted the invitation to five of her sister's closest friends: "Remember your Lewis Carrol and come in costume to a Very Merry Unbirthday Party for Eileen Frazier at my house, 7 p.m. on May 16."

THE DOORBELL rang.

Sis checked the time on her cell as she went to the door, 6:55. Through the glass, she saw the first arrival, the Dormouse—Mickey Mouse ears for real, and a nose and whiskers painted on her face. She threw open the door and hugged the mouse—Addie Frye. "Addie, you are so cute."

The Dormouse yawned. "Yesss, and I am sooo tired. Do you have someplace where I can nap?"

Sis did. A giant teacup she'd found at a secondhand store. Got it for six dollars, as well as two chairs, each shaped like a giant hand, for which she paid ten. Getting them all in her Fiat had been a horror.

She escorted the Dormouse into the living room where she pointed her to the cup.

The Dormouse clambered in. As she let out the first snore, twin bunnies hopped in off the front porch, the March Hare and the White Rabbit—Ellen Wendorf and Monica Warrenton, real-life twin sisters—both with Playboy bunny ears and cotton tails, the March Hair chewing on a carrot while the White Rabbit studied the time on her husband's railroad watch.

Sis, after hugs, pointed them to the unbirthday table that had been set for tea, with a giant Merry Unbirthday cake bare of candles except for one in the center.

The Cheshire Cat sneaked in while all admired the pastry. She tossed a smoke bomb at the floor and, when it went off, stepped through a cloud of smoke for the most dramatic entrance of the evening, an entrance met by applause—Betts Dommerschmitt in a costume she'd borrowed from the community theater's current production of *Cats*.

Someone in the doorway bellowed, "Off with her head! Where's that disrespectful Alice?" The Queen of Hearts—Kitt Sallivar—wearing a ball gown with a hoop skirt. On her head, a paper crown from the Burger King. She carried a scepter topped with a ruby-red crystal heart. The Queen swept in to bows from her subjects. She peered at the unbirthday table. "And where is the Mad Hatter?"

Sis reached under the table for a box. She opened it and took out a red-and-white striped Cat-in-the-Hat hat. "This is the best I could find," she said as she put it on.

The doorbell rang for a second time.

Sis shushed everyone, then went to the door. She opened it, and there stood her sister gaping at Sis's Cat-in-the-Hat hat.

"What's that for?"

"You'll see. Now put your hands over your eyes."

Eileen sputtered but did so. "If this is a birthday party—"

Sis pushed her through the entryway and into the living room. "You can take your hands down, now."

Eileen peeked through her fingers. She gasped and swung on her sister, hissing, "Sssisss, you're out of the will."

"But it's not a birthday party." Sis spun Eileen around and gave the downbeat, the guests howling out, "A very merry unbirthday to you. / A very merry unbirthday to you . . ."

Note: It was this year that, for the first time, I sold my books at Chicago's Printers Row Lit Fest, a huge event spread over six blocks. While there, the Midwest chapter of the Mystery Writers of America held a flash fiction contest. The writing prompt intrigued me: "Digging a hole six-feet deep was harder than he thought." We had a half an hour to write, so I entered. I don't remember who won. It wasn't me, but nonetheless the judges enjoyed my story as did the audience.

Wanted: Grave digger
– 2011 –

HE GOT a one-word response when he rapped on the door of the Rest in the Bosom of Jesus Cemetery Association, the response: "Come."

He eased the door open, the door squalling on its hinges, not the best sign, he thought. "Ma'am," he said, holding out The Tribune's want ads, "you're lookin' for a grave digger?"

He gave a ripple to his shoulder muscles beneath his skin-tight Marines tee, figuring that might make for an impression.

It didn't because the woman never glanced up. Instead, she thumbed over her shoulder at an office door with PRESIDENT in gold script on the glass.

He stalled. "I should go in unannounced?"

She gave him the cold eye, and he took that to mean that's what he should do. So he sidled past her and opened the second door. There sat a cadaverously thin man smoking a rum-cured crook cigar at a roll-top desk the likes of which he had seen only one time before, on the Antiques Road Show.

The man rose and extended his hand. "I'm Colonel Little," he said, ashes flicking away from his bent stogie. "Colonel, my father gave me that name, can you believe it?"

He clamped onto Little's hand and pumped it like he was trying to raise water from a well, Little's face twisting at the pain. "You've got a real bone crusher of a grip there, Mister—"

"Daggett. Kenny 'Dig em' Daggett. I got my nick because I could dig a shelter hole faster than anyone in my squad."

"Soldier, huh?"

Daggett brushed the front of his tee. "Marine. I need me a job, Mister Little. Yours is the thirty-second place I've called on since I mustered out. Seems nobody wants to hire us guys who've done two tours or more in Afghanistan. They think we're nuts."

Little surveyed Daggett from the toes of his camo boots to the slashing scar on his forehead. "Well, son, if you can dig holes like you say, I'm willing to give you a try. Not many people want to dig graves."

"I just want a job," Daggett said, "any job."

"Well, we've got a burial scheduled for tomorrow, so I need a grave opened right now." Little set his crooked cigar in an ashtray shaped like a skull. He tugged a map out of a pigeon hole in his desk and unrolled the map in front of Daggett. "See here? This one—" He tapped the map. "—the grave must be eight by four by six feet deep."

Daggett ran his hand over the map, orienting himself with the front gate. "Do I use a backhoe?"

Little's long face became even longer as he stretched his lower jaw. "Oh, I am sooo sorry. The section of the city where this cemetery is has gone green, so we can't use motorized equipment. You get a spade. You'll find one in the tool house. It's marked there on the map."

He rolled it up and handed the map on.

Daggett stuffed it in his back pocket. "Then a spade it is. I assume I get paid by the hour."

"Right, and a bonus if the deceased's family compliments your work." Little walked Daggett to the door. "Now I want you to be as inconspicuous as an ant while you work out there because we've got a burial today. The grave for that one is already open."

DAGGETT STOPPED at the Kwik Trip at Eighty-Eighth and Halstead on his way to the Rest in the Bosom of Jesus Two. There he fortified himself with a jug of kiwi-flavored Muscle Milk.

At the cemetery, he found the tool shed right where it had been marked on the map, and the lot, too. Someone, he saw, had spray painted DIG HERE in red letters on the grass.

Daggett stripped himself out of his tee and set to work shoveling. Forty-five minutes in and sweat running in rivulets down his chest, he struck rock, a shelf of rock as he worked along the bottom of his hole only a miserable three feet deep.

Daggett stopped. He leaned on his spade's handle and listened to a pair of orioles warbling while he considered his options. He had seen a pick and a sledge hammer in the tool house. Good, he thought, and hiked back to get them.

Daggett hefted the sledge to his shoulder.

That's when he saw it—a stick of TNT and a roll of fuse cord. "It's sure not Semtex," he said to himself, "but I can use it." With that, he gathered up the dynamite and cord with the new tools and meandered back to the shallow grave.

There he chipped out a hole in the rock. Daggett tamped the TNT in, lit the fuse—extra-long for safety—and ran. He dove into an open grave. While hunkered down there waiting, he heard cars drive up, followed by doors opening and slamming shut. Daggett peered over the lip at a funeral party moving his way. He threw himself out the grave ready for occupancy and raced back to his grave, to stomp out the fuse.

When he saw it sputtering up to the stick of explosive, he dove back into the second grave a second time. A volcano erupted, showering dirt and rock over the mourners, the priest, and himself.

Daggett shuddered as he hauled himself up and out of the grave. Damn, I've sure blown this job, he thought. No pay and sure no bonus. It's like I never left the Marines.

Note: It started with a picture.

Memories
– 2012 –

HE FOUND THEM after his mother died, a dozen photo albums packed away in a Golden Guernsey milk crate. Yes, that milk crate. They were farm people.

His mother was a picture taker. He knew that. What he didn't know was that she also was a picture saver.

He sat in her room paging into the first album. A memory book for his mother . . . photos of her parents and grandparents, sisters and brothers, pictures of growing up in the lead-mining towns of southwestern Wisconsin, pictures of school events and of his father as a young man. He studied those for a while, deciding after some time that he indeed looked a lot like his father when he was that age.

The second album, family . . . his brother and him. Somewhere in or about the middle, a photo slipped out. It dropped to the floor.

He scooped the picture up.

A print of a photo taken with her Brownie Hawkeye. He could still see that camera sitting on top of the piano where she kept it always at the ready.

The print? A picture of him as a nine-year-old, something poking up out of his shirt pocket.

Oh my gosh, he thought. Squeak. A baby squirrel. He had forgotten him.

He had found Squeak abandoned in the yard. Probably the squirrel had fallen out of a nest in the hickory tree. The little guy would have been cat food if they had left him, so his mother and dad agreed he could keep the squirrel. He, of course, would have to feed him and take care of him.

One Sunday, he put Squeak in the inside pocket of his suitcoat and took him to church. Those were the days, yes, when men and boys, too, wore suits to church.

Squeak stirred occasionally, but for the most part slept through the service until a thunderous chord on the organ announced the singing of the Doxology. That chord must have woke him and, curious, he crawled out of the boy's pocket far enough that he could peer around the lapel. At that moment, a woman in the pew ahead turned around. She saw Squeak . . .

And screamed.

Scared him. Squeak leaped out and ran. The father dispatched the boy with an angry look to catch the squirrel, and the chase was on. The two ended up outside which was probably just fine with everybody else. After church let out, the boy got the lecture—Squeak was never to be taken out in public again.

Never.

Ever.

Again.

But that didn't save him.

Sometime later, the boy's family was to host a 4-H meeting at their house. The mother was cooking a big pot of chili. They were going to serve chili and crackers, and he couldn't remember what else, to the 4-H kids and their parents. The boy came into the kitchen with Squeak on his shoulder. As he played it back in his memory, either Squeak had a hankering for chili or he had a streak of flying squirrel in him because he launched himself from the boy's shoulder and splashed down in the chili pot four feet away.

That was it. The boy's father had banished Squeak from church and now the boy's mother, after words he had never heard her say before, banished the squirrel from the house.

Squeak was now almost fully grown, and he could fend for himself, so the boy gave him a bath. If you, reading this, thought it was fun giving a cat a bath, you've never tried giving a squirrel a bath. After he got Squeak dried off, he took him outside, out in the yard to the hickory tree and set him free.

Did the boy, now an old man, ever see the squirrel again?

He couldn't remember.

Probably, he decided, the other residents of the hickory tree didn't care for this new stranger and banished Squeak, too, sent him packing to find a tree of his own.

In the man's memory, though, Squeak survives equal to the other memories brought back by his mother's photo albums, Squeak peering out through a sepia-toned past.

Note: Ah, yes, H.G. Wells, the father of science fiction. He was so imaginative, so far ahead of his time in envisioning worlds and machines that might someday become, well, real. It got me to wondering, what if someone's son or daughter built a time machine for a science fair project . . . and old Dad took it for a spin?

OMG
– 2013 –

IN LITERATURE, H.G. Wells did it first. In 1895, he had a character named Time Traveler invent a time machine and try in out, riding in the machine back to a prehistoric world.

I knew about it because I had read the novella back in high school, but not my son. He took this time-machine thing on because it was an assignment from his physics teacher . . . build a time machine for this year's Odyssey of the Mind competition.

I think his teacher was laughing up his sleeve, but Tony consulted with his big brother majoring in electrical and computer engineering at MIT and, OMG, they came up with this contraption that whirred and dinged and the lights on its control panel danced a Tango when Tony pressed the ON button. But he never pushed the ENGAGE lever.

I did.

And the damn thing took off like the Tardis, settling me some minutes later in a white sand desert at twilight. The date and time on the control panel read 3-2-1947, 8:26 p.m. PST—Pacific Standard Time—as I stepped out, my Hush Puppies crunching down in the sand at the side of a highway, State Route 375 a sign said.

A silvery, saucer-shaped craft whistled out of the sky and settled on spidery legs hardly a stone's throw away.

Wells' *Time Machine?* Wells' *War of the Worlds?*

In my mind I assembled the pieces and knew where I was. Nevada's Mojave Desert, Arear 51.

A portal opened in the side of the craft.

A projection shot out, a hologram that glimmered and glowed. "You ordered the Poppa John's Intergalactic six-cheese, roasted Brussel sprouts, spiced pineapple, artichoke, bacon and barbecued prawns pizza?" it asked.

Note: The Ogle-Winnebago Literary Society sponsored a short story contest in which the writing prompt was "this is the only story I'll ever tell or the only story that one of my characters will ever tell." At this time, we had been involved in a war in Afghanistan for 13 years and, when this book comes out, it will be 19, the longest war in U.S. history, a war that was won in the first year and then lost.

The Letter
– 2014 –

THE OLDER MAN laid his arm across the younger's shoulders, both men in dark suits, white shirts, and ties expected for a funeral, their boots buffed to a high gloss, the collars of their suitcoats turned up against the prairie wind. "I've got something for you," the older said.

The younger, his eyes dewy, his hair flicking this way and that, poked at the sod with the heel of his boot, the sod not yet greened up. "We just put my dad in the ground. I really ought to stay with Mom."

"Your sister can do that. Look, I was your father's lawyer. This is important."

"I suppose." The younger wagged a finger at a woman near his age in a storm coat closer to the still open grave, his finger directing her toward an older woman in black, strands of silver visible in her hair, the woman dabbing at her eyes with the corner of a silk handkerchief.

He got a nod in return, so moved away, off to the side of the funeral party and under a maple tree bare of leaves. He and the older man stopped, quarter to one another.

The older planted his cattleman's hat on his head, then drew an envelope from the inside pocket of his suitcoat. "I've had this letter in my safe for a month. It's from your father. His instruction to me was to give it to you after he died."

"After he killed himself, you mean."

"That's the way it turned out, yes. I'm sorry." He held the envelope up. "I really think you should read this."

"Now?"

"Your father said it's important."

The younger took the envelope. "Do you know what's in the letter?"

"No."

He tore the end off and blew into the envelope, the way he had seen his father open envelopes so many times. The sides puffed out. He reached in with two fingers for the folded paper. He snapped the paper open and read, the only sound around him that of the restless wind:

February 12, 2014
My son –
　　If you're reading this, I'm dead.
　　Forgive me for having made a fast exit from this life. Getting help from the V.A. has been damn hard, such long waits for appointments with the shrinks. To them, rank means nothing. And when your head, pardon me, my head is all screwed up...
　　I was career Army, as you know – 20 years. And you know the highlights, the good stuff. The early and late

years were good. But the middle years, one year in particular, one three-month period, late September 2001 to December…

I've never told your mother this or you or your sister Gwenny, but for those months I was in Afghanistan, one of two dozen Green Berets and how many CIA guys I don't know charged with leading the Afghan Northern Alliance in their drive to rid the country of the Taliban. We Green Berets all spoke Farsi, fluent Farsi. That's why we were selected.

We rode in on two Chinook Nightstalkers flying so damn high to get over the Hindu Kush Mountains that we all had to suck on bottles of oxygen or we would have died. I shared my O-2 with my war dog, Werbly. I know, it's a sissy name for an almost fully black German shepherd that would rip someone's leg off when ordered, so I called him Wolf. After 11 hours in the air, the chopper crew put us down in some farmer's field in the Dari-a-Souf Valley at O-200. It was just 39 days after 9-11, and we boiled out of our chopper ready for a fight, but there was no one. We had to walk for a day and a half before we came on a couple guys on horseback, scouts, it turned out, for the Northern Alliance army.

We had $3,000,000 with us, cash money in hundred-dollar bills with which to buy the loyalty of the warlords, crates of money that we slung between us on our march. Damn lucky we didn't walk into a Taliban ambush. Had we, we might have ended up making the enemy rich.

The Taliban – the T-Men, that's what we called them – were as bad as bad men come, bandits and killers, and they still are. Those T-Men of my generation conquered their country in the name of Allah, they said, took it after the Ruskies pulled out and after seven years of civil war. They established Sharia law. Harsh law. Terrible law. They would cut off your hand for breaking it or kill you. If you've never read up on Sharia, you should. Just google it.

Most of us in my unit, the 595 – the Army's Operational Detachment Alpha 595 – and our sister unit, the 555, dressed like Afghanis, robes over our desert camos. Some of us had full beards and long hair, and half or more of us wore pakols, the soft, round-topped hats that Afghani men wear. We lived like the Afghanis with the Afghanis. We rode horses everywhere, a hell of an experience for me, a towny, because the only time I ever rode a horse was on the merry-go-round with you and Gwenny when you were little tykes. But in the mountain north, horses are the only way to get around.

We were the cavalry.

We could and did move fast with our Northern Alliance brothers, 10 to 30 klicks a day.

I got the thrill of a lifetime – actually, I thought I was going to die – when we were picking our way down a mountainside on switchback trails sometimes only a foot wide. My horse must have decided he'd had enough because he turned in the trail, faced down the mountain, crouched like a cat, and sprang into the air. He must have flown 20 feet down the mountain before his hooves hit the ground and then he raced the rest of the way down like someone had jammed an electric prod up his butt and lit him up. All I could think to do was lay back, whip my feet up by his neck, and hang on. At the bottom, that wild stallion leaped across a gully and, apparently pleased with himself, stopped. Shaking, I slid off the saddle and kissed the ground. I really did.

It was the better part of a half an hour before the rest of the 595's and Wolf came off that mountain and caught up with me. I got a new nickname out of it: Rodeo…Rowdy "Rodeo" Gurnholt. No longer was I

"Gurney," the nickname you'd have got tagged with had you joined the Army.

Rodeo. Sometimes Rodie.

Most of the battles we engaged in were small ones – firefights – but there were two massed assaults. In October, the General – what was his name, Dostrum? Can you believe it, that's Afghani. – he led 1,500 Northern Alliance horse soldiers and an equal number of ground pounders against the T-Men dug in at Bishqab. The T-Men had a couple tanks, several anti-aircraft guns, and a half-dozen APCs – armored personnel carriers – all of them bristling with cannons and machine guns, a lot of killing power…and us with just horses and M-16s. Well, we had a surprise for them, a couple forward air controllers who called in a squadron of F-16 Falcons. They pounded the town with missiles and bombs.

Still we had to ride across a mile of open ground to get at the Taliban. From the air, it must have looked like Picket's Charge or the Charge of the Light Brigade. We made it, but we lost 14 Northern Alliance fighters in the charge. Without the 16's, it would have been in the hundreds, maybe a thousand or more.

The next day we rode against Cobaki and overran the T-Men again. So much killing in two days, we of them.

We had been told we would be in Afghanistan a year, but after three months, the Taliban we didn't kill fled to Pakistan.

Good riddance.

Our job was done.

But we lost some, too, outside of those two big fights and the small ones. The suicide bombers who are creating so much hell now, I saw them first in Afghanistan. When we had the T-Men on the run, they turned loose the fanatics willing to blow themselves up if it meant they could kill us and the Afghanis we led. We got good fast at spotting the men, so they sent in the women, and that we never expected.

One, coming from a market with a big basket of produce and fruit, offered to sell what she had to a claque of our allies. She had 5 armed men around her, bargaining, haggling, when she set off her explosive belt. Cut herself in half and killed those five.

I saw it. God, I was a witness to it – the slaughter, the carnage. That night, we of the 595 gathered behind the mud walls of a compound and agreed we'd never let that happen to us, that we would kill any women in burkas who came at us, who would not stop when we ordered them to do so.

Two days later, a little Afghani woman ran at us. She ran from a couple with whom she was walking, ran straight at us, and I had to cut her down. I killed her with a burst from my M-203 because she wouldn't stop.

Only she wasn't a woman. When we got her face covering off – her face veil – we saw she was only a kid, a girl maybe 12 or 13. And she didn't have a bomb or a suicide belt.

A girl not yet a teenager.

I threw up my guts.

One of our 595's got the couple aside. They had been yelling at us in Farsi not to shoot and now they were wailing, grief stricken. He asked who was she? And the man, in a rage of anger, shouted she was his daughter. She was deaf. She saw Wolf – loved dogs – and only wanted to pet him, that she was impulsive. She could not hear us or her parents.

That girl, Tom, she haunts me to this day. At night, that's when it's the worst. Try as I might, I have not been able to shake her from my mind. And I've tried it all – Oxy, whiskey, head doctors, and more Oxy. The stuff's easy to get if you know who to ask.

Three months into the war, the diplomats set up a civilian government, and we were ordered out of the country, ordered back to our bases, the 595's to our base in the Kuwaiti desert. Wolf was killed there. We were playing catch with a frisbee. Once he ran out for it and triggered a land mine left from the first Iraq war. The engineers had missed it. There was nothing, absolutely nothing to bury, not even his collar. I cried the rest of the day and all that night.

Suck it up, they tell you. Sometimes you can't.

The civilian Afghan government turned out to be no better than the Taliban. They were really corrupt, stealing everything they could. So the Taliban returned.

But that wasn't the 595's concern. We were out of there. We had done our job. Others screwed it up.

While we were there, Tommy, we snatched what comfort we could where we could. I took a bullet in one firefight and had to lay out a couple weeks. A family lived in the hut where the Northern Alliance put me. They conscripted the hut and ordered the family to take care of me. We became friends in time, laughing a lot about the silliest things. And the girl – well, young woman…you know where this is going and why I've never told this story to anyone. I loved her, I really did. You've never been in a war, so I know you can't understand how that could happen in so short a time. Nine, ten months later, I got a letter from the head man, telling me that I had fathered twins. Tom, you have two sisters you never knew about.

I couldn't get them. I couldn't get their mother. By then some crazed uncle had killed her, her father wrote. An honor killing. There was no honor in that. I had family here – you and Gwenny and your mother – so I arranged to send the man and his wife money, so much a month so they could take care of their grandbabies – my babies –

because the family had so little. And I've done that every month since for 12 years now.

You will find in my will that you have an inheritance. I want you to do one of two things for me with that money, either continue to support my Afghani girls where they are or go bring them home and adopt them. Ten years and they could be through college and on their own.

The first, Tom, that's not asking much. The second, I know that's asking you to do what I could not force myself to do but should have. You're a good son, Tom. I trust you. Be stronger than I was.

Now what you choose to tell your mother, well, that's your decision. Just know that I will not be hurt.

Because I'm dead.

Dad

He folded the letter.

"Well?" the older man asked.

The younger looked away, across the rows of headstones, to the hearse leaving the cemetery. He raked his fingers back through his hair rippling in the wind. "Dammit. Dammit to hell, I'm gonna have to go to Afghanistan."

Note: I'm a short story writer, as you know, so it's hard for me to pass up a short story writing contest. This time the Writers Police Academy was the sponsor. The writing prompt they put up was a photo of two plots in a cemetery. Said the instructions, the story must be 200 words precisely, including the title.

Super sale
– 2015 –

I AM a businessman. I specialize in adjustments.

You are feeling threatened? The competition is pounding you into the dirt? I can make an adjustment on your behalf. Close-up, a .22 to the heart.

When business is slow, I bring out my two-for-one sale sign. I will off your competitor and your brother in-law for the same price.

For a modest additional charge, I'll provide side-by-side cemetery plots and midnight interments. No grave markers, complete anonymity, and that is what you want. Find me at AdjustmentsDotCom.

Yes, there are others in my line, but it never occurred to me that my specials might rile them.

The other night, after I had bagged the first of my two-fers, I felt this cold steel against the back of my neck.

"Gimme your email and website passwords," a husky voice said. I recognized that one—Arnold Martindale. There's no arguing with The Slug, so I coughed it up: one-eight-one-ADjustNOW.

He thanked me and said he would plant me in my extra plot since my customer's brother-in-law wouldn't be needing it.

How thoughtful. It beat being run through a woodchipper, Arnold's usual method of disposal.

Note: I like walking through supermarkets, looking to see what's new on the shelves. This day, August 14th, I picked up a box of Jordy's Farm Fresh Flakes, the collector's edition box no less. There on the front was an artist's rendition of Jordy Nelson in his Green Bay Packers uniform, number 87 emblazoned on his jersey. This got my attention. I'm a Wisconsinite, by birth a Packers fan. So I flipped the box to the side panel and read a rundown on Nelson: "Did you know #87 has been farming longer than he's been playing football? That's right, before Nelson became a World Champion wide receiver for Green Bay, he was working on his family's farm in Leonardville, Kansas." Holy moly, Leonardville. That puts Nelson just down the road from fictional James Early's ranch. Nelson today, in the off season, still goes home to work his parents' place, now his. He grazes a thousand momma cows on his pastureland. All this got me to wondering, what if my James Early were still alive? He'd be 102.

Second note: The Packers released Nelson in March of 2018. The Oakland Raiders picked him up two days later, gave him a two-year contract worth $15 million. He played one year, then retired.

This One's for You, James Early
– 2016 –

MASON DODGE motioned toward a sign beyond his pickup's windshield, the sign reading Jordy Nelson Charity Softball Game. "We're here, Grandpops. You doin' alright?"

James Early peered over the tops of his half-moon readers. "Will be after I get out and stretch my legs."

Stretching his legs, that was his exercise at a hundred and two. Early's age made him the second oldest man in Kansas. Sound of mind and body, he liked to tell his doctor. Sound of mind and body, but shrinking. At his best, when he was sheriff of Riley County a half-century back, Early stood five-foot two in his stockinged feet. Now he needed the heels on his boots just to reach five-one on the doctor's measuring stick.

Early laid aside the map he'd gotten at a welcome center when his grandson rolled his rig into Wisconsin, his rig, a Chevy crew-cab dually pulling a Bighorn fifth-wheel travel trailer.

Dodge touched the redial icon on his truck's screen. He and Early heard a ring and a second, then someone picking up. "Jordy, here," came a voice through the speaker.

Dodge glanced at the screen. "Jordy, this is Mase. We made it."

"Good. Just follow the arrows around to the parking lot. I'll meet you there."

The call clicked off.

Dodge guided right at the first arrow. He passed the ticket windows for Appleton's Fox Cities Stadium, clusters of families standing in lines there. Further on, he hauled by the infield bleachers, then the outfield on the first-base side. Next came a snow fence that marked the limits of the softball field and, a dozen feet further, the outfield wall for hard ball. Beyond that, a parking area.

Someone in a Packers jersey and cargo shorts at the end of the third row rolled his hand for Dodge to keep coming on.

Dodge zipped down his window, and the scent of newly mowed grass swept in. When he drew abreast of the traffic director, he stopped. "Hey, Jordy."

Jordy Nelson, smiling like he had the day the Packers and he won the Twenty-Ten Super Bowl, looked in past Dodge to Early in the shotgun seat. "Hey, neighbor, you don't know how proud I am to have you here. Been a long time since you've seen me play."

Early grinned. "It is. Last time was football when you were a student at K-State. Today, it's baseball, my game."

"Well, our game's only softball and slow-pitch at that. I've got seats for you right behind our dugout." He flicked his gaze to Dodge. "Meggie with you in the fifth wheel?"

"Afraid not. Somebody had to stay home and run the ranch with the kids."

"Sorry to hear that." Nelson stepped up on the running board and cupped a hand under the top of the window frame for security. "Mase, swing in here, then go down to the traffic cones."

"Gotcha." Dodge cranked the steering wheel to the left as he pressed down on the gas pedal. "Many people come to this thing?"

"We've sold more than eight thousand tickets. Now at the next cone, hang a left down to the first row and left again. I've got a bunch of spaces blocked off for you."

Dodge, holding his speed, rapped his knuckles against Nelson's fingers. "What say we tailgate after the game? I've got a charcoaler in the back of the truck."

"Good deal. I'll bring the brats."

Early leaned across Dodge. "Buddy-boy, no steaks?"

Nelson ducked down for a better look in. "Mister Early, you're in Wisconsin."

"Well, I did have some German bratwurst back during the war. That was—my Lordy—seventy-five years ago."

Dodge wheeled his rig into the first turn.

"Mister Early," Nelson said, "cheese brats cooked in beer and barbecued on the grill, that's what we call good living here. Of course, we've also got jalapeno brats, if you like a little heat."

Dodge chortled as he cranked the steering wheel for the next turn. "You're making me hungry."

Nelson hopped down. He ran ahead, collecting the traffic cones that marked off a series of empty parking places. He threw the cones into the back of a golf cart that had a giant football helmet for a roof.

Dodge eased his rig into the string of parking places. As he got out, Early pushed himself off the high seat on the passenger side, down to the running board, and down once more to the ground. He reached back for his cane.

Nelson came around. "A cane, Mister Early? I didn't know."

"Aw, Mase and Meggie insist. They don't like it when I fall, though I can't say as I mind it much. See, I get some of my best exercise picking myself up." Early hooked the crook end of his cane around his cattleman's hat left on the seat. He pulled the hat to himself and planted it over his thinning hair the color of salt. Early swept a hand back along the curve of the brim. "Brand new. Got me this Stetson just for this trip."

Dodge also came around. "Jordy, Grandpops has had only one cowboy hat for most of his life, that one work-worn, sweat-stained, and beat to heck, a real embarrassment to Meggie. She told Grandpops she'd burn it if he didn't get a new one."

Nelson stepped up to Early. He adjusted the hat for a jauntier, just-so angle. "Mister Early, you do look smart in this one."

"I do, don't I."

Nelson stuck out his elbow. "Take my arm and we'll walk together to the cart."

Early hesitated until he saw his grandson giving him the cold eye, then he latched his big-knuckled, boney hand over Nelson's forearm the thickness of a telephone pole. "So what do you do this game for?" he asked as they strolled along.

"Charity. The Packers' offense plays the defense. We've been doing this for four years now. This game's gonna rake in more than a hundred thirty thousand dollars."

Early looked up, really up. Nelson, walking beside him, stood a good two heads taller than he. "So who's this charity?"

"Young Life. In the Green Bay area, we match adults with kids who need mentors, middle school through college. It's a great thing."

"Helpin' kids, yup, you can count on me to chip in for that. Mase, too. His momma—my daughter—raised him to do right."

"Come on, Mister Early, the two of you are my guests. You keep your money in your pockets."

Early shrugged.

Nelson helped him into the golf cart, then took the driver's side. Dodge settled on the rear-facing seat at the back.

Nelson stepped down on the accelerator.

Early glanced at him. "Pretty quiet, this machine."

"The cart's an electric."

"Kinda guessed. You've heard they're wantin' to build electric trucks now, right?"

"That's progress."

"If Mase had one, think how long a power cord we'd have needed to make it here." Early snickered.

Nelson, grinning, leaned forward, his forearms across the top of the steering wheel. "You want to meet our quarterback?"

"Aaron Rodgers? Mister Number Twelve? I've got one of his shirts in the truck. Maybe he'd autograph it for Meggie after the game."

"I'll see to it. Aaron's a real autograph machine. Right now I've got him warming up our outfielders." Nelson swerved the golf cart through a break in the fence by first base and cruised on down toward home plate.

Rodgers, at the plate, flipped a ball into the air. It came down, and he drove it high into left field, the left fielder scrambling to get under it.

Nelson waved to Rodgers. He beckoned him over. "Want you to meet some friends from back home."

Rodgers trotted up, toting the bat in his left hand. He stuck his right out to Early. "Jordy tells me you're his next-door neighbor back there in cattle country."

"That I am." Early gave Rodgers' hand a smart pump.

"You've got a good grip there for someone who's older than my father."

Early chuckled. "Probably older than your grandpa, too. Say, I've got a shirt with your number on it back in my grandson's truck."

"I'd be glad to sign it."

"Just one question, if I might, Mister Quarterback. Can you really throw a football through the window of a pickup truck passing by on the road like I've seen in those television commercials, or is that fake?"

"Not fake, sir. I really can do it. But I'll be honest

with you, it took three tries."

Nelson touched Early's arm. "We've gotta get this game going. I'll take you to your seats."

He motored the cart on to the dugout while, behind him, Rodgers let out an ear-splitting whistle and spun his hand over his head for the players on the field to come in. They sauntered his way, gabbing among themselves, peeling off into two teams, one lining up on the first-base line, the other on the third-base line.

Nelson, after he got Early and Dodge seated, picked up a wireless microphone. He strolled to home plate. There, as he brought the mic up, he gazed over the crowd in the bleachers. "Ladies and gentlemen and all you tons of kids, thank you for coming. Thank you for supporting my charity. We're gonna play a little baseball for you now and, when the game's over, I want you to come out on the field. Aaron and all the players, we've got our Sharpies. We'll autograph whatever you have."

A wave of applause rolled down from the stands, plus stomping and cheers as people came to their feet.

Nelson took off his cap. He held it over his heart. "Remain standing, please, for the National Anthem."

TOP OF THE FIRST.

A three-hundred pounder shambled out to the pitcher's mound as the defense took the field. He turned and, chewing a cud, arched a ball up over the plate, letting it slap into the catcher's glove. A practice pitch.

The catcher, almost as hefty as the pitcher, fired the ball to the third baseman.

Early watched the ball go from player to player around the infield and back to the pitcher still working his cud. The pitcher spit to the side.

Early cupped a hand up to his mouth. "Jordy-boy! A

question."

Nelson came away from the coach's box at third base.

Early pointed at the pitcher. "I knew baseball players chewed, but I thought you football guys were more health conscious."

"Some of us chew." Nelson grubbed a pouch out of his back pocket, the pouch labelled Big League Chew. "Mine's bubblegum. Want some?"

"But the pitcher?"

"He prefers Redman, but sometimes he chews snuff. Our team doctor has given up trying to talk him out of it."

Early shuddered. After Nelson went back to his position, Early leaned into Dodge. "Who is that big horse out there on the mound anyway?"

Dodge paged into his program. He touched a picture. "Tommy Scott, starting center for the Packers for ten years."

"Hmmm, guess that's why he's so big, so whoever's opposite him can't move him. And the catcher?"

Dodge turned to another page and touched another picture. "Andrew Wiley, backup center. Says here he's been on the roster for six years. Played football for Missouri."

Rodgers stepped into the batter's box. He dug his sneakers into the dirt, pounded the plate with his bat, crouched, and cocked the bat over his shoulder. He squinted at the pitcher. "Come on, Tommy, show me what you've got!"

Scott lofted the ball. It arched down in the strike zone.

Rodgers swung hard, connected, and sent the ball climbing into the sky between center and right field, the center and right fielders dancing to their sides, gloves up. They collided and fell in a tangle of arms and legs, the ball coming down beyond their reach.

Early elbowed Dodge. "Who they got playin' out there, Laurel and Hardy?"

TOP OF THE FOURTH.

Nelson came trotting in from third base. He made a show of jumping on the plate with the umpire shooting his hands out to the sides, signaling safe.

Early turned to the scoreboard at the outfield fence. The scorekeeper—Nelson had announced the girl in short shorts and a tank top as another player's twenty-year-old sister—hung a new number for the home team, a one where a zero had been, making the thirty, thirty-one.

Early bumped shoulders with Dodge. "Second homer for Jordy. How about that, a three-run lead."

The pitcher—Scott—spit out his wad. He hauled a bandana the size of a bath towel from his back pocket and mopped the sweat from his face. He pulled off his cap and wiped his bandana back over his hair as well.

The catcher sauntered out to him. After several moments of talk punctuated with a flurry of gestures, the catcher got out his tobacco pouch. He held it open to Scott.

Scott forked up a mess the size of a golf ball. He stuffed it into his cheek and went on yammering, chewing and spitting. Appearing to Early as exasperated, he threw a fistful of fingers in the direction of home plate.

The catcher—Wiley—shrugged. He walked away, back toward his position, diverting a bit to a trash barrel where he threw something in. When he got back behind the box, he settled into his crouch.

A batter stepped in.

Scott lofted the ball, putting a spin on it.

The batter slapped at the ball and sent it over the

shortstop's head into left field. He hoofed it for first.

Scott turned away. With his forearm, he swiped at the sweat glistening on his forehead.

Early elbowed Dodge. "That boy don't look too good, does he?"

Scott's knees buckled.

He fell.

Gasps came from the stands, Early, Dodge, and others rising.

Nelson raced to the downed pitcher, the infielders as well. They huddled over Scott. Nelson came up, a cellphone in his hand.

A moment later, an ambulance tore onto the field from behind the stands, two paramedics bailing out.

Early shook his head. "Mase, this has got to be damn serious."

"Yeah, look, they're loading that guy in the meat wagon."

The doors closed on the ambulance, and it ripped away, its emergency lights blazing.

Nelson walked to the plate, and batboy dashed up with the microphone. Nelson took it. He waved to the people in the stands. "Please, everyone, please sit down." He looked at his microphone, tapped it, the tapping coming over the stadium's speakers. "It's okay, the mic's on. Everybody, Scotty's gonna be alright. He just collapsed. Could be heat stroke, we don't know, so we've sent him to the hospital to be checked out. Now I know Scotty'd want the game to go on, so it will. But I promise you this, everybody, as soon as we find out anything, I'll stop the game and let you know."

SEVENTH INNING STRETCH.

Nelson, microphone in hand, stood at the pitcher's

mound, the teams gathered in a loose semi-circle behind him. "I want you to meet someone," he said into the mic. He pointed his trigger finger at James Early and Mason Dodge. When they stood, Nelson waggled his fingers for them to come over to the head of the steps coming down to the field.

While they made their way there, Nelson went on. "James Early is my neighbor from Kansas. That's his grandson, Mason Dodge, with him. Mister Early is one hundred and two years old. I'm younger, that's pretty obvious, but we share the same birthday. Please, everybody, make my neighbor welcome."

Most in the stadium crowd came up, pounding their hands together.

Early waved, waved his hat to them.

Nelson trotted in and up the steps as the applause continued. He put his arm around Early's shoulders. "Mister Early, you want to run the bases with me?"

Early pulled the microphone to himself. "At my age, Jordy, walk is the best I can do. Even at that, if I made it to first, you might have to carry me the rest of the way around."

"How about you ride then?"

"In your golf cart?"

"No, on a horse." Nelson swept his hand toward first base where a woman stood with a tacked-up horse. "Your horse, Mister Early. Molly the fourth. I had her and your granddaughter-in-law flown here this morning by jet transport."

Meggie Dodge, leading the horse, hustled to the base of the steps. "Poppy, how's this for a day?"

Early wiped the back of his hand at a tear. "Mase, you know about this?"

"I'm as surprised as you, Grandpops."

Molly the fourth pushed her muzzle into Early's

chest. He responded, rubbing her face.

Nelson guided Early down a step and helped him swing a leg across the saddle. "Mister Early, show us your stuff."

He reined Molly around toward first base. Early clicked his tongue, and she launched herself into a lope. From first, they went around second and third and on toward home plate, Early, like a rodeo star, waving his hat to the crowd. From home, he fast-walked Molly back to the steps and, with Nelson's help, dismounted, his eyes glittering. "Jordy, how's that for an old man?"

"There's nothing old about you, neighbor." Nelson pressed a piece of paper into Early's hand. "How about you present this check to my charity?"

Early gazed at the numbers. "A hundred thirty-four thousand, six-hundred eighty dollars. Mind if I keep it?"

Nelson shook his head as he looked up into the stands. "Here to accept the check," he said into his mic, "is the president of the Green Bay chapter of Young Life, Eldon Smith, and a busload of kids and young adults who are a part of the program."

A torrent of people poured out of the first-base bleachers. They came running, Packer players waving them into their semi-circle. One came to the steps and up to Nelson, a man with silvery hair flowing out from beneath a Packers' ball cap.

Nelson pointed his microphone at him. "Mister Early, this is Eldon Smith."

"Do I really have to give him the check?"

"You really do."

Early squared up beside Smith, both, at Nelson's prodding, turning to the crowd. "Mister Smith," Early said into the microphone, "Jordy tells me you can use this. The money comes from all the people up in the stands and I'm told from the Packer players, too."

He handed the check on, then took out his wallet. Early removed a bill from its depths. "This is from me, Mister Smith. When I cashed my first paycheck after I became a sheriff back in Nineteen Forty-eight, I got this hundred-dollar bill at the bank. I've carried it with me ever since, so I'd never feel poor. Please accept it."

Nelson put his hand on Early's arm. "You don't have to do this."

"I do. I'm not gonna live forever, Jordy. It's time to put this money to work." He handed the bill to Smith.

Smith gazed at it and at Early. "Mister Early, this donation is one of the most special we've ever received. It comes from the heart. On behalf of everyone associated with Young Life, I thank you."

As the event broke up, one of the Young Life kids, a girl—Early guessed her to be about nine—came to him. "Can I pet your horse?" she asked. "I've never seen a horse close up before."

Early winked at her. "How about goin' one better? How about goin' for a ride?"

Nelson, listening, swept the girl up and deposited her on the horse's saddle.

She, all grins, grabbed hold of the horn.

Early, grinning too, went down the steps and led Molly the fourth and the young rider to the first-base bleachers. There she slid down and, after she stroked Molly's broad face, she kissed Early on the cheek.

TAILGATING.

Nelson nestled a brat into a bun and handed it to Early.

Early studied it. "Big thing," he said and took a bite.

Other players and their families milled around in the stadium parking lot, talking, joking, waiting for brats to come off Dodge's grill and three others donated by the Johnsonville Brats people, one of them manned by Aaron Rodgers.

A police car rolled into the grass lot. Two people got out. Early glanced at them while he chewed. Nelson, beside him, filled another bun. "Mister Early, one of those two is our team doctor. I called him in to see to Scotty. The other man I don't know."

Both made their way to Nelson. One of the men, wearing a Panama, took his hat off. "Jordy—"

Nelson handed the brat away. "Doc, how's Scotty?"

"Jordy, I'm sorry."

Nelson stared at him. "Sorry for what?"

"I'm afraid Scotty's dead. He died half an hour ago."

"Are you sure?"

"I was there, Jordy."

"Heat stroke?"

"Doesn't appear likely. There are a couple things we think point to poisoning."

Players nearby crowded in.

The man rolled his hat in his hands. "I know that's hard to believe. We won't know for sure, though, until the M.E. does an autopsy."

"Poisoning? But how?"

"Maybe some bad food, something he ate." He thumbed to the man next to him. "This is Josh Condey, a detective with the city police. Anything suspicious, they have to investigate."

Early, finished with his brat, brushed crumbs from the bun away from his mustache. He extended his hand to Condey. "Young man, I'm a sheriff from Kansas, long retired. Not that I want to horn in here, surely not at my age, but could the man have died from something he chewed?"

Condey massaged his lower lip. "It's possible. At this

point, anything's possible."

"I'm told the man was a confirmed tobacco chewer. If I wanted to get rid of someone like that, I might be tempted to doctor his chew. Before he collapsed, his catcher gave him a new load from his pouch. Now I'm an old duffer, sir, but I've got good eyes, like Missus Fletcher on *Murder She Wrote*. Love that program. Watch all the reruns. Anyway—" Early waggled a hand toward the dugout. "—if you go to the trash can there, you'll find the catcher threw his pouch in there. Probably figured nobody's notice, but I did."

Nelson rubbed the back of his neck. "Wiley? Why would he do that?"

"Jordy, if you'd been riding the bench for six years as he has, waiting for the starting center to break a leg or be traded away so you could get the starting spot, so you could play, you might consider doing him in, too."

A car started. It spun out of the lot, throwing up a shower of grass clippings as it sped away.

"That's Wiley's car," someone shouted.

Early raised his hands. "I'm not chasin' him. I haven't driven a car in twenty years, but I'm willing to deputize somebody."

Note: I wrote this story to be read during the children's service on Christmas Eve morning at the church Marge and I attend. While the intended audience was children, adults listened, too.

A Child's Christmas
– 2017 –

"PAPA, can we go to church tonight?" the girl asked as she and her father walked along, he burdened by a load of firewood he carried on his back.

The girl? Aria Rodriguez, age eight, living in a cave because a hurricane had blown away her home . . . living in a cave with her parents and her baby brother Luis.

What little light that was left in Aria's father's face dimmed. "Ari," he said, "you know the storm destroyed our church, just like it did everything else in our village."

"But the walls are still standing. Father Bernardo showed me."

"They could fall, Ari. It is dangerous."

"Papa, it is the night for the Jesus child. Father Bernardo said so. We should be there."

Aria's father found a large rock. He laid his load aside and sat down. After a moment's rest, he lifted Aria onto his lap. He hugged her. "Ari, we would be the only ones there. You know we have buried many of our neighbors. And those few who survived, they have left. They have gone down the mountain, hoping somewhere to find food and water and someone to help them."

"But we haven't left, Papa."

"No. No, Ari, we have our plot of land, our garden. We have our cow and she has grass in the meadow, so she can survive. And yesterday, yesterday, Ari—" Jose Rodriguez's eyes brightened. "—yesterday I found a spring at the edge of our meadow where we never had a spring before. God's gift perhaps. I cleaned it out and lined it with stones, to keep the water clean for you and me and Momma and little Luis and our cow."

Aria looked up into her father's face. She let her fingers play over his massive hands, gnarled and scarred from working the soil and cutting wood in the forest. "Father Bernardo says we are blessed. Are we?"

"Father Bernardo says that to everyone, Ari. But maybe we are. Our garden, Ari, we have our root crops. And our seed, it is safe in the cave, so we can replant, grow a new garden, grow new crops of corn and melons and beans. Our neighbors, they didn't have a cave, so they lost everything."

Aria cast her gaze down at the straps on her sandals. "I miss Ettien."

"I miss him, too, and his momma and papa and all their children. But Ettein's papa told me they had to go down the mountain. He thought maybe he could find work helping rebuild if they could get to Arecibo. Maybe one day they will come back."

A mongrel dog, tan from the tip of his tail to just shy of his black nose, ventured into the meadow, hesitant. When the dog saw Aria and her father, he broke into a run, whipping his tail as he came, grinning with his lips turned up. The dog slid to a stop at Aria's father's feet, wiggling all over.

Aria slipped down. She hugged the dog. "It's Dario," she said. "It's Ettein's dog. Can we keep him?"

"No, Ari. It would be one more mouth to feed."

"But he hunts. Ettein said so."

"Hm, perhaps that could be useful, Ari. If anything survived in the forest, it is the wild pigs. We could hunt them for their meat. What we didn't eat would be Dario's." He riffled his fingers through Aria's hair. "Ari, you may keep the dog."

"Thank you, Papa."

"But you will have to explain this to your momma. She does not like dogs."

Aria jerked her face up, surprised. "Is that why we never had a dog?"

Her father nodded. "Come, we must get home," he said as he stood and re-shouldered his burden of firewood.

WHEN THEY neared the cave, Dario the dog bristled. He let out a bark. Just one.

Aria turned in the direction the dog stared. "Papa, there's a man over there by what's left of Ettein's house."

"Yes, I see him."

"He looks hurt. Maybe we should help him."

"I don't know, Ari. He is a stranger."

"But Father Bernardo says—"

Jose Rodriquez frowned. "Ari, with you it's always Father Bernardo says this, Father Bernardo says that." He slung his load of firewood down and took out one stick that he handled like a club. "Just in case," he said and moved out for the rubble that had once been a house and the man poking through it, as if he were searching for something. Ari and the dog hurried to catch up.

"Hey, there," Jose Rodriguez called out. "Can my daughter and me help you?"

The man, dressed in little more than rags, his arm in a sling, looked up. At the sight of Jose Rodriguez's club, he staggered back, tripped and fell among the rubble. "Please, sir," he said, his voice weak, hardly more than a whisper, "I was just looking for something to eat. I meant no harm."

Jose Rodriguez threw his stick aside. "Where are you from?"

"The other side of the mountain. My village was all destroyed. I have been with the dead. The way out was blocked, so I came here."

"How long?"

"Three days."

Aria's father motioned for her to come with him. Together, they helped the man stand. "We salvaged what little food we could find from the houses of the dead in our village, added it to our own supply. My daughter would be disappointed if we did not share."

The man, thin as a reed, gazed down at Aria beside him. His haggard face softened. "Bless you," he whispered.

"Maybe after supper," Aria said, "you could come to church with us. It's the night for the Jesus child."

"The Jesus child, yes, I'd like that."

ARIA, SWINGING a flashlight and with Dario beside her, ran ahead of her father and her mother carrying little Luis, and the stranger limping along with them. She ran across the village square swept free of debris by the storm that had devastated everything else, ran to the church where Father Bernardo stood in the doorway waiting for anyone who might come. "Father Bernardo," she called out, "we've brought a friend with us."

"Thank you, Ari." He came down the steps, his arms opened out in greeting. "It is so good to see you, Jose and Maria and little Luis." He touched the baby's forehead, and the baby grinned at him.

Father Bernardo looked over at the stranger. "And who do we have here coming to our humble little church tonight?"

"His name is Cristo," Jose Rodriquez said, "from the village of San Mateo. The only survivor."

Father Bernardo smiled. "Like us, yes. God does looks out for us, doesn't He? Come. Come inside." He helped Cristo up the steps and down the aisle to the front bench. "Since there are so few of us, we may as well all be together."

The stranger sat down and the Rodriguez family with him. Maria Rodriguez said something to Aria.

Aria set her flashlight on its base on the bench, the flashlight's beam shooting up into the night's sky. She took baby Luis from her mother and rocked him in her lap.

Father Bernardo, his back to the altar, a lone candle burning there, faced his tiny congregation. He raised his hands. "I cannot but believe that God is looking down upon us, pleased that we have come to His house on this the night of the Jesus child."

He turned to the cradle beside him meant to be a manger for a Nativity. "The doll that has been our Jesus child for so many years, it is lost somewhere. Maria, perhaps you would loan us little Luis?"

She motioned for Aria to take the baby to Father Bernardo. He accepted the baby and knelt and laid him in the cradle.

At that moment, a brilliant light shone down from the sky, illuminating the cradle and everything around it.

"The Christmas star," Father Bernardo said, his voice barely audible. "The Christmas star."

That was followed by a whup-whup-whup-whup and the light moving to the side and disappearing.

Outside in the square, a swirl of wind and dust swept up and through the door, flickering the candle whose flame Father Bernardo protected, as Aria protected the baby Luis.

Then silence.

Before Father Bernardo or anyone else could gather their words for what they wanted to say, a man in blue coveralls, a flashlight in one hand and a medic's bag in the other, dashed into the church, followed by a woman dressed as he was.

"We saw your lights," the man said. "We were flying back to Arecibo, looking for survivors on our way. Can we help you?"

Jose Rodriguez gestured toward the stranger. "We have this man—"

But no one sat where the stranger once did. Only a piece of paper held by a flat stone on one corner, the paper fluttering there on the bench as if it were alive.

Aria went to it. She pulled the paper free and handed it to Father Bernardo.

The scrawl on the paper glowed iridescent. " 'In as much as you have done it to the least of God's children,' " Father Bernardo read aloud, " 'the lost, the hungry, the injured, you have done it unto me. My blessings to you.' "

Aria peered at the note. "And he signed it."

"Yes." Father Bernardo put his arm around Aria's shoulders. "He signed it Cristo, the Everyman."

Note: This piece grew out of a writing challenge in my Beloit writers group: Write a letter or an email to someone who supported your writing career, whether that be a friend, a family member, a teacher, or an author you've never met but has been an inspiration to you. I chose a friend, Robert W. Walker. Rob's a prolific writer. As of this date, he's published more than 80 books, most of them mysteries in the horror and thriller genres. You've heard of that great Scots hero, Robert the Bruce. Meet Robert the Good.

Robert the Good
– 2018 –

Rob . . .

We've been friends and colleagues in the mystery writing business for the better part of two decades now, and it just occurred to me that, in all that time, I've never said thank you. Well, I did once, and I'll get to that.

Do you recall how we met?

It was in a parking lot in Chicago. When was that, the year 2000? The Dark & Stormy Nights mystery writers conference had just adjourned, and I was headed to my car, to drive back home to Wisconsin. You ran me down and said I really needed to come to a different conference the next year, Love Is Murder, that I'd find more help there.

I didn't know who you were, and you didn't know who I was. Neither of us were wearing our conference name badges. Neither did I know at the time that you had published twenty mysteries. Me? I hadn't published any. I was just a newbie, as your friend Joe Konrath would say.

I took you up on your suggestion and found that you were right. Love Is Murder was a better conference.

I became a regular and sat in on every workshop you and Joe ran over the next several years.

You were there in 2006 when Tom Keevers, who had critiqued the first 50 pages of my mystery, *Early's Fall*, told John Helfers—John, who had placed all of Tom's novels with Five Star—that "you have to buy this manuscript." Six months later, John did and placed it with Five Star. You blurbed the book. I thanked you then for that, and I thank you again. Nineteen books and a pile of blurbs later, yours is still the best:

> "Jerry Peterson has created one
> of those characters you can't
> look away from. If James Early
> were on the screen instead of in
> a book, no one would leave the
> room. Peterson has a raw, sparse,
> no-nonsense style that sparks
> like spurs bouncing off pavement
> with every beat of this story. He
> joins the ranks of a writer's
> writer—that is, an author other
> authors can learn something from,
> as in how to open and close a
> book, but also how to run the

```
course. Great character, great
story, great writer. What else
can one say?"
```

That blurb ran on the back cover. From it, I lifted this for the front cover. The publisher placed it at the top:

```
"If James Early were on the
screen instead of in a book,
no one would leave the room."
```

That blurb, that abbreviated blurb, has sold a lot of copies of *Early's Fall* for me.

Two thousand-six was a special year for a second reason. You came to Madison for Bouchercon. While you were here, you had dinner with several members of my writers group. We made you an honorary member following that. Over the next two years, I asked you to write a series of articles for our newsletter, articles that today we would call 'first aide for writers.' You did, and I thank you for that. Our members learned a lot from those pieces.

We've stayed in touch, even after you moved from Chicago to Beckley, West Virginia. A couple years after that move, the Mystery Writers of America announced a theme for an anthology they intended to bring out. You suggested we each write a story for it. My story was a stinker. I didn't even send it in. But yours—you titled it "Rules of Fog"—you made it sing.

You asked me to read it and I did. As you know, the editor in me took over, and in a long critique I pointed out a number of things that needed fixing, several that needed expanding, and a couple that could be cut . . . snip a word here and tuck a phrase there.

You rewrote the story, then paid me a high and unexpected compliment. You added my name to the by-line as your co-author.

We were both disappointed that the anthology's editor didn't select your story—our story—for inclusion in the book, but years later you published it as a novella and I published it in a collection of crime stories I had written.

All these years, Rob, you have been an encourager, a cheerleader, and a friend. I thank you most sincerely.

Jerry

Note: You know what we all fear? Yes, the unknown. The knock at the door at midnight when we aren't expecting someone.

Baseball Bats and Wedding Bells
– 2019 –

THE KNOCK at our kitchen door—and it was a knock-knock-knocking knock, not a pounding, hammering knock that demands that you race downstairs or else they'll shoot your dog—was enough that we flipped on the porch light.

"Who's there?" I asked through the crack between the door and the doorjamb, my wife keeping behind me.

If it had been daytime, we wouldn't have asked. We'd just have opened the door. But this was night—I mean really late night, Stephen Colbert had signed off hours ago. It was a time when all good people should be in bed which meant that whoever was out there could be an axe-wielding escapee from the asylum for the criminally insane.

I picked up my Nelson Cruz-autographed Louisville Slugger that I keep by the door and hefted it like a cudgel.

A man's voice answered. At least it sounded like a man's voice, a youngish man. "Our car broke down and my cell's dead."

"So?"

"So, mister, I know it's late, but we're stranded. Can we use your phone to call for help?"

"Who's we?" I asked.

"Me and my girlfriend. She's pregnant."

"Not about to give birth, is she?"

"Not for another couple weeks. It's cold out here, mister."

My wife nudged me. She tilted her head toward the door, as much as to say this is serious, kiddo. Open it.

I did.

Over the shoulders of the couple who stood before us, the couple togged out in winter gear, I saw an old Kia near the end of our driveway, its four-way flashers pulsing.

"Come on in," my wife said.

They did, he helping her along, she waddling, her stomach pooched out so far I thought she might have triplets hiding under her coat.

He eyed my baseball bat. "What's that for?"

I looked at the bat, feeling a bit sheepish now for having picked it up. "It's our boy's. He's always leaving stuff around." I set the bat behind the door. "Phone's on the wall by the fridge. What happened to your car?"

"The motor coughed a couple times and died."

"Out of gas?"

"Filled up yesterday." He nodded to our phone, and I gave an underhand wave.

He went to it. He punched in a series of numbers, calling who I didn't know until someone picked up on the fifteenth ring. "Dad?" the kid said into the mouthpiece.

"Dad, I've got car trouble. Can you come pick up Tina and me?"

He listened for a moment, then turned to me. "He wants to know where we are."

"Twenty-two forty-eight County A. Six miles east of Janesville."

He relayed the information, listened again for another moment, then hung the receiver back on the wall phone. "My dad'll be here in half an hour," he said to me. "Thanks for the use of your phone. We don't want to impose any longer, so Tina and me, we'll go wait in the car."

My wife raised her hand. "No, you won't. It's freezing out there. Would you like some coffee? I can make a pot for the four of us."

Before he could answer, his girlfriend/significant other/partner for the moment/whatever, sucked in a quick breath. She squeaked out, "My water just broke."

He jumped. "You're not gonna have our baby, are you?"

"Bry, it's not like I've got a choice."

She looked down, as did we, water dribbling down her legs, puddling on the linoleum.

My wife, already at the girl's side and her arm around the girl's shoulders, barked at me to get a towel. "I'm taking her to the guest bedroom. We're not having a baby on the kitchen floor."

I bolted away to the bathroom where I dug out an armload of Cannon's best bath towels. I raced for the bedroom and threw them at my wife who really only needed one.

She set about drying the girl's legs. "Go to the garage, Robbie. I want you to get that roll of plastic sheeting—"

"Plastic sheeting?" I asked. "Like we covered our back screen door with?"

"Exactly, only you're going to cover the bed with it, then put down a flannel sheet, and this mother-to-be is going to lay down. And tell Tina's guy to boil some water."

"Water, right." I ran for the kitchen. There I grabbed the kid and shagged him to the sink. "My wife says you should boil some water. Use the big pot under the sink."

"I'm gonna have a baby?"

"Kid, you aren't. Your Tina is." With that, I thundered onto the garage. I found the plastic in the rafters, pulled the roll down, and galloped with it back to the bedroom where I found my wife had stripped the pregnant girl out of her clothes and had wrapped her in a terrycloth robe.

My wife glanced at me in the mirror, at my reflection. "Robbie, she's having contractions. They're coming fast. Where's the boiling water?"

I slapped my forehead and raced back to the kitchen. I slid up to the boy who stood frozen like a popsicle in front of the sink, mumbling, "I'm gonna have a baby. I'm gonna have a baby—"

"Kid," I said, "we've been over that. It's Tina. Kid, have you given any thought to marrying that girl?"

He worked his fingers against the edge of the sink, like he was massaging it. "Marrying? We just never got around to it."

"You can fix that tonight. I'm a minister, by the authority vested in me by the State of Wisconsin—"

"We don't have a license."

"You can take care of the legalities in the morning at the courthouse." I dragged him with me toward the bedroom.

"But what about the boiling water?"

"My wife's an obstetrics nurse. She calls for boiling water in these home deliveries to give the man something to do to keep him out of her hair."

We rounded the corner and rolled into the bedroom. My wife was crouched in the baby-catching position, Tina on the bed, her knees up. "Push," my wife commanded.

The girl bore down, sweat beading out on her forehead.

"How soon?" I asked.

"Any minute now."

"Do we have enough time to marry these two before the baby comes?"

"If you're fast."

I leaned into the girl's face. "Tina, do you want to marry this guy?"

"I do," she said as another contraction hit. She grimaced and followed that with panting.

"That's the right answer," I said. I slapped her clammy hand in his and gazed at them both. "Dearly beloved, we are gathered here in the sight—"

My wife shot me THE LOOK. "Cut to the chase. This baby's coming."

I kicked up the pace of my delivery to that of an auctioneer. "Do you, Tina, take this man, Bry, Briars— Bryan, is that it?—to be your husband, to love, honor, and obey for so long as you shall live?"

"Yes!" she screamed, my wife ordering, "Push!" and adding with quiet assurance, "We've got us a head."

"Do you, Bryan, take this woman, Tina, to be your wife, to love, honor, and obey for so long as you shall live?"

"I do."

"Push!"

Scream.

"Shoulders! Push again."

"I can't do this!"

"Yes, you can. Tina, push one more time!"

A new contraction, and a third scream.

The baby squirted out. My wife caught it and gave the infant a quick once-over. She peered up at the newlyweds. "Congratulations, it's a boy. A healthy boy."

The woman screamed again. A new contraction had hit. My wife looked down, then up at Bry/Briars/Bryan—whatever. "You're gonna have to ditch your mini-Kia for a minivan," she said. "You've got another baby coming."

The kid turned green. He shot his hand to his mouth as he scratched away toward the kitchen where I heard him throw up.

"You hit the sink, didn't you?" I called after him.

Note: We get challenged from time to time. In one of my writers groups, we were instructed to write a story about a risk we once took, a risk that we've rarely talked about. For you who have gotten to this point in the book, this is a gift, a bonus story—the 81st candle.

In Defense of a Principle
– 2020 –

IT'S HARD to believe in our age of "me too-ism'—2019 when I'm writing this—of the drive for appropriate and fair treatment of women in the workplace and elsewhere, that less than fifty years ago few women held positions of authority anywhere.

Men were the bosses.

Back in 1974, I was working for Kansas Farm Bureau. I had been promoted to director of the communications department—a two-man enterprise with a secretary, a woman. I had hired my replacement. A man. Ed.

Our workload grew rapidly because of the things I wanted to accomplish. So it became apparent to Ed, Marie, and me that we needed a third staff person. I went to my manager and got clearance to hire someone and approval of a salary I could offer. What I didn't tell Don was that I intended to hire a woman for this staff position. There were no women in staff jobs—salaried jobs—in KFB or our affiliated companies. There never had been.

I found the person I wanted, the assistant director of public relations in Oregon University's athletic department—a Kansan who wanted to move back home. I hired Norma, then told Don who said are you sure you want to do this? She won't be accepted here.

I assured him that I did want to do this, that I had the backing of the personnel department. I expect Don ground his teeth, but he okayed the hire.

The next year came time for the annual staff retreat. All the staff members from our three companies would go to a golf resort in Oklahoma for three days of planning conferences and relaxation.

By this time, we had two women staffers in our companies. Don informed me that neither could go to the retreat, that the word had come down from on high that Norma and Mary—the other woman—were out.

I went to Norma and told her what had happened. "This is wrong," I said. "This is a retreat for all staff. All staff, not just men. Do you want to fight Don's decision?"

"Yes," she said.

I told her I'd set up a meeting with the executive vice president, that she'd be there with me, that I'd lay out the discrimination inherent in Don's decision, that I'd ask Ward to overrule Don, that if he didn't or if Don continued to maintain that this was a retreat for men only, we'd both quit, that that was our leverage.

Ward, who had headed our insurance company forever and had been the executive v.p. for our three companies for a couple years, surprised me. This old conservative who had never rocked anybody's boat gazed across his desk at us and said, "You're right. This is wrong. Norma, you're going to the retreat with all the rest of us."

The next day, Don came to me and apologized and said Norma would be going with us.

That day that Norma and I had gone over the head of my manager to the chief of staff, we had put our jobs on the line for a principle, that women must be treated fairly in our workplace, that they must be given every perq that men are given, that they must be paid the same salary as men in the same positions. It was a risk. We could have lost, but Ward—bless his soul—agreed with us . . . and change was instituted.

Note: When you're my age, the government, through Medicare Care, wants you to check in with your doctor at least once a year so he or she can see how you're doing. Enjoy this gift, a second bonus story and the 82nd and final candle.

Visit to the Vampire
– 2020 –

"I'D LIKE to get some blood work done on you," the doctor said. "It's all a part of your wellness visit. We want to check on your cholesterol and some other things."

I agreed to it, reluctantly. You see, I've got this thing about my blood. Stick me to take a sample and I tend to pass out. It's happened. I'm laying on the floor, and the nurses are gathered around, debating whether they should pick me up or leave me there. One always says, "We can step over him. He'll be all right."

The doctor handed me the work order for the lab on which he'd noted all the tests he wanted run on my blood. To me, the list looked like every test known to the medical profession. "Take this with you," he said, "and remember, you've got to fast for eight hours before you go to the lab for the blood draw. Can't eat anything or drink anything other than coffee or water, got it?"

Got it.

"The lab opens at seven in the morning," he said.

"Seven? Okay, I'll skip breakfast and be there."

Now it snowed overnight, so I had to shovel out. Made me fifteen minutes late. I walked into the hospital, to the information desk, and said with my best smile to the person there, "I'm here to see the vampire."

She pointed her bony finger into a cavernous hallway. "Down there at the end."

She didn't return my smile. That told me she'd heard this vampire line before, lots of times before.

"Check in at Urgent Care," she said.

Urgent Care, that's a hoot. Go there only if you're prepared to wait three hours to see a doctor. There's nothing urgent about our hospital's Urgent Care.

The vampire, though, will see you much sooner.

Wait time for me, five minutes.

She escorted me down another hall to a small cubicle in which there was a torture chair. Big, wide armrests on the thing and a bar that swings down in front of the armrests, locking you in so you can't escape.

"Push your sleeve above your elbow," she ordered.

I did.

She whipped this rubber clamper around my bicep, just above my elbow.

"Now straighten your arm and make a fist."

She had me captive, so what choice did I have?

I squeezed my eyes shut and bucked up my courage for what I knew was coming.

I swear from the pain that hit me she must have thrown a needle the size of a harpoon at me from across the cubicle.

A motor ginned up, followed by slurping sounds . . . the extractor sucking the blood out of me and into one vial after another, each vial the size of a peanut butter jar.

Done, she hauled the needle out of my arm and slapped a gauze pad over the wound. "Hold that there," she said. "We don't want you leaking on our carpet."

I didn't want that, either, so I held the pad tight. I had no desire to lose any more blood than the extractor had already taken.

"How's your arm?" she asked.

"Hurts like the dickens."

"I can give you a sling if you think that would help."

"I'll take it," I said.

She harnessed me up, then stepped back and stared at me. "You look kind of green. You want me to get a wheelchair for you?"

I rattled the locking bar. "Just get this up out of the way and I'll crawl out of here on my own."

I did. Not easy to do with one arm in a sling. You look like a three-legged dog, hopping along, but I made it to the front door in twenty minutes and another ten to my car.

ACKNOWLEDGMENTS

This is the twenty first book I've published as indie author, this one under my Windstar Press imprint.

We indies, loners that we are, nonetheless depend on a lot of people to make our stories and books the best that they can be. A superb cover designer at 100 Covers dot Com worked with me on this volume, as he has on several other books.

Just as a knock-out cover is vital to grabbing potential readers, so are the words on the back cover that say this book is one you really should buy. For those words, I turned to fellow writer Marshall Cook.

I always close with a thank you to all librarians around the country. They, like you and your fellow readers who have enjoyed my James Early mysteries, my AJ Garrison crime novels, my John Wads crime novellas, my Wings Over the Mountains novels, and my short story collections, have been real boosters. Without them and you, there would be no reason to write.

A NOTE FROM THE AUTHOR

Novelist, critic, public speaker, essayist, and columnist Orson Scott Card said it: Everybody walks past a thousand story ideas every day. The good writers are the ones who see five or six of them. Most people don't see any.

I see a lot of story ideas. For this collection, I wrote 83 stories in three years.

That's pretty darn remarkable.

Several of the stories have double lives. Those few you may have read or will read in others of my short story collections.

Jerry

Janesville, Wisconsin, November 2021

WHAT PEOPLE SAY ABOUT MY BOOKS

Early's Fall, a James Early Mystery, book 1. . . "If James Early were on the screen instead of in a book, no one would leave the room."
– Robert W. Walker, author of *Children of Salem*

Early's Winter, a James Early Mystery, book 2 . . . "Jerry Peterson's *Early's Winter* is a fine tale for any season. A little bit Western, a little bit mystery, all add up to a fast-paced, well-written novel that has as much heart as it does darkness. Peterson is a first-rate storyteller. Give *Early's Winter* a try, and I promise you, you'll be begging for the next James Early novel. Spring can't come too soon."
– Larry D. Sweazy, Spur-award winning author of *The Badger's Revenge*

The Watch, an AJ Garrison Crime Novel, book 1 . . . "Jerry Peterson has written a terrific mystery, rich in atmosphere of place and time. New lawyer A.J. Garrison is a smart, gutsy heroine."
– James Mitchell, author of *Our Lady of the North*

Rage, an AJ Garrison Crime Novel, book 2 . . . "Terrifying. Just–terrifying. Timely and profound and even heartbreaking. Peterson's taut spare style and truly original

voice create a high-tension page turner. I really loved this book."
– Hank Phillippi Ryan, Agatha, Anthony and Macavity winning author

The Last Good Man, a Wings Over the Mountains novel, Book 1 . . . Jerry Peterson joins the ranks of the writer's writer–that is, an author other authors can learn from, as in how to open and close a book, but also in how to run the course."
– Robert W. Walker, author of *Curse of the RMS Titanic*

Capitol Crime, a Wings Over the Mountains novel, Book 2 . . . "In *Capitol Crime*, Peterson's vivid characters jump right off the page, and his sharp detail and snappy dialog puts the reader right in the middle of Prohibition-era action and one of the wildest schemes ever to take down a bootlegging ring. So buckle up. You're in for a hellava ride!"
– J. Michael Major, author of *One Man's Castle*

Iced, a John Wads Crime Novella, book 1 . . . "Jerry Peterson's new thriller is a thrill-a-minute ride down a slippery slope of suspense and shootouts. Engaging characters, spiffy dialogue, and non-stop action make this one a real winner."
– Michael A. Black, author of *Sleeping Dragons*, a Mack Bolan Executioner novel

Rubbed Out, a John Wads Crime Novella, book 2 . . . "Jerry Peterson's latest thriller gives us, once again, an endearing hero, a townfull of suspects, and quick action leading to a surprising climax. If you like your thrills to be delivered by strong characters in a setting that matters, this one's for you."

— Betsy Draine, co-author with Michael Hinden of *Murder in Lascaux* and *The Body in Bodega Bay*

A James Early Christmas and *The Santa Train*, Christmas short story collections . . . "These stories are charming, heart-warming, and well-written. It's rare today to see stories that unabashedly champion simple generosity and good will, but Jerry Peterson does both successfully, all the while keeping you entertained with his gentle humor. This should definitely go under your tree this season."
— Libby Hellmann, author of *Nice Girl Does Noir*, a collection of short stories

A James Early Christmas – Book 2, a Christmas short story collection . . . "What brings these Christmas tales to life is the compassion of their protagonist and their vivid sense of time and place. James Early's human warmth tempers the winter landscape of the Kansas plains in the years after World War II. A fine collection."
— Michael Hinden, co-author with Betsy Draine of the Nora Barnes and Toby Sandler mysteries

The Cody & Me Chronicles, a Christmas short story collection and more . . . "Jerry Peterson is a fireside tale-spinner, warm and wistful, celebrating what is extraordinary in ordinary people with homespun grace."
— John Desjarlais, author of *Specter*

Flint Hills Stories, Stories I Like to Tell – Book 1 . . . "Jerry Peterson's short stories are exactly how short stories should be: quick, but involving; pleasant, but tense; and full of engaging characters and engaging conflicts. I can think of few better ways to spend an afternoon than being submerged in James Early's Kansas."
— Sean Patrick Little, author of *The Bride Price*

Smoky Mountain Stories, Stories I Like to Tell – Book 2 . . . "Jerry Peterson's *Smoky Mountain Stories* is pure Jerry Peterson magic. His years as a journalist have shaved his prose down to a razor's edge, the kind of flinty steel wordplay that only comes from someone who has logged a lifetime at the keyboard."
– Sean Patrick Little, author of *After Everyone Died*

Fireside Stories, Stories I Like to Tell – Book 3 . . . "Witty and clever, Jerry Peterson spins a tale with a deft pen and an ear for dialogue that you don't find too often. There's an old-fashioned sense of character and craft in Peterson's works that will have you desperate for more."
– Sean Patrick Little, author, *The Bride Price*

A Year of Wonder, Stories I Like to Tell – Book 4 . . . "These 24 short gems run the gamut from humorous to mysterious, including a welcome return of Sheriff James Early. You'll wish that a year had more than 12 months in it so that you could have more of these fine stories! A very good year, indeed."
– Ted Hertel, Jr., recipient of MWA's Robert L. Fish (Edgar) Award for Best First Short Story by an American author

The James Early Reader, Stories I Like to Tell – Book 5 . . . "Jerry Peterson is a master storyteller. *The James Early Reader* is set on the Great Plains of mid-twentieth century Kansas where Peterson weaves rugged, heartfelt magic out of bluestem pastures and stony flint-capped hills. Do yourself a favor and give this book a read.
– J.M. Hayes, author of the Mad Dog & Englishman mysteries and *The Spirit and the Skull*

ABOUT THE AUTHOR

I write crime novels and short stories set in Kansas, Tennessee, and Wisconsin.

Before becoming a writer, I taught speech, English, and theater in Wisconsin high schools, then worked in communications for farm organizations for a decade in Wisconsin, Michigan, Kansas, and Colorado.

I followed that with a decade as a reporter, photographer, and editor for newspapers in Colorado, West Virginia, Virginia, and Tennessee.

Today, I'm back home and writing in Wisconsin, the land of dairy cows, craft beer, and really good books.

COMING SOON

Night Flight, the third book in my Wings Over the Mountains series of novels.

Made in the USA
Middletown, DE
16 August 2022

71464319R00274